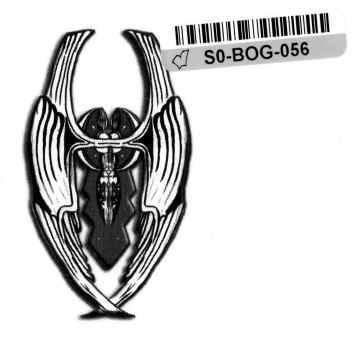

SON OF EREUBUS

GUARDIANS OF LEGEND
BOOK ONE

BY J. S. CHANCELLOR

RHEMALDA PUBLISHING

Rhemalda Publishing
Rhemalda Publishing, Inc. (USA)
P.O. Box 2912, Wenatchee, WA 98807, USA

First American Paperback Edition

Copyright ©2010 by J.S. Chancellor.
Editing by Kara Klotz.
Text design by Rhemalda Publishing.
Cover art by Oliver Wetter of Fantasio Fine Arts http://fantasio.info
Cover design by Rhemalda Publishing.
Author photo by John Pyle Photography, http://www.johnpylephotography.com/

ISBN 13: 978-0-9827437-4-4
ePUB ISBN 13: 978-0-9827437-5-1
ePDF ISBN 13: 978-0-9827437-7-5

Library of Congress Control Number: 2010932949

PRINTED IN THE UNITED STATES OF AMERICA.
10 9 8 7 6 5 4 3 2 1

⊗The paper used in this publication meets the minimum requirements of the American National Standard of Information Services - Permanence of Paper for Printed Library Materials, ASNI Z39.48-1992.

Visit J.S. Chancellor at her author website http://www.jschancellor.com/.
Visit Rhemalda Publishing at http://www.rhemalda.com.

For Bettie Jones and Grace Jordan

ACKNOWLEDGMENTS

Behind every imagined creature, every fantastic race, or castle or invented world, there is a very real one composed of those very special individuals who have influenced, encouraged and inspired. To those who have done so for me, I have more gratitude in my heart than can be rightly expressed through mere words.

To Jeff Groen, who said to me in the most ordinary conversation (on the way to unlock a tanning bed for him), "Think of all the stories that have shaped your life — that you've loved. What if, by never sharing your work, you're keeping us from falling in love with your stories, your worlds." You gave me permission to write with that simple sentence and unknowingly to you at the time, unlocked a door for me as well. I went home that night and pulled out my old notebooks and decided that this story had been in wait long enough. Simply put—you changed my life that day.

To Bettie Jones, who read every word of every draft, more than twice. Had it not been for your persistence in those early days, this book would not be in existence. You were able to see beyond my beginner's prose to the story beneath. Thank you for your honesty, your criticism and your praise and for being my first true fan. Know that your love has taken me from being a girl who wished to write *someday*, to a woman who is and has and will until I am no longer able.

To Grace Jordan, for believing in me and for never giving up on my work. Thank you for providing the opportunity for me to learn, through Carolyn Smoot, what I so desperately needed to in order to succeed as an author. Thank you for being proud of me and never being shy about saying so.

To Eric Longworth and Robert Grawburg, who both spent hours in my office discussing plot and characterization and battle scenes. Thank you for reading those early drafts and for always telling me that it would be published one day. Whether I believed you at the time or not, I needed to hear it.

To Robyn Watson, my own personal cheerleader. You are the human embodiment of selfless love and loyalty. Thank you for telling me, with more enthusiasm than I could have conjured on my best of days back then, that you loved my work, my characters and for talking about them of your own accord, simply because you wanted to. Thank you also to Ben Watson, namely for helping me with the logistics of more than one fighting sequence; and of course for aiding me in the naming of one small, plum-chested, dragon.

To Justin Elswick of Sleepthief. Thank you for generously allowing me to use your music on my website and for helping me through more than one mental block.

To Vin Jensen, how can I even begin to thank you? You found me right after I'd left my job and was just about as discouraged as an author can get. You encouraged my blog, helped shape it, taught me what it meant to socially network with other authors and ultimately you gave me the confidence to submit this novel for publication. Though you were unaware of it at the time, you helped fortify my foundation as a writer, reminded who I was and why I started writing in the first place. You were a teacher when I needed one the most. I am eternally grateful.

To my parents, John and Carolee Rowe — for more things than I can name, but thank you specifically for cultivating a wild imagination and a life of limitless dreams.

To my husband, Benjamin, who is the most patient man I've ever known, and the most giving. Thank you for supporting this burdgeoning career, this second love of mine, for listening to me read dialog aloud like a madwoman, for putting up with my nocturnal habits, and for loving not just me, but the worlds I create. You mean more to me than you'll ever know — *you are my Irial*.

To Diana Best Harbour, for being a kindred soul and providing much needed laughter and wisdom and support. If I didn't know better I'd say we're two halves of a whole.

Thank you to Rhett Hoffmeister, Kara Klotz and the staff at Rhemalda Publishing for taking a chance on an unknown, untried author. I hope to prove that your faith has not been placed in vain.

Thanks also goes to a variety of people who have aided in one way or another; Lyn Barfield Ritchie, Jenner Jordan, Micah Green, Josh Harbour, Kristin and Rantz Walters, Lara Adrian, Doug Brown, Kara Ferhman Young, Sharon Walters, Jay Palmer, John Pyle, and many, many soldiers at Ft. Benning who patiently answered my questions about battle strategy and ancient fighting methods and what it's like to come home from war. God bless you and all of our troops!

And certainly not least, a huge thanks to Mr. Fletcher. You're loved and missed. I'd hoped to bring this to you in person, but you'll just have to wait now. Thank you for pushing me, for insisting on my very best and for being the most crotchety, grumpy, awesome English teacher ever. Here's to a box of salt for the slugs.

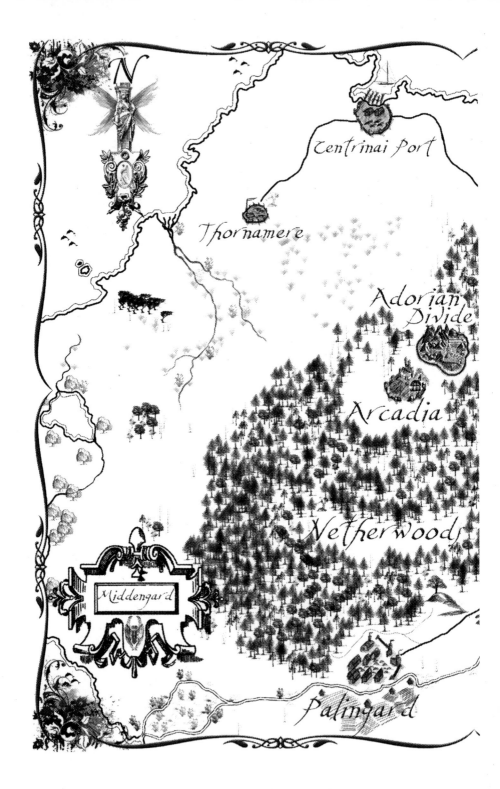

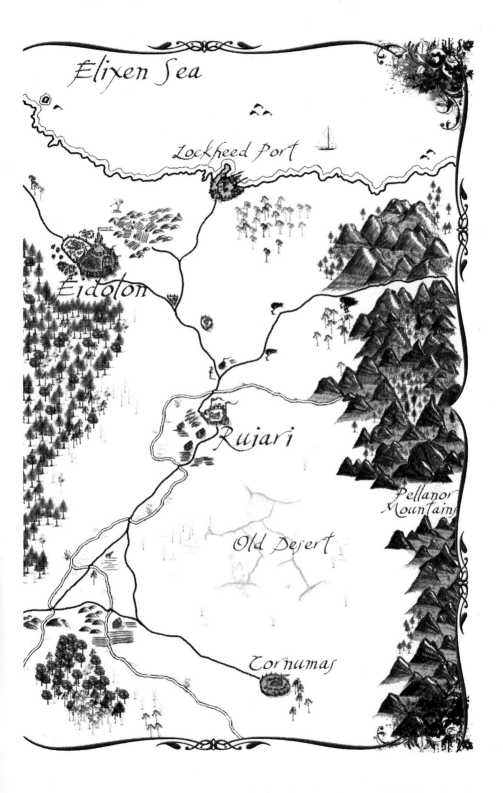

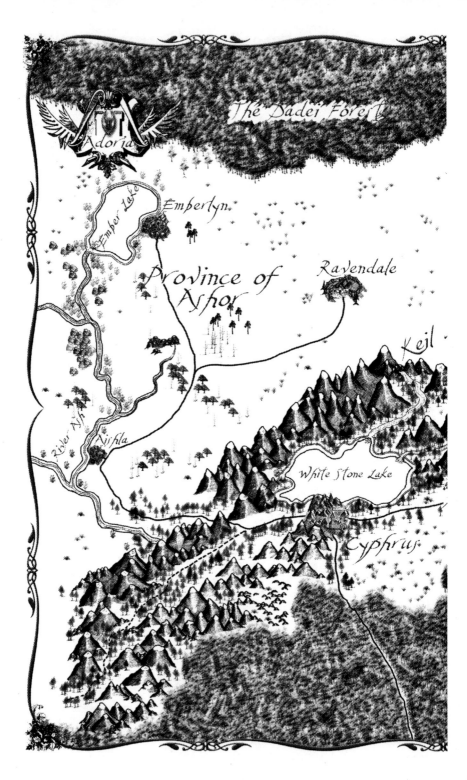

Province of Tyndale

Lipsius

Artesh

Mearai Mountains

Porlace

Mountains

Eve

Kessin Forest

Son of Ereubus

Guardians of Legend
Book One

by J. S. Chancellor

Rhemalda Publishing

THE PROPHECY

How small the world has become. How dark the days of man have grown. Each passing moment is steeped in vile, wicked, and corrupt things that once whispered of power, only to betray. What was once overflowing with life has diminished to a threadbare existence. It was not always this way.

For years, the realm of man, called Middengard, has waged war against the forces of the Laionai. Once human, the Laionai speak as one consciousness — a collective in which nothing of mortality remains. Gifted by the Dark Goddess Ciara with the ability to steal the souls of other men, their purpose is to enslave all who live and breathe in her name.

In the beginning, Middengard was successful in defending its people. But as the first age of war came to an end, its people began to weaken in their resolve, and a fable began to take shape; first in whispers heard at battle's end, then in legends passed down from one generation to the next. Soon, myth became prayer and an unswerving faith in an unseen realm was born.

For thousands of years, that fable fueled the vitality of the human heart, but as the free lands waned and Eidolon's rule overshadowed the few who subsisted on their own, faith faltered. As the last stronghold of man celebrated what little light still existed in the world, few held to the promise of such a fantasy.

There were some among man who would not let die what they knew in their hearts to be true. As they ended their day, they whispered their regards to the winged guardians whose plight was to stand in the stead of mortal man. As they woke, they recited long-held praises for those they had to thank for their freedom.

Though the faith prevailed in some, man was not alone, for among those born into the lineage of Ereubus — the ones who served the Laionai — a prophecy was told:

"Among the souls there is a chosen one, the Oni. Carrying the fate of mortal man, he shall through blood procure their end. He shall be the bearer of all things, bridging the divide between life and death. Through mortal fate eluded, he shall bear witness to those who embody light. This *will be the first sign of his coming. One who has slumbered long shall arise, bringing the Oni the seal that shall forge the final strength of the dark one. This will be the second sign. The son of light shall fall from great heights, spilling innocent blood upon the steps of Eidolon. This will be the third and final sign. All things in alignment, the Oni will then sit at the right hand of darkness."*

With faith placed in things unknown, both Middengard and Eidolon await the future — the Ereubinians, sitting in a throne of power, await the one who will secure their place of sovereignty while man, through the listless eyes of a soulless vessel, awaits the one who will deliver them.

PROLOGUE

The city reeked of sweat and grime. Eidolon's citizens gathered in the chilly, dank air of the commons, their eyes turned to the cloaked figure standing tethered to a post on the center platform. The crowd was boisterous, pushing to gain a better view, all the while musing over the prisoner's identity and the offense he'd committed.

Micah rested against the rain-soaked stone of the far wall, his cloak held tightly to him, trying to ward off the cold he'd felt coming on for weeks. He was tall for his age and could wield a sword better than any of his peers, which was the main reason he was allowed to skip this day's lessons. The other boys would ask and he'd already concocted a dozen exaggerations to relay if the event turned out duller than his imagination.

The prisoner had arrived two days earlier, hood already in place, hands already bound, and apparently gagged, for his only responses to questioning were muffled cries. No one dared touch the hood or even come close enough to examine the undecorated linen shift he wore. Most were content to conjure their own guesses, some stating they knew but had been sworn to secrecy. Micah didn't believe a word of it. They seemed far too interested in what they supposedly already knew.

Urine stained the prisoner's clothing; when the breeze shifted direction, the scent of it and where he'd shat himself filled Micah's nostrils, his congestion doing very little to dull its potency. He coughed and spat, willing away the urge to vomit.

Some had already grown impatient and left, mumbling that the rumor of a public lashing had been just that. He considered leaving, but was too curious. Besides, the crowd alone was more interesting than his studies.

A hush fell over the crowd, every knee bending in reverence as Garren, the High Lord, ascended the shaded stairs beneath the platform. He smiled and walked with a casual stride across the creaking boards, each step echoing in the sudden stillness. He motioned with a turn of his hand for all to rise.

"I see that my display has captured your attention." He clenched the black hood of the prisoner in his fist and jerked it away, revealing the raw, tear-streaked face of Vallor, ruler of the northern realm of Lycus.

A collective gasp was drawn as the magnitude of the prisoner's identity set in. Micah couldn't believe what he was seeing. Had it not been last week that the nobles of the greater houses were singing Vallor's praises?

"Before you," Garren said, "is a reminder that nothing goes unseen. All is laid bare before the eyes of the Laionai and the Dark Goddess — even such trivial matters as paying Eidolon what is rightly due."

Taxes? That's what this is about? Micah was stunned.

Vallor moaned and pulled against his bindings. Dried blood stained his mouth from wrestling with the gag, giving him a maddened appearance. The humiliation seemed rather gratuitous to Micah — surely a simple chastisement or financial penalty would have sufficed.

Garren dipped his head in mock sympathy and placed a hand on Vallor's head. "Perhaps I haven't made myself clear. Lycus has been prosperous …"

As he spoke, a shrill and terrifying cry sounded just beyond the commons. That lone cry became a chorus so dark it sent shivers racing down Micah's skin. *Moriors.* This wasn't a lashing — it was an execution.

Garren continued speaking as though it were nothing more than the wind they were hearing. "Yet, my generous gifts of land and privilege are not enough for him."

The Moriors had black scales and fleshy wings that extended twice the breadth of their body, their man-like countenance complemented by a tall, skeletal torso and long talons that extended from deceivingly frail hands. Their feet were hooved like cattle. Shrieking still, they circled the platform before landing.

Garren pulled his sword and Vallor's eyes washed in relief. When the blade sliced through his gag, rather than mercifully beheading him, Vallor lost what little composure he had.

"If I take your head how will I hear you scream?" Garren asked.

"Lord, be merciful!" Vallor's wailing died against the sound of rushing wings and gnashing teeth, but Micah could read his lips and the words chilled him to his core.

Micah wanted to look away — wanted to sink back into the stone of the wall, or retire to his chambers to read a book, or practice his swordplay

— but he could not tear his gaze from the platform as the Moriors ripped flesh from Vallor's bones, eating him alive.

The gruesome scene silenced all who witnessed it, magnifying the sounds of the carnage. Eventually, only bones remained, gleaming eerily white in the waning light of day.

Garren, jaws clenched, eyed the crowd. For several minutes, he flexed his hands at his sides and paced. The Moriors stood sentinel behind him, their heads hung in obedience, though it was not Garren who commanded them, but the Laionai, and none present questioned it.

Micah had never seen them, nor had any ordinary Ereubinian — only the higher ranks had seen the Laionai, and even then selectively, but he'd heard their description more times than he cared to.

The Laionai, their eminence, had eyes that were solid black orbs deeply set into pallid skin. Their hair, thin and white, swept the ground behind them, blending with their robes of the same color. They stood much taller than a man, nearly eight feet. Though they stood as six individuals, they were one consciousness, their words spoken in unison. Once men, they now ruled over Middengard in the name of the Dark Goddess Ciara. Anything decreed from the High Lord's mouth came straight from their eminence.

Garren's laughter shook Micah from his musings.

"Do you take me for a witless fool?" Garren asked.

No one dared answer him.

"Truly, there is not one among you who will admit to flawed judgment? Come, speak openly. Who thought even one small share would go unnoticed?"

Micah looked around at the shocked faces. Some were visibly shaken, others deathly still in their fear. There was not a single heart that didn't flutter with Garren's dangerous questioning.

Garren leapt from the high platform, an unnatural act, and landed on the cobbled street. The crowd parted only to fall again to its knees once out of his way.

He walked up to a portly gentleman with a sandy beard and a bright blue tailored cloak. Tucking his sword under the man's chin, he leaned into his face, laughing low. "And what about you?"

Sweat rolled down the man's face and into his eyes. The cold weather certainly did not make him swelter so.

"My Lord, I have the utmost faith in the Goddess and their eminence. I beg you not question my loyalty," he pleaded.

Garren removed the sword and nodded once. "By your own admission then, you are not guilty of treason." He turned on his left foot and, just as Micah had convinced himself that Garren was going to return to the platform, the High Lord gripped his sword in both hands and with a swift stroke severed the man's head from his body.

Garren snatched the cloak from the ground and wiped the blood from his blade before addressing the crowd again. "Let this be a warning. The lack of faith, and thereby obedience, that once went unnoticed will no longer be so; no matter the nature of the betrayal nor how slight. All will pay for the sins of one, innocent and guilty alike.

One last human stronghold remains, and nothing will keep Palingard from the Goddess' rightful reign."

It was long into the night, well after the High Lord and his forces had departed for Palingard, that Micah no longer heard Garren's words resounding in his head. *All will pay for the sins of one.*

CHAPTER ONE

NOT HUMAN

For years, she'd risen before the sun would even consider it and yet, on the day she was relying upon an unnoticed departure, Ariana overslept. She rolled out of bed, groaning, and reached one hand under the night table to snatch the packed satchel she'd tucked there. She'd changed the night before from her thin evening shift into a well-worn linen tunic and pants that were in an even worse state of disrepair. Her intention was to slip out before daybreak, but sunlight blistered the horizon, washing the room in shades of bright pink and red.

Koen, her canine companion, looked up from where he rested on the floor and sniffed his disapproval.

"I'm not interested in your opinion Koen. You're only in it for the food," she whispered. Shaking her head, Ariana turned to the window and pushed open the weathered wood. *Three days and the winter festival will be over, everything will return to the ordinary and mundane.*

"Are you interested in *my* opinion?"

Ariana sighed, dropping her head. Without turning around, she knew the doorway to her bedroom was occupied by a head full of hair the color of spun sugar.

"Not particularly, but I fear I have little choice in the matter."

Sara seated herself on the bed and folded her hands in her lap. "Let them have their fun, Ari. It does everyone good to celebrate the victory, however small it may have been."

Ariana let go of the window frame and rested her back against the wall. "I don't need to remind you who was lost in that *victory.*"

Sara gave her a graceful smile. "Hiding won't bring her back. Wouldn't she want you to enjoy this time with us?"

Ariana unconsciously toyed with her mother's necklace as she considered this, then tucked it safely into her shirt. "Perhaps — but I am *not* my mother, nor am I as gentle a soul as she was." As she spoke, the sounds of the hearth in the main room grew louder as Bella began to cook for the day. This was not going as she had hoped. "Why are you here at this hour?"

Sara giggled. "You think me completely daft, do you?"

Ariana's stomach growled and, as much as she hated to admit it, the smells drifting from below the door had begun to hold her attention.

"I suppose I was coming to bid you farewell. And maybe ask where you were planning on hiding this year, so that if you fail to show up after a few days I'll know where to send everyone."

"Tell them I've gone to Eidolon in search of my father," Ariana grinned. "That should keep them occupied for at least a few days."

"Be serious. Are you really avoiding the whole affair?"

Palingard was not the fortified kingdom of Sara's ancestry. It was squalid in some places and simply poor in others. The festival, while lavish for their resources, was nothing that could rightly be called an *affair*. More than anything it was a complete waste of resources that would be needed sorely in the coming year.

"Sara, we have this same argument every year, and every year the result is the same. This is idiocy — to celebrate a victory some fifteen years old. What have we learned since then? How have we improved our safeguards? There aren't any, and the few who held to what my father taught them are no longer here. Don't you think if your fairy tales were real, they would have come true by now? What about the few seasons running when nearly every crop we had withered and died? What then? Your mythical saviors didn't swoop in to teach us how to rotate crops; we had to figure that out on our own. I just can't be around it right now. It's too much."

The silence was drawn out to what felt like an eternity. Finally, the mild exasperation in Sara's eyes shifted back into her traditional congeniality, tinged with a bit of sadness. "Then at least tell me where you're going so I won't worry about you."

Ariana had a habit of being hard around the edges, even bitter at times, but deep down she was heavy-hearted and regretted her tone. "Sara, forgive me. I have been horrid to you lately. I don't mean to be, it's just — I'm sorry. I'll be near the bluff or just south of it."

Bella called from the kitchen, "Your breakfast is cooling while you take your time chattering away, and don't even think about bringing that troublesome friend of yours to the table." She was referring to Koen, whom she didn't particularly care for. Most of the time he played games with her, like seeing how much priceless bacon he could steal, or chasing the livestock.

Sara made a face at Ariana.

"So like a proper *lady,*" Ariana quipped. She walked past Sara and opened the door into the main room.

Bella was bent over a kettle that bubbled and filled the room with the smell of stewed apples. Mixed in was the scent of freshly baked bread. Ariana, not needing to ask what they were for, walked over and picked a steaming sliver from the kettle, sliding away from Bella's scolding hand.

"They're not ready yet, and they're not for your mouths anyhow."

Ariana smiled, biting into the half-cooked apple. "If you didn't intend them to be for our mouths, then perhaps you shouldn't have made them smell so good."

Bella was a pleasant woman, plump and jovial much of the time. She was rather short with long, fine brown hair that she kept pinned beneath a white scarf, her cheeks always flushed a dusty pink. She'd been a presence in their home long before Ariana was born, first as a shy housemaid, then as Ariana's caretaker after the loss of her parents.

Bella brought a loaf of bread to the table, along with a small bowl of apple butter. "I thought you'd appreciate this, Sara, being your favorite and all."

Sara took the bowl from her, gratitude spreading across her delicate features. She was Ariana's closest friend and had been since they were in school. She was the very definition of beautiful and had no knowledge of it whatsoever. The object of most men's attention in the village, Sara would have been justified in being conceited — she was anything but, her ardent belief in the Adorians giving her an almost childlike innocence. Ariana tried not to condemn her too often for such foolishness, but with the festival approaching, it always became a sore subject between them.

Koen made himself comfortable beneath their feet, having waited until Bella was distracted to make his entrance, and chewed on pilfered bits of bread with the kind of silence that only beasts who eat stolen scraps are able to manage. Ariana reached down to graze the fur of his head with her hand.

"Ari, you'd better not be feeding the breakfast that I just slaved over to the dog, or you'll be eating his supper instead of your own."

"Sorry, Bella," Sara offered, having fed him as well.

"It's not your fault, dear. It's the influence of the spoilt child beside you."

Ariana frowned. "I am only spoiled on Thursdays and that's several days away, thank you."

"What mischief are you off to today?" Ariana knew what Bella meant to ask, and she didn't appreciate it in the least.

"Whatever I'll be doing, I won't be doing it anywhere near here."

"Alright, then. I suppose you'll be leaving me here to patch all of these costumes myself," Bella remarked.

"You know I hate this time of year," Ariana tried to soften her tone, but the words still sounded coarse.

Bella shook her head and turned back toward the hearth, a reprimand rasped under her breath. "It's a shame for such a pretty young girl like yourself to be so sullen all the time."

"What are we celebrating, Bella? Please, tell me it's our ill fortune, tell me that we're celebrating years of near-famine and hardship. Say any word to me, *anything* but victory. Never has there been a word I've loathed more." Why did they all insist on discussing this with her when nothing had changed?

Bella heaved a great sigh. "I just want to see you happy — everyone does. I cannot tell you how many of your friends have made mention of your disposition as of late."

Ariana sat in silence for a moment. She looked at Sara, who cringed. Though Bella's comment wasn't unfair, it still seemed poor taste in regards to her timing.

"I'm sorry to disenchant everyone so. I can keep the anniversary of my mother's death reverent without your help." Ariana rose from the table and started toward the door, when Bella intercepted her.

"Do not leave this house ill with me." She handed Ariana her cloak with a look in her eyes that defied her to refuse it. Ariana, accepting the cloak, reached for her satchel where she'd hung it on the wall and slung it over her shoulder. She had one foot out the door when Bella spoke again.

"I am not insensitive, child, nor have I forgotten your mother. I loved her, too."

"Then be reasonable, Palingard has not been blessed. Ours is a dying realm, in case you've forgotten that as well — a realm that needs to be cautious with what little we have. This festival is nothing but disgraceful when you consider its cost." She dropped the cloak and spun to cross the threshold to the dry dirt beyond.

Ariana walked the short distance to the stables, eager to be free of the whole world as she knew it, at least for a little while.

Palingard wasn't very big. The houses were modest, with thatched roofs and stone walls. All things considered, Ariana had grown up a child of relative privilege. Her father had been an important member of the hierarchy and had led their men against the Ereubinians. He was periodically absent throughout her childhood, but stayed with her more often after her mother died. The last time he had left was more than ten years ago. Most understood him to be no longer living; rumors held that he'd been killed in the Netherwoods by Ereubinian scouts, but she'd never believed that story.

Her father had never met Koen, but would have liked him. She had found the dog at the edge of the woods, dirty and homeless, a short time after her father left. None of the other villagers wanted anything to do with him, he was nearly as big as she was and closely resembled a wolf. Other than livestock and horses, feeding animals wasn't high on the villagers' list of priorities.

Sara leaned over the side of the stall as Ariana tended to her horse, Shadow. "She didn't mean anything by — "

Ariana was not in the mood to hear it. More specifically, she wasn't in the mood to hear it from Sara. Both of her parents were alive and well. "I don't care what her intentions were," she said sorely. "I should just stay out of everyone's way for the next few days."

The streets had already begun to transform. Ribbons reached from the corner of one roof to another, draping down in the middle to create a bright canopy. It wouldn't be long before villagers would start to hang red-leafed wreaths on their doors and once nighttime arrived, each threshold would harbor blood-red candles to be lit in honor of the Adorians who they fancied were their protectors.

"I was afraid you would say something like that," Sara said, "so I took the liberty of telling Jeremy that you would be attending the dance tomorrow evening and were in dire need of an escort."

Ariana took her time responding. "You did not." She wanted nothing to do with Jeremy. He was lazy and a poor swordsman. In fact, there wasn't a single thing about him that appealed to her, save perhaps the sound of his footsteps whenever she was gifted with his departure.

"And just what would you have done had I been telling the truth?" Sara laughed. "I caught that fleeting moment of horror."

"Oh, I don't know, I'm sure I could think of something equally cruel." She'd intended to keep a straight face, but failed miserably. "Like perhaps telling your betrothed in order to marry you he'll have to grow wings — and learn to keep an eye on his opponent." Sara's intended, Jonathan, had lost a practice joust in recent days and Ariana had teased Sara without mercy about it ever since.

Sara frowned. "I was not imagining things. There was a white-winged Adorian knight in those woods as sure as I stand here now. In regards to Jonathan, as I've already stated, it wasn't his fault."

Sara's recollection seemed convincing for a moment, but there was nothing about the hallucination that warranted merit. She hadn't mentioned him in months, leading Ariana to believe Sara's reasoning had won her over. Plainly it had not.

"I'm sure you weren't imagining things. Why wouldn't mystical beings have sympathy for the realm of man? We are such beautiful, brilliant creatures." Just then, several disheveled men tore through the fields just beyond the entrance to the stables, chasing a young boy.

Ariana groaned as she realized who was among them. "Speaking of beauty and brilliance." She grabbed the boy as he skirted toward them and threw him into the stall with her horse, just as the men came around the corner. The men stopped, having lost sight of the boy, their breath coming in staggered pants.

"Have you seen a boy come through here?" Jeremy approached with an instigative look on his face and leaned in as close to Ariana as he could without being improper.

"A boy?" Ariana grinned wickedly, unable to imagine this opportunity presenting itself twice. "What would you want with a boy? Or have you finally grown tired of losing to the other men in your swordplay?"

His left eye twitched as he turned to Sara, "Have you seen him?"

She shook her head, an innocent expression on her face that would have fooled even Ariana if she hadn't known better. "No. What are you chasing him for?"

"It is the stuff of men. Proper initiation, if you must know."

Ariana couldn't help herself. It irritated her that he felt the need to address Sara's question but ignore hers. "Perhaps I've been unfair in my assumptions," Ariana said. She did her best to sound at the very least cordial. "It sounds like such a noble thing. What might this initiation consist of?"

Jeremy smiled and took her acknowledgment as an invitation to move closer. If it weren't for the feel of the boy's breath on her back as he cowered behind her, she would have moved.

"Far too gruesome for a fair maiden such as yourself. It's simply something to prove the boy's valor."

"Fair maiden?" Ariana laughed. "My! Someone has been filling your head with fantasies." She narrowed her eyes at Sara.

"He's probably half into the woods by now, we're wasting our time." Jeremy gave her an awkward nod. She'd quietly moved both herself and the boy a good foot backwards. It wasn't as far as she'd have liked, but it was enough to remove her from the stench of breakfast that lingered on his breath.

"Safe journey then, noble sir. Fare thee well." She said it with more dramatic flair than she'd thought she had available, bending into an obscenely formal bow — careful not to go so low as to reveal their hideaway.

Jeremy's face flushed and he cleared his throat. "Will I see you at tomorrow's dance?"

"No. I'll be in mourning for that poor boy and whatever it is you're planning on doing to him. Though I have to say, it appears that he's already proven his stealth and prowess by eluding you."

Jeremy couldn't find the words to respond, but as he turned to walk away, he touched Sara briefly on the shoulder.

As soon as he was out of earshot, Sara turned to her. "That seemed unnecessary. Jeremy is an acceptable choice for a husband."

She scoffed. "That's rich coming from someone who has pined over a myth for years. I see the look in your eyes when Jonathan is around — it isn't love."

Before Sara could respond, the boy emerged from the stall. "Are they gone?" His face was bright red, his wet hair matted to his forehead.

Sara, having always been more sympathetic than Ariana, brushed his hair out of his eyes, as a mother would have done. "Yes, love. They suspect you've braved the Nethers. What trouble have you gotten yourself into?"

The boy shook his head. "No trouble. Just fun and games really, but I don't like the one who was talking just then. Full of hot air, he is."

Ariana grinned down at him. "Keep that sense about you. Your gut is often smarter than your head."

The boy nodded, shifting his weight from one foot to the other. "Thank you. I'll try to repay the favor one day."

Sara waved him off with a pat on the shoulder, and then turned to Ariana. "What is it that so bothers you about them?"

Ariana didn't have the slightest idea who she was referring to.

"Adorians." Sara spoke the word with more reverence than most would conjure for their dead ancestors.

Ariana groaned as she secured her soft leather bow case with a full quiver of arrows to the saddle. "Something that does not exist cannot bother me, Sara. That's all that it is — myth. We're the last ones left. Even if they *were* real, they are obviously powerless against the Laionai." At the sight of Sara's expression, Ariana added, "That was harsh. I didn't — "

"I know. I just wish that I could make things easier for you."

Ariana wanted to say something serious, something to express her sincere wish to respect Sara's beliefs, but the words just wouldn't come. "Well, you could start by not giving Jeremy false hope anymore. I'll marry an Ereubinian before I'll marry him."

"I'll try my best. Are you leaving now?"

Ariana nodded, calling Koen. "I'll be back before too long. Tell Bella

I'm sorry, will you?"

"I will. Three days?"

Ariana mounted Shadow, smiling. "Three days."

She made it to the bluff in record time. Koen seemed to grin from where he sat in wait below the low boughs of her favorite Elpsis tree. "One of these days you're going to tell me how you do that." She smirked. "I've still got one thing on you though — you don't have opposable thumbs."

After tying her mount to the tree, she pulled a blanket from the satchel and sat down with her back against the trunk. She took a deep breath and looked out across the expanse. Her mind wandered over the previous years, the festivals she had tried to participate in that all had been disastrous, finally coming to contemplate the grave day they commemorated. As she closed her eyes, she envisioned her mother lying on the cottage floor close enough to touch Ariana's hand. She had struggled to lift her finger to her lips, urging her only child to remain quiet and hidden. Her father had come in after it was over, still breathing hard from the battle. It had taken him a few minutes to regain his bearings and crouch down to find Ariana hidden below the bed. She could still feel his strong embrace and the cold metal of his armor on her bare feet.

It had taken years to recover from the loss. The carnage alone was a gruesome scene she was thankful to have only a vague memory of. Even before that day, she had grown up hearing dark tales about the inhabitants of Eidolon. The Ereubinians were rumored to have the power to steal the human soul and enslave it for their Goddess. But was it true? Those who were knowledgeable spoke only in whispers of Eidolon, often referred to as the City of Shadows, and of the Laionai. Though Duncan, her father's closest friend, used to entertain them with stories of great battles and lore, her father abhorred any mention of either Adoria or its fabled war with Eidolon. She was lost in her thoughts when she heard a sound.

At first it sounded like thunder, a great rumble far in the distance. Then the sharp, piercing cries of the Dragee grew distinct. She hadn't heard the sound in so many years that its foreignness kept her pinned to the tree.

It can't be!

She slowly opened her eyes, praying that she had fallen asleep and that it was some terrible nightmare stirred up from her thoughts of the past. She was not so fortunate.

The horizon overflowed with riders, the Moriors darkening the sky above them in a thick black mass, the Ereubinians each astride their Dragee, a creature not quite horse or dragon, but an unsettling combination of the two. They screamed as their hooves pounded the dry ground. Her heart felt stuck in her chest, devoid of blood, and despite all her talk of readiness, it took her a moment to shake herself out of disbelief.

"Koen, run!" She tore the reins from the tree branch while mounting and dug her heels into the steed's side. She heard them as if they were already upon her, so many of them — far more than she remembered from the last time.

Please, Shadow. Ride swiftly.

As she came to the edge of the village, she jerked hard on the reins. There were enemies in Palingard. It must have been an advanced group. Shadow reared at the sudden pull on the bit, but she steered him hard to the right, toward the Netherwoods.

She couldn't see much from where she rode, but what she glimpsed was a losing battle. She pulled her bow from the case and pivoted in the saddle enough to nock and aim an arrow. She struck a black-cloaked Ereubinian in the left side of his chest. Another shot and then a third were let fly in succession, several more Ereubinians falling, before she felt a tug on the bow. Suddenly, it was ripped from her hands by some unseen force and tossed beneath Shadow's feet.

What the ...?

She gasped as a hooded rider appeared beside her, as if born of thin air. There had been no one near her, she was certain of it.

He shook his head.

She dug in her heels and sped through the thicket at the edge of the woods, small limbs and twigs hitting her face. A Dragee was much faster than a horse and she realized as she heard him growing ever closer that she couldn't outrun him this way. As much as she didn't want to do it, there were areas in the Nethers that were simply too dense for the beast. Her decision had been made for her.

She closed her eyes, took a deep breath, folded her arms across her chest and slid her heels from the stirrups. Then, tucking her head, she braced herself and turned sharply to the right, where she executed an under-practiced rolling dismount.

She slid as she fought to get solid ground beneath her feet. Just as she'd found it, a sharp pain sliced through her ankle and she bit her lip hard enough to bring the metallic taste of blood to her mouth. She blocked out all feeling as she darted through the wild overgrowth, focusing only on the sound of her pursuer.

The root was thick — so thick that she might have seen it had she not looked back. It twisted upwards from the dirt and back down to form a perfect loop, which her injured ankle found with ease. Her back met the forest floor with rib-breaking force, stealing the breath from her lungs and clouding her vision with black swirls that threatened to pull her under.

Within seconds he was beside her, panting, his sword pointed at her neck. Once he'd caught his breath, he straddled her waist with a knee to her right and a foot planted on her left, careful to keep the blade at her throat.

He was dressed fully in black. Leather guards adorned his wrists and shins, connected by various plates of armor. Dragon's heads served as shoulder plates and extended to his elbows. His hood covered an elaborate helmet that shielded all of his face except his eyes, which flared bright violet.

"I should tell you," he said, "that I *am* impressed that you made it this far. I'm not easy to outrun, but you must already know that by now."

"The threat of having one's soul stolen tends to quicken one's feet," she hissed.

He removed his glove and placed his hand on her cheek, perhaps to keep her from turning from him in fear, though she wasn't about to grant him that. Her gaze did not waver from his masked face.

Unimpressed, he ignored her bravado and closed his eyes, speaking in a language that she didn't recognize. It wasn't a very harsh-sounding phrase, but she could tell it wasn't meant for her benefit. She contemplated an attempt to pry her ankle from its snare, but found even a slight shift impossible.

He abruptly stopped, seemingly mid-word, though there was no way she could tell for sure, and sat upright to slide the hood back and remove his helmet, revealing a black shirt below his breastplate that rose and clung to his neck. His jaw was strong, his profile defined. But the look in his eyes as they grew ordinary brown in color, the expression, was what struck her — he was not just handsome, but *known* somehow. It made her chest ache.

An acrid thought crossed her mind that the odd emotional reaction he was invoking in her was somehow related to the Erubians' rumored power to steal a human's soul.

"You are not human," he murmured, scowling in an unsuccessful attempt to conceal his shock.

"Of *course* I'm human," she said, "do you not see me bleeding?"

"Adorians also bleed. Why are you *here*?"

She assumed that it was a rhetorical question, but before either of them could speak again, a cry pierced close to where they'd entered the woods.

Garren glanced back toward the sound of the Morior's cry, visions of the Laionai's justice filling his mind. He'd seen death come slowly by their hands for much lesser sins than this.

"If I am what you say I am, then I'm your mortal enemy, am I not?" When the girl spoke, there was acid in her words and none of the timidity or outright dread he had come to expect from others in his presence.

He turned back to her with narrowed eyes, his lips twisted in an incredulous smirk, and laughed below his breath before he could speak. He couldn't begin to imagine her reason for antagonizing him, especially considering what she was. "You don't fear me?" She started to answer him but he cut her off. "Before you speak, perhaps you should know to whom you are speaking."

"I don't care who you are. Your arrival has told me enough of your allegiance, that's all I need to know."

He really wasn't certain what to say. Before he could reply, the Morior could be heard coming closer and he saw, finally, fear in her eyes. He expected to be pleased by it; instead, all sound left his head and his sight blurred. His gut felt uneasy.

She lifted her gaze to the sky above them, took a deep breath, and with no small portion of reluctance, acknowledged her defeat by gracing him with a faint smile. It wasn't sarcastic. All traces of amusement had fled her winsome features. What it was, however, was so much worse; she'd resigned herself to leave this world on her own terms regardless of the circumstances. Her expression was perhaps the sincerest he'd ever seen.

He lowered his eyes, weighing his decision. "Can you walk at all?" The words came out as a forced whisper from his lips.

She looked at him, dumbfounded. "You intend for me to walk to my execution? I think not. If they want me, they'll have to come for me here."

He exhaled sharply as he leaned down and lifted her with one arm while reaching to free her ankle with the other. As she struggled against him, he placed a finger over her mouth to silence her and motioned toward the thickest underbrush. He let his fingers slide beneath her chin as he whispered, "Go there, and do not move until nightfall. We'll be gone by then. Do you understand me? Do not move until then."

She nodded, remaining still and wordless as he picked up his sword. As he rose, his eyes met hers again and lingered warmly for a moment before cooling. He tightened his jaw, stunned by his own actions. Without thinking, he shrugged the cloak from his shoulders and shoved it into her hands.

"Go," he whispered, then turned back and disappeared into the thicket.

Just before he emerged on the other side, Garren took his sword and slid it quickly across the gap in the armor at his left leg, blood spilling onto the metal and down onto the cuff of his boot. He clenched his teeth, sucking in air as the stinging subsided, and walked into the clearing.

Tadraem approached with a wry smile on his face, Garren's Dragee cantering beside his own. "My Lord, tell me that you haven't met your match in such a tiny opponent."

Garren took the reins from him and mounted the Dragee, repositioning his helmet as soon as he was seated. "She paid for it with her life," he growled.

"No matter, my liege, one less soul will make little difference to our spoils."

"Let us pray that the Laionai and her most Holy will be pleased," Garren said it just loud enough for Tadraem to hear it. He hoped his old mentor, now his second in command, hadn't detected the hitch in his voice.

CHAPTER TWO

SAY THE WORDS

The woods were deep and still. Ariana had watched the color of the sky progress from bright blue to a bruised and bitter color and finally saw the sun sink below the tops of the trees. It felt like hours, but she couldn't be sure how much time had passed since darkness had fallen. She tucked her arms against her chest, her back against the base of a tree. It was ironic how frightened of this place she'd been as a child; now the recesses and alcoves felt somewhat comforting.

The moon was still a night away from being full, a thin sliver perceptibly missing from its side. It peered back at her from its place in the sky, sending pale rays like silk threads through the forest. Gingerly moving branches aside, her walk back to the village was almost reverent, as if leaving nothing wounded by her presence would somehow save those she had been unable to.

The place she'd taken for granted for years grew new form. The trampled leaves, twigs, and roots seemed foreign to her, rolling from under the overgrowth and snaking along the forest floor to trip her already unsure footing. She knew better than to imbue inanimate objects with hostility, but her gut recoiled at the mere whisper of a thought related to what had befallen her morning. She went back to cursing the wild, unkempt underbrush.

Gregor is never going to hear the end of this when I get a hold of him. This should have been clear-cut months ago.

The absurdity of her thoughts hit her and made her throat dry. A voice murmured in her mind that she would never have the chance to throttle Gregor properly for his negligence.

There is no sound, nothing, save your own fettered breathing. There is nothing left.

She almost tripped on it. Absently, she picked up her satchel from where she had thrown it to the ground in dismount and slung it over one shoulder.

Listen ... what do you hear?

She shook her head against the question. She couldn't let herself think this way, she had no reason to. Then, her internal ramblings halted with her breathing and any threadbare hope she'd held that Palingard had in any way been spared. She crossed over the densest part of the forest to see clearly what she had been hearing, and ignoring, for a few paces ...

The flames danced and licked angrily at the night air, spiraling upwards toward the waxing moon. Any trace of the festival décor was long gone, and scant pillars remained where modest cottages had once speckled the clearing. Those on the outskirts smoldered, while those in the center remained viciously ablaze. There were no survivors; no one picking up the remnants to begin again, no weeping and mourning, no scurrying of animals to find new shelter. Her vision blurred, her eyes glossed over with unshed tears. Her thoughts were as barren as the devastation before her.

What she could see beyond the destruction was the scene she had once tried so hard to forget, the one she had been clinging to anew with hope. As if on top of what was real and in front of her, she saw Palingard as it was fifteen years past. The village was reeling from the aftermath of the last siege — shouts of pain and grief heard in equal measure.

Shock turned to anger as she pictured her savior's face again. He'd known. The Ereubinian had not spared her life out of goodness or mercy. This had been a game for him.

What good are his spoils with no one to suffer for them?

"Was this what you were waiting for?" She wailed. "To see me fall apart?" Her resolve weakened and the ground rushed to meet her knees. Tears rolled down her cheeks and sobs choked her words of clarity. "Why didn't you come back sooner? Finish us off before we had a chance to recover?" She rested her cheek against the soil as she wept.

At first she thought she felt his breath, the Ereubinian's — that he had returned to revel in his win — but she realized the very idea that he would have knelt down to lie on the ground beside her was lunacy.

"Koen," she moaned. Grabbing the dog by his nape, she pulled him to her and buried her face in his matted fur. "You left me, you useless coward."

Her brief joy was sobered as she fought another round of tears, this one stronger than the first. Keeping one hand on Koen, she lowered her head into the other hand and tried to slow her breathing as her father had once taught her.

I can't do this now. I can't let this paralyze me. She didn't trust the Ereubinian to keep his unspoken promise of respite. She waited another minute before trying her legs. Once she was secure on her feet, she limped back to the edge of the woods, where she stood for a moment, peering into the darkness of the Netherwoods. A wind whipped through the boughs of the trees above her, bringing a chill to her skin. She moved to pull her cloak tighter to her when she realized whose cloak she wore.

Ripping it off, she held back a string of curses that would have made a seaman blanch, but couldn't bring herself to drop it to the ground.

It doesn't matter whose it is, it will still keep me warm.

She swallowed a healthy measure of disgust before grudgingly wrapping it around her shoulders again. Koen seemed to look at her with approval.

"I don't want to hear it from you," she sounded ill, but was more than pleased he'd run from the fight. She'd seen nothing but what appeared to be charred carcasses of both man and beast. No doubt Koen wouldn't have made it.

He looked up at her and sneezed, as was his tradition when she spoke to him as if he had the ability to answer.

"Not that you would have been able to do much anyhow," she murmured. Though she played a one-sided conversation, her mind was already elsewhere. *Father, where are you?*

She'd heard for three years counting that Palingard was the last stronghold and it had been at least nine years or more since they'd stopped trading with the city of Ruiari. *Could we really be the last?* Her intuition told her that somewhere there had to be smaller camps of those, like herself, who'd managed to evade capture.

Surely Father is somewhere among them, maybe without sense or memory of where he is from. As much as she avoided others and feigned little interest in what Palingard called society, she now found herself wishing for the world of Sara's parents to be real, for Ruiari to be intact, for anyone to be out there in the darkness other than those who'd taken her life from her.

She imagined as she trod along that she would find the University still stood, and that maybe the village leaders in Palingard had been misinformed.

They were hard-headed, ill-read and it wouldn't have been entirely out of the question for them to take the words of one mistaken messenger to heart. Had they even bothered to see for themselves? Given the extent of their preparations, they couldn't have. Then she recalled hearing something herself from Sara. It *had* fallen. She was being ridiculous. Even Jonathan, whose family was as lofty as Sara's in what had once been Ruiari's royal court, had spoken of its fall.

She traveled for several hours, until the depth of foliage hid the light from the moon. Only when she could no longer see did she stop and take refuge beneath the overhang of what appeared to be a large rock formation. Finally, she was left with no choice but to contend with thoughts of Sara and Bella that she'd previously held back; she surrendered to another bout of tears.

When she woke the next morning, she found she'd slept so deeply that it took her a minute to gain her bearings.

"Koen?" What she'd thought to be stone was in the light of day a huge root. Standing, she found that she could observe nothing but the walls of dirt that blocked her view. "Koen!"

As she climbed to the top of the embankment, she was overcome with awe. Ravines wove their way deep into the ground, dipping from trees whose bases were larger than the home she'd been born in. Moss clung to the winding roots and made their way in strings to the forest floor. The varying hues of green and specks of pale violet flowers left her speechless. The effect was stunning. She had grown so accustomed to the simplicity of her village, the rugged cliffs and barren stretches of land, that a new definition of the word "forest" was beginning to form.

"Koen!" Still hearing nothing, she shook herself from her stupor and began to tread through the maze around her with staggered progress. Her ankle, still swollen, throbbed.

She spied her companion a few paces ahead, hopping from one root to the next. "Koen!" He howled in recognition of his name.

After walking a bit, her stomach overturned her will and forced her to admit she was hungry. She'd argued with herself for some time, insisting she was too shaken to eat and digest anything properly, but in the end, the growling in her gut won.

Untying the satchel, she pulled from it bread, dried meat and a small bit of cheese. Koen refused when she broke off a piece of the bread for him.

"Suit yourself, but don't whine later that you're famished. We could have a long journey ahead of us." She took her time eating. Her ankle needed the rest and her mind began to wander.

Surely the waterfront villages had been stronger than Palingard. She was aware that she was reneging on every point she'd ever made in her arguments with the men in the village when they'd tried to convince her that Palingard was not alone and that there had to be other strongholds farther from Eidolon. That had sounded ridiculous to her at the time. Why *would* Eidolon have wasted its efforts on a little tract of land like that? Palingard had nothing of value and what they did have they accredited to their damned Adorians.

She tore off a piece of the dried meat, feeling her hunger more as the spice of it warmed her mouth. *Ah, the faithful.* Their eyes had been trained on looking for imaginary friends when they should have been wielding weapons. How many times had her father told them to take pride in fighting for themselves and not to believe in such fables? He'd been right, of course. He always was.

But her parents and a few of her father's closest friends had been a minority in the voice of Palingard. Even Bella and Sara believed in the Adorians. Sara's parents had been students of the University and knew better than to keep their faith in the ways of the past, especially when it had done so little to preserve their world.

When she finished eating, she and Koen found a stream and filled the small flask with enough water to sustain them for the rest of the day. For the first few hours of their trek, she vented her frustrations to Koen. As it grew later in the day, however, she fell deeper into silence, lost in remembrances of her past.

Following her mother's death, she'd traveled with her father. They'd gone as far as the sea, to a small province north of Ruiari. She could still remember the smell of the salt in the air and the strength that seemed to radiate from the sailors. Her father had told her they were mostly from the kingdoms in the northern realm of Lycus, his homeland.

So far from Eidolon — is that where you have gone?

Exhausted, she slowed her pace and finally stopped to rest against a tree. This would have been much easier with her horse. She'd heard stories of loyal steeds that searched out their masters long after they had been separated by warfare. Not Shadow. He was only good for spooking and stepping on her feet.

She looked down to see if Koen seemed as worn out as she felt. Just as she turned her head, she saw something entangled in the weeds and ivy that wound around the tree. She lifted her hand to brush aside the foliage, but as she turned, it vanished. Startled, she stepped back, nearly tripping over Koen.

"Did you see that?" She regained her balance and leaned forward, then, ever so lightly, she touched her fingertips to the leaves. Shimmering like sunlight on the surface of water, bright silver came again into view. Shocked, she pulled a sword free of its prison and held it up, examining the intricate designs etched into the gleaming gold blade. The hilt was what she had first seen, an ornate cast silver with two dragons whose tails curled around the hand grip. It was unlike any weapon she'd ever seen. The men of the village had crude swords forged of metals easily found in the surrounding areas. Even her father's chosen instrument was a weapon of simple design.

This was a broadsword, nearly half her height and much too heavy for her to actually wield against an attacker, but she couldn't bear to leave it behind. She was also quite conscious of its strange appearance. There was always the chance that she'd imagined it to be hidden and, in her delirium, envisioned that it was revealed at her touch. She couldn't deny its impressiveness. Perhaps she was much closer to civilization than she thought.

She glanced at Koen long enough to motion him onward. Just a few miles farther, they reached the edge of a city. It was grand — high spires draped with marble carvings rose in the distance, overshadowing smaller yet similarly adorned buildings. The stone was cut in a fashion that gave a sense of great wealth. This was once, if no longer, a flourishing city. What struck her, though, was the lack of movement, the lack of any sound except of creatures scurrying in the woods behind her.

Had she thought at all that she weren't alone, she wouldn't have gone closer. After a few moments of observation, she was certain. She made her way past the wooden doors and into the city itself, wandering for a bit before pausing to take in the magnificent temple in the center of the city. She opened her mouth to say something to Koen about it, when she realized he wasn't there. Not in the least surprised by his disappearance, she continued on.

Removing her dagger from where it was strapped to her thigh, she stayed close to the buildings that lined the main throughway. The sword in one hand, useless for anything but intimidation, and her dagger in the other, she thought briefly to herself that her father would eat his words if he could see her now. He abhorred her interest in archery and would have killed Duncan with his bare hands had he known his friend had tutored her not only to shoot with startling accuracy, but to throw hand blades with equal stealth. Surely, her father would have seen the benefit of her having such skills now.

There was an eerie stillness about everything. As she passed the shops, she noted they were devoid of settled dust, rotted food, or any other signs that there had once been life. She also noted that not only were there no humans or Ereubinians present, there was not one thing living past the wooden doors. Nothing. No bugs, rodents, or animals had found shelter in the city's abandonment.

Something is wrong, something feels so very unnatural about this place.

Despite her growing concern, she couldn't stop herself from entering the temple. The closer she came to its enormous doors, the more compelled her feet were to pass through them.

As soon as she stepped onto the polished stone, euphoria washed over her. She had to grip a small bench to steady her feet. She looked up into the rafters and the carved wood that trimmed the walls, losing herself as her gaze turned upwards. More than ten stories high, the domed ceiling was painted with a bright mural that depicted a multitude of scenes. There were two dragons in battle; one bright silver, the other an almost iridescent shade of white, surrounded by winged beings that she could only guess were Adorians. Another picture displayed a beautiful woman with dark hair standing behind a sandy-haired man, whispering into his ear. He held a book that glistened gold. Farther over was an image of two lovers embracing, tears streaming down their cheeks. She touched her hair, similar in shade to the tresses in the mural, and sadness swept through her.

"Your sorrow is without cause, you have much to be thankful for." A little girl's appearance startled Ariana.

"What?" she murmured. The euphoric feeling strengthened, blending with the grief she felt, making her behave as if drunk.

The girl drew closer and took her hand. "Come, let me show you."

Ariana hadn't the will to say no, nor the clear consciousness to question it. She followed until they came to a low pool of dark water, its surface completely still. A perfect reflection of the painted ceiling appeared on the water's surface, the lovers frozen in their woeful stance.

"Do you believe in dreams?"

Ariana considered the little girl's question as she peered at the water's surface, feeling her chest tighten as the image changed into her parents' likenesses.

"You can be with them, Ariana. All that is required of you is to say the words."

Ariana watched her mother reach out to her. "Mother," she whispered.

"Say the words and this will all be over, a nightmare from which you will awaken."

She closed her eyes, her vision starting to spin. Feeling overwhelmed, she knelt down, gripping the side of the well for support. *This cannot be real.*

"But it is. See for yourself what is offered to you. I can give you anything you desire, Ariana. Anything." Another face appeared in place of her parents, with the opposite effect. In the water she saw Sara.

"Sara needs me," she murmured. "No, this cannot be real. None of this is real." Her voice steadied with resolve and she rose to her feet, fighting the fog that blanketed her consciousness.

The little girl began to back away from Ariana as Koen's foreboding howl echoed in the distance.

"Say the words before it is too late!"

"No!" She screamed, groaning with nausea as the spinning increased tenfold. Suddenly, everything around Ariana decayed, the walls crumbling and the wood rotting. She covered her head and dropped to the ground, watching the drastic transformation.

The drugged feeling lessened only slightly, leaving a haze over her field of vision as she looked around her. A thousand or more years had passed over this place. Stone had not only eroded from rainwater, but thick moss had grown over the walls, or what was left of them. She rose to her feet, alone now, peering out past where the temple doors had been. Ruins. Nothing was before her but the ancient ruins of some long-ended kingdom.

"What?" she whispered. The sun, which had been resting on the very edge of the horizon, had fallen below it, replaced by a luminous pale orb.

Hearing Koen again, she tightened the strap of her satchel and started toward the sound of his howl, through the ruins and beyond the edges of the city, where she paused to take in her surroundings. It took Ariana a few moments to fully understand that what she was seeing just beyond her in the distance was snow.

She had never seen it. Palingard was too far south, and freezing rain was as close as it ever came. *I haven't traveled that far north, I couldn't have.* As far as she understood, the only place within six months' distance where it did snow was beyond the Elixen Sea. Yet, as she trekked opposite of the way she had come, snow fell from the sky and blanketed that which had to have been accumulating for many days.

She stopped and turned, making certain of what she was seeing. The snow stopped just outside of what had been the northern wall. From a few paces away, it looked as though the city had never been there at all.

"Koen!" she cried, feeling fear for the first time since the siege. She shook her head, again putting her hands over her face. "Where am I?" she breathed. "Koen!" her voice echoed through the trees. A large pale moon, now full, cast a bright reflection on the snow that covered the ground. The forest beyond was deep with darkness, leaving little visibility. Koen howled again in the distance ahead of her, and she ran toward him, falling twice as she slid down the embankment at the edge of the clearing.

His eyes were cold. Staring into the well, The Dark Lord Azrian watched the ripples shiver across the surface of the water from where his fist had made contact with the stone. A foul, black curse left his lips in a language he rarely spoke as he leaned over, resting his weight on the centers of his palms, his arms outstretched on both sides. He'd been foolish, he knew. Ariana had been there all along, among the humans, right in the midst of the fray. It was nearly insulting. He wondered if Ciara had felt it too. *No matter,* he told himself, keeping his eyes fixed on her pale skin and fluid blue eyes.

It has begun.

CHAPTER THREE

PREY

Michael had been tracking the wolf for miles as it dodged in and out of the woods, narrowly escaping his line of sight. The moon hung full in the sky, casting a glow off the powder-fine snow and onto the very edge of the forest as he crouched and waited in silence for his prey to reappear.

Michael was dressed in white, the leather of his tunic trimmed with pearl-colored brocade, only his reddish hair and blue eyes visible against the landscape. He was tall with a strong, lean build, and the large white wings typical of Adorian men.

He heard rustling to his left from across the field. He pulled an arrow from his quiver and readied it against the bow. In the darkness, he saw the gleam of two eyes, the same green hue that had been evading him. He watched them look down, then behind. Having seen something, the wolf leapt over a drift and into the light. It was covered in snow, and though Michael could barely see it from such a distance, he could tell this was indeed a different wolf. It was much bigger and less aware that it was being hunted. Michael stood up and eased his way in the same direction as his prey. He remained on the opposite side of the field and when the wolf began to pick up its pace a bit, Michael mirrored its actions. The forest would thin out if they went much farther, this was his last chance. He knelt down and steadied his aim. Releasing the arrow, it flew through the air across the field, letting no more sound escape from the bow than a mere whisper as the string fell back into place. As the arrow approached its intended target, Michael saw a girl move into its stead. He stood frozen for a moment, not believing his eyes, then heard a cry and a whimper from the wolf as the girl fell to the ground.

Dropping his bow, his large wings opened and with a fluid motion he rose into the air and glided across the field to where the girl lay.

"Are you ..." he stopped mid-sentence as he saw markings on her cloak. There was little need to inquire into the girl's lineage.

She seemed unaware that he'd approached her and as soon as his hand touched her shoulder, she reeled from his grasp. Eyes wide, her expression was one of complete surprise. She held her hand to her side and shrank away from his touch.

"You have wings," her words sounded frail and thin, and to his shock, the very moment she struggled to speak he caught sight of the huge sword that lay at her side. A broadsword, it was much too large for anyone of her slight stature to use effectively. She was a wispy creature, with a thin figure and delicate, defined features. Dark red hair, visible even in the shadows, tumbled past her shoulders in thick waves, a stark contrast to her snowy white complexion. It reminded him a little of his own pale coloring. He started to ask her about the sword when her eyes flickered shut and she groaned in pain.

This did not bode well. Fears of how many Ereubinians had crossed over the divide flooded his veins like ice water, but he had no choice. He was scantily armed and alone. If it was a trap, it was too late to back out of it.

He leaned over to pick her up, first moving the sword from her reach. He felt a prick against his neck.

"Stay… away… from…" Another spasm of pain took care of her acerbic tongue, though it did not remove the dagger she held at his jugular.

In all the years he'd been in battle, he had never once seen a woman fight, let alone stumble upon one in the middle of the night in a protected realm, carrying more weapons than he probably was aware of. He quite genuinely couldn't discern what to do first.

A dark red stain was spreading from beneath the hand clamped on her side, soaking her tunic. He took a chance and lifted his hand to hers, prying the knife free, hoping the pain would override her strength of grip. "I need to see how badly you've been wounded."

She was struggling to keep her eyes open, but shook her head. It was mere seconds before her breath grew shallow and she lost consciousness.

After securing her sword at his back, he moved her arm away from her side. It was probably a shallow wound, but it was bleeding steadily. Placing his hand at the base of the arrow, he gripped the shaft with the other and glanced up at her. Leaving it whole would cause more harm than good, but he wasn't certain she was completely unconscious. Her cry as he snapped the arrow off, leaving the tip in place, answered his question.

She moaned and fought him, but he outweighed her by at least a hundred pounds — probably more.

"I have no intention to harm you, nor did I to begin with. I didn't see you," he spoke softly, feeling more sympathy than he cared to. As much as he disdained her world, her whimpering was woeful enough to bring any Adorian to his knees.

He noticed then that the animal he had been so certain was a wolf was in fact a dog. It rose and trotted alongside them as Michael carried her through the woods to his horse. "Is this beast a friend of yours?" he asked her.

"Koen," she whispered. It was the last thing she said before finally succumbing to unconsciousness.

He placed her on the horse first, pulled himself up behind her, holding her around the waist with one arm, and took the reins with the other hand. He had brought his horse to carry the spoils of his hunt. This was far from what he'd expected to return with.

It was not a short ride to the capital, but it went quickly as he was consumed with watching the horizon. His only thought was to gather his men as swiftly as possible and strengthen the border.

The cuts on her face and the bruising were plainly visible as they entered the gates of Cyphrus, but what caused him to wonder more was her clothing. Though she wore an Ereubinian cloak, her pants and tunic were human, typical of the poorer villages.

He slowed his horse to a trot just outside of the keep, stopping as a stable boy approached them.

"My Lord," he bowed, taking the reins in his small hands.

"Wake Jareth and tell him I need his men on the southern border." He turned to one of the two guards who approached as he dismounted. "Summon the Arch Elders. I'll convene with them after I have taken her to the healer." He didn't wait for their acquiescence.

Starting up the stairs to the massive double doors of the keep, a scant smile passed over his lips. There, sitting patiently, as though he'd known in advance where Michael was taking his companion, was the dog.

"Well, come on then, no sense leaving you out here alone."

After navigating a long hallway, he came to a narrow staircase that was easy to miss if one wasn't looking for it. At its base was a small room, lit only by the dwindling light of the hearth. In a chair nestled in the corner was an elderly woman, the healer Aulora, her head resting sideways where it had fallen onto her shoulder.

"*Tu denai nordumbra led estrinigh*," he whispered.

She looked up and studied the girl for a moment before answering him in the same tongue and motioning for him to set her onto the bed nearby.

"Is she human?" Michael asked.

Aulora ignored his question and began to tend to the girl's wounds, chanting softly as she worked. He'd turned to leave her to her art when the healer spoke, "She is not human."

He stared back at her, praying she'd give him a direct answer for a change. "Was she escorted, or did she enter alone?"

The healer hummed a bit more and then smoothed an unruly red curl from the girl's forehead. "No, this one is not human." After patting the girl's cheek affectionately, she pulled the cloak from around her and studied it in the firelight. He hadn't taken the time to examine it, but the markings he'd noted as Ereubinian also indicated authority. Feeling that Aulora had said all that she was going to, Michael took the cloak and started out the door.

None but Adorians were able to pass the divide. All others simply passed over it as if Adoria didn't exist. It had been this way for so long, thousands of years, that the time before the divide that protected them seemed merely legend.

While Michael waited for the elders to assemble, he walked the corridors, running through options in his head. He eventually stopped outside their chambers, waiting to be summoned.

Michael breezed through the doorway into their presence. There were twenty-four of them, both men and women. This had been the governing body over Adoria since the dawn of the first age of war, answerable to the man who once held the title of King. Michael, who currently held the seat of sovereignty, was the son of the Adorians' most honored soldier.

Gabriel, Michael's father, had led many battles and had protected many villages from ruin. He was the last to lead the Braeden — an elite group of male Adorians whose wings were removed at birth so they appeared to be human men. Trained from infancy, they were taught the art of warfare and the customs of Middengard, the human realm. Deadly accurate in their abilities to both wield a sword and shoot a bow, they'd held off the total captivity of man for centuries.

There had once been Adorian women in Middengard as well, but not many. The few remaining who were not killed had returned to Adoria after the elders decreed that the age of guardianship had come to an end, after Gabriel's death. Michael never agreed with this and still rode with his men, doing everything in his power to keep Palingard from Ereubinian reign. In the end, though, his effort simply wasn't enough.

The elders rose from where they sat several rows deep in a circular pattern that was sunken into the floor of the room, as Michael took his place at the center.

"My Lord, we have been informed that forces have been sent to the border?" Jenner's statement — more of a question — was spoken on behalf of the elders. Jenner functioned as the elders' voice much of the time, leading their discussions with Michael, and he remained standing after the others had reseated themselves.

"What you have heard is true. With the healer now is a girl I found near the southern stone, an Ereubinian."

"How can you be so certain she is Ereubinian, my Lord?" a voice asked from behind him.

Michael held up the cloak, clenching his fingers into a fist through the wool. "Not that Aulora needed to comment on her adornment, but she confirmed that our visitor is not human."

Jenner stood wordless for a moment, unable to argue with what Michael revealed. The healer was never wrong. She spoke very seldom, but what she said was never questioned. The Elder's eyes glazed over as murmurs and whispers floated through the room, filling the uncomfortable silence for several moments. "Are there any among us who are not accounted for?"

Jenner's question would normally have irritated him, but on this night, in combination with the Adorians laid to rest at the Torradh just days earlier, it infuriated him.

"Are you suggesting that one of them would betray me, lead an Ereubinian in, then leave her to defend herself, alone in the dark, in a realm she has never seen?" This had been a constant source of dissension for the council, leaving Michael pained as to how best to protect Adoria and yet maintain peace among the various provinces. "Do you believe Eidolon's dark grasp to have traveled so far as to corrupt one of our own? You would believe this before you would believe that they had found a way past the divide? Insanity does not begin to — "

Jenner cut him off. "My Lord, please, I meant no slight to you. This just seems to make little sense."

"Truly, it does not make sense for them to send in a seemingly innocent girl, one whom we would have little wish to harm. Do you not see the logic in this?" He pulled the sword from a sheath at his back and held it aloft for the council to see. "This sword was near her when she fell, she could not have come alone. Sending forces to reinforce the borders will not be enough. You know my sentiments on this." Frustrated, Michael sat down against the large stone that served as the centerpiece of the room. Sighing, he wiped a bead of sweat from his brow and stretched out his wings.

"You cannot lose your faith in the divide, my Lord." Jenner gave Michael a tight-lipped smile, but the attempt at placating him failed.

"This is what the council wishes, for us to sit back and let them destroy all that is left of our world? Or is there another option that you are failing to tell me?"

Jenner frowned at Michael's tone. "We have many ways of defending ourselves, the least of which is militarily. We will re-read the writings of the ancient ones, as tradition urges us to do in such dark times as these."

Michael opened his mouth to respond when the heavy door to the sanctum opened and a young servant girl with the robes of a Bedowyn peered in at them.

"The healer wishes to tell you that the girl is in need of rest but will recover. She is awake, if you wish to speak with her." Michael glanced at Jenner, who nodded and rose to join him.

"We will return and gather again at first light," Jenner said to the remaining twenty-three elders as he joined Michael, who was already standing in the doorway.

The two men walked briskly through the hallway, neither of them speaking. They descended the stairs and entered the small room where Michael had left the girl. She was sitting up in bed, her face just as pale as before, but her cuts had been tended and she wore clean clothing. The broken-off shaft and arrowhead lay on the table beside her, blood still covering its surface. Michael winced at the sight and felt a twinge of remorse over wounding her, but as his suspicion of her lineage returned, his regret faded.

Jenner approached the girl first. She looked to be not much older than twenty-one, twenty-two at the most. At average height, Jenner was not as tall or overpowering as Michael. He knelt down and rested a hand beside her. "I can see that you are weary," he said and turned toward the healer. "Have you given her something for the pain?" The old woman nodded. Jenner rose to sit on the edge of the bed. The girl's eyes were glassy and she was having trouble keeping them open. "Where are you from, child?" he asked.

"Palingard." Her voice was hoarse and ragged from exhaustion, a sound Michael knew well.

Jenner seemed to believe her despite what the healer had said, but Michael's gut told him that her appearance in Adoria meant something grave indeed. "Then you are human? What name have you been given?"

"Ariana."

Michael leaned into the door frame, his chest heavy as he listened to her talk. Suspicion turned to sympathy as she told Jenner about the siege. Her words were formed from a delirium far stronger than what the healer's tonic would have caused. They were lucky she was making any sense at all, considering how jumbled her phrases were. It concerned him.

Michael lifted the cloak and stood closer to her. He took her chin in his hand and turned her toward him. "You were wearing this," he said softly. "Where did you get it?"

"Chased me. Into the Nethers." She furrowed her brow. "I fell. My ankle. He told me to wait until dark."

Michael glanced wearily at Jenner. The girl wasn't in her right mind. They would ascertain nothing while she was in this state. "She is tired, Jenner, far too tired to answer anything clearly. I am still concerned, and you know my intentions when we convene with the others on the morrow."

Jenner nodded, thanking Aulora for her aid with the girl's health, and started for the door. Michael, who'd stepped in front of him, whispered in an Adorian tongue his wish to know whether she had come alone. *"Ne dost narromai denlot ta allolost."*

They had almost made it completely through the threshold when she said it.

"Nigh allolost domay." It was barely a whisper and, had they been any farther past the door, it would have been construed as inconsequential mumbling.

"What did you say?" Jenner asked. Michael was too stunned to say anything and could only watch as Jenner sat down once again at her bedside.

"I said — I entered alone."

Jenner smiled. "My wits, child! You are Adorian. I cannot imagine it. How could you have been left behind?"

"We spoke to each other in this … way. I was little. Before he left. No one but us."

Michael walked around Jenner and took her face into his hands, resting his palms against her cheeks, elated beyond expression that she was not of dark blood. "Tell me. What name was given your father?"

"His name is Gabriel."

CHAPTER FOUR

THE CITY OF SHADOWS

A s dusk settled across the horizon, the Moriors flew like dark shadows in the air. The Dragees' heavy frames pounded the earth, kicking up dirt and mire, leaving a trail of destruction in their wake. Garren was silent for most of the lengthy journey back to Eidolon, stopping as little as possible and speaking only when he was addressed with something that interested him.

Those who survived the siege were imprisoned at the back of the caravan. Held in iron cages, they sat listless, staring beyond their captors. Everything was as it should be, having captured more souls at less cost than many other conquests Garren had led. Yet, he felt ill at ease. He pictured the girl's face, replayed her words. *Her actions were intrepid, if nothing else.* But what disturbed him more than anything was his own response. The sword had been in his hand, he had been ready to strike as he had been countless times before, yet nothing in that moment or any other could have forced him to wound her. Now, he kept envisioning her alone in the dark woods. The more he considered this, the more heated he became. Anger became fury as he outpaced the rest of his men, leaving his guards struggling to catch up.

Was this pity he was feeling? He might have once felt compassion for one of his own, but never for an Adorian.

It had been called the City of Shadows for centuries, and rightfully so. He couldn't recall a time when it had not been saturated in darkness even in the full light of day. The woods, as if consciously aware of the ever-growing power of the Laionai, shrank away from the city's borders. The scent of dampness and choking humidity only intensified as they grew near, the cold rainwater pooling in the barren fields from a lack of warmth to evaporate it.

There were two distinct sections to Eidolon. The outer courts housed the human slaves and the markets. Reminiscent of the poorest living conditions in Middengard, it was not a place where any respectable Ereubinian spent any length of time, aside from the wardens who spent most of their lives among the humans, or vessels, as they were often called.

Beyond the outer courts past the dividing wall was an ornate, richly decorated world full of the finest things any being could be afforded. With the whole of Middengard in service to the elite, no expense was spared in catering to them. There was nothing Garren could not obtain should he want it.

At the very center of Eidolon was the pristine temple of the Goddess Ciara. Built in brilliant, almost luminescent, white stone, it stood out among even the more elaborate structures surrounding it. It represented the Goddess' righteousness and purity.

Garren handed over his Dragee as soon as he entered the inner courts, ignoring the salutations of those who milled about. Having grown used to their subservience, he felt their outward displays of humility no longer deserved his attention.

As soon as he was in his chambers, he summoned Tadraem. He knew his men were all exhausted, but this needed to be dealt with before their feast on morrow's eve.

"My liege," Tadraem gave him a respectful partial bow, smiling as Garren waved his guards from the room.

"You have impressed their eminence with your faith and perseverance," Garren said stoically. "Assuming your acceptance, you will be granted the honor of becoming the new High Priest."

Tadraem tilted his head. "I'm more than grateful, but, may I speak candidly with you?"

Tadraem was older than Garren, having taken him as his charge soon after Garren's father, Seth, died. Though Tadraem rarely mentioned Seth, the two had been close confidants before his death. It seemed fitting, Garren supposed, that Tadraem would have taken the roles as his mentor and guardian after Seth's death.

"Of course you may," Garren thought it unusual that Tadraem would behave with such reluctance. He knew better than to ask permission to be forthright with Garren.

"Are you not pleased with your accomplishment? You seem rather ... distracted."

Garren was irritated that it was apparent. "Indifferent, perhaps. Palingard was much stronger when Ruiari was still a stronghold. It would be a stretch to call this anything more than unfinished business."

Even he wasn't convinced of his answer. Palingard was the last remaining province of any kingdom in Middengard, and while it held very little for them tangibly speaking, it had been of particular importance to Adoria, therefore it was even more important to Eidolon symbolically.

Tadraem had led the earlier failed siege on Palingard, and it was more than significant that they had now so easily destroyed it, especially considering Michael's most recent efforts at thwarting their approach. Garren considered this as he revised his statement, realizing that this was a much larger victory to Tadraem than to him.

"You obtained this for Her Holiness years ago. If it were not for your decision to ride on Palingard then, Ruiari and Cornumas would not have let down their defenses. They made the mistake of thinking us ill-prepared instead of knowing the truth of why Palingard was lost to us in the first place."

Tadraem seemed pleased with this response. "Then I will leave you, if there is nothing further. There is much thanks to be given to the Goddess, and I am certain we all need more rest than we can find before the morrow's events."

"Fair night, then. Please tell my ever-vigilant shadows that I'm retiring. I need to tend to this wound and, as usual, I would like to remain undisturbed."

Tadraem stifled a chuckle as he bowed, then turned and left the room. It was no secret that Garren loathed his guards. Having grown up in near-anonymity, the constant shuffle of armored feet served as an annoyance more than a sense of security.

Garren began to pull at his breastplate. As soon as he was unclothed, he took a wash rag from the basin by his bed and lifted the bloody covering from his wound. Placing the wet rag across the now-open cut, he sat on the edge of the bed and sighed. His back and shoulders felt tight and uncomfortable, his hips and thighs strained from the ride. He removed the rag, took a clean piece of fabric and wrapped it in place. Then, wanting nothing more than to lie down and close his eyes, he washed up and put on his nightclothes.

He lay awake. Having taken the souls of many, Garren's body still pulsated with the strength it wrought in him. He ran his hands through his hair, then rubbed them over his face. His eyes had returned to their usual shade of brown, lessening the violet color that was incurred by using his power, but his own eyes weren't what he envisioned.

Her eyes had been unusually blue, nearly unnatural in shade and depth. They were beautiful, and had it been only esthetics, he might have dismissed his response as a result of his recent lack of physical release. But something else had gripped him as soon as his hand had touched her cheek. It seared him, piercing through years of apathy and indifference to everything save furthering Eidolon's reign. Giving a name to the sensation was as impossible as being in the presence of the Goddess herself. He would find the very edges of it when, just as swiftly as it had seemed tangible, it would dissipate into the inconceivable.

He sat upright, resting his head in his hands. He remained like that much of the night, murmuring prayers to Ciara. He had never faltered like this. Known for his swiftness in slaying the Adorians, his failure began to haunt him. The Adorians had come between Eidolon and all that was rightfully theirs, so justice was dealt out with a righteous hand — his hand.

Garren spent the majority of the morning and some of the afternoon catching up on the less physical responsibilities of being High Lord. By the time evening had come he'd signed more declarations, petitions and judgments than he could count. It left his fingers feeling stiff and cramped. Still, no matter how many redundant papers he read or wrote he couldn't force the questions about who the Adorian girl was, or how she'd wound up in Palingard, from his head. Nothing he could imagine made any sense.

Garren's musings were interrupted by a knock at the door. It was Aiden, one of his most reliable men and his friend. Aiden didn't wait to hear Garren respond before opening the door.

"What are you waiting on? I haven't eaten in two days!" Aiden said.

Garren laughed. Aiden was as tall as he, but thin as a rail. He could consume food endlessly and never gain an ounce. Garren knew for a fact that he had indeed eaten in the last two days — and not a scarce amount by any means.

"I'm sure you're famished." Garren walked past Aiden at the doorway and together they headed toward the main hall. He glanced at his guards, indicating silently that if they valued their lives, they should consider hanging back at least a few feet.

"They are waiting to honor you. Do you feel ill?" Aiden asked.

"I'm weary from the journey. Are you not?"

Aiden punched him in the arm. "Are you getting frail in your old age?" Garren wasn't at all old; he had just recently turned thirty. Aiden was merely two years younger.

When he didn't reply, Aiden stopped walking. "I have been unkind in jest," he said cautiously. "I wasn't serious." He placed a hand on Garren's upper arm. "You aren't acting yourself tonight. What troubles you?"

Garren stared wordlessly at him. He actually hadn't heard his friend's first remark. After a moment, he shook his head and looked off to his side. "I don't know," he lied. "I haven't slept well."

Aiden seemed to accept this explanation though it took him a moment before he replied. "You will feel better in the morning, I'm sure of it. You need to eat. That's really what all this is about." Aiden's tone lightened to playful banter.

Garren could only muster a tight-lipped nod. "Perhaps you're right," he murmured. *I pray you are.*

The dining hall was draped in red fabric that covered the walls and laid in strips down the center of the tables. Garren entered through a large curtain, emerging on a tall platform that rose from the dark stone floor. Those who were gathered kneeled, keeping their eyes trained on the ground as his arrival was announced.

When he gave his approval, they broke into praise and accolades. Giving a warm smile in return, he stepped forward to address them.

"I am privileged to be home on this night, and blessed to be of Ereubinian descent. We have attained long-awaited victory, as the Laionai reign now expands over all of Middengard. Nothing gives me more pleasure than to celebrate this triumph with you. The will of the Goddess has been fulfilled. Rejoice!" He thrust both hands into the air and the crowd applauded and cheered. "Let us eat!" he cried.

As he sat down in his chair, musicians began to play an old tune of which his father had been fond. He remained silent as the food was brought to the tables and the feast began. After prayerfully committing his food to Ciara, he ate and discussed matters concerning Eidolon with the other men. Discussions of this nature always excited him, and as the night wore on, he felt more at ease. The memory of the girl's appearance was replaced by visions of a more powerful realm and the commendation of the Laionai before the coming observance.

CHAPTER FIVE

REVELATION

Michael was unable to speak. Jenner's words came after a long pause and with much effort. "And your mother?" he asked.

Ariana pulled the covers closer as she answered, her lack of awareness showing on her face. "Caelyn," she whispered. "She was killed."

Jenner sat back on his heels. "Could it be?" he asked, looking at Aulora.

Aulora rose slowly and hobbled to them. "Long have you suspected Tathan's daughter to have borne two children."

Michael glared at Jenner, who gave an apologetic nod. "I have, but the thought had little merit until now. She needs rest, and has suffered much. Let this continue when she has had time to recover."

They moved into the hallway. Once they had closed the door behind them, Michael turned to Jenner. "Why would you keep this from me? If you suspected this ..."

Jenner gently cut him off. "It was merely a question in the recesses of an old mind, Michael. I am no longer a young knight, capable of giving room to such a fantasy. You know as well as I that there have been more pressing matters for you to contend with. I had no reason to bother you with an unfounded thought."

Michael felt the tension in his shoulders beginning to loosen slightly. What Jenner said made sense but it aggravated him nonetheless. "We are not finished discussing this. I trust you will say nothing of her identity to the others until I deem it appropriate. I cannot say how she will take it, and I would prefer she hear it from someone who knew Father, who is aware of her existence. If she is from Palingard ..." he paused, a certain Braeden coming to mind. He could tell by Jenner's expression that uttering the name was unnecessary. "I will speak with him tomorrow."

Jenner nodded, "Perhaps it will be some comfort to her considering all that she has lost."

Nearly half an hour after Jenner had left him, the door to the hallway opened. Aulora gazed down at Michael, who sat dozing upright at the bottom of the stairwell with his back against the adjacent wall.

"You can come in now, she is asleep," Aulora whispered, leaning down and nudging him.

He opened his eyes and looked up at her. "You knew I was here all along, didn't you?"

Aulora grinned. Michael often thought she took amusement in her wisdom. His question was answered as he crept back through the door and saw that she had placed a blanket and pillow on the floor in the corner. The dog was sound asleep, having made his bed in a warm spot close to the hearth.

Aulora laughed, mumbling something under her breath as she hobbled over to small spiral staircase that led to the room above. He listened as her footsteps grew faint.

He sat on the blankets and leaned on a wooden chair. He couldn't help but gaze at her as she slept, the firelight dancing on her soft porcelain features. She seemed so small, younger than him by at least ten or twelve years.

Many thoughts ran through Michael's head. He'd known very little about where he was born, only that, as an Adorian male, he had been taken back to Adoria to be raised. Trained Braeden males were the only Adorians allowed stay among the humans. His mother would have held to the account that she had miscarried the child and his absence would never be questioned. Ariana couldn't have known about him unless their father had told her, but apparently he had kept their existences a secret from both of them.

He thought about his father's death, almost a decade ago. That would have left Ariana alone at the age of eleven or twelve, at the most. His heart sank at the realization. As devastated as he had been over their father's death, he had been twenty-four, able to handle something so difficult. She had lost both a mother and a father before she was even a teenager. Gabriel had told him long ago of his mother's death but not the details. Michael figured that if he needed to know, his father would have told him. It wasn't something he had questioned until now. His mother's death had been close to fifteen years ago, the same time as the failed attack by the Ereubinians on Palingard. His father had returned to Adoria several months later, devastated, staying a very brief time before leaving again, which made more sense now that Michael knew his father had a child to tend.

There was a good reason that children who were brought back to Adoria were never told where their parents were. Had Michael known, he would have gone after his father on several occasions. Others would have done the same. Humans were never to witness them in battle or otherwise, so only on a rare occasion had a human seen a traditional Adorian male.

Gabriel, being Braeden, was gone for long periods of time throughout Michael's life. But he was present often enough to hold an important rank in Adoria and to serve with the council of elders.

It made no sense to Michael why his father never mentioned Ariana's existence. Why wasn't she brought here after their mother was killed? What bothered him more was the likelihood that there were others of their kind who knew, but had kept silent.

"You must have had a reason," he whispered.

Koen stirred beside the fireplace and lifted his head. He sat up, stretched, and ambled over to where Michael was sitting.

Michael stroked the dog's head and neck. He was a rather large animal, with a blackish-brown coat and white paws, ears that stood straight up, deep black orbs for eyes, and an indescribable presence, as if he carried all the secrets of the world.

"You knew, didn't you?" Michael whispered, scratching behind Koen's ears. Koen panted happily in response. Michael had a dog once; he had looked similar to Koen except it had a much smaller body and a distinct reddish coat of fur. Michael had found the dog wandering outside of the Iidolis, where he grew up. It was a school of sorts, where the male children of the Braeden were raised. Originally they were trained in the same manner as the Braeden, in offensive warfare. This was before the Elders had ended the Age of Guardians.

Michael, after growing up and leaving the Iidolis, remained a mentor despite his duties as Archorigen. The education had changed purpose since Gabriel's death, focusing now on more defensive techniques. Their existence now was more for the protection of Adoria, should it be needed, than for foreign warfare.

The select few who were chosen to become Braeden were raised in the

Aidolis. Similar to the Iidolis, it housed the boys as they were trained in intensive warfare. There were only a handful chosen each year and they were never the sons of Braeden, so as to not place the burden of loss too deeply on any one family. In keeping with custom, they were never told who their parents were, their allegiance rested on their leaders alone. Gabriel had been the last to guide them. The Aidolis now sat barren, its hollow shell the subject of heated debate concerning its future use.

Michael moved the chair and repositioned his pillow and bedding. His body was telling him how late it had become. Laying down, he heard Koen scratching and shuffling around part of the blanket, exhaling noisily as he settled in.

Michael closed his eyes, picturing as he drifted into sleep what his mother might have looked like. He imagined that Ariana favored her a great deal.

It was mid-morning when Michael opened his eyes. The room was still dim, the fire having died down, but Michael could see a thin ribbon of light filtering in from beneath the door. Koen had moved and was sleeping on the end of the bed with Ariana.

The air had chilled during the night and he rose to place more wood on the fire.

Ariana stirred as the bark on the firewood scraped together, bits and pieces falling to the floor below. She had burrowed beneath the covers as far as she could, leaving only the top of her head visible.

Michael stopped for a moment before putting the logs in the hearth and glanced over at her. He could barely see her without the glow from the fire.

He turned and arranged the wood, picking up some kindling and stuffing it beneath the heavier pieces. There were enough embers left from the night before that with a few breaths it sparked back to life. Visibility returned to the room, tiny flecks of light dancing over the deep red hue of Ariana's hair. His dark blonde hair had a tint of red to it. His skin was also pale like hers. Adoria was blanketed in snow for most of the year, so unless an Adorian was half-human, his complexion was naturally light.

The homes in Cyphrus, the capital city, were nestled along the cliffs of two large mountain ranges leading down into the valley. The castle that housed the elected sovereign, all members of the council and retired members of the Braeden began in the valley, built along the edges of the mountain, and extended upwards to a high point on the far north side.

The buildings were all cut from the radiant white stone of the Keil Mountains. Ornate carvings lavished the exteriors and rich colors from tapestries and paintings, all crafted by the ancients, adorned the interiors. Deep hues of blue with patterns of silver were woven into the rugs that ran the length of the halls in the castle. He had stayed there with his father when he was home, the only child who had ever been allowed to come and go from the Iidolis. He remembered his father teaching him how to wield a sword and shoot a bow. It was nothing like the training that he had received from his instructors — his father was unquestionably more skilled.

He had only seen Palingard once, and it had been from a distance. Several years ago, he had detoured from his men on the return voyage from a brief skirmish near Cornumas, which lay south of Palingard.

He had ridden at dusk through the Netherwoods, aware that it was risky coming so close. The other men had stayed far aside, riding straight through to Adoria, but Michael was curious. He had wondered how different their world was from his. He had met Ereubinians on too many occasions, every one of which was unpleasant. They were still humans, in a way. The two races had the same lineage thousands of years ago. But he had never actually seen a real human village, though he had been defending them and learning about them for as long as he could remember. He had slowed his horse as he approached the edge of the woods. The light from the fires illuminated the villagers with a soft glow. They were celebrating something.

It had appeared to be a wedding of some sort. He was intrigued. It was nothing like a wedding in Adoria. Their weddings were very sacred matters, held in private. Michael had watched as the couple stood together holding hands in front of a man dressed in dark clothing. Everyone was silent as the pair was prompted to repeat things to one another. A few moments later, they had turned to face the crowd, and everyone cheered. Michael smiled. They all began to sing and dance. Long tables had been set out with food and drink. He couldn't make out details, but he could see decorations had been put up everywhere. They were so full of life. He had spent so much of his existence focusing on duty and responsibility that he couldn't pull his eyes away from them.

As they had rejoiced, it had struck him why the Braeden were so different when they returned home. Once the young Braeden were ready to leave Adoria, they weren't allowed to return for at least ten years.

He had watched them for a moment, imagining what it would have been like to live among humans for so long. In the brief time that he had witnessed their private world, he felt extraordinary loyalty to their cause. He could not imagine how intense it would have become had he been there longer. Michael left, feeling a renewed sense of purpose. He had believed and put faith in his father's words, but it was different seeing the very core of what he had been taught to protect. He would never be the same.

Michael was still deep in thought when he heard her move. He was sitting on the floor, leaning against the side of the bed, staring into the fire. She shifted beneath the covers for a moment, before growing restless and sitting up. She looked around the room, trying to get her bearings, her brow furrowed. Michael looked up at her and placed his hand on the bed.

"It's alright," he said. "Do you remember where you are?"

CHAPTER SIX

You Look Like Him

His stomach was already coming dangerously close to being unsettled. Garren tried to drown out the sound of those who escorted him as he made his way through the keep, past the baths, and into the temple of the Goddess.

Night had fallen and the high glass dome that topped the entryway appeared as black as ink above him as he passed the red-robed vessels, his boots loudly echoing off the stone floor. Polished to a high sheen, the floor had a mirror-like effect, catching the candlelight and sending it out among the pillars and carvings that flanked the walls, lighting everything as if the room itself were aflame.

There was no need for his guards to be told they were not allowed past the great doors into the inner sanctum, nor would they have wanted to go if they had been invited. Garren didn't normally feel so ill at ease approaching the Laionai, but his insides churned, fearful of what they would sense in him. *Will they know of my betrayal?*

He clenched his fist before motioning for one of the vessels to usher him in, falling to his knees the instant he was in their presence.

He never grew accustomed to it. No matter how many times in the past he had been witness to it, no matter how many moments he spent questioning it, he would never find himself used to hearing their voice, devoid of an echo, as if time itself had no hold on them.

"You have pleased Her Holiness, High Lord, with both your faithfulness and valor."

Garren felt his stomach coming undone and coiling in on itself as they spoke. His pulse quickened, sending blood rushing through his body, lower extremities going numb as the blood pooled at his middle. He kept his head lowered as he responded.

"I pray that I have pleased you as well, your eminence."

Their eyelids slid over black orbs, fluttering unnaturally before reopening. The movement seemed nearly human, but forced as if the skin was trying in some way to respond like it was still marked with responsibility, still burdened with the tasks of keeping the organs functioning, but finding it unnecessary as it performed them.

"Yes, High Lord. We find your appointment appropriate, as we believed when we gifted it to you. In light of your recent achievement, it is time for you to be joined with a breeder. It is the Goddess' will to reward you for your efforts. We trust this gratifies you?"

The Ereubinians had been held to eugenic law for centuries. He understood the reasoning — it was the only way to ensure the continuation and eventual purity of the lineage. Humans were not allowed to bear children of their own, but a select few were chosen as breeders to carry the blood of Saint Ereubus.

"Yes, your eminence. Deeply."

"We trust you have seen to the position of High Priest?"

Garren nodded, "Yes, your eminence, I informed Tadraem upon my return from Palingard."

A smile erupted across the thinly stretched, translucently pale skin of their lips, revealing an absence of teeth. They laughed; a low and guttural sound that sent shivers across Garren's flesh.

"Very well, very well, son of Ereubus. Then as custom dictates, may the High Priest choose one among the daughters of Middengard for you and those of your men whom he feels are worthy of the blessing."

"Yes, your eminence."

The shuffling of feet filled his ears, scraping and eating at the floor as they came to surround Garren. He swallowed before lifting his eyes to see what they had brought him.

The Ordakai, childlike in stature, were deceiving in their guile and agility. Servants to the Laionai, they scurried about the keep and courts like diseased rats, eating what food they could find, and stealing what caught their fancy. Without language or gender, Garren doubted they would exist at all if not for their masters.

Their horned heads turned, looking him over. A fat, clumsy one stumbled forward, holding a chalice in its hands and cooing as Garren pulled it from stubby, crusted fingers.

Always cool to the touch regardless of the climate around it, the chalice had been blessed by the Goddess for use in worship and was half-filled with a pungent red wine. He held it in his hands, as he had done thrice a year for nearly five years, waiting.

A side door squeaked open, the rusted pins groaning with the weight, and four vessels ushered in a bound human who futilely thrashed about, hissing his anger through his bloodied mouth.

Their eyes met, and to Garren's surprise the man seemed almost grieved that the High Lord was present, a noticeable withering of his spirit visible in the lines of his face.

"You look like him," the human whispered.

Garren rose to his feet and approached him, amused at the meaningless chatter. The moment he touched the man he knew. "Adorian." Confused, he looked to the Laionai.

"A new age has begun. This night's worship, and this Adorian's blood sacrifice, celebrates a turn of the tides for Adoria. An army of humans, legions of those whom the winged ones have for so long protected, will rise against them. Do not question the divide, High Lord, for Her Holiness has spoken in faith that it will fail them when they need it most. Your commanders have been given one year's time to ready this army."

"Then blessed are you to be consecrated this night." He glared at the Adorian and the vessels that struggled to hold him. "Tadraem has chosen well." Dismissing them to the sanctuary, Garren turned back to the Laionai, and knelt before them. He repeated the prayer of Saint Ereubus, the sound of his words almost overpowering the sound of their exit as he was left alone.

With nothing but the familiar walls of the inner sanctum to keep him company, he lifted his lips to the rim of the cup, sipping a small portion. A smile deepened across his face as he stood. He extended his arms, speaking the words to dedicate the spoils of his victory and the communion wine to the Goddess. As he did so, a light surrounded him, shimmering golden in the darkness. It started from the floor at his feet and wound its way up his body like a great snake, twirling and hissing as it went. He could feel the power surging through his veins, connecting him to the great Mortal Coil just as the Goddess had promised her chosen ones so long ago.

But as he opened his eyes, just beyond the radiance that enveloped him, the face of another peered back. Her hair appeared as a burning red flame swirling around her face, her eyes a piercing blue. She wore a deep purple cloak, its hood concealing only a fraction of the light, far stronger than his own, that shone forth from her.

Dropping to the ground, he brought his arm over his eyes in a poor attempt to shelter his face. A voice came from the vision, speaking what he thought to be Adorian, leaving his body shuddering in fear as he listened. Only when he felt both his own strength and the girl's dissipate from the room was he quieted.

Still trembling, he dropped his arm by his side and stared out into the shadows. His breath came fast and heavy, his chest burning from the exertion. He rubbed his hand over his breast, clenching his teeth. He had yet to regain his composure when he heard another voice outside of the room.

"My Lord?"

The guards. Garren struggled to his feet and rushed to the door, grasping the iron handle with his hands and bearing his weight against it to keep it closed. His tone belied his answer.

"I am in prayer!" he barked. Garren felt his knees go weak, falling to the floor with his back against the wooden door.

They made no protest. It meant nothing to him that the very act of doing so would likely gain him an entirely new set of faces to detest — ones far less willing to abandon him at his request. It was a wonder any of his guards lived to old age. It wasn't until he looked down at his hands and saw the red hue staining his breeches that he realized what he had done.

What little of the wine was left had settled into a shallow puddle on the floor. Groaning, he made a futile attempt to salvage it. Once it finally occurred to him that it was useless, he pulled a kerchief from his pocket to soak up what hadn't seeped into the stone.

Frustrated, shaken, his head filled mercilessly with the girl's voice, he made his way to the kitchens with as much discretion as possible, considering his position. He found a suitable wine, allowing one of the Ereubinians serving there to refill the chalice.

Garren hesitated in the doorway to the sanctuary before entering. It looked like service had begun long ago, but he had just entered the inner sanctum. Hadn't he? He grew disoriented, unsure of how much time had passed.

Candles were lit along the pews, revealing rows of vessels dressed in white robes behind all those of the lineage who attended. He had seen the humans in this attire for observance his entire life, knowing that though he would not live to see the day, it would come to pass; eventually humans would no longer exist in this state. There would be no need for separation, for they would all be of Ereubinian descent.

Garren entered. He had taken no more than two short steps when, in complete accord, every human turned at once to face him. The room grew quiet as prayers hushed, the attention causing a succession of heads from the front of the room to turn also in his direction. Startled, he froze, trying to understand what had happened, but realized he would do better to ignore any significance in the event. After shaking himself from his shock, he walked to his seat beside Aiden, just a few rows from where he'd been standing. As he sat down, he realized that he had been holding his breath.

"Garren," Aiden whispered. He appeared horror-stricken at the humans' recognition of Garren. "I believe we have something to discuss."

Garren said nothing. He remained unmoving, his head bowed, following along with the recitations.

"Did you hear me, Garren?" Aiden asked.

Garren glanced at him, narrowing his eyes. "We will talk about it after service." He bent his head back down, his eyes staring listlessly at the floor. He felt his friend lean back onto the pew and join voices with the others. After a few minutes, the room again grew quiet as the candles that lined the pews were blown out one by one. All that remained alight was a single flame on the altar. Garren lifted his head and watched as a tall Ereubinian approached, kneeling in front of it.

The black-robed Ereubinian raised both hands into the air and spoke in the language of the Laionai.

"*Nech ordai neroman,*" the words echoed in the sanctuary. From the sound of his voice, Garren recognized him as Kolevar, the retiring High Priest. From the center aisle, two more figures in similar garb entered the room with the captured Adorian between them, his head peering at the floor. The Adorian was clothed in white and wore a gold cloak. The cloth of his shirt had been gathered at his neck, revealing only his pale face, framed by the hood that rested on his shoulders.

Garren watched, speechless, at the willingness of the Adorian, who was left standing untethered at the altar before Kolevar, who had risen. Was this not the same creature he'd beheld?

Tadraem, who had been announced earlier in observation as the new High Priest, had already been given the blade that would take the Adorian's life. As he came to stand next to Kolevar, his gaze turned to Garren, who suddenly realized that in his truancy, he had failed to bring the chalice to the altar.

"My Lord Garren, it is only fitting that tonight's sacrifice come from your hand, for no other is as proven in service or faith to Her Holiness."

When the knife was placed in his hands, he should have felt pleasure. When he lifted the chalice to the Adorian's lips, he braced himself against rebellion, only to see him accept it of his own accord. Garren should have felt peace. Instead, the blade rested like a leaden weight in his grip. He swallowed an unnerving and unwelcome measure of disgust as he looked into the Adorian's eyes, to see that beyond the façade of subservience was something far less understandable.

You look like him, the Adorian had said.

Unwilling to show reluctance, Garren did not hesitate in sliding the blade across the Adorian's throat, spilling blood onto the unblemished sacrificial garment. Before taking his seat again, he paused for only a moment to allow the denial of any merit in the words.

Aiden hit the floor hard. Garren rushed upon him, picking him back up by his collar, pinning him to the wall next to them, their eyes level.

"You will not address me in that manner. Friend or foe, I will not accept it."

Aiden wordlessly lowered his face, peering down. The blood from the Adorian was still shining wet on the leather of Garren's boots.

"Our discussions are my preference." Garren said, leaning in closer. "What brings on this insubordination from you?"

Aiden lifted his head to face him. "They turned to you, Garren. Are you denying this?" Garren slowly moved off his friend's chest, allowing him off the wall and to dust himself off.

"They fear me. Perhaps you should give credit where it is due," Garren said between gnashed teeth. Aiden took a short breath, rubbing his arm where Garren had grabbed him and thrown him to the ground. They had just entered the south hall, behind the sanctuary, when Garren had come at him.

"I'm sorry, my Lord," Aiden said. Garren scowled.

"I have never asked that you refer to me as Lord in private, but you are still to know your position. You may very well be my friend, but you haven't the right to feign authority over any commanding officer, or counsel, or least of all me." Aiden stood quietly, waiting for Garren to direct the conversation. "Don't do this, Aiden. Don't put me in this position. You know what my options are." Garren knew that Aiden would not need him to finish his sentence. The Moriors dealt swift justice to those who stepped beyond their station. Aiden swallowed hard.

"I understand." He bowed his head in submission.

"Then we are finished here?"

Aiden nodded, and without another word, left Garren alone in the hall.

Garren retreated to his chambers. He pulled off his boots, taking the dirty rag from where he had tended to his wound earlier and wiped some of the blood from the leather. He sat on the edge of the bed and rested his head in one hand as he let out a sigh. He felt the length of the day in his muscles and bones. His whole body was tired. If it weren't for Aiden's defiance, he might have fallen right to sleep, but his pulse had quickened as if from a nightmare and a raging headache made his eyes feel like they were being pulled from their sockets. He pulled off his shirt and pants, leaving them in a pile on the floor.

Leaning over the night table, he blew out the flame from the lamp, blanketing the room in darkness. As he slid beneath the cool blankets, his mind raced. What manner of madness were these visions — this behavior? He'd been in the inner sanctum, and still her presence would not leave him. He dared not reveal his concerns, as he didn't have the luxury of truly trusting another. He knew there were far too many who were more than ready to take his place.

Frustrated, he bolted upright. The air hit his exposed skin and he realized that he had broken into a sweat. It poured down his bare chest and back. He rose and stumbled in the darkness to a vial that sat on the window ledge in the corner, next to a large wardrobe. He pulled the top away and lifted it to his lips, letting the liquid slide down his throat. It felt warm on his tongue. It was not something he used often, but as his power grew, he felt his body lessen in its ability to fall asleep on its own. All the strength in the world, and yet he could not keep his own eyes closed.

CHAPTER SEVEN

WHERE IS HE?

"It's alright. Do you remember where you are?"

Ariana's side felt stiff, the skin pulled taut. When she shifted positions, a sharp stabbing sensation spread through her back. She glanced around the room, too groggy to comprehend much of anything and confused as to where the question had come from or what had just startled her.

"I'm not so sure that where I am exists," she murmured.

"What's the last thing you recall?"

She turned to see the disembodied voice had taken the shape of a winged man seated on the floor beside the bed.

She thought back, working her way forward and found that very little of what she recalled *could* be real, including her current circumstances. After much internal debate, she decided she'd been killed during the siege, maybe even falling to her death in dismount from Shadow, and this was some twisted version of an afterlife. For whatever reason, this struck her as funny.

She lay back down, staring up at the ceiling, and faintly smirked, too tired to put any real effort into it — besides, if this absurdity was to be her eternal fate, what difference would it make?

"I suppose if I were to narrow it down, the last thing I clearly recall was a city — nay a *kingdom* — " she paused, giggling, "that crumbled into ruins before my eyes. This was of course prior to stumbling into Adoria."

He rose and sat beside her. He seemed tense, which normally would have concerned her. All things considered, she couldn't have cared less.

"Ariana, you are not dreaming," he said softly.

"Oh, I'm certain that I'm not," she mused. *I don't have the imagination to conjure swords hidden in the overgrown confines of trees or a well in which you can see mystical images — or men with wings.*

He reached down, picking up something from the floor, and rested it in his lap. "*Nigh narro iasc kier sellot tolay.*" *I know this sword cannot be yours.*

She shook her head, responding before the tongue he had used dawned on her. *"Tu, ath ortho kulet ..."* *No, it was hidden ...*

His head tilted sympathetically toward her, "The language you speak is dead to many of our own kind, and yet you speak it not only with fluent elegance, but use it when incapacitated."

Suddenly feeling both claustrophobic and flustered, she looked around her for anything that might serve as a weapon. Nothing. She found absolutely nothing around her save bottles of various liquids and dried plants hung along the entire length of one wall. She supposed she could try and beat him with some of it, but wasn't quite sure how that would turn out in the end.

She could tell by his clothes that he was wealthy. *But is it just arrogance or does he hold a title? He had to know Father if he speaks this tongue.*

"This is overwhelming for you, I anticipated it would be. But I sense that you're concerned for your safety, are you not? "

She sniffed. "I can defend myself, if that's what you are asking."

"I noticed." He grinned, rising from where he had been seated to lean against the wall nearest the hearth, casually tucking the sword behind him. "There are few who could lay claim to pulling a blade on me."

"In equal number perhaps are the women with whom you've had such spectacular precision of aim," she snipped.

His wide smile lessened to a tight-lipped grimace. "My deepest apologies. I see you do remember some of your journey."

She felt a pang of remorse at his response — not his words. The distress in his eyes made her regret her terse speech. *So much like Sara.*

Slowly, details began to crystallize. She realized that not only was he aware of her father's language, the one she'd always understood to be of his homeland and shared by only his closest allies, but he'd been addressing her by her given name.

"You said my name."

He gave her a partial bow. "And I have failed to tell you mine. I can hardly expect you to recall a conversation in which you weren't really a participant. My name is Michael."

She held still, waiting on him to finish. "Just Michael? Just plain

Michael?"

A trace of amusement returned as a lilt in his voice. "Actually, since you ask, my full name is Michael Loren of Cyphrus, Archorigen of Adoria, begotten of Gabriel Briony of Leiden and Caelyn Edessa of Lipsius."

He studied her, holding his breath as he awaited her response.

She said nothing at first, staring at him dumbly, even more convinced that she was no longer among the living. "Archorigen?" Not knowing where else to go with his statement and wanting to avoid any more awkward silences, she found whatever word would come to her mouth and spoke it.

He shook his head, catching a deep breath. "Cyphrus is Adoria's capital, where an Archelder from each of the twenty-four provinces resides. The Archorigen is the elected sovereign." He moved away from the wall. "Did you hear what else I said?"

"Our parents have strikingly similar names — fascinating," she remarked dryly. "Let us assume for prosperity's sake that Adoria exists, that I am not hallucinating your extra appendages. It still means little considering my mother was from the Sutherlands and my father from somewhere in Lycus."

Michael's gaze lowered to the floor, his voice somber. "Caelyn … Mother," he corrected, "miscarried a child about eleven or perhaps twelve years before you were born. A male child."

The room started to grow smaller, shrinking until Ariana found herself short of air, the heat from the fire intensifying and her chest felt as if it would burst.

Michael continued, "I cannot venture to even imagine why he chose not to tell you your true lineage, or any of us here about your existence. But, Father was vigilant and sage in his discretion. There must have been a purpose." His brow knitted, and he glanced away from her. "He couldn't have foreseen his death. I don't believe it was his intention for you to find out this way."

She shook her head, still pressed for breath, and struggled to express her thoughts clearly. "My father isn't dead. I'm sorry, but we speak of two different worlds. I am not, nor have I ever been, a part of this one. I need air."

"It's cold outside," he said gently.

"And stifling in here." As she turned to slide off of the opposite side of the bed, a biting pain ripped through her lower back and shot up to her shoulder blade. Her eyes squeezed shut, a whimper slipping out.

Michael came over to the bed, touching her arm. "You need rest, maybe this was too soon. I'm — not very good at this sort of thing."

You imagine lost relatives often? She mused. "I just need to be outside of this room for a little while," she rasped. Koen lay asleep in the corner, his legs shaking as he dreamt, no doubt, of some great chase. She spied the cloak laying folded on the chair next to him.

Her head spun as her feet found the floor and her vision momentarily swirled black. He was right, though she wouldn't dare admit it now.

Holding back a groan, she walked carefully to the chair and had the cloak halfway over her shoulders by the time Michael reached her.

"Here, take mine. That one isn't suitable for the weather here, not to mention the panic you would cause by walking around in it." He slid his fur-lined cloak from his back, undoing the ties where his wings divided the leather. "I'm genuinely surprised you found it. Their elite are well trained and difficult to overcome. Palingard must have put up a fight to have killed one of such rank."

She remained still while he wrapped the cloak around her, angry that he would automatically assume she'd pried it off of some dead, unfortunate Ereubinian. She stepped back, holding out her hand.

"I could care less about the sword, but the dagger I want returned to me." She paused, and when he made no move to retrieve it, she felt the edge of her restraint crumble. "It has sentimental meaning, and it's rightfully mine. I think exchanging what is plainly more valuable in return for something that I've had for years, a gift mind you, is more than fair — it's outrageously generous."

Astounded, he turned and opened the drawer of the night table, pulling out her dagger. She took it as soon as it was offered and started toward the door.

"And just to make certain that you understand, I didn't find the cloak." *Duncan would be more than entertained if he were alive to hear this.*

She had pried the door partially open when he stopped her.

"Was this given to you?" he asked sharply, motioning toward the cloak.

She contemplated a sarcastic answer, but his expression belied his composure. Sighing, she turned back around to face him. "What else would I have meant?" she huffed. "He followed me into the Netherwoods, I fell, and after — brief conversation ..." her mind wandered for a moment, his words coming back to her. *You are not human.* "He told me to hide until nightfall and shoved the cloak in my hands."

Michael's eyes for a split second lit with unbridled anger before returning to meticulously maintained stoicism. "What did he look like?"

Beautiful. "Dark hair, strangely colored eyes — violet. He had a scar." She traced her jaw, seeing it in her mind for the first time as she pictured him.

"Garren," Michael growled. "His motives were not benevolent, I assure you."

His sudden intensity led her to accept his gesture and she pulled his cloak tighter around her shoulders.

A knock at the door interrupted as she opened her mouth to thank him.

"I thought I heard voices," a gray-haired Adorian peered in, greeting them with a poignant smile. "Ah, the child is awake." He said melodiously. "Michael, have you spo…"

"No, I haven't." Michael waived Ariana over the threshold, motioning for the other Adorian to follow. "Do you mind escorting Ariana someplace where she could get some fresh air? Something has come up that needs my attention."

Jenner nodded, placing his arm around her shoulder. "I would be delighted. In fact, I know just the place." He looked down at her. "Though only if my lady wishes it."

She nodded, feeling at least somewhat at ease with him. "Please."

Michael, without another word, breezed past them, making his way up the stairs and around the corner before they'd touched the first step.

"Are you feeling better?"

She smiled. "I suppose."

"Good, good. I cannot imagine you remember my name. It's Jenner."

She nodded, relieved to be free of the cluttered room, its suffocating warmth, and Michael's chatter.

As they walked, she noted the shades of Jenner's hair varied from light silver to a sooty black, falling neatly plaited just below his collarbone. Despite the softness about him, the gentle touch of one arm on her shoulder, she could not mistake the scars that marred his neck and hands.

He laughed, noticing her scrutiny. "He wasn't always this grave, and I wasn't always so old. Michael has lost a wife, as well as a mother and father." He straightened the hood from Michael's cloak, patting at the fabric once it was in place.

"This life — these sacrifices take a toll on all of us." He ran his finger across a particularly deep scar on his forearm. "Though bearing in mind those whom we have become united with under such trial makes it bearable, if not pleasurable. Give Michael time. This is not easy for either of you."

They came around the corner, passed through another door, and exited to a courtyard. The air nipped at them, whipping Ariana's hair around her face and neck. She considered correcting what had become a shared delusion, but decided against it. He seemed pleased to imagine her one of their kind, and she didn't have the heart to seem ungrateful for their hospitality. She had a hard enough time believing that their world was real and not some figment of ancient man's patently bored mind. She'd deal with the rest of it when she had time to let that thought grow conceivable.

They walked in pleasant silence for quite a while, wandering through well-kept winter gardens with snow-covered statues, all the while staying near the keep. All she could think about were the stories Sara had delightedly recited to her over the years, the wonder and faith that had been ever-present in her smile. *Where are you now?*

Passing through an arched doorway into a partially open pavilion, she heard a ruckus followed by grumbling, and what sounded like the pounding of a nail in wood.

Off in the far left corner, a wingless being stood, the apparent source of the displeasured ranting, a shadow obscuring all but the outline of his figure. As they neared, another — this one winged — stood next to the first, clutching rolled papers in his hands.

"All this time. All of this effort spent on … Doesn't he have someone else who can do this?" He pushed away the papers that had been held toward him in an uncoordinated gesture. "No, I don't have time to listen to it. It's meaningless anyway. You see what we have become. Slaves, servants in a realm that supposedly know nothing of slavery," he griped.

"But my Lord Braeden, it is the proposal of the Archorigen, and his wish for you to consider it."

"I was fighting battles before the boy was drawing breath. Archorigen or not, if it's that important to him then he can speak with me himself."

Mere steps were all that remained between them. Light streaming in from the octagonal opening attached to the lower spires of the keep illuminated tan skin, and weathered, war-worn features. He continued to mumble, oblivious of their arrival.

Ariana didn't notice Jenner's retreat as her hand gripped the dagger that she had pulled from her sleeve. She drew back and hurled it at the post, pinning the man's sleeve.

He wrapped his hand around the dagger to yank it free, when he slowly uncurled his fingers, exposing the gilded handle.

"You should recognize it," she spat. "Or has it been so long ago that you left us that your memory is dull?" She blinked back tears that were clouding her eyes, angry when she failed to keep them from rolling down her cheeks. The confusion, pain, and loss she could handle in due time — even the outrageous claims of familial ties, but this was too much.

Without turning around, he lowered his head to where his sleeve was pinned, and rested his head upon the post. "Ariana," he whispered.

"You might have been better off pretending that you haven't any knowledge of me, of any of us," she choked, "Where is my father?"

He removed the dagger and turned to face her. "I thought you were ..." his voice faltered and faded against the sound of its echo.

"What, Duncan, dead?" she laughed bitterly. "I was told as much concerning your whereabouts, as well as father's. That lie is abundantly clear."

He started forward, a shamed expression on his face. "Ari, please forgive me."

"I'm not even certain what to forgive you for!" she said angrily.

She looked back at Jenner. "You led me here on purpose," she accused. "Do not act as though I am incompetent or too faint for truth."

Whirling back around, she glared at Duncan. "You knew better. Of all who have known me, you couldn't have forgotten what little patience I have for lies. Is what Michael speaks about me true?"

Duncan hesitated and she winced. Her exaggerated movements and the strain on her throwing arm had irritated her side. Biting back the pain, she snapped, "Answer me!"

"Yes," Duncan said gravely. "You are and will always be a full-blood Adorian."

The air seemed devoid of oxygen, her chest struggling to hold its own against her shock. The sharp, undeniable pain felt far too much like betrayal to be anything else.

He continued, "Ari, you have to understand that we were sworn to keep your existence from the Ereubinians. Your father had good reason for his actions. I never questioned that."

She shook her head. "My father can speak for himself. Where is he?"

His eyes glossed over. "I'm sorry, truly. I thought — I assumed you knew."

Had she been able, she would have left them then, gathered what little she still possessed, and taken Koen as far from this place as she could go. Though she wanted — willed them even — her feet would not move.

"How would I have known?" she asked softly.

What a foolish, foolish girl I've been. I should have listened to them. How many days, years were lost imagining that my father lived, believing that those who had told me otherwise were wrong.

Jenner rested one hand on her shoulder, turning her face toward his with the other. "I should have expected your father's spirit in you. Michael and I both thought a familiar presence would comfort you, not wound you. It seems perhaps we have not fully considered your feelings."

She turned cold eyes toward the man who had been like a father to her. "There was a time it would have."

CHAPTER EIGHT

SHE WILL DO

Completely circular, with a dark stone floor, the room held ninety of Garren's officers awaiting his arrival. Without any natural light, it was pitch-black save the faint glow of the sconces that lined the outer walls.

As soon as Garren entered, the Ereubinians knelt down before him, the sound of their swords brushing the floor mingled with the soft scuffling of his guards' boots falling into alignment at the threshold.

"You may rise," Garren said. "The Laionai have commanded that a new regime shall be brought forth against Adoria. An army strengthened by the hands of men. You shall depart to each of the provinces of Middengard and gather the strongest among the vessels. Train them in our methods — equip them with our weapons. You have been given less than one year's time to complete this preparation."

"My liege, has it been decided which of the provinces we are each to attend to?" Jules asked. He was one of a handful of seasoned officers, well set in his ways. His overzealousness to please often annoyed Garren, but today it seemed slightly more palatable.

"I have drawn up scrolls for each of you, sending you to a province according to your ability. Each of the regions has its own natural strengths and I have decided accordingly."

"And what of you my Lord? Will you be in charge of a region as well?" Aiden asked. Garren could barely see him from the back of the assembly, his face shaded by darkness.

Surely he won't question my authority here, now.

"As High Lord, I fail to see where my dealings are of any concern to you." He gritted his teeth, his blood boiling just below the surface at the boldness of the question and the mere suggestion that he needed to answer it. He desperately wanted Aiden to shut his mouth, but this streak in him made Garren wonder where his friend's loyalties were. There was one sure way to find out.

"As for your assignment, it is to be in the southernmost region. I expect all of you to ride out at dawn."

Aiden stepped out of the shadows. "The southern region is almost desolate. Only Ruiari remains intact, I would be of better use elsewhere."

A chill fell across Garren's features. "You seem to have lost your wits today, Aiden. Go back to bed and pray to the Goddess you awake with better sense."

Aiden seemed to consider this, but his body grew rigid and he took an aggressive step forward, his hand balled into a fist, evidence that he'd decided against his better judgment.

Garren closed his eyes, willing Aiden to fall back before it was too late. "*Rese fixous necromai.*" He lifted his hand, gesturing toward Aiden, pausing just long enough to give him one last chance to back away.

"*Eritrev chorak.*"

The final word of the reprimand crossed, as a whisper, over Garren's lips. He opened his eyes and though his expression displayed nothing but righteous anger, his heart ached for what he had done.

The others froze as they watched Aiden fall to the ground, his body twisting unnaturally, sending his arms and legs into strange contortions. Mangled words came indecipherably from his lips as he writhed in pain.

Garren stood over Aiden in silence for a moment before speaking to him. "It's your speech that leads you into such dissonance, so you shall be without it."

All were silent as they watched Aiden continue to seize, unable to open his eyes or speak. Blood began to drip from the corner of his mouth, trailing down his chin to form into a puddle on the dusty floor. Aiden reached up and clasped a hand around his throat, coughing and gagging. A sickening cry erupted as he tried to speak and found himself without a tongue.

The others had backed away far enough to kneel and still appear under Garren's command, but their eyes were trained on Aiden. Tadraem, clothed in the elaborate robes of the High Priest, was the only man present who kept his proximity and likewise his ability to hear the High Lord's hushed words.

Garren leaned down, whispering into Aiden's ear. "I consider it a measure beyond grace that you're still breathing, despite your inability to take seriously the corrections I generously offered you. Don't disappoint me again, or this will seem but a pleasant dream."

Rising, he motioned for Tadraem to see to Aiden.

"I will get him cleaned up, my Lord. I have left the scrolls in each of the officer's chambers," Tadraem said, lifting Aiden. With staggered steps, they made their way to the guards, who escorted them into the hall.

"Do not mistake me. Compared to the Moriors, my kindness is more than unmerited." Garren paced in front of them as he spoke. Not a single one dared utter a word in response. "Do you think my judgment unfair?"

Jules stepped forward, and knelt. "Your commission by the Laionai is without question, my Lord. Your command through the Dark Goddess is unquestionable; therefore your judgment is as well. Blessed am I to be among your favored."

Garren would have rolled his eyes, or even chastised Jules for taking patent advantage of the situation, but even the ingratiating proclamation was a respite from the actions Garren had just found unavoidable.

"Your allegiance has earned you Aiden's position," he said soberly. "The Southern region would be my support, training with my forces in Eidolon. Considering Tadraem has retired from his command, a commission is in order. That commission was to be Aiden's, but now you shall step up in his stead."

Jules kept his head bowed, smiling as Garren revealed his decision.

"I am honored my Lord. You will not regret my appointment."

"For your sake, let us hope that I don't."

Garren's head pounded, partly from tension, partly from lack of sleep. "I release all of you for now. Go, read over your decrees — *Nech ordai neroman.*"

Voices joined in a reverent echo as they left him.

Aiden had never so much as whispered a word of defiance before. Garren felt a twinge of remorse as he realized that he'd never hear his friend speak again, but his words weren't worth hearing if they were going to invite insolence against him.

Suddenly unable to contain his frustration, he grabbed a chair and smashed it against the wall.

"Are you ready, my Lord?" Tadraem asked, as he returned to the room. "Aiden has been taken care of."

"I had no other choice." Garren had never before felt the urge to justify his actions to anyone, let alone Tadraem.

"My Lord, I have been expecting this for some time. Jules is a much wiser choice for my former standing. He is more reserved in his opinions and though he's a bit pompous, he's reliable." He walked over to Garren and glanced at the floor. "Did the chair say something offensive as well?" he mused.

"No, I'm redecorating." Garren gave him a half grin.

"With one less voice to cause disunity among the forces, you'll feel at ease before long. You sensed this as well. You haven't been yourself since our return." Tadraem began walking with Garren toward the door. "I chose to avoid the topic with you, but it seems now that you were simply being cautionary. I owe you an apology."

Garren considered telling Tadraem about the girl and his visions of her, but something kept him from speaking the words.

"Is there something on your mind, my Lord?"

"What would my father have done?"

Tadraem took a moment before answering. "He would have made the same choice, had he the ability."

As they made their way through the courtyard, Garren thought of his father, Seth. He'd never known his mother. She died early in his childhood, though it wouldn't have made much difference had she lived. She was human and would not have been allowed to spend much time with him. He recalled very little of either of his parents, his father having lost his life in battle with the Adorians around the same time as his mother's death. Tadraem, Seth's friend and commander, took Garren as his charge. He'd practically raised him.

"If it suits you, my Lord, I will sit with the two of you. The Goddess shines her favor upon you with this union, and I would not dream to offend her holiness or your wishes by my choice. I trust this meeting will address any changes that may be necessary." Tadraem paused before the threshold.

"How long has it been since she lost her soul?"

"She was taken from Ruiari." Tadraem opened the door to the outer courts, and without further conversation, they made their way to the temple. Once inside the sanctuary, they passed the altar and the pulpit, walked through a high-framed doorway and entered a small room beyond. There, the girl sat at a crudely carved table, her hands neatly folded in her lap.

"Her name is Cadence." Tadraem pulled a chair out for Garren to sit across from her.

"I am privileged to be here, my Lord," she said. Her voice was hollow, devoid of emotion or sentiment — the words were nothing more than meaningless sounds to her.

He'd not only expected this tone, he'd heard it thousands of times before, making it so much more than ordinary. But somehow, beholding it in such a private setting disturbed him. He kept a still countenance as his mind wandered. He'd asked her a few menial questions, mainly concerning various family traits and illnesses, when he lost control of his thoughts.

"What would you say if I were to threaten your life?" His body raced with adrenaline as he realized what he was in the midst of doing. The girl looked at him blankly, her eyes as clear and motionless as still water.

Garren reached for his dagger and rushed over the table, bringing its blade to her neck. "Tell me, do you value your life at all?"

The girl didn't so much as quicken her breathing as she considered his question. "I value what I may be to you, my Lord. Do with me as you will."

Tadraem's hand sank deeply into Garren's shoulder blade as he pulled him back down into his seat. "Are you looking to dishonor yourself?"

He couldn't recall the last time Tadraem had braved such a tone. Speechless, Garren stared through the woman before him, seeing a vision of another.

"Undress yourself and stand before him," Tadraem commanded.

Cadence stood and stepped out to face them. Without reluctance, she reached behind her neck and opened the clasp to her dress, letting it drop unabashedly at her ankles. She stood blushless before them, looking straight ahead. Her coal black hair fell about her shoulders, her blue eyes set against a complexion as smooth and pale as Orbus root.

"Does she suit your needs?"

Garren still had trouble finding words. The girl was beautiful, and on any other day he would have been more than pleased that such a breeder would be his possession. He'd waited for this honor for some time. But as he looked into her eyes, he was reminded of another's, a far more piercing blue, fierce in tenacity and insistence.

"She'll do." Garren rose from his chair and had started to leave the room when he turned back around to address Tadraem. "I have some other matters to contend with before the day is out. Forgive me, I'm still feeling a bit fatigued from the journey."

Tadraem nodded, "Then you are pleased with her." Then added almost as an afterthought, "My Lord?"

"Much so," Garren lied. "I will convey my appreciation to the Laionai when I go before them tomorrow to discuss our progress with the preparations. I'll be out attending to something this evening, so don't expect me at observance."

Garren made it a point to leave the room before Tadraem had the opportunity to inquire as to what it was he would be attending to.

CHAPTER NINE

MORE THAN
WHAT APPEARS

M ichael gazed through frosted glass to the pavilion below. Duncan's form appeared pained as it stiffened with Ariana's approach and subsequent response.

He pressed the hinge so the pane gaped at the edge, just enough for him to hear the conversation, and found it disconcerting.

So far, she defied every assumption he'd made. Unruly, dangerously loose of tongue and a hair on the bitter side — her mannerisms supported his notion that Garren's mercy had been purposeful. As far as they understood, little infuriated the High Lord like rebelliousness, and he could not fathom her either begging for her life to be spared, or his offering her freedom willingly. Which meant only one thing. Garren knew whose blood he was relinquishing. *But why?*

Garren's own forces had obliterated Palingard — everything Ariana had ever known. *Surely he couldn't fancy this would buy him an ally behind the divide?*

Turning from the window, he started toward the hall of scrolls, grateful for the silence. Though there was little need for formal guard within their borders, he was still rarely unencumbered by the well-meaning populace he governed, often bombarded with those wishing to do everything for him from cleaning his weapons to lacing his tunics. He did at times enjoy the company, but more often than not, he regarded their intrusion with respectful silence. Since their return from Middengard, he'd insisted on his solitude — considering the Torradh had laid to rest a good many Adorians, his wishes went unchallenged.

For the remainder of the day, he left Ariana's care to Jenner and his wife and busied himself with re-reading Gabriel's journals, searching, hoping for something he might have missed. He lost count of the hours.

Sighing, he dropped the seventh leather-bound book onto the table, causing loose papers to fall into disarray about the floor, disappointed for once at his father's meticulous prudence. He rubbed his tired eyes, missing sorely the days when his bones felt less aged, and his spirit unbroken.

He jumped slightly as a knock echoed loudly through the room.

"My liege?"

"Approach." Michael shook his head, more in frustration than displeasure for the interruption — but it apparently displayed the latter.

"Forgive me, my Lord. I mean not to bother you, particularly after ..."

Michael hushed his prattling with a slight lift of his hand. "Never mind all of that, you've not bothered me in the least. What is it?"

A man, bent over with age, stepped beyond the Adorian, genuflecting as he did so. Personable, he smiled politely at Michael, keeping his hands shyly clasped together at his stomach as he stood.

"My Lord, this is Bronach, a historian on loan from the House of Childress in Artesh. If it pleases my liege, he has been assigned by the Council of Elders to the restoration of the Saeculum."

Michael nodded, vaguely recalling some business of the sort that he had delegated to several of the smaller provinces. "I see the old ways are not totally forgotten. I imagine if the mythologies were real, Bronach might be pleased that you bear his name in such a profession. Tell me though, clearly you are human, were you raised here?"

Michael knew the remaining Braeden, if not by name, by face, and he had never seen this man before.

Bronach nodded. "It is as you say, my Lord. I fear I have never known my birth name. I was brought here as a youngling."

Michael gathered several of the journals into the crook of his arm, patting Bronach on the back as he brushed past. "While you are here, you should acquaint yourself with Jenner. He finds the past absurdly titillating and would more than enjoy the company."

He was almost to the door, having nodded his agreement with the arrangement, and had resigned himself to finding answers elsewhere, when Bronach spoke again.

"Am I to take it then, my Lord, that the past is of little interest to you?"

A smirk found its way to Michael's usually still features as he pivoted to face them. "The present and the future concern me far more than the past, which I can no more change than live eternally."

A peculiar grin lit up the historian's face, highlighting his bushy blonde brows and unsettling amber eyes. "Well spoken, my liege," he said warmly, "If you find there arises the need for an old man such as this humble servant in any other ways, I believe you know where to seek me. My labor is yours, as my loyalty is to our great realm."

The room was resplendent, far richer than anything she had ever seen — even the doorknobs were made of precious metal. At the northernmost corner of the castle, nestled into the side of the mountain, the view revealed a landscape she couldn't have conjured in her wildest dreams. Instead of the plain, earthen rock of Middengard, Adoria's white-stone mountains shimmered like crystals that had been thrown by a god onto the horizon.

The ceiling alone was over thirty feet high. Thick blue velvet curtains hung floor to ceiling and were pulled to the side of a wall that was made entirely of glass.

Past the threshold was a seating area that had been furnished with several finely fashioned chairs and a chaise, all facing a large fireplace in the center of the room. Ariana walked to it and bent down to get a better look, discovering that she could see through it to the other side. A smile lit up her face as she peered around the corner.

Behind the fireplace was a canopy bed made of gleaming silver. White linen curtains embroidered with delicate designs along the hems were hung along the canopy railing. Ariana ran her hands along the needlework, lightly fingering the elegant trim of the pillows.

"This room once belonged to my daughter, and Michael of course."

Expecting Jenner's voice, Ariana was startled to hear a woman.

"Ariana, this is my wife, Lady Elspeth."

Ariana couldn't recall how to curtsy, though Sara had taught her once, so she hugged her arms to her chest and did her best to look regal. "Thank you for your kindness, Lady Elspeth. May I assume you are human because you do not have wings?"

"Please, call me Elizabeth." She placed her hand on the small of Ariana's back and ushered her toward a tall wardrobe. "It was my name in Dullanan. I am human, however, only Adorian men have wings. Perhaps

Jenner will bore you with the story of our meeting another day."

Jenner was older than his wife, though Ariana could not tell how much so. If she had to guess she would say twenty years, certainly enough to be considerable.

Though Ariana was still seething, infuriated with Duncan, she was engrossed with the events unfolding around her. Elizabeth opened the doors, revealing more clothes than most of the young women in Palingard had owned collectively.

"These were Genevieve's," she said, touching a deep green dress with a scarlet cloak that hung beside it.

"Does she have no further use for them?" As the words tumbled thoughtlessly from her lips, Jenner's comment concerning Michael returned to her. "Oh, forgive me," she murmured.

Jenner smiled a small, sad smile. "She died several years ago, but rest assured, she had a loving spirit, and would have delighted in your use of them. And do not concern yourself with Michael; it was he who suggested it."

"Thank you," she whispered, ashamed that she had been so involved in her own misery that she had failed to hear Jenner when he'd told her of Michael's loss — of their loss.

"Rest. Aulora will be up shortly to change the dressing on your wound." He paused, smiling. "Though I sense you will fight us on this, a chambermaid has been chosen for your service. Her room is connected to yours." Jenner pointed to a plain wooden door to their left. "Her name is Kaitlyn, and she's there should you need anything."

Ariana looked down at Koen as soon as they were alone, her sentiments shifting from anger to gratitude to a deeper sorrow than she had ever known.

"He's really gone, then," she murmured, her thoughts returning to her father. She sat down on the chaise closest to the fire's warmth, curling her legs beneath her. "If it is so, then why does my heart fail to believe it?" Absently, she petted his head and neck and moved over when he settled his oversized frame next to her.

"I feel him now more than ever." Again, the distinct feeling of betrayal edged too close and she pushed it aside, unwilling to give it a foothold when she had barely enough strength left to deal with the grief she already shouldered.

For some time she stared at the flames, trying to rest, working against the tension that coiled in her muscles. The unrest served only to urge her to action, and it took everything in her to will the feeling away.

Later in the day, just as Jenner had said, the healer returned to see to her. Ariana lay on the bed, gazing at the paintings on the wall as Aulora added more salve to the wound on her side.

Her eyes wandered over depictions of great battles, several of the keep itself. One in particular caught her attention. As soon as Aulora was finished with her, Ariana rose and stood before it.

The city was the same save the presence of life in the painting, where it had been absent in what she had come to assume was only a hallucination.

"I have been here before," she lifted a hand, stopping just before her fingers touched the canvas, and traced the outline of the temple in the air.

The healer came to her side. Ariana could feel the warmth radiating from the elderly Adorian, despite the chill in the room. "One of two nearly identical cities. Arcadia is what you see before you, Eidolon is its twin."

Ariana nodded. "Ruins, now. Is that all that is left?"

Aulora grinned, turning from her, and lifted a weathered hand into the air. "Ah, but perhaps there is more than what appears. Not everything in existence is visible to mortal eyes."

Emotion swept strangely over Ariana, rushing up her spine and feathering out to her hands. Something rested on her tongue, caught just before her lips could form it into words like the image of a dream awoken from too quickly. It remained there long after the healer had left, leaking into her dreams as she napped in the chair.

Their robes flowed unnaturally, like living things encircling their frightful forms. Eyes like onyx moved in unison over the expanse of the room and the dark-haired figure that knelt before them. It was Garren.

A dull groan began to sound low in her mind as they spoke, intensifying and drowning out the clarity of their words.

Suddenly, she watched in horror as an all-too-familiar face was brought to stand before Garren.

Gregor. He fought wildly, failing to pull himself free.

The sound grew sharp and piercing, the pain blurring her already obscured vision.

"Who? Who is it that you think you see before you?" She heard Garren's voice, though his lips remained motionless. Straining to listen, she was troubled by the sudden grief on Gregor's face — true sorrow, and not for his own circumstances.

Dark things moved among the shadows, tilting their heads and hissing as they turned in her direction. They could see her.

"Garren!" She called out to him, but he lowered his head, lifting a chalice to his lips. The liquid appeared as black as night, fanning out upon his skin in tangled veins the moment he drank of it.

A golden spiral burst forth from the ground, like two great arms, wrapping around his body — feeding from the darkness.

"Who are you?" she asked him, surprised when he opened his eyes. He gasped, shielding his face with his arms and letting go of the cup. It crashed loudly, spilling its contents to the ground.

Ariana opened her eyes, lifting herself from the chair to look nervously about the room. She was breathing hard, an echo of the shrill sound still reverberating in her head.

A clearer image of his face was burned into her memory than she saw in her dream. Her skin seemed still to tingle with the feel of his hand on her arm, her cheek with the touch of his palm. She thought of it as she tried on some of the dresses, changing from the plain garments the healer had replaced her bloodied ones with into a pale blue gown, trimmed in gold, so fair in color it seemed almost silver in the right light.

It had not occurred to her to look into the mirror before now. Having seen her reflection in a looking glass only once, the uncertain likeness on water's surface was all that was afforded her in Palingard. She passed by the dressing table and it pulled her back to sit. A countenance gazed at her that she had not seen since she was a child. She had never realized how much she looked like her mother, despite how often she had been told.

A young girl, whom she assumed to be Kaitlyn, came to the door to announce Michael's arrival and ask if Ariana minded his company.

Michael set down a platter of food and seated himself.

"I'm not used to such formality," she said softly, still looking at the mirror as she made light of it. "What would she have done had I declined?"

The lack of color in Michael's face, contrasted with the red-tinged whites of his eyes, belied his exhaustion. "I suppose she would have ushered me away." His dour expression shifted as he took note of her apparel.

"Fits wonderfully, as I thought it might. Are you comfortable? Do you need anything? I was told you were taken to Duncan."

She turned to look at him. "I'm pleased to hear you aren't passing off the meeting as chance. I'm not some spoiled frolicsome lady of your courts so let me spare you the idea of treating me as such."

A pregnant pause hung over them, leaving Ariana unsure of what to say next. Finally, Michael rubbed his forehead with his thumb and forefinger, replying quietly as he did so, "You certainly are worldly for having been raised in such a sheltered place. Would I be correct in assuming that he was adamant about your education as well?"

"Do I strike you as dim-witted?"

Michael was on his feet, courteously excusing himself before she could speak again. She managed, however, to laugh with enough enthusiasm that it stopped him before he made it out of the room.

"Wait, wait, come back. That was said purely in jest. I know perfectly well what you meant, and no he didn't. Duncan and Bella and certainly Sara's family concerned themselves with my education." Her heart ached to think about Sara's well being.

Michael reclaimed his seat, surprised to discover that it was no longer his alone. Koen, gangly limbs and all, had made himself comfortable in the chair's fleeting moments of vacancy.

Michael awkwardly repositioned himself, seemingly wary of inciting more pithy comments from Ariana by asking the beast to move.

"What little I know of Eidolon was told to me so long ago that I hardly know the truth of it," Ariana plaited several strands of hair as she spoke, fastening each braid together like Sara used to do for her on occasion. "Is the soul of man so ephemeral that it may be stolen with simple words?"

Michael shook his head, his eyes turned downward. More thoughts flickered in his eyes than his reply indicated.

"Not so simple. Words are spoken by the Ereubinian who takes the soul, but the act itself is accomplished through what has physically become of the Laionai, through their connection to what is known as the Mortal Coil. The blood of Ereubus was bound to shadow by the Goddess before the ancients walked Adoria, but the Lineage are merely a conduit for transferring the souls to the Coil and because they do so, they in turn are granted power by it—the greater the number of souls collected, the greater the power. If the writings are to be believed, the Laionai feed from the souls taken. It is a dark web indeed that the Goddess Ciara has woven."

"Why is Adoria spared when Middengard has fallen so far?"

"I can't say that we have been, Ariana. The divide that protects us is an unknown thing, unspoken of in any of the histories or scrolls. We can't count on its strength in all situations — though some would tell you differently. The Adorian language is a living language, sustained by light, and can't be spoken by those who are born of Middengard, whether they are of dark lineage or not. We are the only ones who can pass the divide or usher another in. We know that the divide and the language are tied together, but not how."

Rising to his feet, Michael motioned toward the untouched food. "You really should eat something, or at the very least try."

She nodded, "Are you leaving so soon?"

Michael nodded apologetically. "The winter festival approaches. Rumor, I'm afraid, has already begun about your arrival. I had hoped to let you settle in a bit first, but the council has suggested formally introducing you on the eve of Lisida Olein, when there will be a feast and the celebration of the winter moon. I agree. I think you'll enjoy yourself, maybe see a lighter side of our realm."

She nodded, remaining silent as he left. All she could think of was Sara. Here, Ariana sat in embroidered finery, and her dearest friend — if she'd survived the siege at all — may fear her every breath.

She did not sleep well that night.

CHAPTER TEN

INFANTILE EFFORTS

Garren paced in front of his Dragee's stall. He'd been there for over an hour, trying to decide whether to ride out or not. Finally, he leaned against the wall and looked down at the dirt floor of the stables.

Just as it was prior to their departure for Palingard, it had remained. He removed his glove and touched the cool earth, letting the dirt fall through his fingers. It felt the same, smelled the same. Perhaps his whole world hadn't fallen apart, and yet, when he thought about it, it wasn't so much that his world had changed, but like he'd stepped into a world he'd never seen before. The closest thing he could liken it to in his experience was the immediate relief upon waking from a nightmare.

He paced the Dragee at first, moving quietly through the back roads of the city. His path, covered in shadow, helped him evade his guards. He neared the gates to the city, and came upon several watchmen who fell to their knees at his approach.

"My Lord."

Garren, in no mood for idle chatter, didn't pause to acknowledge the salutation. He picked up the pace as soon as he was beyond their sight, rushing through the barren landscape. It was late in the day and the sun had begun to fall below the horizon. The hours had felt long since the previous evening's observance and the countless moments he'd spent in the sanctuary following it.

The crisp air stung him as he rode. The farther from Eidolon he traveled, the colder it became, the bite of the winter wind taking his mind off what truly had him shivering.

As he came to the edge of the field and entered the peaceful woods, he slowed his Dragee to a walk. He had been riding through these parts of the forest since he was a small boy. He remembered playing among the trees. He could still smell the pine and hear the snap of the branches below his feet as he ran.

He had been about ten at the time. Tadraem had walked with him to the stream and the waterfall that day. They had crawled to sit on an enormous log that had fallen across the expanse of the falls and had gotten soaked from the spray of the water. Garren could not recall all of their conversation, but a few bits and pieces remained. Tadraem told Garren things about his father that he'd never mentioned before — things that he would not speak of again.

They had sat peering over the waterfall, the roar filling their ears and making it difficult to hear one another. Garren reached into his pocket and took out a handful of rocks. He picked them up, one at a time, to throw them. Tadraem patted him on the back, causing Garren to stop for a second, soaking in the affection. Tadraem, though much like a father to him, didn't openly show affection.

"You remind me of your father," Tadraem had said. "Have I ever told you that?"

"No. But you have described him to me before. He had dark hair like mine, and was tall — like I want to be when I grow up. Is that what you mean?"

"In a way. But there is more to a man than his appearance. You have his laugh for example, and you are just as stubborn as he was. You do have his hair color, and you have the same brown eyes, but you physically favor your mother."

"I thought you never knew my mother."

Tadraem had looked out over the water and then back to Garren. "I knew your mother well." He sighed deeply. "Your father fell very much in love with her."

"But she was a human," Garren had cried, bewildered. "They can't think or reason as we do. You have told me that much yourself."

"I have told you many things that are perhaps not always true. Without a soul, one can do very little outside of subsisting. Your father very much had a soul and therefore, the ability to love. Just because it is forbidden does not mean that it does not exist. Ereubinians may not be allowed to be companions to one another, but have you ever heard of two that have had feelings for each other?" Tadraem had asked.

Garren had not hesitated to answer his question.

"One of the boys in my lessons ..." he had paused with fear in his eyes.

Tadraem had leaned over and cupped Garren's small chin with his hand.

"You may say anything here without repercussions. I have told you things that I have never said before and you may do the same. Today, we are honest with each other."

"One of the boys in my lessons kissed one of the girls last week; no one saw it but me, but I didn't tell anyone. I didn't want them to be mad at me."

"No, I suppose you wouldn't," Tadraem had laughed. "You did the right thing in not telling on them. Emotion is not something that's easily kept away, even with laws and punishment. Your father fell in love with your mother, even upon fear of death."

"Have you ever known love in this way?" Garren had asked.

Tadraem had curled his hand to his chest as he spoke. "Without fault. Without question, or hesitation." He had closed his eyes. "I love but her and her alone."

Garren had struggled to understand what Tadraem was talking about, the expression on his face displaying his confusion.

"I cannot tell you her name or anything more. But I can tell you there will come a day when you will be given a choice. Two paths will be laid before you and one of them will be against everything you've been taught."

"But you'll be there with me, right?"

"I cannot promise that. Don't forget what I have told you. Put these things out of your mind for now and ask me not about them later. Set aside this memory for that day."

They'd continued to talk for some time, but past that Garren could recollect very little. In fact, he hadn't thought about that conversation for years and had never recalled it with such clarity. Tadraem must have briefly doubted the Laionai — this was several years before he had failed his crusade against Palingard. He'd become weak in his faith and it had cost him his victory. Garren gnashed his teeth, the hard muscles of his jaw stiffening in response. *I will not let the ramblings of a lesser Ereubinian keep me from what is rightfully mine.*

Very little stood between him and Adoria. The barrier between the realms would become inconsequential, just as the Goddess had foretold.

It was only a matter of time. With their realm no longer protected, Adoria would begin to crumble. Even their best fighters couldn't contend with an army as strong as the one the Laionai had just commissioned.

The Ereubinians knew there were some who didn't have wings. They had run into them on occasion and suspected their involvement anytime a human village won against them.

There was a long history of bad blood between Garren and Michael, their fight now having become a matter of personal vengeance. Their last battle had been particularly nasty, leaving Garren with a deep scar at the line of his jaw. Michael was foolish for not killing him when he had the chance. There was no honor in clemency and it had sickened him to see it in Michael's eyes as he rose from where he had pinned Garren to the ground. Michael had left him with an idle threat, slicing Garren's skin as he pulled the sword away: "Next time, I will not be so merciful."

Garren could feel his adrenaline rushing as he thought of Michael. Garren would revel in Adoria's fall and would see to it personally that Michael was kept alive long enough to see his empire destroyed. The Adorians' involvement with the human realm was nothing more than an elaborate facade. They were only interested in power for themselves. He remembered the reactions of the few wingless men whom he'd encountered over the years and though the Adorians' compassion appeared real enough, he wasn't deceived. He vividly recalled an instance in particular with one of them.

The Ereubinians' efforts to take Ruiari were hindered greatly by several men well trained in the art of combat. Garren had begun to suspect they were in fact not human at all. He rode near one of them and grabbed the first human he encountered — an adolescent girl. She had screamed and tried to free herself from him, but Garren was much stronger and held the girl without any struggle on his part. He looked over at the Adorian and brought his knife to the girl's throat. The Adorian noticed it right away and rode closer. Garren turned toward him and pressed the knife barely into the girl's flesh. She cried out in pain, which only provoked the Adorian even more.

"Let her go and I will lay down my arms."

Garren laughed. "Do you take me for a fool? Tell me, being not of this realm, what significance does this girl's life have for you?"

The Adorian threw down his sword and rode with his hands held above his head in surrender. "It's of no consequence to you what this girl means to me. I offer my life for hers — more than a fair trade. I'll go without resistance, I give you my word."

"Your words are meaningless, but you may have confidence in mine. Your interference in Ruiari has cost this girl any pity I might have had for her. Perhaps this will teach you to leave matters alone that don't concern you." Garren lowered his knife and drove it into the girl's side. He watched as the expression on the Adorian's face grew cold. The Adorian tried to force Garren from his saddle by charging his horse into the Dragee. The Dragee easily resisted the charge by craning his long neck, grabbing hold of the Adorian's horse with its wicked jaws and tossing it to the ground. The Adorian landed in a pile of broken bones and armor. Dazed, he cried out in Adorian and crawled toward the girl. Garren rode on, turning around to see the Adorian cradle the girl's lifeless body in his arms.

Garren was still deep in thought when he came to a clearing. He turned right to go around it. He hadn't realized how long he'd been riding. The sun had set and he was miles from where he had entered the woods. The moon shone brightly in the sky, casting a blue glow on everything in the forest. He hadn't gone too far when the Dragee began to resist his lead. Garren pulled the beast's head toward him with the reins and saw clear agitation. The wind blew through the trees, creating a hollow moan that echoed through the darkness. He stayed frozen, his hand resting on his sword, and within minutes he heard what the finely tuned ears of his Dragee had perceived. The earth shook with the rumbling of hooves. He jumped to the ground, pulling his sword from its scabbard. Searching his surroundings, he was shocked to find nothing. He peered into the woods but detected no movement save the slight sway of the trees against the breeze. He remained still, all of his senses fixed on discerning the source. As the sound grew closer, he leaned into his Dragee and whispered a command, *"Tradekh ealo."* The Dragee lay on the ground and rolled onto its side. Garren crouched, laying one leg over the beast, across the saddle.

Suddenly, from the middle of the field, a group of ten Adorian riders emerged. Garren stared wordless as the men materialized out of thin air. They tore through the clearing and into the dense woods on the other side.

After seeing what he assumed was the last of them come into view, he tugged at the reins. The Dragee rose to its feet and Garren slid back into his saddle.

As he raced through the woods, his eyes flared momentarily violet as he cloaked himself and the Dragee in a spell of silence. He wove through the trees until he was parallel with the closest rider and ran him through with his blade. The Dragee dipped its head and dug its teeth into the horse's leg, pulling it to the ground.

He pulled his second sword from its sheath as he ran between two more riders. Deftly brandishing the blades, he slew both men with one fluid cross-swing. Their severed bodies fell from their horses. The Dragee recoiled then gathered momentum and leapt in front of the horses, tearing at the throat of one with its claws and sinking its teeth into the chest of the other.

The sounds of the slaughter alerted the others, who turned in their tracks. Garren slowed as he came upon them, blood still dripping from his weapons. He glared at the seven remaining riders, his Dragee emitting a guttural growl. One of the riders who had been farthest from Garren moved in front of the others to face him. Garren recognized him as Caedmon. These weren't just Adorian riders — these were Michael's men.

Caedmon aggressively extended his wings, casting a shadow in the moonlight. Garren slid his swords back into their sheaths as Caedmon's horse grew restless, stirring beneath him.

Garren sighed and draped one hand over the other. "You are indebted to me; I've just relieved you of three of your most pitiable fighters."

Caedmon pulled on the reins to settle his horse, then held up a hand to his men. *"Louthairo toul eralaun doe aronai."* All but one of the men seemed to agree with his command.

"An tiroknow toul eralaun, nigh allolost," the second Adorian yelled. Caedmon looked at him, but before he could respond, the soldier rushed forward, unsheathing his sword as he came at Garren.

"Perhaps you would be so kind as to deliver a message for me," Garren said, narrowing his eyes.

Without warning or any action on Garren's part, deep slashes cut across the charging Adorian's face. Crying out in pain, his hands flew to cover his bleeding skin, dropping the reins.

The other men were still as blood poured down the Adorian's face. Unable to see and shuddering in anguish, he slipped from the saddle.

"Please inform Michael that I grow weary of his ineptitude and that if he intends to continue this game, he might consider not insulting me further by sending such infantile efforts."

Garren did not wait to hear a reply as he headed for Eidolon.

CHAPTER ELEVEN

DEAD BY DECREE

I t felt like a lifetime had passed since Palingard's fall. Ariana was fairly sure it had been mere days, but it could've been weeks for all her tired bones knew.

She stayed mostly in her chambers, resting and healing from both her twisted ankle and wounded side. Michael checked on her frequently, joyful one moment and grievously brusque the next. As if his silence concerning all things of value to her — namely Adoria's intentions for Middengard — weren't enough, his tremulous moods aggravated her almost beyond bearing.

Also irritating was the adolescent chambermaid who gushed incessantly about one young Adorian or another. How quickly Ariana had forgotten what it was like to be so young and how grateful she was to be beyond it.

Avoiding Kaitlyn wasn't easy — the girl took notice of just about anything Ariana did or said, remembering it with startling and annoying accuracy. As soon as the girl was otherwise engaged, Ariana made her way in cloaked anonymity to the outer hall. Wandering the corridors, she took the path she recalled having walked with Jenner, finally coming to the pavilion where she'd found Duncan.

Her father's dearest friend had asked to see her on more than one occasion and she'd found herself, for once, pleased to have someone to turn guests away at her whim.

How could he? After everything, all of his stupid empty promises, the time he spent teaching me skills that he obviously learned here.

Ariana laughed indignantly, more than a little mystified at her father's disdain for what he had told her were crutches for those unwilling to fight for their own dying world. Not only was Gabriel wrong, he was a hypocrite. Perhaps he was ashamed of her, wanting nothing of her brash, untempered gracelessness to stain his revered homeland.

She shook her head, anger welling in her gut, and walked into the open. The wind hit her face, threatening to push back her hood, so she held it close with one hand. She had begun to hate the cold but felt trapped whenever she was inside for very long.

As her brother already suspected, rumors concerning the arrival of Gabriel's daughter had quickly spread through Cyphrus. If she didn't know better, she'd think Michael was King and not a powerless figurehead as he claimed.

She came finally to the markets, which, unlike in Palingard, were located on long cobblestone alleys to shield them from the fierce winter. Blazing fires lit the middle of the street to warm shoppers.

She took a deep breath, enjoying the sound of life and the smells of breads and fragrant fruits that she would venture to guess did not grow in Middengard. Michael had given her a handful of gold tokens soon after she had arrived, and she had spent only a few, treasuring what was left despite Michael's promise of providing whatever she needed.

He simply couldn't understand. They came from different worlds. She knew nothing, save what very little Sara had shared, of court life. She didn't know how to be anything other than the boisterous child of Palingard that she was. It saddened her a little to think that this would be her new existence and she wondered if Sara would feel at home here or just as lost as she did.

Smiling, she picked up a warm, round loaf of bread, dropping a coin into the Adorian woman's palm. Then, surprised by a whirling gust of wind that whipped around the corner of the street, she gasped, clutching her hood too late to keep it from falling back, revealing fire-red ringlets that tumbled in long strands well past her shoulders.

There was no doubting who she was. She had been told that red hair wasn't common in Adoria's capital, appearing mainly in those who were related to her mother's kin.

All talk hushed into whispers, which alone made her feel uneasy, but when they fell to their knees, her stomach lurched.

Bowing her head, she tried to will the blood that welled in her cheeks to leave them a more reasonable color than the vibrant scarlet hue they no doubt displayed. Mumbling apologies as she pushed her way past the masses, she ducked into the darkest doorstep she could find, discarding the bread as she entered.

The crude wooden sign that hung from rusted chain above the door should have warned her, but at the time, she didn't care where she was going as long as it was away from the unwelcome attention.

Inside the establishment, the Braeden stopped their chatter. The tinkling of glass mugs being set down on tables forced a groan from her. *Please, let me just get out of here without further notice.*

Duncan stood from where he sat near the front, a gentle smile gracing his usually grumpy features. He was thinking that she'd come to find him. Sighing, she didn't have the heart to refute what his face plainly showed he believed. He was lucky she'd had a little while to cool off.

"I'd hoped you would make your way down here at some point, though I can't say your brother will be too pleased you're here."

"Is that because he is supposedly my brother, or because I am a *lady*?" she asked dryly.

Before he could answer, another voice — one she hadn't heard since she was very little — answered for him.

"Can a lady not be her brother's ward as well? Not that any man or Adorian will ever have any hope of keeping a true eye on any female in your family."

"Roahn," his name fell solemnly from her lips, breaking her heart as the enormity of her sense of abandonment washed over her.

His hair was much lighter than when she'd last seen him, gray streaks blended with chestnut, the scar that ran from brow to cheekbone far less prominent and his skin much fairer now than when the harsh sun of Palingard had tanned him.

"Ariana," he rose from his seat, his walk slow and deliberate as he made his way to her. "Were it within my ability to ask your forgiveness I would, but I know, as do we all, how deep was the love your father felt for you, how limitless, and to ask for such a thing would be to deny what I know was a decision made out of great strength. He wanted nothing but to have you here."

"You knew of their advances on Palingard. Did you think of that endless love of his when you knew my fate and decided my life wasn't worth saving?"

Roahn paused, restraint evident in his handsome features. His face wounded her deeper than she'd imagined it could. Lifting a hand in an angry reflex, her palm was inches from his face when he caught it and lowered their clasped hands to his chest. He held it her hand there for a moment, stilled against his heart beating in his chest.

She closed her eyes, wishing away the memories of how many times she'd been held there as a child, letting out a breath only when he pulled her to him. A steady arm held her waist while he rested his cheek on the top of her head.

Duncan touched her back. "Don't think for a moment that we wouldn't lay down our own lives for you."

"I know you are wounded, Ari," Roahn whispered. "I also know there are no words that are strong enough salve to mend what you believe to be broken. But you're here, and if there were ever a time to remember the faith you once had in him, it would be now." Roahn lifted her chin. "You were spared for a reason."

Still in his embrace, tears spilled down her cheeks. Perhaps her tears were for those she'd long since mourned and laid to rest in her mind, or for the realization of the magnitude of how much of her life had been a lie, maybe even a little of both. She cried until her throat was raw, fears for Sara and Bella — for all of Palingard — mixed with the overwhelming grief of losing nearly everyone she'd ever known.

Eventually, a mug of ale was placed in her hands; she emptied the glass in seconds.

Duncan laughed louder than the rest of them, patting Ariana on the back. He looked at Roahn and smiled. "I once fancied you merely brave. Had you spent the last fifteen years in Middengard, I'd call you irrefutably fearless."

Roahn's laugh rolled from his belly as he chuckled. "And why is that, if I may ask?"

Duncan grinned, ducking his head as if he were about to share a secret of great importance. "If you had, you would've known what you risked by pulling a furious, armed Ariana into your embrace."

Roahn stepped back, looking her over in mock horror. "What's this?"

He shook his head, clicking his tongue in disagreement, "I think our friend has had too much to drink, eh?"

Duncan took a step back, holding his hands up in a helpless gesture. "I warned him."

Roahn looked at her sideways as she pulled a dagger from her belt, letting it play in a nimble dance through her fingers, snatching it away as soon as he reached for it.

He looked at Duncan, then back to Ariana, astonished. "Dare I ask, but can you use it?"

She smiled, all the while taking aim at a gamesman's board that hung on the wall. Letting the hand blade go, she crossed her arms as it hit dead center. "What would you say?"

Laughter abounded and another drink was sent her way, leaving her feeling light-headed and, for a short while, relaxed.

"So, you were supposed to have wings?" Ariana asked Duncan.

"We all were."

"And, you're not furious about that? I'd be furious. You have to ride and walk everywhere while they get to fly? Seems unfair."

Roahn groaned. "Well, there are moments where it chaps. There are games we can't play for lack of wings, but at the end of the day it isn't so different. It's not like you think, Ari. You ride horses and walk, even though you are fully able to run. Why? Because running wears you out. So does flying. The wings aren't like birds'. Adorians have arms and shoulders and a human body structure, but you won't notice too many flying unless they have to or unless there is some immediate benefit in it." He paused, something unreadable in his eyes. "You definitely won't see your brother fly much. Your father instructed Cademon and him to fly in retreat the day he died and though Michael had no choice in the matter, he's never forgiven himself for it."

"I don't want to know the details, not now." Ariana was already feeling woozy and wasn't in the mood for such talk.

"Then tell us what you've been up to since we've seen you last," Roahn said. "I'm sure you caused all sorts of trouble for Bella."

She entertained them with stories of what had changed in Palingard since they'd last been there and in turn listened as Duncan told his own tales of teaching Ariana the weaponry her father had forbidden.

"It amazes me that the very beings who left my sister for dead, by decree of what they believed my father swore them to, would so flagrantly go behind his wishes to educate her on what he plainly wouldn't have allowed."

Michael's voice silenced the pub. Roahn cleared his throat and bowed to Michael.

"My Lord. My discretion was questionable. I should've reasoned that you wouldn't appreciate her being here."

Ariana looked up at Roahn and then to Duncan, whose hand rested on her shoulder. She'd had far too much ale to take any of them seriously, let alone someone she'd just met days ago, whether he claimed they were related or not. Duncan cringed as she opened her mouth.

"I resent that." She hiccupped, giggling softly to herself. "I am a free woman and can go anywhere I please."

Michael stepped forward and took her by the arm. "You are an Adorian sovereign's sister and your father would be more than mortified had he found you here — he would have strung up every last one of your accomplices by their feet and watched with no remorse as they were tarred."

She giggled again. "Creative. I think I might like to see that — it could prove rather entertaining. It's quite dull around here isn't it?"

The Braeden tried not to laugh, but Ariana's irreverence toward Michael proved too much. Their restraint crumbled, leaving Michael's face stern as he walked her out of the pub, pulling the hood of her cloak over her head as they entered the street.

"Are you ashamed of me as well?" she mumbled.

He stopped, whirled around, and took her face in his hands, steadying her unsure gaze. "It's your comfort that concerns me, not hiding who you are." He paused. "You're drunk."

She shook her head. "I believe I was drunk an hour ago."

Flustered, he dropped his hands and turned back toward the keep. "I suggest you lie down for awhile lest you wake with the headache I fear will keep you close company this evening, though I question your ability to do much of anything reasonable at this point. Kaitlyn will call for you when the feast begins."

"I resent that, too," she quipped, proud of herself for holding what she hoped was a reprimanding scowl on her face. "I'm *reasonably* able to call myself to the feast!"

CHAPTER TWELVE

BLOOD IS BLOOD

Garren walked into the chilled night air, his boots scraping against the dirt and stone, the sound echoing in the stillness. His head felt clouded and heavy, his vision hindered by disorientation. He could recall nothing of where he'd been before then.

Eidolon was illuminated by the glow of the moon. Shadows were his only company as he wandered past one deserted building after another. After a while, he found that he'd wandered to the oldest part of the dividing wall, made of iron and covered in thick ivy. It was unremarkable for a few paces, but as he approached an aperture, he caught a fleeting glimpse of red through the leaves.

He tore the ivy away and saw nothing for a moment. Then, just ahead of him, he caught another flash of moonlit red and he ran after it, tearing at the ivy every few feet in an attempt to catch her. Finally, he reached an opening, and though it wasn't the gate that he'd recalled, he found himself face to face with her.

He was speechless. She apparently was, too. If he could just see clearly — everything seemed so distant, so hazy. She stood in silence, her blue eyes not quite as bright as they'd been the last time he'd encountered her. He pulled his glove from his hand and reached through the bars, certain that she'd shy away.

She remained still as he swept his fingers across her cheek, her skin warm to the touch. He started to speak, but though he stood right in front of her, his very flesh upon hers, her presence felt like a beautiful illusion and some part of him feared that if he spoke, she'd vanish. He'd just parted his lips, willing to take the risk, when he heard a sickening scream.

At first he thought it was coming from the castle, but, to his horror, he saw the Moriors approaching her from behind. He pulled his hand back and tried the iron, finding it as solid as it appeared.

"Garren." Her voice trembled.

He tried to climb the wall, but every foothold failed him. He attempted in vain to use his powers to remove the wall between. His sight spun as he clung to her through the bars, her hands fastened on his arm so tightly that she broke his skin. As the sharp claws of the Moriors pierced her chest, he cried out.

Sweat poured over Garren as he bolted upright in bed, his heart beating hard. He ran his hands through his hair, trying to get his bearings. As he brought his hands back down to his sides, he felt a sting on his right arm and when he looked down, he could barely make out, in the faint light, a bloody tear where hands had clung to him. He traced it with his fingers, expecting it to vanish at any moment. His pulse quickened further as it dawned on him.

She said my name.

Michael was downstairs with Jenner when Kaitlyn tore around the corner.

"My Lord," she leaned over with her hands on her knees as she caught her breath. "She's screaming! She's asleep, but I can't wake her. I just know something's wrong."

Michael didn't wait to hear anything else. He grabbed Jenner by the arm and started up the stairs toward the north hall.

As he approached the back corridor, he heard her crying out and ran faster. It was a terrifying scream, sounding more from pain than fear. He reached the doors first and as he swung them open, he could see her thrashing about on the bed. As soon as he reached her, he took her by the arms and called her name, but just as Kaitlyn had said, Ariana didn't respond.

Jenner stepped forward. *"Nor dunto lathoro toul verdet et antonai."* As Jenner spoke, Ariana began to struggle less against Michael's hold. Her breathing stayed the same, as did the level of distress in her expression. *"Navi lavotu ahnorno nigh say entiron laithos."*

She fell limp against Michael.

"Ariana," Jenner said softly.

She stirred, turning her head, as if she were trying to push the dream away. Once she finally opened her eyes, she saw Michael first and clutched the sleeves of his shirt.

"Ariana," Michael turned her face to his. "You were dreaming."

Ariana couldn't speak right away. He pulled her to him, this time wrapping his arms around her, but felt his skin grow wet and warm. He lifted his hand to the light, and saw that it was covered in blood. Horrified, he looked to Jenner.

The elder reached over and pulled at Ariana's gown to expose long cuts that tore through her skin. They were superficial wounds, little more than scratches, but quite real.

Michael's eyes darkened, "Ariana, what aren't you telling me?"

She tried to speak, but her voice came out as a sob instead.

"Leave us," Michael said softly.

Jenner motioned for Kaitlyn to follow him into the hall. "Would you have me postpone tonight's affair until tomorrow?"

Michael looked at Ariana doubtfully. "Begin without us." He watched them disappear through the doorway before he turned back around. He could see in her eyes the hesitation to reveal anything and almost scolded her for it, but behind her reluctance was clear and unmistakable fear. He swallowed his disapproval and tried his best to be patient.

"What did you see in this dream?"

Ariana shook still but had calmed down enough to speak. "I saw Garren — Moriors — a place that I can only assume is Eidolon."

Michael's face hardened.

"He didn't do this to me," she whispered.

Michael closed his eyes and bent his head to keep from showing his fury. He could tell she was afraid to provoke him and he needed her to be honest with him. It was frustrating that she would consider the High Lord innocent in any way.

"Don't be foolish! He has no benevolence. Dark to his very core, whatever poison he is using to tempt you into thinking of him in any other way is straight from Ciara herself. Why didn't you disclose this before? I assume that this isn't the first time you've seen visions of him?"

"What could you have done?" she asked, quickly showing regret for her words.

"What would I *not* have done to prevent this?" Michael glanced away, reining in his emotions. "He's inflicted horrible deaths upon our people out of sheer spite. He's slain without consideration of gender or age — infants, women, children — it makes no difference to him. Blood is blood." He let go of her and rose from the bed. He walked to a small cupboard near the washstand, where he withdrew a washcloth and an unadorned green bottle. He sat back down on the bed beside her and motioned for her to lie down.

He moved aside the torn shreds of her gown with as gentle a touch as he could muster and tended to her wounds. He started to comfort her, but he couldn't say the words. Anger outweighed his sympathy. In all fairness, she was right, he didn't know what he could have done, but not telling him was unacceptable. She naturally would be guarded, given her childhood and the events of the last few weeks, but it wasn't an excuse to harbor such secrets. This, even for Garren, was extraordinary.

The cuts looked much better with the blood washed away. He placed the top back onto the bottle and laid it with the washcloth on the night stand.

"Are you angry with me?" she asked, her voice not much more than a murmur.

"I'm not pleased with your discretion, but I wouldn't use the word anger," he lied, not wanting to say much more for fear of revealing his real sentiments. She didn't respond, but lay still and wordless instead, as though she were waiting on his permission to move. He put his hand on her shoulder. "If you're well enough, change clothes. I will meet you in the hall. You are under no obligation to go if you aren't ready. There is always another night."

She shook her head. "I'll be ready in a few minutes." Her back was to him, her breathing still shallow.

He rose from the bed and walked toward the hall. Once outside, he leaned against the wall, his arms crossed on his chest. Blood throbbed in his head, blurring his vision. How could he intervene when the enemy was miles away? He'd expected the Ereubinians to grow in strength with their victory in Palingard, but this was unlike anything he'd ever witnessed. They'd displayed moderate powers of a trivial nature, like levitating objects or a mild persuasion, but nothing this malevolent.

He hadn't noticed the dog before, but Michael suddenly felt hot breath on his legs. Koen was sitting next to him, whimpering. He must've been locked out of the room. He ran his hand down the dog's head and back. "I think she would appreciate the company." He cracked the door enough for Koen to go through. Though it was muffled, he thought he heard Ariana cry out Koen's name and his heart sank. Was it really necessary for him to have been so harsh with her? She was miles away from what she'd known as her home, and though he felt he'd known her forever, she had more to take in than just his existence. She needed time to get used to everything — to get used to him.

As he waited, he paced back and forth through the hall. It was a habit of his. He'd worn furrows in the floor when Genny was ill. But this was so different. He'd at least known what to expect with her sickness. He couldn't begin to prepare himself for an enemy who could injure from afar.

Michael had stopped pacing and was leaning against the door when it moved behind him. He turned to see that her eyes were red and puffy. The gown she'd changed into was a deep navy blue with a silver beaded bodice and a white fur-lined cloak. Her hair fell in blood red ringlets past her shoulders.

It took him aback to see her in the dress, having only seen Genny wear it on one occasion —the ceremony for Michael's father. There'd been no body to bury, so they had held a vigil, lighting candles in his honor. All of Adoria had been united on that day.

"Ariana ..."

"Not right now, please." She looked tired.

Nodding, he started to put his arm around her shoulder when she stepped out of his reach and walked ahead of him.

It was for her own good that he remained distant in his sympathies. As rightful ruler of Adoria, he couldn't entertain any notion of Garren's virtuousness, no matter how much it pleased his sister to do so.

CHAPTER THIRTEEN

A THOUSAND YEARS

The room was filled with people. Michael had told her that it would be, but somehow it hadn't readied her for their reception. As she and Michael entered, every Adorian fell to his knees. He held her hand outstretched as they descended a wide set of steps. All eyes were on her and she felt vulnerable, naked. As upset as she was with Michael, she gripped his hand like it was the last thing she'd ever do.

The room was vast, stretching three stories to a cathedral ceiling made entirely of stained glass. Tall, white columns framed the edges of the room and set off several sections in the middle. Open balconies were mounted on all sides. She was in the process of wondering about the stairs when she saw several Adorians fly to take their places. It certainly explained why the ceiling was so high.

The décor was intricate from the doorways down to the designs on the marble floor. Painted tiles were scattered across the walls among paintings and tapestries, much like those in her room. She heard music and singing coming from somewhere behind the crowd.

The elders greeted them at the foot of the stairs. Their robes were dark navy, matching Ariana's cloak. She recognized Jenner, who emerged from the group first. He took Ariana's hand in his as he bowed, and kissed it. She wasn't sure how to respond, and was grateful when he rose to face them.

"Lady Ariana, begotten of Gabriel Briony of Leiden and Caelyn Edessa of Lipsius, we are honored to welcome you home. *Antu oinai worno ethomos.*"

All of the elders then came to her, one by one, to grant her the same Adorian blessing. When they were finished, everyone cheered.

Michael leaned over to quietly inform her they'd be moving into the dining hall. She walked beside him, still keeping a firm hold on his hand. Although she was anxious about being the cause for so much fuss, she couldn't get Garren's face out of her mind and it brought heat to her cheeks. Michael mistook it for nerves.

"It's alright. You should feel loved. You're a part of this realm now, a daughter of Adoria." He smiled, but she couldn't even bring herself to nod in acknowledgment, nor could she force the feel, from the dream, of Garren's hand on her cheek. Her cuts stung despite the salve that had been used and she wasn't in the mood to hear Michael's idealistic banter. It wasn't that she didn't think he believed what he was saying, he appeared to take every word of it as absolute truth, but after seeing the dissolution of so many promises in her life, Ariana couldn't recall the last time she'd had faith in anything substantial. How could she just accept that everything was going to be fine when nothing ever was?

They walked through a large set of doors into a room of identical proportions, filled with long rows of tables. A separate table was set on a large platform at the far end of the room, no doubt for Michael's and Ariana's use. Michael approached the table and pulled out a chair for her. They sat down, facing the room.

Servers brought out many kinds of game — pheasant, venison and quail — and other animals that she couldn't begin to name and had no interest in learning. It was a shame that she still had no appetite. Scores of Adorians came to speak to her as the night progressed, repeating their names over and over in the hopes that she'd remember them. It was hard enough to appear interested in what they were saying, much less keep track of their identities and the purpose they served in Cyphrus.

Michael must have sensed her state of mind and leaned over to check on her several times throughout the meal. She nodded respectfully each time, but declined to enlighten him further. She was pleased to see Duncan, who came around the table to hug her. She held on tightly this time, happy to see a familiar face.

He kissed her cheek. "I know this is all strange to you. It's nothing like home, but you'll come to love it here, I promise. Are you settling in alright?"

Ariana shrugged, hoping that her lack of a response would answer his question.

"If you'd like, we can ride sometime soon. I can show you a bit more of Adoria."

"I would love nothing more," she said, giving him a genuine smile in return.

"Then it's settled. Tell me when you're ready." He gave her one overzealous pat on the back, unaware of her wounds, before he turned to leave.

"Wait, Duncan?" She swallowed back the newly revived pain that spread now from one side of her back to the other.

"Yes?" he asked, kneeling down in front of her.

"Do you think any of them are still alive?"

"Garren had a particular loathing for Palingard." He leaned against the wall behind them and looked away for several moments. "I wish I could tell you differently, but I seriously doubt that if they're alive, it's a good thing." A profound grief clutched at his words as they left his lips. He'd loved Palingard and though the other Adorians she'd met had expressed regrets, it wasn't the same. None but Duncan, Roahn and a handful of Braeden understood what had been truly lost. It was more than just a stronghold, or a name on some map. It was home.

She could tell by Michael's attitude toward the Braeden that he felt they were languid in their character, simply by not disagreeing with the elders. This aside, when she'd finally let go of her initial anger, their presence here above all others made her feel at ease. The Braeden had been in Middengard with them — or with the humans. She still couldn't think of herself as an Adorian.

"I have so many questions, but I suppose now isn't the time."

He nodded and looked as though he wasn't going to speak again, but turned back just before leaving. "I'll make time to answer anything you want to know later." He cleared his throat and absently swung his hand, hitting the door frame, as he breezed out of the room.

Michael leaned toward Ariana again. "You barely touched your food."

"I'm alright."

He kept his arm on the table beside her, unimpressed with her answer. "It seems you and Duncan have made amends."

She nodded in silence.

"I was never able to see Palingard except at a distance," Michael noted. "Tell me, what was it like?"

She'd been playing with her fork, and when Michael finished his question, she dropped it beside her plate. She still wasn't interested in talking, but realized that he was going to press her until she gave him some sign that everything was alright.

"It was different. It's hard for me to explain how. Everything was simpler, less elegant." She took a deep breath, pausing before saying anything further. "I was raised by a friend of our mother's, her name is Bella. I've known her since I was born. She helped mother around the house and in the fields in return for room and board. Then, when mother died, she tended to me while Father was gone. Eventually, she was all I had left."

"What about your lessons, what were they like? Is there a school there?" He seemed genuinely interested, but she'd have preferred to finish her meal, or rather play with her meal, in peace and quiet.

"There were few children left after the first siege, so we were all taught by the same teachers. It was a small building near the center of the village. The older children helped the younger ones, and though it was nothing like what you have here, it worked for us. Mother read to me when I was little, and while he was still there, Duncan taught me all sorts of things." A slight smile forced its way to her lips. "I tried to teach Sara a few words of what I now know was Adorian. Certainly explains why she was never able to grasp it. She'd tell me stories that she'd heard over the years of winged men. It was all fun and games to me, nonsense, but she really believed it."

"I take it Sara was a close friend of yours?" He asked.

"She was my closest friend." She was terrified for Sara, and though Duncan had said it would be worse if she were alive, Ariana desperately, selfishly hoped that she was. She pushed the thought of what Sara would be going through out of her mind; it was too much to bear at the moment.

"She told me once that she'd seen an Adorian. We'd just finished celebrating a wedding, and just as everyone had readied for bed, she came tearing through our house yelling for me. I'll never forget her face. At the time I thought she'd gone mad, but, I suppose she could have seen one of you."

Michael lifted his head. "What did she say to you of this Adorian?"

"She said she was walking through the woods, looking for flowers for a wreath, or something equally ridiculous, when she spotted him from a few yards away. She went on about this for weeks, well, years afterwards. The armor he wore, his horse. Even after she'd gotten engaged, she still talked about it, all weepy eyed and sappy."

"Did she marry?" Michael asked.

Ariana thought the question odd. She shook her head. "No, the wedding was set for a few months from now, though if you want to know my opinion, I don't think it was ever going to take place. They didn't get along very well." A smile crossed his face. It had a quaintness to it that caught her interest. "Am I missing something?"

"I saw Palingard once from a distance, as I said earlier. It was at dusk after a ride from Ruiari and when I approached the village, as I shouldn't have done, I witnessed what I assumed to be a wedding. It was several years ago. I think your friend may have seen me."

Ariana wasn't sure how she felt about this. "Are you serious?"

He nodded, looking a bit self-conscious. "I'm afraid so. No other Adorian would have ventured that close. I deviated from my riders because I had the authority to."

Ariana thought it over for a moment and found the revelation saddened her. It may have been the only time that Sara would ever lay eyes on him. "You would have really liked her." Ariana closed her eyes to keep from crying. "She was the human embodiment of trust and loyalty."

"Ariana, there's someone I would like to introduce to you."

She opened her eyes to see Jenner, his hand on the shoulder of an aged, pleasant-looking human. At least, she assumed as much — he didn't have wings and didn't have the build to be Braeden.

"This is Bronach."

The man bowed, a generous smile lighting up his features. "My Lady, it is truly my pleasure to meet you. It seems your name is all I hear these days."

She rolled her eyes. "Don't believe a word of it. I'm not nearly as feisty as they would lead you to believe."

Bronach laughed as he patted her hand. "Fair enough, but I should tell you that you are every bit as lovely as I was told. You remind me very much of someone I once knew. Perhaps I'll tell you about her sometime."

"Bronach is a historian," Jenner said. "I imagine he could tell you far more about Adoria than any of our elders, myself included."

Bronach nodded. "If you could stand the company of an old man, grumpy and sardonic in his ways, then I will teach you anything you wish to know, child. All you need to do is ask."

Ariana was intrigued by him, relieved by his humor and his humanity. "I'll take you up on your offer. Just remember that you made it."

Michael leaned back relaxed in his chair. "Bronach has begun the restoration of the Saeculum, which I have no doubt you'll find interesting. It might eventually lead to excavating the old world, but we'll see what comes of this first."

Bronach eased a chair out beside them, settling himself against the high, thin back — fashioned so for those whose wings would fall to either side. "In due time we'll tell you all about it, though I cannot imagine why a spry young thing like yourself would bother with dusty, overgrown ruins." He appeared well aware that such a choice of words would do nothing but pique her interest all the more.

"Spry indeed, my bones say otherwise. I feel well over a thousand years old these days."

Bronach's face stilled. His rounded eyes and bulbous little nose paused only long enough for her to catch it. "My deepest sympathies for your loss, this cannot be easy to bear." He looked to Michael then. "Have you taken her to the Garden of Dedication?"

Michael shook his head, "I haven't. Too much has been weighing on our list of considerations lately. Palingard will be dedicated with a statue of its own sometime in the coming months. I think you'll be pleased. Every village and city has been — "

Ariana abruptly rose from her seat, the legs of the chair screaming against the polished floor. She didn't intend to be rude, but the finality of his words fell on her like a hundred stones.

Memorial. Remembrance. Sara is not lost! Bella is not lost!

She started to explain her sudden change of emotion, but found herself without the words. As she turned to leave the dining hall, she heard Michael start after her and Jenner's voice telling him to let her go.

As she walked deeper into the keep, down one corridor to the next, she sobbed. She missed Bella and everything else about home. She missed the smells and the sounds, and all the things that she'd longed so desperately to escape. Michael had meant no harm in his questions, nor Bronach in his teasing. But Adorians and the few from Middengard who were raised in Adoria didn't seem to really understand humans. Everything in Adoria was a matter of principle alone. Things in the human world weren't always that simple. She couldn't explain why she kept thinking about Garren, but whatever the reason, she couldn't just shut off her emotions. He had released her. The look in his eyes, both that day and in the visions where she'd encountered him since, wasn't malicious, wasn't evil. His hold on her was far from being in her control, even had she wanted it to be.

She wandered through halls and rooms of various sizes and purposes, until she came to a heavy wooden door in the corner of a broad gathering area. She was pleased to discover it was a library.

She took a lit candle from the hall and carried the flame to the sconces that were fastened along the wall, revealing immense bookshelves and several generous chairs. She pulled a couple books out, flipped through the pages, surprised to see there wasn't much dust on any of them. Adorians, she gathered, were enthusiastic about education. It made her feel a bit lacking. She remembered hearing about Sara's mother and father, who'd gone off to school in Ruiari years before Sara was born. Ariana's father had told her those schools were no longer in existence, having been turned into orphanages, or training camps for human soldiers. The humans had made an effort to protect themselves — it just hadn't held a candle to the forces of the Laionai.

She ran her hands along the shelves, feeling the bindings of the books. They were deep with artistry, metals woven into the trim and decorative designs embossed into the leather. She was so involved with inspecting them that she wasn't paying attention and ran into a rolling ladder that was attached to the wall. It made a loud squeal as it was jarred to life. Startled, she stepped back, only to bump into something else behind her. She turned to see not *what* she'd run into, but who; a very well-built, pleasing to the eyes,who.

"Forgive me, my Lady. I didn't mean to frighten you." He was tall like her brother, but had skin that more closely resembled Duncan's, tanned enough to give him a healthy glow, his hair a light brown color, with just a hint of auburn to it. He seemed to be about her age, or maybe a few years older. He leaned against the bookcases with a smug grin on his face.

She found herself blushing as she realized that she was staring at him. "You should feel honored, I don't frighten easily."

"So I hear." He laughed. "I'm Jareth. And I do believe I am the last one in Adoria to make your acquaintance." He took her hand and brought it to his lips, bowing his head as he did so.

She would have to at least give Adorian males credit for being a lot more civilized than any of the men in her village, who were barbaric in comparison. "Well, Jareth, I'd very much appreciate it if you didn't address me so formally." As soon as she said the words, she heard a noise that sounded very much like a dragon, which made no sense until she looked down and saw that it was indeed a kind of dragon. A small creature with jade green scales and a plum-colored chest sat at Jareth's feet. He crowed as he peered up at her.

Jareth gestured to his little friend. "I'm sorry, I forgot to introduce you. This is Cryx. He's my faithful companion, useless in the most important of assignments, but comforting in the least of them. He tends to have a bit of a temper, so he'll pitch a fit if you don't pet him. And the bit about formality — understood."

She smiled, having never heard of or seen a dragon so small before. She leaned down to pat him on the head. He cooed, leaning his head into her hand so she could more effectively reach behind his pointy ears.

"Wherever did you find him?" Cryx thumped his foot on the floor as she found a ticklish spot below his chin.

"Being such a ferocious beast, he scared off my prey on a hunt several years ago and has been my ward ever since." He knelt to see Ariana eye to eye. "I've been close to your brother for a long time. He took me as his student years ago, when we were still at the Iidolis. Eventually my antics won him over and he became more than a mentor, he became my friend. I introduced him to my sister."

"Genny." Ariana was excited to be able to follow a conversation.

Jareth was surprised. "Yes, Michael doesn't waste any time does he? So you must already know that Jenner's my father?"

Ariana nodded her head. "Indeed, and I've had the pleasure of meeting your mother as well. They're both lovely. So, am I to assume, since you said Michael was your mentor, that you're commissioned in some way?"

"Yes, I'm one of his commanders. Caedmon and I are his closest advisors, though you haven't met him yet, either. He's scouting Eidolon's outer regions." He rose, offering his hand to her. "Your hands are freezing."

She didn't get a chance to respond. The door opened and Duncan rushed into the room, interrupting them.

"They've returned. Michael has requested our immediate presence." Duncan was out of breath, his words striking the air with a vehemence that was almost tangible.

Jareth started toward the door. "*Louthai ere erothim, tay callesto —* "

"Hold your tongue lad, she speaks Adorian. I'll leave it up to Michael to decide what he wants to disclose. Forgive me, Ariana, we must go, I can't tell you anything just yet."

She nodded, not wanting to test his patience by pressing for information.

Jareth looked over at Cryx, who'd made himself comfortable beside Ariana. "He knows the way back to the main hall and can find his way back out to my cottage from there. Do you mind him staying with you for a bit? He doesn't really like to be alone." Ariana nodded. Why not, she was already caretaker to one beast, why not two?

"I have someone who might like to meet him," she whispered to herself as the men's boots echoed down the corridor and into the main hall.

CHAPTER FOURTEEN

THE ONI

Michael sat in an ornately carved wooden chair near a fireplace at the back of the room. His boots tapped erratically on the floor as he waited for everyone to arrive. Only five elders, who were of the bloodline to the original monarchs of Adoria, were present for these meetings.

Caedmon sat beside Michael, his face a perfect reflection of his grief. He and his men had arrived nearly an hour before, the three dead among them having been buried in an unmarked grave where they had fallen. Michael had been shocked to see Caedmon arrive back so soon, but was more alarmed at Garren's newfound abilities. It compounded the fears he was already wrestling with after the ordeal with Ariana. He was caught up in his thoughts when Duncan and Jareth entered the room.

"What's happened?" Jareth asked as Michael stood to greet them.

"I will let Caedmon describe the encounter to you."

Caedmon stood, wiping a hand over his forehead. "Garren was waiting for us in the woods when we emerged from Adoria's northernmost border. Before we were even aware of his presence, three of our men were slain. Once we confronted him, Riedar rushed him against my orders and, without touching him in any way or so much as moving a hand, Garren scarred Riedar's face beyond recognition."

"Did you not hear him coming?" Duncan asked. Michael could tell he was trying to put the question delicately, but it offended Caedmon anyway.

"Do you think that I'd have three dead Adorians if we had?" Caedmon approached Duncan. "I'm in no mood for your mouth, *Braeden,* not tonight, not — "

Duncan placed his hands on Caedmon's shoulders. "Friend, I meant no offense." Caedmon shrugged off Duncan's gesture, and slumped back down into his chair, holding his head up with one hand, the other held across his chest.

Michael closed his eyes, drowning out the voices of the elders as they argued back and forth about what their course of action ought to be. Garren had always been a sage fighter, knowing Michael's next move before he made it.

"Perhaps the time of the Oni has come," Michael offered.

"If you believe this," Jenner asked, "then why did you spare his life when you had the chance to take it from him?"

Michael swallowed hard. He simply couldn't answer that question. "I chose to be merciful to him out of honor. He was pinned to the ground without arms. Hardly the demise I'd intended." Michael rose to pace the outer edges of the room.

"Your hatred of Garren does not change his fate," Jenner said. "It makes no difference what dishonor or accolades he has received from any mortal. The Oni is mentioned as being among the souls — Garren is Ereubinian — he cannot be the Oni, for the soul of his lineage was sold for power. Have you forgotten the history of these things?"

Michael cocked his head sideways. "Have you forgotten the wounds inflicted upon my sister as she slept?"

As Michael said this, Jareth raised his head, having been staring at the floor. "What happened to your sister?"

"Ariana's been seeing visions of Garren. In a dream this afternoon, she was scathed by Moriors, her back ravaged with claw marks. It took Jenner to pull her from its hold on her."

Michael gave his words a moment to sink in before he continued. "Though the realm of man has begun to diminish, we are not free from our duty and obligation to be its steward. Keeping this in mind, we're of no use to them if we place ourselves in peril."

Jenner objected, as Michael had expected. "My Lord, the divide has never failed us. You must have faith in its hold. And while Ariana and Riedar's injuries are cause for concern, they hardly constitute bringing all of Adoria into open warfare with Eidolon."

Michael flexed his wings. "Duncan, are you willing to reunite your men?" He'd hoped to hear his father's closest friend come to his aid, but even Duncan, it seemed, had lost the will.

"I've tired of the human realm. They've done little in response to all that we have lost for their sake. Jenner's right; the divide has never failed us. No matter if Garren is the Oni or not, let Man save himself." Duncan sighed. "The Braeden can't aid you in this, whether you make it a matter of obedience or not."

"The elders," Jenner said, "would do everything allowed by law to prevent such a command. We cannot allow Adoria to wane in the shadow of Eidolon. Lead your own as you see fit, but we will send for our brethren still in Middengard to return home and a mandatory severance between the worlds will be decreed. For all others, we shall leave the permission to cross over to your discretion alone."

Jenner had risen from his seat and now faced Michael, one hand on his shoulder. Michael was stunned and by the look on his face, Jenner knew it. The council had clearly discussed this — without his presence.

Jareth came to Michael's side, looking his own father in the eye. "I'll stand beside you, regardless of Elder rule."

"I'm at the mercy of our Elders. The last thing this kingdom needs is division among its citizens." Michael paused, reining in his disappointment. "We have nothing left to discuss here."

Duncan followed him into the hall. "Don't be angry with me Michael. If you only understood …"

Michael stopped but didn't bother turning around. Regret dripped from Duncan's words, but it made no difference. "When the human realm ceases to exist, I would think your kind would mourn it most, and yet you fail it first. What else is there to understand?"

CHAPTER FIFTEEN

NOBLE BLOOD

Garren had been awake for several hours and lay staring at his ceiling, images of the girl running through his mind. He couldn't quite summon anger, his apprehension continuing from the night before. He rubbed his arm tenderly; the red marks had almost dissipated. He should have killed her when he had the chance and yet, as the words formed in his head, he felt sick, his stomach knotting at the thought. He ran his hands through his hair.

"Enough," he murmured, rising from his bed to dress. When he'd finished, he made his way to the sanctuary.

It was empty. Black stones laid on the floors and walls. The cherry wood pews were inlaid with intricate white stone designs. The walls bore several large stained glass windows depicting scenes from when Ciara first entered Middengard. A likeness of Saint Erebus knelt in front of a large white dragon. When Ciara was shown in that form, her body was outlined in bright silver, her scales iridescent.

Garren began to whisper prayers as he approached the altar and knelt, feverishly reciting as many verses from the sacred epistles as he could. Suddenly, he jerked his head up. It had been a test. He looked around at the various depictions of Ciara, some human, some animal, and felt regret wash over him. He'd failed her. That had to be what was tormenting him.

He lay completely prostrate before the altar and was perfectly still, chanting a prayer of repentance. But while he'd started the prayer with conviction, he began to doubt his assumption more and more with every word that passed his lips. If she were indeed Ciara, it would certainly explain his affinity for her, but how could she have expected him to kill her? A picture briefly crossed his mind of his mouth touching hers and he recoiled. He squeezed his eyes tighter and tried to refocus himself. Trial or not, he'd failed both the Laionai and the Goddess by having mercy on an Adorian.

Did she not know she was Adorian?

It made no difference whether she'd been abandoned in the world of man or not, Garren argued with himself. Adorian blood still flowed through her veins.

I love but her and her alone. The words weighed as stones in his head. He could still see Tadraem's face as he'd said them.

"And what, my Lord, are you repentant of?"

Garren didn't move, convinced that he'd fallen so deep into his mind as to audibly hear his thoughts, until Tadraem stepped close enough to nudge him with the toe of his boot.

"I have been watching you pray in this manner for over two hours now."

"Has it been that long? I didn't see you when I came in."

Tadraem sat in one of the pews beside Garren. "I was in the back, you wouldn't have noticed me. You needn't suffer in silence, Garren, I have no need to compete for your position. I've waited many years to be High Priest. Whatever burden you are carrying is not yours to carry alone."

Garren raised himself from the ground and sat with his legs stretched out in front of him, his back against the end of the opposite pew.

"I have committed a sin," Garren said, watching Tadraem's expression darken. He lowered his head and took a deep breath before continuing. "The girl you saw me pursue into the woods in Palingard wasn't human. I had my sword in the air, no opposition, and yet I couldn't strike her. I heard the Moriors coming and left her in hiding. I released her, Tadraem — an Adorian."

Tadraem was still for a time. "An Adorian female in Middengard is unlikely. How do you know she was not human?"

Garren looked up from the floor. "I couldn't take her soul. The only other possibility is that the Goddess was testing me."

Tadraem shook his head. "She would not have done so. Your reputation alone speaks for itself. The girl could have had a spell of protection about her, though I've never met an Adorian with such privilege. If she was of noble blood, perhaps?"

Garren furrowed his brows in disbelief.

Tadraem continued. "There are legends of Adorians who have such powers. I cannot say for certain, but considering their secrecy, it wouldn't be unimaginable. If a female had been allowed to enter Middengard, it would seem reasonable. I can't imagine why she would have been there, though, particularly considering the Adorians were aware of our advances on Palingard. Anyway, the spell could not have been strong enough to make the girl invincible, but it would have been enough to affect your judgment."

Garren wondered if it had been prudent to speak with Tadraem at all. Something felt wrong about the High Priest's reaction, though he couldn't say what. He decided it would be unwise to divulge that she'd continued to plague him.

"Did my father ever speak like this to you?" Garren knew as soon as he'd asked that he shouldn't have.

"Why do you ask?"

"You spoke of my mother once, years ago. That you knew her well — "

"Garren, I never knew your mother, you know this. What's this occasion that you speak of?"

Garren suddenly felt like the floor had been pulled from beneath him and he placed his hands, palms down, at his sides. "I was but a boy, playing in the south woods, when you came to me. We walked to the falls and you spoke of my father. You said that I reminded you of him. I must've made the assumption then that you knew my mother as well."

"That's all that I said to you?"

"You asked me not to bother you with such questions," Garren lied. "I was probably asking you things that would seem trite to an adult — it wasn't important enough for you to remember."

Tadraem sat back and seemed to be satisfied with Garren's answer, but he was sometimes difficult to read. "Don't concern yourself anymore with this incident. The girl is of no importance. You've followed your orders from the Laionai and pleased Ciara. Nothing else is of any substance.

"I have prayed to the Goddess and it has been decided that Aiden will also be wed. Considering his wayward attitude as of late, it is more than charitable. This will at least give him something to occupy his time. I feel it should be you who chooses his intended." Tadraem rose from his seat.

"Do you think I'm ready for what is ahead?"

Tadraem turned to face Garren. "My Lord, you have always been ready. You're nothing like your father. I cannot imagine what would have possessed me to say such a thing to you. His weaknesses are your strengths. He had little faith and lost his life because of it. He questioned his beliefs and it led to his eventual ruin."

"He lost his life on the battlefield, at the hands of an Adorian — you've told me so yourself, many times."

Tadraem walked back toward the center aisle. "He did lose his life because of an Adorian. He died because of Michael's father. There was little choice for us."

Garren's chest tightened as Tadraem spoke, and he almost didn't ask — but he clung momentarily to the hope that it would not be so.

"You turned him over to the Moriors?" Garren clenched his teeth.

Tadraem stepped closer, but stopped as Garren held out his hand. "Garren, you would have done the same. Don't let familial ties cloud your perception. He had the opportunity to do Ciara a great service but he chose instead to aide Gabriel in defeating some of our own men. It was treason in its most elementary form."

"What is the difference between what my father did and what I have done?" Garren crossed his arms over his chest.

"There is much difference, Garren. You are on your face, begging repentance for something that wasn't in your control, whereas your father intentionally led our forces into harm's way. You are Aiden's friend, yet it didn't stop you from doing what needed to be done to continue in the faith. He stepped out of line and you corrected him as you had to. You and I are not so different."

Garren felt ill. "Perhaps not," he said, forcing a smile. "As always, I value your council and your friendship."

Tadraem bowed his head. "Thank you, my Lord. I am blessed to be in your favor." He turned on his heels and ducked out of the doorway, leaving Garren alone in the sanctuary.

Garren felt a chill run across his flesh as he considered his father's death. Tadraem could have killed him more mercifully than the Moriors; he wondered if Tadraem's condemnation had been warranted. If Tadraem had seen his father becoming more powerful than he, as his commander, he would've felt threatened. It would've been far too easy to make up lies. He couldn't fathom his father having sympathies for Adoria.

CHAPTER SIXTEEN

JUST A DREAM

I t was late by the time Jareth made it to his cottage, only to discover that Cryx wasn't there. He smiled, happy to have an excuse to call on Ariana.

He knocked on her door, fully expecting to be met by her chambermaid, but Ariana herself answered. She looked surprised to see him. "Time got away from me. I should've sent him home hours ago."

Jareth laughed, leaning into the door frame. She'd changed from her dress into brushed-suede pants and a simple white cotton top. Her boots were made of leather, thick fur at the cuffs. They were fitted over her pants and extended almost to her knees.

"It's fine. He must have been having a pleasant time." Cryx scurried to the door at the sound of Jareth's voice. Behind him walked a rather large dog. "Who might this be?"

"This is Koen. He's been tormenting your little friend here. It's been tremendous entertainment." Ariana motioned for him to enter. "Why don't you come in, have a seat."

Jareth seriously considered it. "I would love to, more than anything in the world. But even as Michael's best friend, I'm afraid he would feel there is no hour early enough in the day to warrant any male in your chambers other than himself."

Ariana rolled her eyes. "Alright then, suit yourself." She started to close the door, but Jareth obstructed its path with his foot.

"Perhaps you could join me for a walk? If you aren't too tired."

Her face lit up. "Let me get my cloak." She disappeared into her chambers and he overheard her talking to someone. He assumed it was to let the chambermaid know where she would be. Moments later, she appeared with the same white fur-lined cloak that she'd been wearing earlier. Her blue eyes stood out against a backdrop of unruly red curls and made Jareth's stomach flip-flop. He leaned over her shoulder and pulled the door shut behind them.

"Where are we going?" She played with the ties from her cloak, swinging them back and forth.

"Well, I assume your brother has already shown you the center courts and I heard a rumor that you've already found your way through the courtyards, so I thought I might show you something a little more unique to Adoria. Consider it a surprise."

Ariana smirked. "What if I don't like surprises?"

Jareth laughed. "You don't exactly have much of a choice, unless of course you've been here before. Don't worry. I won't take you anywhere Michael wouldn't."

"Is it true that he wasn't always this way?" she asked.

He tilted his head. "What way?"

"Was he always this serious? So burdened?"

"No. He was never this serious, not until Gabriel died. Genny grew ill shortly after and then with his newfound responsibility, he had no choice but to put his childish ways behind him. Don't misunderstand me, he was always wise, and he's always had a sense of prudence about him. There wasn't any question as to who was to take Kael's place. That's who held Michael's seat prior to — "

"I'm not that dull, Jareth. What other place could you have been referring to?"

He bit back a grin and gave her a terse nod. "Are all the women in Middengard as sarcastic as you are?"

She appeared, falsely, to think this over before responding with, "Well, don't tell anyone. It'd be positively dreadful for that to get around."

"I'm sure it would be." He smirked. "Dreadful indeed."

As they reached the end of the hallway, he led her to a large wooden door, cool to the touch. He reached out and thrust his weight against it. The door slowly budged and a cold draft blew past them. Ariana pulled her cloak tighter around her.

"So this is it? I survive Ereubinian siege, wander in the Netherwoods, cold and hungry, recover from being shot by my own brother, and this is how I meet my end — by walking willingly into some dank dungeon under innocent pretenses."

Jareth laughed louder than he expected to. Whether she had grown up around Michael or not, there was definitely a trace of his former wit in her.

Suddenly it dawned on him what she'd actually said.

"Wait — did you say he shot you?" A wide grin spread across his face. Ariana looked horror-stricken. Perhaps she hadn't intended to reveal it.

"I didn't mean to say that."

"Too late now! My lips are sealed, but you have to tell me the rest or I'll herald it from the rooftops." How could Michael, most arrogant of all archers, have possibly aimed so poorly?

"He was trying to shoot Koen. I suppose he thought him to be a wolf. It really wasn't his fault. Please promise me you won't mention it. He's moody enough as it is."

This was royal, such a shame that he had to relish in it alone. It would be much more enjoyable in Michael's presence. As Michael was teaching Jareth how to wield a bow, he'd put up with a tremendous amount of criticism. Among many of Michael's more reasonable sayings was, "Aim so you may never be unsure of your intended target. Only the weak miss their objective."

"I'll do my very best to never utter even a hint of your indiscretion."

She shot him a wayward look. "You sound so convincing."

Jareth motioned for her to enter before him, a gesture that she didn't seem to care for.

"If you're planning on locking me in there, you'll have to be more creative than that."

"If it were my plan to hoard you away for malevolent purposes, you'd have little choice. I simply don't want to obstruct your view by entering before you."

She narrowed her eyes. "Little choice? I wouldn't be so sure of that. I'm smarter than I … my view?"

"There's a rail you'll need to hold onto." He placed his hand on the small of her back and eased her closer to the doorway. She grabbed the banister, and after a moment's hesitation, they both descended into the darkness.

Gradually, closer to the bottom of the stairs, a light began to swell in the room. He reached a hand over her shoulder, pointing toward the corners of the cavern. "It comes from the rocks."

She ducked her head as they came to the bottom and crossed under a low overhang. Coming out onto the other side, she gasped. Lights of all colors — pinks, blues, yellows, lavenders, greens, every color imaginable — filled the once-dark cave, growing dim the farther they walked, new ones sparking to life ahead.

"I doubt anything like this exists in Middengard," Jareth remarked.

She just shook her head.

"They are much like butterfly wings" Jareth said. "Too delicate to touch." He picked one up, watching for her dismay as it grew dim.

"What causes the rocks to light up?"

"We aren't really sure. There is a legend of beings who once lived in these caverns, long before Adorians existed. They were supposedly immortal and eventually transformed into insentient stone, having grown tired of this world."

She held out her hand and Jareth almost thought to take it when it dawned on him that she was asking for the rock. He tossed it into the air and snatched it back before she could catch it.

"And do you believe such fairy tales?" she asked, her eyes trained on the stone.

"I don't know. I did as a child. We used to sneak in here and steal them, but you see what happens when they're touched. It took quite a few tries to convince us that we hadn't simply chosen idle stones."

He tossed the stone again, this time letting her catch it. "Didn't you ..." His voice trailed off as he tried to comprehend what he was seeing. He blinked, then looked again and sure enough, the stone had come to life in her hands.

"Maybe you just aren't any good at this?" she laughed, unimpressed by the feat. "Do all of the caves look like this one? What's beyond here?" Ariana leaned against one of the walls, then jumped back upon discovering it was damp.

Jareth wasn't sure he could find his tongue to answer her. "They're extensive. The largest area, where I played most as a child, isn't far from here."

She pitched the stone back and forth from one hand in the other, like it was a child's tetherball. "Well, unless you have somewhere better to go, perhaps you should show me."

He shrugged, figuring that at the very least he could find out more about her and how in Hothrendaire she was doing what she was doing.

They continued deeper into the caves, the air growing heavier as they went. It smelled good to him, reminded him of more blessed times. They walked for a few minutes until they came through a tunnel into a huge cavern. It was about sixty feet high and nearly twice as wide. He'd expected Ariana to be stunned, so her reaction surprised him. She walked out toward the middle of the cave, and turned to face him.

"I've seen this place before." She looked down, trying to pull something from memory. "In a dream maybe, I don't know. It seems I say those words quite often these days."

A dream? Jareth wasn't so convinced, especially after hearing about the Moriors injuring her while she slept. He'd forgotten about it until just now.

"Is your back alright? I shouldn't have asked you to walk so far."

"They're nothing more than scratches." She looked uncomfortable and he regretted bringing it up. Why did he always speak first and think things through later? It was moments like this that he envied Michael's restraint.

He tried to change the subject. "So what did you see in your dream — about this place?"

"A room that looked like this one, huge white stones encircled it, between ten and twenty of them."

Jareth's eyes grew wide as she spoke. He couldn't believe what was coming out of her mouth.

"There was a large stone in the center. Really, it was just a dream."

"Did you see anything else?" he asked, trying to hide the astonishment in his voice.

"No. That was it — all I can remember anyway. Why do you ask it like that?"

"There were stones where we now stand, fourteen pillar stones that were arranged in a circle, and one center stone. They were removed many years ago, long before even our great grandfathers were alive. My father once told me they were found sometime after the doorways between the realms were opened."

"Where are they now?" she asked as if she were afraid to hear the answer.

"Mounted along the borders of Adoria. You passed one of them as you entered, though it was probably covered in snow. The center stone sits in the heart of the elder's assembly." He shook his head in amazement. "You baffle me — such a mystery."

She shrugged, but there was a smile tugging at the edges of her mouth. "Sorry to disenchant."

She'd done anything but disenchant him. He'd only known her a few brief hours, but already she intrigued him. She was nothing like an Adorian woman, bold and outspoken — everything he would've imagined in a female sibling of Michael's. And of course there was always her apparent persuasion over his childhood fascination. As he started to respond, a strong male voice sounded from behind him.

"I thought I might find you here." Jareth didn't get a chance to tell Michael that Ariana was with him. "My disagreement with your father has nothing to do with you. Though I'm honored by your loyalty, please be more prudent in the future with how you show it. Before long, a dissolving of the separation will become warranted."

"What separation?"

Jareth cringed as he heard Ariana speak.

Michael raised an eyebrow at Jareth as Ariana stepped into view. "A new order will be put into place, initiating a severance from Middengard. It will be decreed at daybreak."

A horrified look crossed her face. "Michael, there are humans still alive. I was under the impression Adoria held some oath of loyalty to Middengard's people. Surely you're not going to just surrender?"

Michael's face faltered, though it was so subtle a shift that Jareth doubted anyone else would've notice it. He felt as his sister did, but would never have been so candid if he'd known Ariana was there.

"You must trust us to govern these matters. We will do all that we are able." Ariana started to respond when Michael threw his hand in the air. "Enough. These matters don't concern you."

Jareth was surprised to hear Michael sound so harsh. However, Jareth had never seen his father overrule anything that Michael felt was provident. This of all council meetings would have left him sore.

Ariana appeared hurt and more than a tad outraged at his abrupt dismissal. She tossed the stone back to Jareth. "Thank you for walking with me, it was lovely."

Michael started to put his arm out to stop her as she breezed past him, but didn't follow through.

"I'll send Cryx, I assume he can find his way home," she shouted.

"He'll be fine." Jareth heard her footsteps grow faint as she made her way closer to the castle.

"That went well," Michael said, rubbing his forehead with his hand.

Jareth started toward him. "She reminds me in some ways of Genny."

Michael laughed. "You must be thinking of someone else. Genevieve never questioned a single word I said. She was the most cordial creature alive. Ariana manages nothing but resistance. Father must've had a time with her."

"She reminds me of Genny in her apparent ability to test you. She may not have verbally challenged you, but she certainly did me. She constantly bit at my ankles. This is what having a sister entails. You aren't always the hero — in fact you're more often than not the villain. I saw that look in your eyes when you realized she was here with me. My intentions couldn't be nobler, yet still you questioned them."

Michael grinned, tilting his head to the side. "I questioned who, knowing whose sister she is, would lure her into the caverns in the dark of night? You're fortunate that I don't doubt the integrity of your *intentions,* whatever they may be."

Jareth heard the words escape his lips too hurriedly to stop them. "True. Knowing whose sister she is, I could've had such foul intent as to use her for target practice. What was it someone wise once said to me? Ah, aim so that you may never be unsure of your intended target." Tears came to his eyes, he was laughing so hard and it became apparent that he couldn't have contained himself, no matter how ill a response he received from his friend.

Michael glowered at him.

"I'm sorry. I even promised her I wouldn't." He said it between breaths, his chest still heaving.

"Funny." Michael said.

"Yes, yes it is." Jareth was just beyond Michael in the caverns when Michael reached back and took him by the arm.

"Tell me my eyes were playing tricks on me."

Jareth backed up till he could see Michael face to face. "You realized what she was holding? You were asking about the reasoning behind your father's secrecy? I think we've found — "

Michael, who'd been holding his breath, exhaled. "What we've found, I suspect, is barely the beginning of it."

CHAPTER SEVENTEEN

A VIRGIN MANNER OF DECEPTION

I t was a special observance. Four humans stood at the front of the sanctuary. Garren, flanked by Aiden and several others, stood behind the pulpit. They were clothed in black, save the thick red cloaks that hung at their shoulders. Tadraem led the evening prayer and then summoned the Ereubinians who were to participate in the ceremony. Garren walked out with Aiden, the other two Ereubinians following on the opposite side. They faced Tadraem from behind the Breeders.

A young Ereubinian boy, carrying an armful of white robes, walked up to Garren and handed him one. He did the same with the remaining three. Tadraem walked around to Aiden, after instructing the humans to turn around, and began to dedicate a human to him.

This had always been a curious ceremony to Garren. It was a high honor. He could feel the excitement swell in his chest. He watched as Tadraem took a small blade, the same one that was traditionally used in sacrifices, and held it to the girl's throat. He let it hover there for a moment, then gently sliced the skin, just enough for a drop of blood to form on the surface of her flesh. This was to signify that she had been saved for the noble purpose of continuing the lineage.

Garren was happy with his choice of a vessel for Aiden. While he didn't owe Aiden an apology, he didn't carry any malice toward him, either. He'd aided Garren in his victory and deserved rewards. The vessel he'd chose was one of the more attractive girls he'd seen recently. She was tall, with long blonde hair and tan skin. He'd been told that her name was Sara.

As Tadraem repeated the tradition with each couple, he robed the human in white, signifying the Ereubinian's ownership of the breeder. He finally came to Garren and Cadence. He did something that surprised Garren. Instead of dedicating her himself, as he'd done with all the others, he held the blade out for Garren to take.

"My Lord, I believe it is fitting for you to make this dedication, as it is your will that now determines her life and death." Tadraem pushed the blade closer toward him. Garren slowly reached out, taking it in his hands. It seemed an unusual thing for Tadraem to have done, but having never been through the ceremony himself he couldn't readily correlate the High

Priest's actions with malevolence. He turned his attention back toward Cadence. Her eyes were deep, colorless wells. They reminded him a bit of the Laionai, and it made him wonder if the Laionai had souls. Or if they, too, were simply slaves to another's will. As the thoughts passed through his mind, Garren shuddered. *Sacrilege.* How could he even conceive such things in a house of worship?

He took the knife and placed it across the smooth skin of her neck. He could see a reflection of the candles burning. He began to recite the prayer of dedication.

"Mani suche dost nousmaede ..." As the words sounded in the air, he kept his focus on the tip of the knife, fearful of bearing down too deep and ending her. He watched the flickering of the tiny orange and red flames dancing in the distance.

"Lio treksthis mordoutai ..." his hand began to shake. He couldn't take his eyes away, nor could he finish his sentence. A clear image of the Adorian girl shone where Cadence's reflection should have been. There was no missing the fire in her hair or the ice in her blue eyes. He breathed slowly and steadily, reigning in his alarm. This was not the place to be haunted by such apparitions.

He continued speaking aloud the prayer, careful to make it appear as though he'd merely been reverent in his sudden silence. He finished pulling the knife across her neck, and held it down at his side. Tadraem took the cloak from his hands and placed it around Cadence's shoulders, pulling the hood over her head, as he'd done with the others. Garren barely listened as Tadraem ended the ceremony. The congregation then knelt, reciting prayers of thanksgiving to Ciara.

Garren stayed still as the others exited the sanctuary. The ceremony had taken a little over an hour, but it felt like mere minutes to him. After everyone had left the sanctuary, Tadraem came to Garren, who was still standing silently in front of Cadence. "My Lord, are you ill? Shall I call for someone?"

Garren shook his head, his heart pounding in his chest. He hoped his words would not reveal how out of breath he was.

"I'm simply overwhelmed with anticipation — honored to receive such a blessing." Tadraem didn't show any doubt in his expression, but instead smiled and gestured for Garren to leave with his new bride. Garren started to move, but felt his knees go weak beneath him. He leaned over to the railing behind him. "I think we will stay here for a time, to thank the Goddess for her generosity."

Tadraem seemed pleased with this answer and turned to leave them alone.

Garren knelt at the altar. His hands shook as he clasped them tightly together. He motioned for Cadence to kneel with him. He closed his eyes and began to pray. His whole body ached, sore from the tensions of the past few days, every muscle stretched taut along his bones. His head pounded and his skin felt cool and clammy. He was both angry and terrified. Nothing had ever felt beyond his control, and this was something that not only could he not command, he couldn't even begin to understand it. This was a night he was supposed to relish, and yet he was on his knees, begging for mercy. He became unaware of the words that were flowing past his lips, his prayers becoming fluid as they formed in his head. It was almost as if he'd fallen asleep, because he came to with a firm hand on his shoulder.

"What form of desecration is this?" The hand jerked him backwards, and Garren hit the floor on his side. He looked up to see Tadraem, who'd leaned down to face him. "What blasphemy do you speak?"

Garren jumped to his feet, drawing his sword. "Have you caught Aiden's sickness or have you just gone mad?"

Tadraem looked back at him, shocked. "Garren, you cannot feign that you are unaware of what just came from your own mouth." Garren looked at him doubtfully, not responding. "You were speaking in Adorian!"

"No Ereubinian has the ability to form the words! Do you think to make up lies about me as you did my father?"

Tadraem reached out to push the blade away from where Garren had it pointed at his chest. "Garren, my Lord, I have no reason to be dishonest with you. I speak the truth — Adorian speech just passed your lips."

"This is certainly a virgin manner of deception. First Aiden, and now you? Don't mistake my allegiances."

Tadraem started to respond, his hand rising in the air in a show of dispute, when he withdrew it suddenly, cradling it against his chest. He howled in pain, shrinking back from Garren to collapse into a pew a short distance from the altar.

Garren walked up to him and peered down, watching Tadraem as he shook with pain. He thought then of his father and the demise that Tadraem had arranged for him.

"Please, my Lord." Tadraem begged.

"Surely, you don't expect me to have pity for you? I believe your words were that you would do the same. So, I suppose you do speak the truth. Don't cross me or you will regret it."

Tadraem's cries subsided and he sat quietly as he rubbed his hand. Though there was no hint of discomfort any longer, the memory of it would without question last. Garren took one good look at his former mentor before turning to leave the sanctuary, studying the eyes that he'd once held as wise and prudent, the hands that had instructed him. He gazed at the man he'd once revered like a father and found him a stranger.

Garren entered his chambers with Cadence behind him. Humans were never allowed to live alongside Ereubinians; this would be the only night that she'd be permitted to be in his room. She would be remanded to the other side of the wall for everything except observance.

He walked over to the window and opened the glass pane. Cold air spilled into the room. He breathed in deeply, his chest having tightened again as he made his way from the sanctuary. He paused there a second before turning around and finding Cadence unclothed, standing wordless in the center of the room. He didn't say anything to her as he tried to unravel his emotions.

"I am yours, my Lord. What is it that you wish from me?" Her face was turned toward his, her eyes trained on him, but she was not looking *at* him. She was looking through him. She was soft on the eyes, flawless in every physical way, yet seeing her so vulnerable made him feel disquieted.

"I wish for you to clothe yourself."

She had a slight hint of displeasure on her face, though it was subtle at best, merely an echo of what she would've once been able to express, perhaps. "Have I done something wrong, I do not …"

He interrupted her. "You've done nothing wrong. Do as I ask." She nodded and redressed. He walked over to the bed and pulled down the sheets. Humans, on their wedding night, slept in the small, unadorned keeping room that accompanied each main chamber. He started to undress himself, tired from the day, when he stopped. He glanced back at his bed, then again at Cadence. The smaller room would be much colder. A picture passed through his mind of how chilled the air had been the first night after the siege, how cold the Adorian girl must have been. He slammed his fist on the wall behind the headboard, having grown tired of seeing such reminders. Cadence jumped as his fist smacked against the bare stone of the wall.

"I'm sorry." Garren walked toward her. He almost expected her to shy away from him, but she made no motion. Perhaps it had been instinct. "You will sleep here tonight, I will stay in the outer room." She gave no response. He watched her move to the bed and lie down, pulling the covers around her neck.

Garren pushed open the door to the other room. There was indeed a cold draft, as he'd suspected. He shivered a bit and pulled his cloak tighter. There was a simple bed, with a wool blanket and a washstand that supported a large empty basin for water. He approached the bed and picked up the blanket. He hadn't been in this room in a long time; dust had settled heavily. He should've known to ready this room as soon as he'd been told that he would wed. He shook the blanket out and wrapped it around himself as he lay on the mattress.

He lay awake for some time. Just days ago, he would have disregarded any hint of sympathy for a human, yet here he was, undoubtedly distressed over being unable to be fully a part of this night. He'd waited so long for this — what was the cause of this unrelenting doubt? It infuriated him that Tadraem would make such wild accusations and yet a sliver of fear crept into his consciousness that Tadraem had been telling the truth. He could think of no reason for Tadraem to lie to him. Garren didn't completely trust him, but it wouldn't benefit Tadraem for Garren to fall from power. Either Jules or Aiden would be in line now that Tadraem had accepted the lifelong calling of High Priest. Neither of his two probable successors regarded Tadraem with much loyalty, though he'd begun to question Aiden's loyalties all together.

It was bewitchment — there was simply no other explanation. The girl was using whatever power had persuaded him to release her to also ensnare his emotions. There was no logical justification for him to care anything about whether an Adorian or a human lived or died. There was no moral reason; Ereubinians were the only ones of true blood. He wished his father were alive. It would be great comfort to be able to speak with him and clear up any misgivings surrounding the last battle.

He had a fleeting thought of trusting Aiden with what he'd discovered about his father, before it crossed his mind that Aiden wouldn't be able to reply. He thought of all the times he and Aiden had exchanged jokes.

Garren finally felt his eyelids grow heavy. He was apprehensive of sleep, the dream from days before still haunting him. He wanted nothing more than to be rid of the Adorian girl and to have things as they once were. Yet, each time he saw her, he was overwhelmed with the same sentiment that held him captive in the woods. He couldn't harm her, he could barely maintain the ability to speak in her presence, let alone relieve himself of her encumbrance from afar.

CHAPTER EIGHTEEN
THE FATE OF ALL OTHERS

"You going to be alright to ride?" asked Duncan as he leaned over in his saddle.

"I'm fine. I wish everyone would stop treating me as if I were made of glass," Ariana said.

Duncan laughed. She truly hadn't changed a bit since the last time he'd seen her. Maybe she looked a little older, like Caelyn, but that spirit — that brilliant, wild spirit of hers that was so much like her father's — hadn't changed one bit.

"You'll find that Adorian males in general are that way. Try not to take offense, it's their nature to be a pain in the ass."

Ariana grinned. "If you say so."

They trotted through the snow, through the gates of the main township. The wind was cold, but it felt good on his skin. He'd been up late the night before, irritated by his argument with Michael. He understood Michael's reasoning, but Duncan had spent far more time with humans than Michael had. After Michael left him in the hall, he'd returned to the room to discuss the matter with the rest of the group. He sometimes envied the allegiance of Michael's men, wondering if his own men would have been so bold.

"You don't consider yourself an Adorian man?"

Duncan turned his head to look at her. "Why do you say that?"

She smiled. "Because you said *their nature,* not our nature."

"I do and I don't. It depends on the day. I've spent so little time in my own realm that at times it feels foreign to me. Beautiful, but strange still. I understand how lost you must feel. I'm sorry about Palingard. You must be tired of hearing that, but I grieve with you."

Sadness crossed Ariana's face, and he wondered whether he should've brought it up at all. "Maybe we should find another subject to — "

"No, you're really the only person that I care to talk with about it. You knew Palingard. There are things that I can speak of all day long to others, yet they can't relate to any of it, especially the things that are so apart from this place. It's ironic, I was always seen as the grave serious one back home, and now I find myself almost too light-hearted to belong here.

Everything has a coolness in this realm."

Duncan remarked, "Adoria has been held to such regimented ideals for so long that she's lost some of her former spirit. It saddens me, but just look at the evidence of what was. Did you notice all of the paintings and the woven rugs and the sculptures? That was all left for us by our ancestors. You've perhaps heard them referred to as the Ancients. They are the Adorians who existed before the fall of man. They decided our role as guardians. If you'd like, I'd planned on riding out to some of the less populated areas today. The place I'm thinking of isn't far from here."

"I'd love to."

They rode in silence for a while, passing forests thick with snow and the frozen lake.

As soon as they'd slowed down, Ariana turned to him with an inquisitive look on her face. "You mentioned the ancients — did they write the scrolls that I've heard Bronach speak of?"

Duncan nodded "Some are letters written to the former monarchs, and others are more expository in nature. That was a big word — are you proud of me?"

Ariana laughed, as he knew she would. He'd studied human history and warfare in school. Very little time had been spent on grammar lessons, though he still felt as though he could hold his own with any Adorian. "Why do you think Father never told me of Adoria or its history?"

Her question shouldn't have surprised him. It wasn't as if he hadn't thought of it many times himself; he had just never considered how she might feel about it. He didn't know what to say, there was no clear answer. He shook his head.

"I'm genuinely unsure. I know his intentions were always for your good, so you needn't worry about that. You're all he talked about when we were away. Not that Michael is the jealous type, but I think it might hurt his feelings if he really knew how much your father adored you."

Her eyes filled with tears and he briefly paused, unsure of whether he should continue.

"Please, tell me more about him."

"Though he was Braeden, his soul was true Adorian. He was bound to the same principles as your brother. The word 'compromise' didn't exist in his vocabulary. If it needed to be done, it would be done, no question. The only time I saw him outside of his character was when your mother died. Your father never let go of the fact that he wasn't there."

Duncan cleared his throat. He'd been more wracked with emotion in the few weeks surrounding Palingard's fall than he'd been in his whole adult life. He really didn't know how to deal with it.

Duncan's mind wandered. The last time Duncan and Gabriel had spoken, it had concerned Ariana. They'd returned to Adoria mainly for the Braeden to assemble. Anxiety had deepened for several of the smaller villages in the outer regions.

Duncan had been in the pub, which was the only place in Adoria that even remotely resembled Middengard. Gabriel had sat down in the booth across from him. His eyes looked tired.

"Of all the places in Adoria, how did I know you'd be here?" Gabriel had motioned for the barmaid, who approached their table carrying a pitcher of ale. She refilled Duncan's mug.

"I'll bring you a mug, dear, just one moment," she had said to Gabriel.

He had grabbed her on the arm as she turned from him. "Thank you, but I'd prefer kestath juice instead."

She had nodded, smiling a little before turning to fetch it for him, probably because Gabriel had been the only person to order the nonalcoholic beverage in awhile. Duncan, personally, hated the stuff. It stunk like old leather and tasted even worse.

"You knew I'd be here because it's the second stop I make every time I come into this realm. Call me homesick," Duncan had said.

Gabriel had just laughed. He had a deep baritone voice, its timbre almost a purr. "As am I, my friend. As am I." He had looked down and begun to fiddle with a stick that he'd pulled from his pocket. It was twisted in such a way that it had appeared to be some sort of animal. Duncan had been able to make out four crude legs made from bent pieces peeled from the body of the twig.

"Should I ask?"

A smile had spread across Gabriel's face. "It's a dog. At least, I assume it's a dog. It was left for me with a note on my shield before I left Palingard. It's just about the only time I see the little girl in her anymore. She's so solemn these days, her behavior far more mature than her age dictates. Not that I blame her. She's been through more in this lifetime than many who are thrice her age. But it's nice to see her laugh now and then."

Duncan had understood perfectly what he meant by this. Ariana had been nothing like the human girls. She had perceived things the other children were too busy or frivolous to notice. "Perhaps it's time to tell her. She's only as her Adorian nature dictates."

Gabriel had shaken his head. There always had been a seriousness that radiated from him whenever this subject was brought up, but Duncan couldn't help himself.

"I know that I ask much from all of you to keep this unavowed, but I've never needed your help more. Her existence cannot be made known. Trust that I have more dire reasons than I can express — *please*."

"You know that none of us would do anything to betray you."

"Even if it meant holding a pledge beyond my death?"

Duncan had been taken aback. "Certainly. But what talk is this?"

"Simply talk of what will come to pass. This is a reality for all of us; I am not excluded." Gabriel said. "Eidolon grows in power each day, with every stronghold they overcome. Middengard is vanishing before our eyes. We may no longer count on our victories as our ancestors once could." Taking the twig from the table, Gabriel had tucked it with care into the inside flap of his cloak.

"True, but you've never spoken like this before. What's brought about this change of heart?"

"I wouldn't call it a change of heart, Duncan. I've always carried these sentiments, but my dreams have been dark of late. My heart is heavy for the future. I see my son, my vision in his eyes, and my sweet daughter. It reminds me of the things that I never wanted for them. I envisioned a world without darkness and ruin, as things once were in Middengard." Gabriel had shifted in his seat, placing his back against the wall, stretching his legs out in front of him. "Palingard will be the last to fall, but it will fall."

Duncan had looked at him, bewildered. "Don't be so pessimistic, there's still hope for its survival. As long as there exists one kingdom in the world of man — "

"Palingard's fate is already sealed. Middengard's enslavement under Ciara has been established irrevocably."

"Then what have we been dying for? What purpose can be found in preventing the inevitable? If we don't have faith the Laionai can be overthrown, we're more than wasting our time — we're sacrificing all of Adoria. Braeden or citizen, it makes no difference. Every Adorian has been touched by loss in some way due to this guardianship. Are you telling me all of that is for naught?"

Gabriel said nothing for what felt like an eternity. "The spell separating our realm from Middengard is powerful, but it isn't eternal. Once Ciara has spread her sickness unto all of man, Adoria will not be far from her path. I've told you on more than one occasion that I believe her intent has never been carried in human souls, but in Adorian power. Our realm, carrying the seed of immortality itself, has far more worth to her."

Duncan had scarcely been able to believe what he was hearing. Gabriel had never been so forthright. "You are grave. Whatever ails you, I pray it passes. Have you lost faith entirely?"

"The very nature of faith is to believe when all else fails — when reason or logic cannot provide proof of hope. It's easy to leave with nothing left behind. A true test of character is if one is able to willingly leave what means the most to him, his very heart, for the sake of a greater cause. This is the fear that creeps into my thoughts when I set it free from my subconscious. I didn't come here to burden you — these things are of no consequence to you yet."

"You speak in riddle this day, friend." Duncan had laughed. "Just send me in the right direction with arms, and I'll serve you well." He hadn't known how else to answer.

Now, Duncan rode in silence as he thought of the irony of their conversation. He never had the chance to mention it again. Gabriel was killed soon after. Any death wrought by Morior hands was a violent, merciless death and he shuddered to think of it.

Ariana's gaze was fixed upon the scenery, in deep thought as well.

"You are thinking about Palingard," he murmured.

"Are you not?"

CHAPTER NINETEEN

TOURNE ETHLIS

Michael's horse was a few lengths ahead of Jareth and Caedmon. He'd roused them early to ride with him. He wished to find out why Garren had been riding alone — it wasn't like him and it bothered Michael. He sensed dark intents being set into motion. They sped across the field into the woods. Every muscle in his body was tense, his senses trained on his surroundings. He'd given the two Adorians a stern lecture concerning their attentiveness before they'd saddled their horses. If any blood was shed this day, it wasn't going to be Adorian.

They rode in complete silence for hours. Michael tried his best to clear his mind and focus only on what was at hand, but that in and of itself was a cause for irritation. Everything surrounding the death of his men should've shown his reasoning for heightened protection over their realm. His father would have felt the same way. He could almost hear the words coming from his father's lips — "There is much reason for provision," he would have said.

Michael felt a hollowing in his gut. It had been awhile since he'd thought about Gabriel. Since finding Ariana, he was more aware of his father's presence. At times it was as if he were in the room with them. He wanted to go back in time, do things differently, say all the things that he'd never had the chance to say. It pulled at him constantly now.

Over the years since Gabriel's death, he'd often had nightmares of the Moriors entering Adoria. He could smell their stench as they flew past him. He would always be unable to move; he could only watch helplessly as they destroyed everything in their path.

The same dream always repeated itself in Michael's mind. He would wake up, sweating and out of breath. He supposed it was the result of how his father died. Now to have Ariana wake up, scarred in any way whatsoever by them, only motivated him more. He'd avenge his father's death and keep her safe, if nothing else. He still felt in his heart that Middengard was not beyond saving, but should fate be against it, he'd at least restore what had been taken from his own flesh and blood.

It was no wonder the terrifying creatures gave him nightmares. The Moriors' wings were thin, fleshy sheets covering brittle bones. Their scaled skin appeared rotted, hanging from their skeleton in patches, exposing cavities devoid of living organs.

Their faces were their most disturbing feature. They had a human cheek structure, dark seething eyes, and their teeth were uneven in length. They tore flesh into pieces, a single bite a condemnation of death. Their bodies were long and thin with abnormally narrow torsos. Piercing claws extended from hands whose strength had surprised many Adorians over the centuries. Hooves descended from thick, muscular legs.

Jareth and Caedmon sped up to Michael's side as they came to the edge of the woods. Beyond them lay the plains that marked the border of the outer regions. Several smaller provinces surrounded this area, including Ruiari and what was once Palingard. Michael slowed down, dismounting near a large series of stones. The other Adorians did the same.

"Do you hear it as well?" Jareth whispered to Michael. Michael nodded. There was a low rumble in the distance. As he looked closer, he saw a cloud of dust on the horizon.

"Riders," Caedmon growled. He had pale skin and bright blonde hair and a warrior's build, with broad shoulders and strong limbs. His wings were larger than average. Respectful in his mannerisms, he was always well thought of by any under his command and certainly by Michael.

Michael motioned for the men to tie their horses behind the shelter of the rocks. They'd be less visible if they were aloft.

Rising into the air, Michael stretched his wings, the wind carrying him higher. Michael and his men flew swiftly along the forest canopy. They would be virtually invisible to anyone on the ground.

The riders from Eidolon followed the edges of the plain. He guessed there were about twenty of them. Several miles later, the Adorians came to Ruiari. Characterized by its dark red clay, once it had been a thriving center of culture, renowned for its pottery and sculpture. The buildings were still there, the majority of the city intact. Even though humans still populated it, it was nothing but a shell of what it had once been.

They watched as the leaders of Ruiari met the riders at the city's gates. They'd been expected. Michael, Caedmon and Jareth settled themselves in trees as close as they could. For a moment it appeared to be a visit of little importance, perhaps just a checkpoint for the riders on their way to somewhere else. But Michael's blood ran cold as he watched human soldiers fall into perfect alignment before the riders, heard the click of their boots as the men pivoted on their heels, stamped their feet to the ground and turned to face the Ereubinians. It took him a moment to take in was happening before him. There were hundreds of men, all of them built for war, standing motionless as one of the riders walked between the rows. Michael leaned in closer to see if he could recognize the Ereubinian's face. He narrowed his eyes, and though he could be mistaken, it looked like Jules. Not Garren's worst commander, though no less vile than the rest.

Jules observed the humans as he walked between them. He occasionally found one who didn't please him; he would tap the human once on the shoulder and a second rider would slay the human.

Michael, hearing Jareth mutter in disgust, held up his hand to quiet him.

It was a long time before Jules finished his inspection. He handed one of the Ruiari leaders papers bound by twine. Michael feared what the documents might contain. The riders then mounted their horses and turned toward Eidolon. Michael stayed fixed in his position until he was certain the enemy had all retreated behind the walls of the city. One by one, Michael, Jareth and Caedmon dropped from their perches.

Jareth was the first to speak, which wasn't unusual. "They've left the bodies of the slain men to rot in the sun?"

Michael was surprised to hear this question. It was something Jareth should've known. Caedmon responded before Michael had a chance.

"Their souls are already in captivity, what importance do the empty vessels carry if they aren't fit for servitude?" Caedmon's tone was dark, changed since he'd returned from his confrontation with Garren. Reese, one of the fallen, was his cousin. "Had I the ability, I would bury them myself."

Jareth leaned over, and squeezed Caedmon's arm. "And I would aid you, my friend."

Michael was too distracted by his thoughts to comment. There was only one reason for Eidolon to commission a human army. He'd already started to rise back into the air when he spoke again. "Fly swiftly; it's not wise to linger here."

They returned to where they'd hidden their horses. Michael could see one. It stood unmoving before one of the rocks, having pulled its reins loose from the tree. Jareth skipped as his feet touched the ground, landing closest to the horse. He walked up to it, placing his hands on the reins.

"How did you manage to free your ..." he stopped as, suddenly, the horse fell to the ground, its body completely gutted of bones and innards. Jareth stepped back in horror, his mouth open.

"Such a pity. All three beasts seemed to have been fine specimens. Though, I do believe you'll be missed a bit more than your horses." Jules, along with the other riders, materialized before their eyes. They were completely surrounded.

Michael had been close on his estimation. He now counted twenty-two of them. He drew his sword, bending his knees as all three of them backed into the center of the circle, keeping their eyes on the opposition. Michael ran through their options in his head. He'd seen too many Adorians assume flight was an appropriate course of retreat, only to lose their lives to the arrow of a crossbow. That's when he saw the movement in the trees beyond.

"Nethlo lai werndt ados." Michael tightened his grip on his sword.

Caedmon murmured in response. *"Tourne ethlis."*

Jules laughed as he stepped forward. "Your commands will do your companions little good, Michael. No matter the meaning behind the words, you are marked for death."

A grin spread across Michael's face. Garren wanted Michael to cease with his infantile efforts? So be it. "You arrogantly assume to know both the purpose and directive of my commands." Michael folded his wings behind him, a sign of ease. "It isn't my immediate companions to whom the words were intended. It is to my legion."

Jules watched with horror as seven hundred Adorian fighters descended from the trees and surrounded them on all sides. A rumble sounded as several hundred more, mounted on horseback with their swords held readied in their hands, emerged from the forest.

Kendall, one of Michael's commanders, dropped to the ground nearby to address him. "I received word of the High Lord's undetected advance on Caedmon's men and figured there was a good chance that His Loathness wasn't the only one with newly formed abilities. I am well aware of the severance, my Lord. The elders can rot in Hothrendaire for all I care."

Michael stepped forward, torn between gratitude for Kendall's loyalty and quick thinking and frustration for his having gone against the elders' wishes. At the moment, gratitude was the greater of the two emotions. He looked at Jules.

"I could choose you, but perhaps I will offer you clemency. Pick for me your weakest soldier, his life in exchange for your freedom." Jules paused a moment, hesitant to trust Michael's words. "The choice is yours. Do you not have a single dispensable soldier among them? Or are you telling me that you're willing to die for your men?"

Jules scanned the lot of them, finally resting his eyes on one who stood behind Jareth. He was one of the younger, thinner men. Jules, his hand shaking, pointed him out.

"You're certain? This is whom you've appointed to whatever end I deem fit?"

"I don't understand the reason for your mercy, but I'm indebted to you."

Michael took the fated one by the shoulders, looking down at him. He was but a boy in a man's suit of armor. "As you should be, Jules. I'm granting you freedom from a long lifetime of depravity and wickedness."

A brief shadow of fear fell across Jules's countenance.

"Tourne ethlis!" Michael shouted.

Jules never had a chance to respond. Michael raised his wings around the boy, shielding him from the carnage that roared around them.

Michael made eye contact with the boy. "I need you to deliver a message for me."

CHAPTER TWENTY

THE VERY FOUNDATIONS

"You are not finding Adoria palatable?" Bronach's voice, though unexpected, did not startle Ariana. Its depth filled the small reading room with a feeling of near-reverence, everything else falling away in his presence.

Ariana had begun to notice this — the manner with which he seemed effortlessly to navigate the world around him. It wasn't wisdom or the maturity that comes with age — not even peace, for sadness seemed to dog his steps. She turned in her seat, studying him as he walked into the light, grateful for the interruption.

"Adoria, yes. My taskmaster of a brother, no."

Bronach laughed, "I have heard he has taken it upon himself to be your warden. It is the way of things here, you mustn't take it quite so personally."

"Perhaps." She took an unladylike bite of kestath root, sucking on it for a moment, letting the bitter spice soak her tongue before chewing. "You've studied all of this — have you knowledge of human history as well?" Ariana asked. She half-expected Bronach not to have understood her words since she barely did herself. She swallowed and put her snack away.

"They intertwine much more than most realize. Middengard and Adoria have always been tethered in one way or another. But I see more deliberate questions in your eyes. Have you not yet learned there is nothing unworthy of asking?"

She wondered for a moment if he would think her raving mad. Gesturing to a picture drawn in one of the leather-bound books in front of her, she said, "This picture, I've ..." She let her fingers play across the image, remembering how she'd felt upon first seeing it. "I've seen this before."

Bronach dropped the bundle he'd carried into the reading room with him, sending parchment maps and loose papers scattering to the floor.

"My, my, these old bones of mine. Forgive me," he said as he scooped the majority of them into his arms and sat down beside her. He almost missed his chair, his eyes were so locked onto her. "Continue, please. My clumsiness does little good for those with the unfortunate task of being around me. What were you saying?"

"Just before I came into Adoria, I — you'll think me delusional — it's nothing."

Bronach placed a hand over hers, giving it a tender squeeze. "Child, speak, there is no harm in telling a brittle-minded old man."

"I found a city just before I came here, though it couldn't have been real. I went into a temple and saw this image, among others, painted on the ceiling."

"Why do you believe your sight false?"

"Because the stones fell to ruin before my eyes. I saw a child there, beside a pool of dark water. She showed me images of my parents, and spoke nonsensical things. 'Say the words.'"

"You found the sword outside of the city walls, if my guess is correct."

"Yes, did..."

"Michael has left the sword in my care for now to research its origin. Tell me, what have you read of the immortals?"

"Very little, they're scarcely mentioned in the books I've been privy to. This book makes a couple references, but they're vague at best."

Bronach turned the book so the picture of the lovers was visible to both of them. When he spoke, his mouth trembled with age. "The two you see before you are Irial and Èanna. Remember their names well, for before the world was as it is now, a great love was lost. It is because of their sacrifice that we stand not in the depths of Hothrendaire.

"Darkness has many names and has worn many faces. None has brought him pleasure, only pain and suffering, which he has gladly shared with the mortals of the created realms. He wants for nothing, every indulgence may be granted to him upon a whim, save the one thing his heart truly longs for — Èanna, the daughter of light. Knowing this, her father, the creator, kept his only daughter safe behind the infinite gates to the realm of light and for a time she lived contentedly.

"It came to pass though, as he had feared, that she caught a glimpse of the created worlds and those who reigned in sovereignty — the immortals. She watched them, curious of their ways, and remained at a distance until she saw Irial. After such a thing has stirred the heart of one so innocent, it is irreversible. She could not cross over to touch his brow, or hold his hand, or even whisper his name so that he thought it more than the intimate whisper of the trees. She begged her father for his consent to enter the created worlds, but he refused her, and threatened to take away her ability to view them if she spoke of it again."

"The immortals were all given gifts, some to use for good, and some to protect from the Dark Lord's hand. One had the gift of nature, and created all that you see around you. She could imagine lakes, and mountains, and forests; some that mortal eyes have never beheld. Another had the gift of music. Every melody sung by bird or mortal came from his thoughts. Yet another had the gift of language, and all things spoken, or written came from her hand. Bronach was granted the gift of sorrow, and was the only immortal who could freely enter the realm of light and commune with the father, for he was the eldest — his gift borne from the creation of Hothrendaire itself.

"Bound in duty by the creator, the immortals ruled among the creatures and balanced the power of the darkness, for the seeds of darkness had long been sown in the realm of man, though at that time few understood how firm evil's foothold was. They fought for the perseverance of goodness and virtue against the nightmares of the dark realm. None could imagine a world where light did not prevail in the end."

"Bronach felt Èanna's sorrow and petitioned her father, begging him to see for himself the depths of her love for the immortal. When he did, he saw he had no choice, and despite his will, he granted her a mortal form."

"Èanna said nothing of her true form, but Irial knew the moment he laid eyes on her. They fell in love. It was a love deeper than that felt by any other, and stronger than the power of both light and darkness. It was felt from the foundations of the world, and beyond that even to the dredges of the dark realm itself — awakening in the Dark Lord an even greater hunger for her, an obsession that drove his every breath."

"Two things of great importance had been entrusted to the immortals, the Sword of Death and the Book of Life. The Sword of Death was too dark a creation to rest within the realm of light, and too dangerous for it to be within the Dark Lord's grasp. The Book of Life had in it the prophecies said to have been spoken by the Oracle, the great one who lived before all mortal creatures were in existence."

"Dairinn, the immortal with the gift of strife, was guardian of the sword and the book. It was his betrayal that plunged all who lived and breathed into shadow. Ciara, the immortal with the gift of language, wove her tales as the Dark Lord had tempted her, and she opened the forbidden pages of the Book of Life, and touched them with the blade of the sword, tearing out the Prophecy of the Oni, and stealing the sword just as Dairinn was caught in his treason."

"Condemned to Hothrendaire with Dairinn and two others who willfully betrayed the creator, Ciara began to cultivate the darkness that had long lay in the realm of man. She promised power and immortality in exchange for service to her, and her free entrance into their world. They opened the gateway between Hothrendaire and Middengard, sealing the fates of all mortal and immortal beings. In the Dark Lord's hands now rested the power to take lives for eternity, leaving no soul to either Hothrendaire or the realm of light."

"Knowing how greatly the Dark Lord coveted her, Èanna made a trade — her life in exchange for the lives of all others."

Ariana kept her eyes on the image, understanding now the expressions they wore. "What a dark tale. Is that the end of it?" she asked.

"*For now,*" Bronach whispered.

She laughed, shutting the pages of the book. "Your parents must have had a sense of humor. Who would name their child after what might as well be the God of sorrow?"

"It was not always this way. The name used to mean something very different, but we will save that story for another time. I believe you have an engagement this evening."

"Don't remind me. I couldn't feel farther from home than when I'm near the women in this place. They make me feel downright savage."

He smiled, patting her hand again, "Don't let these little things weigh on you. You are of far greater worth than you know, child. Much more."

"Your kindness I think may be misplaced, but it's certainly appreciated." She rose, turning to face him as she reached the door. "What do you think it meant — the temple, and the little girl?"

Bronach remained silent for a moment, "It is said that Ciara sometimes sends strange dreams to toy with mortals. I cannot imagine she would favor the child who has so effortlessly swayed her highest commander."

"Perhaps ... who told you about Garren?"

"He spared your life didn't he? In Palingard?"

Ariana leaned against the door frame. "Did Michael tell you? Jenner?"

"And he touched you, which was not necessary, when he tried to take your soul?"

She came back and reclaimed her seat at the table. "I never told them that he touched me."

"You have seen him since, in visions, dreams. You have heard of his deeds and, while your mind may understand the gravity of them, your heart sees someone else entirely." Bronach took her hand in both of his, clasped it with clear emotion, but didn't look at her directly. Several moments passed before he spoke again. "Jenner told me."

She stared at him, his gentle, unassuming features; his quiet, respectful nature evident in the lines of his eyes, and noticed that the pages in the book had turned, likely from the draft she'd felt from the moment she'd entered the room. It had landed on a portrayal of the immortal Bronach.

He let go of her hand and as she rose from her seat, he did as well. "I merely mean to point out there may be far more significance in it than you think. That's all."

Again, she made it to the door and turned around. "You aren't going to tell me what that significance is, are you?"

"If only I could, child."

"Jenner told you?"

Bronach listened until he heard Ariana's footsteps fade, before he turned around to address the question. "What was I supposed to say?"

The figure emerged from the shadows, "You saw her reaction to Garren first-hand, why did you need to see it confirmed?"

Bronach nodded, his features shifting in the flicker of the candlelight from the wizened visage of an old man to the ageless features of his true form. "So did you. Yet I know you were watching her response just as carefully as I was. And who went to Garren as a child? Spoke to him in the guise of his guardian, of choices he'd be making in the future? You speak of taking risks, but perhaps you should consider your own indiscretions first." When he didn't receive a response, Bronach added, "Why didn't you tell me that Azrian had found her?"

"Would it have made a difference?" The figure came around the table and sat in the chair where Ariana had been moments before. "The Dark Lord cannot reach her here. Have faith, friend. You've said this to me on more occasions than I can begin to recall. Why do you have doubts now, of all times?"

"The winds have changed. If Azrian knows where Ariana is, he knows where Garren is. This may have always been a possibility, but if we had — "

"There is no way we could have foreseen the effect of their meeting in this mortal plane and that's the only way the Dark Lord *could* have found her. But, you are forgetting something — that same unpredictable power means their love is far greater than even you or I could ever have imagined."

This didn't lessen Bronach's fears at all. "Or that Garren's darkness as a son of Ereubus is so great, the very foundations of the immortal world shook when he touched her. His mother's Adorian blood combined with that of the lineage may have made things worse."

CHAPTER TWENTY-ONE

WHY IS THERE NO BLOOD?

G arren had just fallen into a deep sleep when Tadraem burst through his door. He sat up, rubbing his eyes.

Tadraem stopped just a foot from Garren. "They are all dead, my Lord. One, a mere boy, was left alive."

"You're going to have to be more specific." Garren rose from the bed, and pulled his cloak tightly around his shoulders. He was so cold, his fingers felt numb.

"Jules and all of his men. They were returning from Ruiari when they were slaughtered. Michael spared only one of them."

Garren's eyes grew wide. No Adorian had ever behaved in such a fashion. They usually avoided bloodshed as much as possible — it was their greatest weakness. He knew Michael would be angry over the loss of his men, but he hadn't foreseen this.

"Are you certain it was Michael?"

Tadraem nodded. "The boy has said little else, but he was certain Michael was in command."

Garren started toward the door. "Take me to the child."

Tadraem led Garren to a smaller room at the end of a long corridor and down several flights of stairs. Pushing open a heavy wooden door, they passed the humans who were tending to the boy. One was putting away his armor; the other was preparing fresh clothing for him.

Garren looked at them, pointing to the door. "Leave us!" he barked.

The boy's clothes were covered in blood, though it did not appear be his own. Still, he shook violently in his chair.

"What's your name?" Garren placed a hand on the boy's shoulder, leaning over him as he spoke.

"Micah, my Lord." he stammered. He was so small. It surprised him that Jules had chosen him for any venture outside of Eidolon. As the boy looked at him, he began to recognize some of his features. He guessed the boy to be in his early teens. He had the same gray eyes that his father had, and same mousy brown hair that fell in curly ringlets about his face.

"Jules was your father?" The boy nodded weakly. He looked as though he wanted to say something, but was hesitant to open his mouth. "What happened to the other men, Micah?" Garren questioned him with as much gentleness as he could muster, but he didn't have time to coddle the youth. If the winds in Adoria were changing again, he needed to know.

"We surprised them after we found their horses tied behind a large set of stones. There were only three of them at first; a really tall one with huge wings and another with light brown hair. Michael, who spared me, was the third."

Garren assumed the other men to be Caedmon and Jareth.

"We had them surrounded, when out of nowhere there were hundreds of them, a thousand maybe. They came from the forest and fell from the trees." Micah drew in a deep breath, and then said in nearly a whisper, "He asked that I speak only with you."

Garren nodded and looked back at Tadraem, motioning for him to leave.

"You cannot be serious, my Lord. There's nothing that cannot be said in the presence of the High Priest."

Garren narrowed his eyes. "Do you need another reminder of how to bite your tongue?"

"No, High Lord," Tadraem bowed with clear reluctance and left the room.

Garren lowered himself to meet Micah eye-to-eye. "What happened?"

"He asked my father to choose one of us in exchange for his freedom."

Garren was surprised to hear this. "And he chose you?"

The boy's eyes welled with tears. "Yes, my Lord. When Michael pulled me back from the rest of the group, he told my father that he was freeing him not from death, but life. Then he asked me to deliver a message to you."

The boy pulled a small scrap of worn leather from his pocket. It appeared to be some shred of clothing. It had writing from coal upon it. "I wrote it down so I wouldn't forget.

"'I know not your reasons for sparing my sister, but continue to torment her and it will seal your fate. This is nothing in comparison to the judgment that will be dealt in the event any further harm is afforded to her at your hands.'"

Micah lowered his head and stared at the floor.

Garren was too shocked to respond.

No. She can't be.

He could feel pressure building in his head, his heart pounding in his chest. He placed a hand over his mouth, leaning into it while resting his elbow on his knee. He realized his knees had buckled and he was now sitting flat on the floor by the boy's chair.

"I'm sorry about your father."

Micah remained silent, fearful. It was a look Garren had come to expect from those who delivered bad news to him. This time, however, it grieved him to see it.

Garren lay back on the ground, placed his hands over his eyes and sighed. What had Michael meant by further torment? His emotions flitted wildly from fury over the death of his soldiers to an unwanted feeling of fear for her — the same fear he'd felt upon seeing her in the dream. He'd naively assumed that she was the source of the visions. She was obviously experiencing the same strange connection.

Michael's sister. The very thought of it sickened him. Their loathing for one another ran so deep, it was ironic that Michael's blood was leading Garren astray. He again wrestled with his anger. He'd never felt so lost. Everything that was once so simple had, in such a short period of time, grown so complicated. Though he wouldn't have dared to consciously acknowledge it, he'd developed a desire to somehow bring her to Eidolon to be with him. This desire now became a stark impossibility. The one thing he was certain of about Michael was his fierceness to protect those who were under his command; the ferocity with which he protected his own blood was even stronger.

Garren lay still. His chest rose and fell with heavy breaths as he tried in vain to push her face out of his mind. He remembered leaning over her, holding the blade to her throat — and yet she'd remained strong. He could still feel the touch of her skin as he'd lifted her from the ground, the look in her eyes as he retrieved his sword. *She did not fear him.* There'd been no hint of it in her expression if she had. He should have seen the resemblance. Now, knowing, he could place her cheekbones and the tenacity in her voice as almost identical to Michael's. It made no sense that she had been in Palingard alone, unless she'd been there without his knowledge. Even that didn't explain her reaction. She didn't appear to know that she was Adorian.

Then he considered Micah. Garren had thought a lot about his own father since discovering his brutal end. It pained him to imagine being sent by his own flesh to be slaughtered. He looked up at the boy.

"How old are you, child?"

The sadness in Micah's face was excruciating. "Thirteen this year, my Lord."

Garren nodded, he'd suspected as much. Micah's shoulders were narrow, his build not fully developed. He wouldn't reach his full height for several more years. The boy was far too young to have been on any battlefield. Most Ereubinians didn't make their first kill or take their first soul until they were sixteen years old.

"I have failed you, my Lord." Micah said. "I didn't fight them."

Perhaps the boy was braver than Garren was giving him credit for. "No. You've done no such thing. It would have been imprudent to make any other decision than to do as they asked."

The boy brightened as Garren spoke, but he could still see the beginnings of a deep scar forming. Micah would now be well acquainted with the burden of betrayal.

Then, from where he sat, Garren noticed a pile of cloth hidden behind the boy's chair. He reached out and pulled it close. It was a deep royal blue cloak, with two very distinct slits along the back for wings. "Did you take this from one of their fallen?"

Micah nodded. "Yes."

Garren could tell he was lying. "Then why is there no blood?" he quickly rose to his feet.

Micah looked at him with panic in his eyes, but said nothing.

"He gave this to you." Garren's voice softened as he spoke. "You were accompanied on the journey back here." Garren turned his back to Micah to walk toward the window. He peered through the glass.

Michael was out there. It would take little effort to summon his men and ride out after them. But he couldn't. A rare opportunity to avenge his men and kill his mortal enemy, and yet his feet were frozen to the floor.

Michael's sister.

CHAPTER TWENTY-TWO

THE HEART
OF MY PEOPLE

The smell of burning flesh hung in the air. Michael walked back toward the rock where he'd told the boy to stay. They'd rounded up the bodies of the twenty-one men and burned them, burying everything that wasn't consumed in the flames. Several smaller fires had been scattered in various places for the Adorians to burn the blood from their weapons and dispose of their soiled clothing. As Michael walked to where the boy had been, he truly expected him to be gone. As he approached, he saw the boy wasn't only there but was repeating words beneath his breath. Leaning in closer, he realized that it his own words the boy was trying to etch into his memory.

Michael tore a piece of leather from his tunic. He reached for a small piece of burnt wood that had cooled, and handed it to the boy. "Take this and write the words. This has been a dreadful day, you can't be expected to remember anything while dealing with your grief." The boy took the burnt wood and began to scribble Michael's message down. "What name have you been given?" Michael propped one foot on the rock next to him and leaned onto his knee.

"Micah." The boy didn't face him as he answered.

Michael could see the boy was shivering beneath his armor. His clothes were soaked through with blood. After the fight was over, he'd released the boy and watched as he'd wandered for a moment among the fallen men. He stopped when he'd reached Jules's body, and to Michael's surprise, he knelt beside him, weeping. He decided out of respect not to question him as to how he could mourn a man who'd so quickly delivered him to what was supposed to be his end. After allowing it to go on for some time, Michael pulled him to his feet. He'd instructed the boy to wait at the rocks.

Eidolon would be a long journey for any man or Adorian on foot, let alone a young boy fresh from a massacre. He looked around, scanning the crowd for a moment, when Kendall noticed.

"Who is it you need summoned, my Lord?"

"Please tell Jareth and Caedmon that I'm accompanying our young survivor back to Eidolon."

"Alone?" Kendall asked. A voice interrupted them before Michael could say a word in response.

"No. I'll be journeying with him."

Michael turned to see Caedmon and nodded, glad for the company. He was well aware it was risky, if not outright daft, for a sovereign to do such a thing alone, or even with the accompaniment of just one other soldier. Kendall's expression indicated that the fact had not escaped him, either. Yet, something in his gut told him that he needed to. Something about the boy.

Michael mounted his horse and leaned down to help Micah join him; he was about to let go when the boy pulled from Michael's grasp, then turned to race through the trees to an Adorian whose arms were full of clothing to be burned. Michael cantered to him, watching as the boy tenderly pulled a tattered sleeve from the remnants. It was embroidered with a coat of arms that had somehow managed to survive the slaughter without a trace of blood on it. Michael recognized it as the crest on Jules' shield.

He leaned over once again and helped the boy into the saddle in front of him. "You don't have to answer this, but your superior was willing to trade you for his own life — why would you grieve him?" Micah was quiet, and at first Michael suspected pure indoctrination as the root of his apparent loyalty.

"He was my father."

The words fell like stones from Micah's mouth. Michael looked at Caedmon, who'd followed him. They both felt pity for the boy, Ereubinian or not. It was a shame they couldn't take him back to Adoria with them. Michael desperately wanted to, but no Ereubinian could be trusted, no matter how innocent they seemed.

Michael motioned for Caedmon to follow as he dug his heels into his steed, galloping quickly through the remnants of battle and deeper into the woods. It would be better for them to make as much progress as possible in the remaining daylight.

The boy was quiet during most of their ride. Michael leaned down on several occasions to check on him. Finally, once they'd stopped to rest their horses, he had a chance to speak to him.

"I am sorry that you were witness to this. I did not set out on this day intending to — "

The boy's voice was soft and laden with sorrow as he interrupted him. "You had no choice but to do what was best for your people."

Michael felt uneasy hearing Micah's words. It was unlike his lineage to say such things. "You've been taught many things about us, I imagine. Do you believe everything you're told?"

Micah seemed to be choosing his words with care. It was a smart tactic considering that Michael, in his eyes, was the enemy.

"Don't be afraid, you don't have to answer that either. I am just curious what things Eidolon has taught its youth."

"What could I possibly fear you'd do to me if I didn't give you an answer and you'd fancied one mandatory? If you were going to kill me, you'd have done it by now."

Caedmon laughed before Michael could even smile. The boy hadn't meant it to be funny, but it had made brilliant light of Michael's mannerisms. Sometimes he was polite to a fault.

Micah shook his head, irritated, and continued. "We're taught that you purpose to take the Laionai's power for your own. I was told that Adorians are deceitful and weak; that you value your own lives above all else. Your reason for being in Middengard is to gain human sympathies in order to use them against the Goddess."

"Do I seem deceitful to you?" Michael truly hurt for him, for the lies that he'd been taught.

"I don't know you well enough to make that judgment." Micah's voice trembled as he spoke. His eyes were still puffy from crying and he wiped at them.

"What your father did on this day was dishonorable and should prove to you that everything is not as it seems in your world. An Adorian couldn't have even conceived of something like that. We don't enter into bloodshed unless it's forced upon us and ..." Michael's voice hitched as he questioned his own reasoning. "Surrender isn't an option for your kind. Jules would have fought to the death."

"What you haven't been told is that three of my Adorians, our own flesh and blood, were mercilessly killed without reason. Your fearless leader, who is worthy of anything but reverence, committed this sin. I've seen him slay much younger youth than you. It is he whom you should fear, not us. We won't harm you. Our purpose in Middengard is to protect those who are not able to protect themselves. Garren would have left you to survive the journey alone and on foot if he had left you alive at all. It's your well-being that leads us through these woods with you, not the words you carry."

For a long while, Micah said nothing. He ate what was given to him from Caedmon's saddlebag and drank from Michael's flask of water. Then, just as they were about to mount and start onward, he spoke. "What is Adoria like?"

"It's much colder, with snow covering the ground most of the year. High mountains and valleys make up the majority of the landscape. No one is in servitude or has any reason to fear our leaders. We value all life, not just those who are deemed worthy. Adoria is bound in duty to protect Middengard because Adoria is not so different. Our sorrows and joys were once very much like that of man."

"Are they different now, your sorrows and joys?"

"Generations of sacrifice have been made for the sake of man. Adoria is a more somber place now than it once was. A burden lies at the heart of my people, the desire for things to become as they once were, for life to be revered again in Eidolon. It, too, was very different once upon a time. I suppose they've neglected to tell you that as well?"

Micah look up at him. "What do you mean?"

"Eidolon was once a city filled with life. Don't be fooled by the power of the Laionai. You are but a tool for evil's foothold. The Goddess has no interest in the human realm; it's of little consequence to her. What she wants is beyond our borders and she needs the aid of the Laionai to get it. You may be treated as if your lineage is favored, but it will not always be so. Once you've served your purpose, she'll discard you as your people have discarded humans."

"I've been told to not trust any Adorian."

"See for yourself when you return. Go among the humans and you will see traces of their will to survive. You'll have to pay close attention, but when you do, remember my words. Recall the mercy that's been shown to you, and ask yourself if any in your realm would do the same."

Michael had been told by the Braeden that most Ereubinians don't take their first soul until they're sixteen. He guessed the boy to be several years younger, which explained his relative innocence. He hoped Micah would never see that day — that somehow this epic war would come to an end before he was of age. Michael had never felt compassion toward any Ereubinian. Most he regarded with a soldier's distance; they were all just nameless faces on the battlefield. But this boy he could not disregard so easily. Michael had felt it the moment he'd seen Micah, and he still wrestled with the desire to bring the boy back to Adoria instead of returning him to Eidolon.

Their conversation was limited the rest of the way. They finally reached the outermost borders of Eidolon as the last rays of light sank below the horizon. The air was much cooler than he'd anticipated; it almost felt like Adoria. Without second thought, he pulled his cloak from around his shoulders and handed it to Micah. The boy didn't refuse, taking it and wrapping it tightly around his shivering body.

"You should be alright to travel on foot from here. Remember what I've said, all of it. Speak to him and him alone." Michael helped Micah dismount and watched as he started to walk away. The boy was a few yards out when he turned around, staring wordlessly at the two Adorians. Michael couldn't read the expression on his face, but he hoped that something had begun to stir within whatever soul Micah still possessed.

The woods were quiet as Michael and Caedmon journeyed back home. A brief thought passed through his mind that it would be quite possible for Micah to tell Garren that they'd brought him back to Eidolon. It would be a swift ride for a Dragee, leaving them in peril's way until they reached Adorian borders. Michael looked over at Caedmon, motioning for him to pick up the pace.

CHAPTER TWENTY-THREE

TRY NOT TO BREAK YOUR NEW TOY

Tadraem turned from where he'd leaned against the door. He'd heard enough to affirm his suspicions. *Michael's sister.* He rushed to Aiden's chambers and entered without knocking.

Aiden lay back against the headboard of his bed, his new bride sitting naked, rubbing his feet with oil. She had a bloodied lip and a newly swollen eye.

Tadraem sat on the bed and let his eyes wander over her. "Her name is Sara?"

Aiden nodded.

His mouth watered at the site of her. It had been months since he'd visited the temple and taken care of his physical needs. Still, those vessels were worn out — used. They were nothing like this human, whose innocence was so strong he could almost taste it. He touched the slender column of her neck and then massaged one breast, flicking her nipple with his thumb. Having lost her soul so recently, he could almost feel the fear radiating from her. It pleased him.

"Jules and twenty-one of his men have been slain," Tadraem shifted to rearrange himself, uncomfortable from his erection. "They encountered Adorian forces upon return from Ruiari."

Aiden leaned forward as Tadraem spoke, not the least bit bothered by Tadraem's attentiveness to his new plaything.

"Now is the time for the revenge of yours that I spoke of. I'm sending the remainder of Jules' men, through what will appear to be your authority, into the outer regions with instructions to slay every human that resides in the lesser provinces. We've more than enough of them in the main cities to make up our forces against Adoria, the rest are of little use to us."

Aiden grabbed a piece of paper and a pen from his bedside table, handing it to Tadraem when he'd finished with it.

How is this revenge?

Tadraem tore the paper, letting it float in pieces to the floor. "Your allegiance is to me now, which means you must unquestionably follow what I say. Upon waking tomorrow, you'll find that speech will flow freely past your lips again. Once those who already question Garren's abilities hear of Jules and Garren's failure to avenge him, it will be enough to secure their faith in your commands. Tell no one of this. Garren's forces at large mustn't be aware until after the humans are dead. Then we'll see where Garren's loyalties lie. I believe it to be only a matter of time before his own men turn on him and you will be there waiting to claim their loyalty, having already avenged our fallen by power of the Goddess, your miraculously recovered speech as the proof of it."

Aiden smiled as Tadraem made his way to the door.

"And Aiden ... try not to break your new toy. It would be a shame."

CHAPTER TWENTY-FOUR

NOTHING
OF IMPORTANCE

"Have you seen Ariana?" Michael approached Jareth from behind, causing him to jump. "You really ought to work on that."

"No. Not in the last few hours. And why be on guard in a protected rea… nevermind."

It had been almost a week since Michael's encounter with Jules. He'd returned home to discover that Duncan had given Ariana yet another weapon, this time a bow and arrows, which both worried and angered him. It would be one thing if it were recreational archery that she fancied, but he had the sinking feeling that she had no intention of using Duncan's gifts for sport.

"I've heard her mention exploring the old world on more than one occasion — don't give me that look Michael, I didn't encourage her."

Michael grimaced. Keeping up with her was going to be the death of him.

"Let her go," Jareth laughed. "She's not a child."

"It's not her age or maturity that concerns me. Has she said anything more of Garren to you?"

Michael hated to ask him this, hearing anything about her attention toward Garren seemed to make Jareth's skin crawl, but Ariana had taken to confiding in Jareth. Michael tried his best to not let it hurt his feelings that she hadn't spoken to him.

"Thank you for reminding me. She's managed to not mention him in over a week." Jareth scowled. "You're going to look for her aren't you? Do you want me to come with you?"

Michael considered it for a minute. "You mean, 'Can I come along pretty please because I'm in love with your sister?' Sure. I could use the company."

"You, my friend, can be an ass sometimes." Jareth stood with a telling grin on his face. "Duncan told her about the entrance near the Aidolis.

That might be the first place we try. We aren't going to let her know that we were looking for her, are we?"

"No. If she knows I'm trying to keep an eye on her, she'll be that much harder to manage."

"Has it occurred to you that she might not need managing?"

"Has it occurred to you that my father might have spent her entire lifetime lying about her existence for no reason — no? It hasn't occurred to you because the idea is ludicrous. Thus, her protection has my full attention."

Jareth shrugged. "I'm just saying that perhaps you should consider seeing her as an equal, trust her with your thoughts, your concerns. That's all."

"My equal? You mistake me. That sword I was telling you about? It matches perfectly the description of the fabled sword of Ereubus, said to be hidden just beyond the borders of Arcadia."

Jareth smirked. "You seem to be under the assumption that I stayed awake for ancient human history. Allow me to correct you."

"Jareth, I am not saying these things lightly. That sword took the first human soul and hasn't been seen for nearly three thousand years. She saw Arcadia as it once was — no doubt through the power of holding that very sword. Bronach said a being spoke to her there as though life and death itself rested in her hands. You saw her touch the Aurora stones, and while she thinks it bears no meaning, she's wrong and so are you. She is not my equal. She is worth more than all of us combined and Eidolon knows it."

Jareth seemed to understand this. "We'll need to take a lantern with us."

They reached the entrance to the cave. Jareth turned the wick up on the oil lamp as they descended deeper into the shadow. Michael kept his ears open, hearing nothing but their steps. It was a long way into the old world from that entrance. It did eventually empty into a courtyard, but it was after nearly a mile of darkness. He hoped she had taken Koen with her.

He was grateful for the beast, no one could come near her without its approval; it amazed him. He'd never seen an animal so attentive before.

It was low at first. Michael was in front of Jareth in the narrow opening and motioned with his hand to quiet him. "Lower the flame," he whispered. He heard someone talking ahead of them, and assumed it to be

Ariana speaking to Koen. He couldn't make out any words, but it certainly sounded like it could be her.

Light burst the darkness in front of them, so intense that it appeared as though the sun had sunk beneath the ground. It happened so suddenly that it caused Michael to stumble back onto Jareth, who fell to the ground. Michael quickly regained his footing and ran toward the source.

As they approached the end of the tunnel, Jareth grabbed Michael's arm and pulled him back into an alcove. "Wait," he whispered, "look."

Ariana stood with Koen in the center of the immense room. It was hard to tell where the light was coming from. It was shining from every crevice. It appeared similar in color to the aurora stones, but it was much more intense. Jareth put out the flame from his lantern and set it down.

Ariana was speaking, but he couldn't understand the tongue she spoke. She lifted her hand toward the ceiling. A small, rotating ball of light hovered above her palm, growing in brightness as the words left her lips. Michael was speechless. As the light spun faster, a beautiful humming sound started to emanate from the walls around them.

Jareth gripped Michael's arm, astonished. Another light, even brighter than the first, abruptly exploded from the center of the room, causing both Michael and Jareth to fall to the ground, covering their eyes. Then it dissipated, leaving them again in relative shadow.

Michael rose to his feet first. He could make out the shape of Ariana's body on the ground beside her lantern. He stumbled to her, Jareth at his heels.

Kneeling beside her, he cradled her upper body and patted her cheek. "Ariana?"

She brushed his hand away, her eyes still closed.

"Ariana, are you all right?"

She slowly opened her eyes, a confused expression on her face. She looked around, trying to get her bearings. "Where am I?" She looked over at Jareth, then back at Michael.

Jareth laughed. "Are you playing with us or do you really not know where you are?"

She frowned at him, pushing herself up from the ground and out of

Michael's arms. "Oh, because looking helpless would really benefit me? What's going on?" Michael looked over at Jareth, willing him to keep his tongue stilled. "Always the discerning one. Forget it, I'll figure it out for myself." She started to turn around and lost her balance.

Jareth caught her. "You're in the old world. I was setting out to look for you when I ran into Michael and asked him to accompany me. I figured you might be here."

Ariana turned to Michael. "Your friend's loyalty is endearing. Though somehow I find fault in his story." She rubbed her eyes. "How did I get here?"

Michael had no intention of telling her what they'd just witnessed until he'd had a chance to discuss it with Jenner first. "That I truly can't answer. You appeared to be awake when we found you, but I suppose you were sleepwalking."

Koen trotted over to Ariana, making a low whining noise.

"How glad I am to see you! You abducted me didn't you? That's it, you wish to steal me away and keep me all for yourself. If you needed more attention, all you had to do was ask."

Jareth laughed as she spoke. Michael wanted to feel endeared by her innocence and playful nature, but he was too stunned.

"I used to sleepwalk all the time in Palingard, but Bella always heard me," Ariana admitted. "Though I don't recall lying down to rest today."

Jareth put his arm around her shoulders and leaned into her. Michael couldn't hear what he said to her, but whatever it was it made her smile.

Ariana held up her lantern, illuminating the area around them. "Considering the length of time I've begged and pleaded with Jareth to show me this place, I suppose it would do for one of you to at least show me a little of it, seeing as we are already here?"

Jareth shot Michael a sideways grin. "Told you I didn't encourage her."

Michael took the lantern from her. "Well, some of the old world we won't be able to access from here. What we can reach is unremarkable. There isn't much left that isn't dust and rot. Perhaps we can still see some of the architecture."

He wiped dirt away from the carvings on the walls. The old world had fallen into even more disarray since he was young and it was in bad shape then.

"How could Adoria let something this incredible fall apart? I've seen how everything else is kept up, why let this place turn to rubble?"

"I couldn't agree with you more. Perhaps, considering the separation, our people will have more time on their hands for renovation. This is partially why Bronach has been brought here from Artesh." Michael placed his hand on her shoulder, hoping that this would make her smile, but it didn't.

"Bronach's said as much. But why bother? Why not let this barren, desolate place symbolize what's left of Middengard — considering the separation?"

"Michael, come look at this!" Jareth was several feet from them, peering down into a stack of what looked like rocks.

He pulled away from Ariana to walk closer. "What am I missing?" Michael asked, leaning in to line his vision up with Jareth's. He couldn't have cared less about whatever it was Jareth was trying to show him, but he couldn't take any more of Ariana's sarcasm. He agreed with her and it was only a matter of time before he'd slip and tell her.

"Appears to be pieces of old pottery."

Michael looked closer and saw that mixed in among the rocks were pieces of shattered plates and goblets, some of them almost whole. He turned around to call for Ariana and realized that she wasn't there anymore.

"Ariana!"

Jareth jumped to his feet, echoing Michael's call. "Ariana!"

Suddenly, it dawned on Michael what part of the cavern they had wandered into. Further down the narrow opening to their right was one of the few borders to Middengard that could be reached from underground. He looked at Jareth, who seemed to have come to the same conclusion.

Taking the lantern with them, they walked a short distance to the opening and came out onto the other side. There, she knelt in silence, looking out across the field.

There were thousands of corpses. It appeared they'd been there for at least several days, which added to the stench of the decay.

Michael clenched his fists at his sides as he sat down beside her.

Jareth walked over to the rocks and threw up. Michael was too angry to be overwhelmed by the smell and it appeared that Ariana was in shock. He touched her on the shoulder. "You don't need to see this."

She surprised him by putting her hand over his. "Do you see where Koen is?" He was pacing around and around a particular body, whining.

Michael nodded. All his senses told him to get Ariana away from there as fast as possible, that they weren't safe perched on the rocks. But he couldn't move his feet. He supposed he was shocked as well. This wasn't the only border the Ereubinians knew of. He wondered how many others had been slain and left to rot.

"I recognize the blue from her dress." Her voice was hollow.

"Is it your friend Sara?" He didn't want to hear her answer.

"No. Bella." Ariana turned hard, tearless eyes to him. "Why would Garren have done this?"

"He needs no reason for his depravity. I've told you this."

"It seems to me that with every human being at their mercy, they wouldn't be so wasteful. She was alive, Michael. She was still breathing before now. Servant of the Laionai or not, she was still alive! Something provoked this."

As much as he wanted to be self-righteous, and as badly as her comments stung, he couldn't help but wonder if he'd made an error in judgment. He had certainly felt convinced that killing Jules and his men was warranted, but had it really only been out of vengeance? Could he have let them go, resulting in the same message being sent? He looked out across the landscape, laden with death and the casualties of hate.

Jareth coughed and wiped his mouth with his sleeve as he came up beside them. "Garren killed Caedmon's cousin and two other Adorians, slayed them brutally and without reason. We were ambushed by his men last week and had our own not been as loyal as they are, we wouldn't be here. We left only one of them alive."

Ariana looked at Michael again. He was silent, his body aching from both anger and regret. She leaned in to whisper to him, "You want me to be candid with you, and yet you disclose to me nothing of importance."

He placed one hand on her cheek. "I am guarded in what I tell you because I care for you. Nothing else matters to me but your safety and that of Adoria."

"And had you not returned home last week? What then? Don't you think I'd mourn your loss? Or worse yet, go on thinking you were alive — searching for you until I was sure that you were either dead or unconcerned with me?"

"You thought Father left and didn't return because he didn't love you?" He reached to pull her close but she rose to her feet. "Ariana, that's not true."

Koen had returned, no doubt at the sound of Ariana's distress, and rubbed his nose against Michael's arm, whimpering.

"Duncan has already told you that Father spoke of you nonstop when he was away from you. I certainly hope you don't question that you are loved by me and by all of Adoria. Don't misunderstand my caution as anything more than what any brother would do. Genny had to bear the same from Jareth. If she were still here, I would keep her at the same distance from things of this nature. It isn't personal." He lied. That wasn't quite true. He'd had less to worry about with Genny. Ariana's little display back in the caverns alone would be enough to elicit several discussions with Jenner concerning her heightened protection.

She shook her head, her expression losing its momentary warmth. "And what a wonderful, close, relationship that must have been. How blessed she must have felt to traipse along in your shadow, doing as she was told and never thinking a single thought for herself." Her voice cracked. "There are women on the council of elders, in case you haven't noticed. Some of us are here as more than ornaments in your perfect world!"

Ariana couldn't have been more wrong in her assumptions about how Michael viewed women, how he'd viewed Genny. Truth was that Genny had a weak heart — both literally and figuratively. He'd learned to be careful with her because by the time he'd married her, he'd had no choice in the matter. And in the end, it still didn't do her any good.

Jareth coughed again and clamped his hand over his mouth and nose, making his words difficult to understand. "That's unfair, Ariana. You didn't know my sister and you don't know what kind of relationship she and Michael had."

Michael waved Jareth quiet. Now was not the time for an argument.

Ariana turned toward the caves. "Will you still do nothing to help Sara?"

Michael sighed. It just wasn't plausible. She was likely dead, or from Ariana's description, she might have been chosen as a breeder. If the latter was the case, they would never be able to get anywhere near her.

"If it were within my power to allow it or to rescue her myself, I would. I swear it to you, but I can't. There are greater things at play here that overrule any one human being, no matter her place in your heart."

Ariana nodded only once and he thought he heard her whisper, "OK," as she passed back through the divide, leaving Michael alone on the rocks with Jareth.

It almost bothered him more that she didn't cry. Seeing her caretaker should have elicited more of a reaction than a temper tantrum. He feared that she'd experienced one too many losses. Perhaps not having Sara's death confirmed would work in his favor until he'd had time to decipher everything that was still unknown about her abilities.

CHAPTER TWENTY-FIVE

ADORIAN STONE

It was well into the night when Ariana awoke. Darkness still covered the landscape beyond her window. It had taken her hours to fall asleep, visions of the carnage permeating her every thought. Michael had the best of intentions, this she knew. But knowing Sara was in imminent danger was too much for her to bear. She lay awake, staring at the canopy above her bed. She would go to Eidolon, with or without Michael's aid. Her heart raced at the thought. She'd already been face-to-face with Garren and survived. She'd have to take that chance again, or live forever with the knowledge that she could have done something to save Sara, yet chose not to.

She'd spent weeks with Bronach, reading everything she could find on the history of Eidolon and Adoria. She'd learned much from the writings of the Braeden, and had secured a map leading her there from the northern border of Adoria. She would have to rely on her wit and ability to improvise. A few days earlier she'd found the amulet that had once belonged to her mother wasn't any ordinary necklace at all, but a key of sorts. According to the legend on the map, where an exact likeness of it was drawn, it appeared to be related to the Braeden tunnels below Eidolon. The history she'd read explained that whatever magic protected the divide between Adoria and Middengard had also been forged to protect the tunnels — the Ereubinians would never have known they were there.

She rose from her bed and changed into the only clothes she had that would blend in at all — the ones she wore when she escaped from Palingard. The blood from her wound had ruined her blouse but she'd managed to find one similar. She pulled on her riding boots and a long brown cloak. She looked to see if Kaitlyn had stirred, but the girl lay silent in her bed.

She leaned over and glanced down at Koen, who was sound asleep. She didn't wake him. When he discovered her absence, he'd alert the others. She took one last look into the room before she left. She would have to be more than cautious, as Michael tended to roam at odd hours. She couldn't tell if it was because he'd always had strange sleeping patterns, or if he'd been burdened by a heavy mind since her arrival.

The halls were silent, as she'd hoped. The fastest way to the stables was to pass Michael's door, but she didn't dare take that route. She took the long way, through several tunnels and back through the main dining hall. She finally made her way into the night and around the corner to the stables. She'd been given a horse, a beautiful chestnut with a black mane. A gorgeous beast, it reminded her a little of Shadow, but minus the cowardly demeanor. Ariana patted him on the neck saying, "and that is why I named you Midnight."

She led him out of the stables before mounting him. They made their way through the back passages that would take them out of Cyphrus and into the Adorian woods. It would be some time before they reached the borders.

As she rode, the snow fell fast and heavy. The wind picked up and she wondered if this had been a wise decision. But the image of Bella's body dropped crudely in the dirt urged her forward.

It had been hours since she'd left. The sun was coming up over the horizon, and she had yet to reach the border. She knew Michael and the others would rise soon and find her missing. She squeezed her legs against her horse, and he took off. They couldn't be far from Middengard. As soon as the words had formed in her head, the scenery changed. Her horse stepped down from a two-foot embankment onto the floor of a field. She looked back, surprised. She hadn't expected the ground to be a different height, but it shouldn't have surprised her, considering the landscape outside of the border she had found at the edges of the cavern the day before. Her heart stopped for a moment — this was it, she couldn't turn back now. She wondered, perhaps too late, if the only dangers would be in Eidolon, or if she'd even make it that far. She reached into her saddlebag and grabbed a compass. Comparing it to the map, she turned her horse north and raced onward.

She stopped several times during the first day to rest and drink water. Once she reached the marshes, she slowed considerably, her boots filling with water as she mucked through, leading the horse by his reins.

She dismounted another hour into the journey to rest. According to the map and her estimate of how many miles they'd been riding, she was within a mile of Eidolon. She decided it would be in her best interest to leave her horse there.

Michael would have long since been made aware of her departure and this thought brought a small stab of regret. She didn't want him to worry, but it was unavoidable. She tied the reins to a tree, hesitant to leave her weapons behind. As much as she wanted them with her, she wouldn't be able to conceal them in her cloak. She ran her hands down the mane of her horse and rubbed his nose.

"I'll be back," she whispered. She was trying to convince herself more than inform the horse. She walked in the direction of Eidolon.

It was a barren place, much darker than she'd envisioned. The gates weren't guarded, which made her nervous. She supposed it was because the city itself hadn't been attacked in centuries. The last time Adorians were in Eidolon openly was nearly two thousand years earlier.

Eidolon was expansive, a great black nothingness that seemed to go on forever. There were only small bushes and shrubs to hide in along the edge of the wood. Past that was a barren field of tangled root and mire, where she'd be seen long before she reached the gates.

Ill at ease, she rested with her back against a great rock, covered mostly in moss and leaves. Absently, she played with her necklace, running the amulet along the chain as she wracked her mind for ideas. Though the map had shown her how to get to Eidolon and that there were Braeden-built structures below the city itself, it gave no hint about how to find the entrance or if the amulet was indeed a key at all.

After nearly half an hour, she had convinced herself that crawling along the ground was the only way she would have any chance of entering the city. She'd started to lower herself to the ground when her necklace was snatched from her neck.

She froze, thinking that any moment Garren would again show up out of thin air, but after a few minutes of silence, she started to wonder if she hadn't imagined it. She placed her hand where the amulet had been, and indeed it was gone.

She brushed aside moss and leaves, and dirt, finding nothing but Ezzai worms and Shiela bugs. She was about to give up when her fingers grazed over something that didn't feel at all like stone.

She pulled everything back, wiping the dirt away to uncover an intricate design carved into the rock.

I was right!

More desperate than before, she rooted around until, clutching the amulet in her hands, she crawled back to the stone and slid it into a crevice in the design's center.

Suddenly, the rock shifted beside her and a narrow passageway opened, exposing stairs that led into the ground. Plucking the necklace from the lock, she tucked it into her pocket.

She reasoned with herself that she should feel afraid, but she simply wasn't. She felt more assured now than before she'd left Adoria. *Sara is here!*

Candles were lit along the walls, as though someone stood guard to await her arrival. As she passed through the empty corridors, she saw that paintings adorned the walls, and remnants of life — pots, papers and clothing — still rested in nooks and crannies.

My father was here...

It wasn't long until she found the first door. A faint golden star had been painted on the wall just a few feet back, and she realized this must signify the division in the courts — if what she'd read was correct concerning the layout of the city.

Pressing her hand against the door, she leaned her ear to it, listening for any sign of life on the other side, and heard nothing but her own shallow breathing.

It took a short time for her to gather the courage to pry open the door and peer into the night beyond. She stilled her mind and slipped through to the other side.

Turning to examine the door, she gasped to see that it was no longer there — or, if it was, it could not be seen. Panic momentarily seized her, but a lumbering Dragee nudged her onward before she could give her fear a foothold. She made her way along a darkened corridor until she saw a gleaming white temple in the distance.

Adorian stone, she mused.

She studied the attire of those entering the temple, and found that she had been right in her estimation of what middle-lower-class Ereubinians wore. Bravely, and somewhat blindly, she stepped forward onto the steps and made her way into the temple.

She could tell right away who was human beyond the temple doors. The humans peered out beneath dark scarlet cloaks, but what struck her was how attractive all of them were. Perhaps those who manned the temple couldn't be burdened with the presence of unsightly servants. Or worse, perhaps this place was used for worship of a sexual nature. She seemed to recall a description of a breeder, but hadn't lingered on it long. The very idea made her feel sick.

She traveled deeper into the temple, hearing the curious sound of laughter. Great curtains were hung along most of the walls, to keep the draft down, but it worked to her benefit and she slid easily behind the one nearest the voices. Peering out, what she saw left her speechless.

His wings were bloodied and torn, ragged from beatings and neglect. His face was wan. A collar was fastened around his neck, glowing with a dull amber light. She thought of how she'd seen Gregor in her dream, held by humans in red robes.

"Well done, well done," an Ereubinian whose voice matched the laughter she'd heard came from a darkened corner in the room. Something about his face felt as if she'd seen him before — he favored Garren physically.

He walked up to the Adorian and, to her bewilderment, handed him a blade.

She expected the Adorian to gut the Ereubinian, but instead, at the sound of a single-word command, the Adorian turned on the two humans who held him and took the blade to their guts.

Clasping her hand over her mouth to keep from crying out, she whipped around and closed her eyes with her face against the wall, her heart pounding. She heard a voice telling the Ereubinian that observance would begin soon and waited until they left before forcing her eyes open.

The Adorian remained seated calmly in the room, blood covering his hands and soaking his clothes. She stared at him through the curtain, wanting to do something, wishing there was some way to snap him out of whatever spell he was under.

What foul magic is this?

Mournfully, she turned to leave him, remembering that if Sara had been chosen as a breeder, she would be in observance as well, dressed in white robes.

It felt like an eternity before she was able to find a white robe that would allow her entrance into the sanctuary. She slipped it on just as the humans passed through the doors.

CHAPTER TWENTY-SIX

WHAT HAVE I DONE?

G arren had been hunting all day. His body was tired, but he'd been successful in his efforts, carrying several deer and a wolf back with him. The beasts were tied across the saddle of his Dragee as he walked beside it, reins in hand.

Things had not been well since Jules was slain. The other men were anxious for retribution but Garren needed more time to sort through things, gain his bearings. He'd spent a lot of time in prayer and solitude, neither of which had helped him come to a decision or boosted his men's confidence in him. He re-organized the remainder of Jules' men and placed them under the jurisdiction of another commander. Tadraem had suggested they be taken to the outer regions for training and Garren really hadn't been able to argue — the logic was sound. He'd told his own men they would resume preparations at the beginning of the week.

Garren was wandering through the city when Micah, with whom Garren had spent a good amount of time since the night of Jules' brigade's slaughter, approached him. The boy was out of breath and tried several times to speak, but nothing intelligible escaped his lips. Garren laughed, thinking that like most youth, he was being melodramatic. "Slow down. I can't understand you."

"I swear to you, as sure as I stand here, that I've heard Aiden speak. I overheard him talking with another about the men in the outer regions. The man was reporting to Aiden that his command had been carried out. He said the humans were dead and positioned at the border to Adoria."

Garren's face fell. Micah wouldn't have known of their presence in the outer regions had he not overheard someone else speak of it. "Was anything else said?"

Micah shook his head. "I followed Aiden to see if I could discover anything else, my Lord, but he said little after that."

Garren had disclosed more to Micah than he'd ever intended to. Micah had been brave enough to begin to ask him questions after Garren didn't do as he'd obviously expected upon finding the cloak. He'd asked what Michael had meant about his sister. Garren, without considering it, told him of their meeting, his release of her in Palingard and of his subsequent visions.

"At any point did you repeat anything Michael said to you to anyone other than me?" Garren asked.

Micah shook his head. "No, my Lord. I would never have even considered it."

Garren believed him. Somehow, Tadraem had to have overheard his discussion with Micah. He clenched his jaw and leaned toward Micah. "I want you to keep your distance from me until I come for you. I sense dark intents being set into motion and I don't want you hurt in the crossfire."

They'd been searching for Ariana for hours. Kaitlyn found Michael that morning and mentioned that she wasn't in her room, which didn't immediately alarm him; he was under the assumption that she was with Jareth, as they'd taken several early morning rides. It wasn't until he ran into Jareth in the afternoon that he became alarmed. Jareth hadn't heard from her all day.

They immediately set off looking for her in the caverns. Duncan sent his men to search for her over the cold terrain of the Adorian wilderness. When Michael, Duncan, Jareth, Bronach and Jenner met back at the castle at dusk in the council room, no one had found any trace of her. The only clue they had to go on was that wherever she was, she'd taken her horse.

"She kept her bow and quiver in a case attached to her saddle." Michael said.

Jareth's countenance displayed the same sick expression, though he was trying his best to deny it. "She isn't that foolish, Michael, expel the very idea."

Duncan stepped past Jenner. "What idea?"

Michael lowered his head, almost fearful to say the words aloud lest they come true just by being spoken. "She's had concern over a friend of hers from Palingard. Yesterday's discovery didn't — "

"She's worried about Sara," Duncan interrupted. "They were thicker than thieves. What was the last thing she said to you?"

Michael thought back. "She asked if I was still unwilling to help Sara."

As he said the words, remembered her whispered response, he knew. "She's gone to Eidolon alone."

"Then we've lost precious time looking here," Jareth said. "Assuming that she left sometime in the night, she should be nearing Fool's Marsh." Jareth was right, but Michael's body didn't want to cooperate.

"She has been studying Eidolon's history and customs for weeks," Bronach said, "and I know she has at least one map of the city."

What have I done? She would have been in danger just by being an Adorian, but he'd made it known to his mortal enemy that she was his sister. He lowered his head in his hands.

Duncan cleared his throat. "Then our decision has been made for us. The Braeden will suit up within the hour."

"Ready your men, Michael," Jenner said. "You have the council's full blessing."

Michael was grateful that Jenner had taken seriously their discussion from the night before concerning Ariana's powers. But he hadn't expected this response from the elder. It had been two thousand years or more since Adorians had been openly in Eidolon.

Jenner responded as if he'd read Michael's mind. "We have no choice but to enter into open warfare. Bronach has shown me passages from the scrolls that lead me to believe that Ariana's powers may be related to the strength that forged the divide. If Eidolon knows this, it could be the reason Garren spared her life and has been sending visions to lure her there. They need her in order to usher the human army into Adoria."

The next two hours were a blur as Michael was suited in his armor and readied his weapons. Though typical Adorian armor was all silver, Michael, as Archorigen, wore a gold breastplate that was carved with ornate symbols from the scrolls of the ancients. He knew the symbols signified strength, honor, and power, but despite the carving's archaic meaning and the lightness of the Adorian metals that made up his suit of arms, he'd never felt more burdened or unable to breathe under the weight of it. The main joint of his wings was protected by a series of small plates, made of the same special metal, that allowed him flight and served as moderate protection against Ereubinian arrows.

At last, he leaned against the outside wall of the stables to catch his breath before heading out. He was there only a brief moment before turning; as he did so, he caught a glimpse of Bronach in the distance, his features distorted by the dim light. Eyes, once gentle, looked fierce — his face chiseled with the hard lines of a much-younger man, yet when the historian stepped closer, the torchlight revealed again the soft, humble visage Michael had grown fond of.

Ariana followed in line with the others. They walked through the open areas beyond the wall and back into the temple. She didn't want to admit that fear had crept into her thoughts but she had to force herself not to hesitate as they entered.

They walked through a long corridor and down a narrow flight of steps. She gasped as they entered a large, black-paved room with rows of benches. An altar was at the front, lined with candles. They filed into their seats, mindless drones, keeping their heads down and eyes averted. She braved a glance at her surroundings and had to keep from yelling out. Sara sat at the very far end of the pew from her.

Ariana swallowed hard as tears began to form in her eyes. It took all of her strength not to weep with joy. She looked over again and noticed Sara's cheek was bruised and her hand was wrapped in cloth. Her attention was pulled away as she heard a familiar voice.

"Nech ordai neroman," Garren's voice echoed through the sanctuary and she jumped to her feet as everyone around her rose at his entrance. "We are here for worship. But tonight is a night apart from all others." He turned to the robed Ereubinian who stood closest to the altar. "His Holiness and I are here to dedicate the death of many to our Goddess. Thousands of humans have been sacrificed at Adoria's borders in her honor and in revenge for the loss of our brethren. No longer can Adoria question the hand of the Laionai or the will of the Goddess."

Ariana's blood ran cold.

Garren walked around the sanctuary and for a time spoke in the same tongue that he'd used with her in the woods, what she'd come to learn was Ereubinian. Occasionally, he would pause, and everyone would repeat the last part of what he'd said.

"Norde latresk Ciara mordat." She would have felt the heat of his breath on her neck had it not been for the hood of her cloak. "It has come to my attention that there are some among us who have mixed loyalties — who have agendas of their own to abide by instead of that which the Laionai have set before us."

As he walked away, she turned her head enough to see him saunter to the end of the pew and place his hand possessively on Sara's shoulder.

She's his wife!

She heard many of the Ereubinians shift in discomfort in their seats as Garren continued. "Come, *speak*, you who've led them astray! Show them — show us — your strength!" The vile tone of his voice bit into the air. No one answered him. Whatever he'd just done, it had elevated the level of tension in the room significantly.

Suddenly, Garren laughed. "See, my brothers, you have nothing to gain from following such cowardice. Why would you listen to such a craven, powerless creature?" He released his hold on Sara and made his way back up to the altar.

Ariana tuned out the remainder of the service. Her bitterness clouded her focus, and she had a difficult time following the others. Several times throughout the service, she had failed to rise at the same time or kneel with them. She caught herself within an instant each time, but it wasn't without fear of having been noticed. The service finally drew to a close. After the Ereubinians left, the humans started to file out of the doorway. Ariana watched as an Ereubinian grabbed Sara by the arm and pulled her from the group. She was about to yell out when a hand clamped over her mouth and pulled her into a darkened corner.

"That wouldn't be wise." It was a young teenager. He lowered his hand from her mouth. "You are Michael's sister, are you not?"

She nodded, shocked that he knew her brother. She wanted to ask but didn't have time — Sara was getting away from her.

"It's not safe for you to be here." He said. "Dark things are afoot. I'll take you as far as I can, but you must leave."

"I'm not leaving without Sara," she whispered.

He looked at her sternly. "Don't approach her. Believe me, Adorian, you have no choice but to leave. Doing anything else will get you killed and then what chance will she have?"

Ariana couldn't argue with him. She'd been naïve in her assumptions of Garren. It would take the help of trained Braeden to free Sara from these walls. But how could she return to Adoria empty-handed? Her pride and her love for her friend wouldn't let her acknowledge failure.

"I'm sorry," she dodged his hand as he reached out to stop her and slid unseen across several of the pews, following Sara and her captor from the room.

She was careful to stay as far back as she could as they walked out into the open, shedding the white cloak as they reached the outer walls. She followed until she came right up beside Sara and as soon as the Ereubinian was distracted, she clamped a hand over Sara's mouth and pulled her into an alley.

"Sara, it's me," she said urgently.

Sara had no expression on her face. As Ariana dropped her hand, tears formed in her eyes. "Aiden!" Sara cried out.

"Sara, no ..." Ariana moaned, backing away from her.

A single tear made its way down Sara's cheek as she yelled for him again. "Aiden!"

Ariana contemplated forcing Sara to come with her, but the thought vanished as the Ereubinian came around the corner.

"What have we here?" Even his voice was vile.

She started to run but three Ereubinians intercepted her. Changing directions again, she yelled out in frustration. Suddenly, she felt something thrust into her hands. She paused to look down and she saw that she was holding reins. The boy had caught up with her.

"Go to the east entrance, it's your only chance!" He hoisted her onto the Dragee and hit the beast hard in the side.

The city was congested, but breezing past the humans was easy. However, when they made it beyond the gates, things got complicated. She felt several crossbow arrows whizz past her head.

Oh, you're about to lose this game — you sick bastards.

The first time she tried to turn around, she nearly fell off and it took a moment to regain her balance. She tried once more and found success by keeping her body lower to the beast. She pulled the bow from the case attached to the Dragee's saddle and shot arrows out of the quiver.

She mortally wounded seven of the Ereubinian soldiers before the rest disappeared. Then she remembered Garren's power to go unseen in Palingard and realized she'd been wrong in assuming he alone had the ability.

Unseen, but not totally unheard. She closed her eyes, ignoring more arrows as they missed her, and focused. Drawing back the bow, she listened to the sound of hooves pounding into the ground. She let the arrow fly from her hands and yelled in triumph as she saw one of them reappear and hit the ground with her arrow lodged squarely in his chest.

CHAPTER TWENTY-SEVEN

I WILL COME BACK FOR YOU

Garren didn't take the time to see who'd grabbed his shoulders before throwing the offender to the ground. He spun and saw the look in Micah's eyes, and it brought immediate dread to his gut. "Goddess, Micah, what is it?"

"She was in the service tonight, Michael's sister, dressed as one of the humans. She was caught. I caught up with her and gave her my Dragee, but I don't know how far she'll make it, my Lord. Aiden's right behind her."

Garren didn't wait to hear anymore, he grabbed the reins of the Dragee nearest him, his heart caught in his throat. He'd been so close to her, how could he not have known? And she'd heard every word that he'd said. Even if he were able to get close enough to help her, she'd have every reason not to trust him.

He paid little attention to what he was destroying as they tore through the city. If Aiden reached her first — no, he couldn't think of that. She'd outrun him pretty well in Palingard, but she'd have little chance against as many men as Aiden would bring with him. Garren tore through the gates of the city into the barren landscape beyond.

He passed several who'd fallen, mortally wounded. Perhaps she hadn't come alone. He could only hope. He came upon several more before reaching the edges of the forest — nine in all. Aiden was yet unaccounted for. Just then, Garren realized he wasn't alone. Riders were approaching from the south.

"Don't harm her," Garren struggled with what to tell them. "I have unfinished business with this one."

The riders seemed to heed his command, but, glancing at their faces, Garren realized he didn't recognize any of them. Yet, they were clearly Ereubinian and wore the cloaks of his elite. He didn't have time to contemplate it further as Aiden came into view.

Aiden raised his sword and it fell too quickly for Garren to act. He heard

Ariana cry out as it caught her heels. Aiden pulled her from the Dragee and she fell to the ground. He looked directly at Garren and raised the sword. "Aiden, drop your sword!" Garren's voice echoed through the forest. He watched in horror as Aiden plunged the sword into her chest.

Garren jumped from the Dragee before it had come to a full stop and scrambled to her side. The men who'd ridden with him seized Aiden.

The sword had entered just below her collarbone on her left side. His aim had been for her heart, but he'd missed.

She met his gaze, her face wild with fear as she gasped for breath. He wanted so desperately to tell her that he wasn't going to harm her, but it would prove fatal for them both, considering their audience.

"Have I not done as you've requested, my Lord?" Aiden hissed. "Is it not your will for this Adorian to die? Or do you perhaps wish for her to live?"

Garren wanted nothing more than to end Aiden's existence right then. "It's not my will that's important, but that of the Laionai. This Adorian has knowledge that we may use."

The girl didn't have enough energy to say anything, but managed to grip his sleeve with one hand. He could feel Aiden's men's eyes on him and he brushed her hand away with coldness that made his insides shudder.

Aiden had nothing more to say on the matter, though Garren suspected it had more to do with his being restrained. Garren motioned for the men to take Aiden back to the city. "Keep him in his chambers until I say otherwise."

Garren removed his cloak and pulled off the long-sleeved shirt he wore. He held it ready as he pulled the sword free. Her eyes, hurt and angry, met his one last time before she lost consciousness due to the pain. He tied the shirt around her chest and over her shoulder to stop the bleeding. He clenched his teeth as he saw the reason for Aiden's first blow to her ankles. If she recovered from her more serious wounds, she'd never be able to walk again.

He pulled her into his arms and stood, numb and unsure of his next move. When he felt a hand on his shoulder, he turned to see that a few of the men had stayed.

"I'll hand her to you once you're mounted."

Garren put his cloak back on and then hoisted himself up onto his Dragee and steadied himself in the saddle. Once he was ready, he leaned over as the soldier handed her to him.

He held her with her legs across the saddle, her head against his chest. He could feel her heart beating against him, though it was weak. Her eyes were still closed, but she'd regained an ounce of awareness and struggled against him as they made their way back to Eidolon.

He felt his face heat up as they neared the city gates. He hadn't the slightest idea what to do. Anything he could think of would get them both killed. As they came to the castle, the same unfamiliar soldier who'd helped him before again approached him.

"My Lord, I assume you're taking her to the dungeons below the keep?"

Garren nodded. He'd almost forgotten those particular cells were in existence. They were the least used in Eidolon and the last place anyone would think to look for them. "I didn't catch your name."

"Malachai, my Lord. It's as good a name as any other." The soldier smiled as he turned his Dragee and disappeared into the crowd.

It took him a moment to realize what had just occurred. He knew his men were loyal, but to the point of disobeying the Laionai? And why hadn't he recognized those particular few? He looked down at her again. Her face, once blushed with color, had paled to a lifeless pallor. Fear clutched at his heart as he felt for a pulse. He breathed a little easier as he found it, but it was weak and unsteady.

There were already several others in the cell halls as he came down the stairwell with her. One of the larger guards reached over to take her from him.

He held her firm in his arms, refusing to loosen his grip. "You should be off to more important things. This one poses little threat of escaping."

The guard laughed, his voice coming out rough and coarse from years of pipe and ale. "I suppose she wouldn't be, my Lord. Much of a threat, I mean. Kind to the eyes though, this one is. I haven't seen one quite this young down here in a while."

"The Laionai wish to have an audience with her at dawn, if she's awake.

I expect her to be left alone to regain whatever strength she may still have. I need her at her wits if she's to answer our questions."

"Certainly, my Lord. I'll come back at first light to make sure she is still here." He laughed. "Don't believe she'll be running off though — just like you said, my Lord."

Garren walked into the cell the guard had opened for him. It was cold and wet. There was nothing to lay her down on and he cringed as she sank into the layer of mud that covered the ground. He left her there and appeared to walk around the corner, but had concealed himself instead and returned to stand in front of the cell. It was a useful ability, though he'd come to find it didn't last very long. It was a little like holding one's breath. He watched as the guard hung his keys and walked through the hall to his chambers.

As soon as the guard was gone, Garren picked up the keys and re-entered the cell. Picking her up, he sat with his back against the cold stone. He tore two strips of cloth from his cloak and tied them around her ankles to stay the bleeding, then wrapped what was left of it around her, his own body shivering as the draft hit his bare skin, his chest covered in her blood. Once daylight came, he would be unable to hide his allegiances. The Moriors would hear of it, as Aiden would no doubt get free and summon them, and justice would come swiftly for them both. He sat, weighing the outcome of the path that he was about to take, when Tadraem's words from so long ago rang loud and clear in his ears.

It wasn't Tadraem.

Who could have come to him like that, in the guise of another, knowing years before it would occur that he would find himself here — turning his back on everything he'd ever known?

Could it have been my father?

He questioned then his assumption that Tadraem had been lying to him about his father's betrayal.

Ariana stirred and his thoughts were drawn to her having been in observance. He'd walked the length of the humans' pew — he had to have stood right behind her at some point during the service. She'd been within his reach, and he'd walked right past her. Why was she here? Why was she here alone? She had to be. There was no way Michael would have let her anywhere near Eidolon, with or without escort — unless he was unaware. Then, he found himself hoping that Michael would discover her absence. As sure as it meant his own demise, it was her only hope. He couldn't risk leaving now, not with the attention they'd just brought to the outer courts.

"Michael," she moaned and moved her head, drawing labored breaths. Her bleeding had slowed, but the pain would only intensify as the night wore on.

"Michael will be here soon," he whispered. He touched her cheek with his hand, as he'd done that day in the woods. Had it been such a short time ago?

He stayed awake long into the night, looking at her, hoping that some idea would come to him — something that perhaps he'd overlooked — a way out of all of this. But nothing ever came, and he eventually gave in to sleep.

Sunlight streamed through the small window at the top of the cell. He opened his eyes, forgetting where he was until he heard the loud footsteps of the guard coming down the hallway. Garren laid the girl down, rushed to conceal himself and watched as the guard came into the cell. He leaned down to take her pulse and every muscle in Garren's body tensed as he waited for the guard's response.

The guard lingered for a moment before calling out to his friend, "She's not alive!"

Garren almost lost his composure. The other guard entered the cell and pressed his hand to her neck.

"Yes she is. You couldn't hear it over the rush of hot air in your head!" He stood up and scowled. "Let's go. It's time to eat. I can't be expected to finish my duties on an empty belly."

Garren waited until he was sure they were gone before he bent over her to check for a heartbeat himself, and though it had weakened considerably during the night, it was still there. He kissed her forehead, noticing that her temperature had dropped and she no longer responded to the chill in the air.

He had no choice. He would ready his Dragee and carry her to their borders. He could think of nothing else as a viable option. He tucked his cloak tighter around her and laid her in the driest corner of the cell. There was a small area where the light hit that had warmed it just a bit from the coolness of the rest of the room. He smoothed her hair from her face and whispered, "I will come back for you."

He took the cell keys and raced to his chambers. Once inside, he threw on a new shirt and cloak and filled a small satchel with minor supplies. He opened the doors to his wardrobe and pulled a shield and breastplate from inside. Laying the shield aside, he pulled the breastplate over his shirt, refastening his cloak when he'd finished. He traded his riding boots for a heavier pair, fastened his vambraces and greaves on his forearms and shins. It hit him then that he would be forced to fight his own men if things went badly. He'd grown fond of many of them, oddly more so over the last two weeks. Not that he had been entirely uninterested before, but he had never paid them much attention. Now, he realized all too late they meant more to him than whatever skill they brought to the battlefield.

He grabbed his satchel and headed down the hall. Whenever he heard someone approaching, he concealed himself until they'd passed. Once he'd reached the solitude of the stables, he saw the Dragee were restless. Perhaps they'd sensed something was coming. He felt it too and hoped it was Michael. It would take them nearly a day to reach Eidolon. Garren had reached Adorian borders much faster on the back of a Dragee, but a regular horse was far too slow. The only way for Michael to reach Eidolon faster would be to fly, though he'd never seen Adorians make such a long journey airborne and thus assumed they couldn't.

"Ride swiftly, Michael," he whispered. He thought his words had gone unheard until he felt a sword upon him.

The blade did minor damage when it hit, but only because it struck his breastplate, which was concealed beneath his cloak. He spun on his heels to find Tadraem facing him.

"And to think I once believed you were so different from Seth, incapable of his treasonous ways."

"Treason? What right have you to claim treason when it's you who have been plotting against me? You, who claim to be my mentor and friend — I trusted you once."

Tadraem sneered, "Ah, trust, another of your father's errors, though not his gravest. Not by a long shot. I had such plans for you, Garren. You don't know what I have done for you, how I stood behind you even while the Laionai wanted to strip you of your power. How I spared you the dark truths of your past."

"How you've spared me? Spared me what? The only darkness in my past is how you killed my father, how you betrayed him just as you betray me now."

Tadraem shook his head. "No, Garren, Seth wasn't my friend. He was many things, but never my friend. And you're wrong about the darkness of your past — I'd hoped for years that it wouldn't matter. The moment I heard you utter Adorian, I knew you'd inherited more than your mother's blood. You've inherited her sickness as well; those vile, wretched traits they call mercy and goodness."

Garren's head spun as he struggled to find his bearings. "My mother ... was Adorian?"

Tadraem shrugged. "Don't act so shocked. I know who you harbored at your breast through the night, who you've given up your title for — your life, once the Laionai are told."

Garren tried to summon his powers, anything, but found himself completely bereft.

"The Laionai giveth, and the Laionai taketh away." Tadraem sauntered over to a partial wall, laughing. "You are insignificant in their plans now, expendable. You could have been the Oni and there was a time that we thought you — "

Micah didn't even have to mind his steps; Tadraem was far too involved in his own self-righteousness to hear him. The boy swung fast and hard, the sword held in both hands, its height nearly twice his. The blade came against the soft flesh of Tadraem's neck, the force alone causing the boy to stumble. Tadraem's body fell to the ground in a crumpled heap, headless.

Micah slipped from the wall but managed to catch himself before he hit the ground and grappled with his footing as he lowered himself down the stones to stand.

Garren was too consumed by the echo of Tadraem's revelation in his ears to respond.

"My Lord?"

Garren forced himself to look up but still couldn't speak.

"Forgive me, I thought it was the only way." Micah's eyes grew wide in sudden doubt of his actions.

"No, no, I owe you my life. I..."

"I came to find you because Aiden is on his way to the Laionai. I saw him entering the temple."

"Then I don't have long before they release the Moriors." After a moment's pause, Garren shook himself from his disbelief and grabbed his own sword from its holster on the Dragee. He fastened the sheath over his shoulder. "I'm taking her to Michael. I don't know if I'll return." He turned to face the boy. "I doubt that I'll be received well by the Adorians when I arrive. If I live, I will return for you. Keep yourself in the shadows until you either hear of my death or you see me again."

Micah looked at him, eyes wide. "Can I come with you? Michael won't kill you if you're with me, I know it."

Garren shook his head. "I can't risk it, Micah. I need to focus all of my attention on her right now. If I am to watch out for both of you, I may put all of us in harm's way. Do you understand?" Micah seemed to take his word for it, though it didn't please him. "You have to trust me on this. If it's within my power, I will come back for you, I swear it."

Ariana knew she was dreaming, but even in her sleep she couldn't escape the blinding pain that started at her ankles and radiated to a sharp, hot point in her chest.

"Ssh, ssh, sweet one, I'm here."

Strong arms came beneath her and she was hoisted against something warm and solid — something soft. It smelled good. It reminded her of someone.

"Michael is coming for you, he's almost here. Just hold on a little longer."

"Father?" The sound of her own voice sounded strange, far away. *So far away.*

"Ssh, ssh, stay still, Ari. It's alright." His voice, while soothing to her ears, brought a new kind of terror into her heart because she'd never heard him sound so afraid, so unsure.

"Am I dying?"

For a long moment, the only response she received was a choked sob. She felt his chest tighten and for a moment she thought she heard someone else, someone speaking nearby in a language she didn't understand. It was a beautiful sound, ethereal. But the second voice soon silenced and she could no longer tell if she'd heard it at all.

He kissed her on the cheek and whispered in her ear, "I love you." And everything faded away.

CHAPTER TWENTY-EIGHT

WHY WOULD
I BELIEVE YOU?

N ever had Michael been so frustrated by the slow pace of those who accompanied them. This time it was two thousand elite Adorian knights on horseback. He kept his mind quieted, focusing only on the sound of hooves galloping over earth and mire. Only once did he let his mind consider that he might find her already dead, and it seized his chest so that he couldn't breathe. He pushed it from his head; he couldn't consider that as a possibility. It would congest his thoughts and create vulnerability that they couldn't afford.

The scouts had returned with Ariana's horse only a half-hour earlier, bow still in the case attached to the saddle. This only served to heighten Michael's concern for his sister's welfare. Not only was she ignorant of the ways of Eidolon but she was without the weapons he had once condemned.

They were barely at the edges of the woods near Eidolon when he thought he saw something out of the corner of his eye. They'd lost her tracks somewhere around Fools Marsh but had picked them up shortly after. He slowed his horse and turned around. Trotting back to where he'd seen it, he then dismounted and began to scour the ground. As soon as he saw it, he fell to his knees. Several of the men around him stopped.

Roahn was the first to speak. "What?"

Michael reached for a pile of brown cloth on the ground, covered in a dark red stain. It was torn in several places. His hand shook as he brought it closer to him. He put the cloak close to his face and breathed in. It was hers. He held out the fabric, stretching it to the light to see where she'd been hit.

"It's Ariana's," Jareth said, coming to a stop. He dismounted and stood next to Michael. "If she's been injured, then we're wasting time." He leaned into Michael, whispering. "Michael, this isn't proof of death. If she were killed, she would've been left here. Don't let this cloud your reason."

"Then let us be quick." Michael burst into the air with a quick movement of his wings and was in the saddle of his horse, digging in his heels as they tore off back toward Eidolon.

They'd already discussed positions prior to leaving Adoria. Michael's sole objective, aided immediately by Roahn and two other Braeden, was to find Ariana. Jareth, Caedmon and Kendall led two separate groups of Adorians who were to surround him, clearing the way. Duncan led yet another group of Braeden whose sole purpose was to check all the cells they knew of, entering the tunnels beneath Eidolon from a secret door that Duncan had used in the past. They were all counting on their enemy's lack of preparation. By the time the other Ereubinians were alerted, they'd be well within the city walls.

Duncan and his thirty Braeden headed for the tunnels as Michael gave the order to attack. The Adorian knights took to the skies, leaving their horses in the shelter of the Netherwoods, and crossed the barren field on silent wings. They flew over the high walls of Eidolon with a select group of Adorians assigned to open the southern gate.

Passing through into the human portion of the city, they were met with no opposition as they took to the ground to begin the search for Ariana. They raced through thick crowds of aimless faces. It wasn't until they were past the center wall that they had any use for their drawn swords.

Ereubinian soldiers flooded from the castle. Most were unarmed and scrambled to find weapons. The element of surprise was working well in their favor. Michael's greatest fear though, was not the flesh and blood of Ereubinian lineage, but the Moriors. They would sense Adorian presence before long. The sting of an arrow grazing Michael's forearm caught his attention. He whipped around to see an Ereubinian crossbow aimed at him. He pulled an arrow from his quiver and readied his bow. The reason Adorians had never even considered crossbows were because they were slow and clumsy. Michael had deftly fired two shots, mortally wounding the soldier, before he'd even loaded his second bolt.

Drake and Meridian, the other two Braeden who were with Michael, were pulled away separately by fending off groups of soldiers, leaving only Roahn and Michael together by the time they'd crossed the dividing wall.

Riding as close as they could to one another, Michael looked to Roahn for instruction. The Braeden obviously knew far more about the layout. Roahn pointed toward the castle and yelled something Michael couldn't hear over the sounds of battle. He nodded and followed him.

As soon as they reached the castle steps, Michael pulled his sword from its sheath and dismounted. He spotted Garren.

Garren had blood on his pants and Michael knew whose blood it had to be. Having wounded his sister, Garren must have prepared for this. Rage overcame any rational thoughts and Michael flew at him, sword bared. Garren barely had time to react, raising his own sword in defense.

The loud roar of battle could be heard from all sides, but the fierceness and speed with which Michael wielded his sword was unmatched. Garren wasn't putting up a fight, or so it seemed, but merely deflecting the blows. Michael caught him several times in the arms and torso.

Roahn had his hands full staving off those who tried to come to Garren's aid at the base of the steps.

Garren shook his fist in the air. "Michael! Listen to me."

Michael didn't care to hear a word from his mouth. He swung harder, his blade glancing off of Garren's, screaming metal against metal.

"Michael, she is ..."

Michael didn't let him finish. He thrust his sword again at him, their blades crossing several times before Garren turned and pinned Michael against a large stone wall.

Using his hands and body weight, Michael knocked Garren to the ground, where he slid to a stop against the opposite wall.

Michael swung down on him hard, but Garren rolled from beneath its path, leaving the sword to clatter loudly against the ground.

Garren held his free hand up at Michael, the other still griping his sword. Both were out of breath. Michael paused for only a moment to see that he'd lost sight of Roahn, before coming at Garren again full force.

Suddenly, someone who'd come up unnoticed behind Michael caught Garren's attention. Michael turned around just in time to see Garren duck from Michael's sword and knock the Ereubinian unconscious with the handle of his blade.

"How kind of you, making sure that if I die on this day that it's by your hands alone. Haven't you taken enough from me?" Hot tears stung Michael's eyes, and he angrily wiped them away. He was out of breath, more from his fury than anything else. He'd begun to fight poorly in his rage and he knew it. Garren was just toying with him.

"Michael, I know that you're here for your sister."

"And what is it about Ariana that so cools your blood? What has she done that warrants this? What triumph does her death bring Ciara?" Simply speaking of Ariana quickened Michael's pulse and he lost it. Blind delirium flooded his senses and he could no longer hear Garren's words. It was either Garren's death or his own that would finish it. He raised his sword again.

"Taoth islo shule. Ou toole nertho!"

Michael froze. He'd lost his mind. He stared at Garren, whose lips he saw moving, but it was Adorian speech that he heard.

Garren turned his sword in his hands to point the tip at his own chest and went down on one knee, offering the handle of the blade to Michael. He lowered his head.

"What did you say?" Michael approached him, still keeping his own sword aimed at Garren. He couldn't tell what Garren intended with this move.

"She is alive, please, we have no time for this."

Michael, from a safe enough distance, took the tip of his sword and tipped Garren's face up. "You apparently have no need for such weapons; I've seen your handiwork on the face of one of my bravest Adorians."

Garren closed his eyes. Michael saw frustration and fear. He wasn't sure which confused him more. The amount of blood on his clothes told him the likelihood of this being a lie was better than even, but there was no denying Garren's words were Adorian.

"I didn't ride out after you that night," Garren continued. "I knew that Micah had not returned alone. I could've come after you with an entire army, but I chose not to. Have I ever shown mercy before now? Please, Michael, I know you have no reason to believe me. What I ask is that you have faith in my words for her sake. I'll gladly give you my life after she is taken from here. But let me take you to her."

"Get up," Michael removed his blade from Garren's neck. "Take your sword." He watched Garren slide it back into its sheath.

"She's fading quickly. One of my men reached her before I could and I fear her wounds may be mortal." Garren reached into a side pouch and pulled out a set of keys, then motioned for Michael to follow him.

Garren fumbled with the keys as they came to the cell. Michael could barely make out her figure, curled up into a ball in a far corner. The slightest bit of light fell across her from the tiny window. He rushed in as Garren cracked open the door.

"I stayed with her through the night, she's worsened since then. I was preparing to take her to your borders."

Michael didn't acknowledge Garren's words. He leaned down over Ariana, and pressed his hand to her neck. Garren was right; she was alive. She moved at his touch, taking in small shallow breaths. Her skin was cold to the touch. She didn't have much time left. He lifted the cloth tied around her shoulder, seeing that a sword had pierced through to the other side; it seemed to be the most serious injury. He paid little attention to the smaller cuts and tears to her middle and legs, but paused once he saw the deep gashes to her ankles. It took him a second to start breathing again.

He pulled her into his arms and turned to the cell door to see another soldier standing behind Garren.

Just as Michael had convinced himself that it had been a trap all along, Garren suddenly noticed the soldier as well and turned to face him.

"The eastern gate will be the easiest to get to. The Moriors ... will be diverted to the western side."

Michael was stunned. Garren must have been as well, for still he remained speechless.

"My Lord, there's no deception in my offer, but you'll have to accept my loyalty alone as an explanation for now. I cannot speak for any other than myself, but my allegiance is to you."

Garren took a visibly deep breath. "Malachai, I can't thank you enough, but are you willing to sacrifice your life for this? I can't ask you to do so, unless you assure me that you're aware of the consequences of your actions."

The soldier nodded. "Your friend is waning. Go." Malachai turned from them and headed up the staircase at the far end of the hall near the guard's chambers.

Nothing had played itself out like Michael had expected. He hadn't believed the Ereubinians to have the capacity for loyalty, but he was steadily finding himself wrong about a lot of things. Garren led him through the castle again, out into the open, where he pulled his sword and held it readied in his hands.

Ariana looked much worse in the light. Michael didn't want to admit his gratitude, but he couldn't defend them with Ariana in his arms.

Several men rushed them and Garren didn't hesitate. He fended their advances, using as few fatal blows as possible. Michael looked out across the open courtyard, to the battle at hand. He could see the bodies of several of his men and many still in the thick of it.

It wasn't long before Roahn found them again and had clearly taken note of which side Garren was fighting on.

"You won't be able to take her by horseback." Garren yelled. "You'll never make it in time. Take my Dragee, it's the only way."

Roahn gave Michael a questioning look, but both of them knew that what Garren said was true. Michael acknowledged Garren with a nod and they both followed him to the stables.

It started with one soldier. Then two. One by one those around them, upon seeing Garren defending Michael, began to lay down their swords. The sounds of clashing weapons dissipated as the men ceased blows and an awkward tension ensued as the Ereubinians looked toward Garren in shock. They'd obviously seen his power and were either unwilling to test it or were too shocked to challenge it. Either way, they seemed uncertain whose side to fight on. The sudden lack of opposition stunned the Adorians as well.

Garren led his Dragee from the stall. He'd already saddled the beast, which told Michael that Garren had told the truth about having prepared to take her to Adoria. He handed Michael the reins. After gesturing toward another Dragee for Roahn, Garren then reached out for Ariana. "I'll return her to you once you are settled." Garren pulled her from his arms and held her to his chest as Michael mounted the Dragee. Ariana coughed again, struggling to take in a breath.

Michael leaned down, taking her from Garren, shouldering her against his left arm and holding the reins in his right. Once he was upright in the saddle, he looked down at Garren. The Ereubinian's eyes were red, his face distraught.

Roahn finally spoke. "And what of you?"

Garren glanced around them, a lost look falling across his features. "I'll meet what end I have secured for myself. It's not without cause. My only consolation is that I will follow in my father's footsteps. His last breath was taken by Morior hands as well."

Michael didn't know what to think. He was still hesitant to trust him, but something else pulled at Michael's conscience. Garren had spoken Adorian, pure and simple. A voice whispered in the back of his mind that he should do something, that he couldn't just leave Garren behind. "Saddle one of the other beasts — you'll ride back with me."

Garren looked at them blankly.

"You have nothing to lose. The death that awaits you in my realm will be a much kinder end."

Garren said nothing. He turned and quickly saddled another beast. Michael watched him, never so unsure of a single decision. He wondered what his father would have done and was in the process of answering his own musing when he realized that the voice he'd heard in his mind had been his father's — something Gabriel had said to Michael about Garren on the battlefield many years before — something that hadn't held an ounce of meaning or made a bit of sense until now.

"You want to know why I didn't take his life. You'll understand the truth of the matter someday. Perhaps when you're all he has left in the world. Just remember this; our tongue is a living tongue, spoken only by those whose blood is pure. Never forget this and show mercy accordingly."

CHAPTER TWENTY-NINE

RIGHTFUL NOBILITY

Garren raced ahead of Michael and the wingless Adorian through the city but was still close enough to overhear a conversation between Michael and Jareth, who was questioning Garren's ability to still draw breath.

"You can't be serious. Roahn, has he lost his wits? Have both of you?" Michael didn't say anything in response. "Michael, if you won't listen to me as one of your advisors, then listen to me as your brother-in-law, as your friend. This has to be a ploy to get him past Adorian borders."

"Then you will be more on your guard than you have ever been, I trust."

Jareth didn't seem content with Michael's response. "Hopefully, that was never a question. He gets near her and I'll personally kill him, with or without your consent."

The possessiveness in Jareth's tone told Garren that he wasn't the only one who had feelings for her.

"If Ariana is ever in harm's way, you won't need my consent. Have faith in my leadership, Jareth, you've never questioned it before."

"It's not your leadership that I question; it's the persuasion of one who's brought nothing but death and loss to all who encounter him. Do you not see the result of his work in your arms?"

"Her wounds were not caused by him."

Jareth scoffed. "I suppose the scars on her back were not his doing either? Proximity to him alone brings misfortune. By the Ancients! Roahn, have you nothing to say?"

Garren cringed at Jareth's words, remembering the dream. That must have been what Michael was talking about when he'd said 'further torment' in his message.

Roahn remained silent.

"Jareth." There was a long silence before Michael said anything else. "Keep your eyes open, and your senses fixed. If I'm wrong, then I know you'll be there to come to Adoria's aid. We'll soon travel at a faster pace than your horses can follow. Take heed of the others. Find Duncan and let the Braeden know we're on our way back home. We'll meet upon your return."

Garren couldn't hear Jareth's response, but guessed it to be in accordance with Michael's wishes. They sped faster into the wilderness beyond the eastern border, leaving the others behind them. Garren looked into the sky and did not hear or see any trace of the Moriors. The strange soldier, Malachai, who had approached him the night before and again in the cell, had done as he'd promised. Even upon discovering they'd been misled, the Moriors would be too far behind them to catch up.

Garren felt numb. They galloped through the thickest parts of the woods, everything silent except for the sounds of the large beasts destroying everything underfoot as they tore through the undergrowth. He closed his eyes, letting the wind hit his face.

Ariana. There were so many things he didn't know about her. Had she been married? He wondered if she had children. If she did, had any of them been killed in Palingard? Without warning, a flood of thoughts and regrets washed over him. Visions of every being whose life he'd taken without cause weighed upon him. He also thought of Tadraem. He hadn't had time to think about his death, but with the miles of empty woods ahead of them, he had what could be the very last chance he ever would to look back on his life.

They were nearing the section of woods where he'd been when, who he'd thought was Tadraem, had spoken of his mother. He thought of Ariana dressed as one of the humans in the sanctuary. His mother would never have been suspected if she knew how to behave. But his father couldn't have been the only one to know, and why would his mother have come to Eidolon in the first place? After years of assuming much about the Adorians, he began to realize he knew very little.

He was surprised that Michael and Roahn were so trusting. They'd had every reason to leave him for the Moriors. They had Ariana and Garren was of little use to them now. Perhaps it was to be assured of his death. He couldn't blame them. He thought of the humans who'd been slain and left at their borders. Michael must think it was his doing and Ariana heard him take full credit for it during observance.

Michael at that moment rode up next to him and gestured that they stop to rest the beasts. Garren looked over, wanting to explain, but no words would come.

"It would be in your best interest to stay close to me once we are within Adorian borders. Unless you wish to rush your execution."

Garren nodded, keeping his gaze downwards as they dismounted. He could feel Roahn studying him. Probably wondering what his motives were. He didn't even know himself anymore. He had no explanations for his recent change of perception. "You look as though you have something to say," Michael remarked.

Garren looked at him doubtfully. Would it be worth even saying? "I wasn't responsible for the deaths of the humans who were placed outside of your realm. That was done without my knowledge, or approval. Despite that," Garren paused before continuing, taking a ragged breath, "I've still … if it were within my power to take back the harm I have caused, take back the lives that I …" Garren couldn't speak anymore. Grief overwhelmed him and he closed his eyes, swallowing back tears. His face grew hot as he tried to hide his emotions. "To learn that I've betrayed the very realm that gave life to me — "

"That gave life to you? What do you mean?" Michael immediately looked to Roahn, whose expression gave no hint as to what he was feeling.

"My mother was Adorian. I was just told that our fathers were allies, not enemies, and that my father was sent to his death because of it." Garren rubbed his eyes. "I didn't want to believe it either, but I can't explain what's happening to me any other way."

Michael looked straight ahead, wordless.

Garren didn't expect him to either believe or accept anything that he said. He certainly wouldn't have if the tables had been turned. "Why was she in Eidolon?"

"Probably a vain endeavor, but she was trying to find her friend from Palingard — Sara."

Garren felt sick. "Sara didn't perish with Palingard, but I fear her fate isn't much better in Eidolon. She's been claimed as a breeder by Aiden, the same Ereubinian who wounded Ariana." Her name sounded odd when he said it aloud, as if he had no right to speak it.

"She is alive?"

"I assume Ariana found her. Whether she wanted to or not, Sara would have made Ariana's presence known."

Michael peered down at his sister, a new kind of sadness spreading across his face. "I can't imagine what that must have been like for her, she's already lost so much ... then to feel betrayed by her closest friend. I should have done a better job guarding her. I should have listened."

"Guarding her? She killed nine of my swiftest men before being seized by Aiden, who couldn't have been working on his own."

"Nine?"

Roahn gave a slight nod of his head indicating that this didn't surprise him in the least. It made Garren wonder if Roahn hadn't known Ariana somehow better than her own brother.

"Surely you know this about your own sister. She had the same ferocity the day she evaded me outside of Palingard. Even at the tip of my sword she was brazen. The only reason I caught her is because she tripped, no one has ever outwitted me."

"That scar on your face tells a different story. Though I wouldn't call my mercy a matter of outwitting you." Michael appeared to debate his next words before speaking them. "I wasn't aware of her existence. Nor was she aware that she was Adorian. She was raised as a human and up until that day believed nothing to the contrary." It was obvious that Michael intended to reveal as little as possible on the subject and Garren was in no position to pry.

Michael's lips curved into a disdainful scold. "Don't misread your good fortune. I can't pretend that I would have done anything other than leave you for dead if it weren't for the words that came from your mouth in our mother tongue."

Garren had no idea what he was talking about. His expression must have conveyed as much. "You spoke to me in Adorian, told me that Ariana was alive, do you not recall this?"

Garren remembered Tadraem also accusing him of as much in the sanctuary the week before. "I ... no, I don't. Our High Priest apparently overheard such speech coming from me in our sanctuary several days ago, but I can't tell you that I was in any way aware of it, nor was I aware of it today."

They didn't have time to discuss it further, Ariana's breathing became strained. She inhaled sharply, choking on blood that had begun to spill from her mouth.

They remounted and Garren yelled a command in Laionai aloud to the Dragee. It felt like sacrilege to use the tongue, but he had to. He held on to the reins as though he were holding onto his very life as they quickened their pace.

They finally reached the border and Michael motioned for him to ride close. "Remember what I said!" Garren didn't need a reminder. He rode beside Michael as the three of them passed through.

A moment of disbelief passed between Michael and Garren as he passed through the divide unaided. Roahn was still unreadable.

It was stunning. Despite the lateness of the day, Garren could see snowdrifts and mountain ranges and what felt like the deepest darkness he'd ever seen as the woods around them went on forever. Yet, it was a different kind of darkness — comforting, not foreboding.

Michael was visibly relieved to have Ariana beyond the divide and for a moment slowed down. He leaned to kiss Ariana on the top of her head. "We're home, dear heart. Hold on."

Up ahead, though he could scarcely make out their figures through the shadows, he saw what appeared to be mounted forces awaiting them. As they moved closer, he saw he was correct. Nearly a hundred mounted Adorians, suited for battle, anticipated their arrival.

Michael held up his hand, still gripping the reins. *"Algreto heirthra fornomas, allolost kai louthai dusto. Nouroma."*

An older Adorian approached first, bending his upper body in partial bow. The rest followed suit.

"Isthre eirea lestho?" the older one asked. He didn't seem the least bit shocked by whatever Michael had said.

"Requisthis masthri louthra. Pournai domest." Tears started to well in Michael's eyes as he responded and it tugged at Garren's chest in a way he'd never imagined.

The older Adorian nodded. "Aulora is waiting. Your beasts, though quicker, are winded. Take my horse and we will follow you." He dismounted and walked over to take Ariana.

Garren had assumed that he'd be left there with the other Adorians, when he was instructed to dismount as well and was given a horse. It was Roahn who was staying behind. He'd avoided all eye contact with Garren from the moment they met with the others.

Michael gestured for Garren to come to his side. Garren caught a glimpse of Michael's countenance before they tore off through the darkened landscape. *Rightful nobility.* Michael had commanded respect from those under his command without the faintest trace of aggression. They followed his leadership, not out of force, but loyalty.

They rode for several more hours. It felt like days, each passing mile stretching on forever. Suddenly, Michael yelled out to his horse, digging in his heels. Garren followed, hoping they were close. His hope turned to panic as he heard Michael's faltering voice.

"She's not breathing!"

CHAPTER THIRTY

FORGIVE ME

Duncan jerked his dagger free from his opponent's chest. Blood trickled from the Ereubinian's mouth as their eyes met; Duncan saw the reflection of a mace as it swung at him from behind. He ducked when it was mere inches from crushing his skull and stepped back as it struck the Ereubinian he'd just released.

"Michael has Ariana!" Kendall struggled to land nearby. One of his wings was torn and bleeding. He wore a dark cloak that was fastened high at his neck and covered his chest completely.

As Duncan slid his blade across the second Ereubinian's throat he asked, "Is she alive?" The fact that Michael had been able to find her this soon was good news. Duncan had just heard from Konner that the cells below the keep were empty, which is where he was certain she'd be.

The scent of sweat and death was heavy in the air. The sounds of rage and grief could be heard in every direction. Memories of Duncan's past mingled with his training and instincts; a second battle, this one internal, was waged with equal fervor as the one that surrounded him.

"I don't know. There was a lot of blood ..." Kendall and Duncan both turned as the sounds of fighting grew strangely mute. Whatever was happening, it was just reaching them. "Garren was with them when they left from the eastern gate."

"Good, he'll pay for ..."

"He appeared to be riding with them of his own free will. He was fighting alongside them. Roahn signaled for a rear guard, so I sent Harish and Tabor in their wake."

Duncan looked beyond where they stood to see confusion on every face in sight. No wonder they had ceased blows. Still, loyalty was rare in Eidolon and would no doubt be as short-lived as those who displayed it to the wrong party. "Withdraw now! Get as many of your men as you can out of the city safely, the Braeden can handle themselves. Aerial retreat isn't ..."

"Jareth has already given the order. They'll know when to fly," Kendall smiled wanly as several more Adorian knights dropped down beside him.

"Then why are you still ..."

"We are here to do what you and I both know must be done. Tell Leigh I love her."

"No! Kendall, this is madness! The tunnels — "

"The Moriors will not stop until their thirst for blood has been quenched. This time they'll find more that mere blood and bone." As Kendall spoke, he pulled his cloak away to reveal that he wore beneath it a chest plate identical to Michael's. With helmet pulled down, they looked identical. *"Gahai werndt daios."*

"There is still time!" Duncan rushed him but reached the spot too late. "Kendall! Damn it! I won't tell her, do you hear me?" Furious, Duncan reached for the first Ereubinian he saw, completely unimpressed by the Ereubinians' apparent reluctance to continue fighting.

Rage flooded his senses. He killed without consideration of what his mentors had instilled in him, with no regard to Adorian standards for bloodshed. Eventually, the battle around him caught up with his anger and resumed as if the Ereubinians had never laid down their weapons. In the distance, the first shrill cry was heard as the Moriors were released, but Duncan paid it little mind as he pushed through the battle to the gates.

Jareth caught up with Duncan, cradling his arm to his chest. "Michael and G—"

"I know!" Duncan barked.

"Here, I'll fly." Jareth slid from his saddle and held the reins for Duncan to take. "Have you seen Ke—" Before he could finish, a tremendous explosion rocked the ground beneath them and a huge fireball erupted into the sky on the western side of Eidolon. They both covered their heads momentarily as debris rained from above.

Duncan swore an oath in Ereubinian, loud enough for any of the blessed within ear shot to have heard him. "Yeah, I saw Kendall. So did the Moriors — right before he blew them and himself to Hothrendaire."

Jareth, having caught sight of an approaching Ereubinian, swung the hilt of his sword into the man's face with as much force as he could muster. As soon as the Ereubinian instinctively grabbed for his injured head, Jareth cut it cleanly from his neck. For a moment, neither Jareth nor Duncan spoke.

Overhead, a veil of smoke shielded them from the arrows of Ereubinian crossbows and the Adorians were able to fly out of Eidolon. Duncan felt his face and neck flush with heat and his heart rate increase.

"Damn you, Kendall," he whispered, "and damn your heroics!"

Garren sat for what felt like an eternity. Michael had taken Ariana past two enormous doors, shaped like butterfly wings, that might as well have led to the afterlife. He guessed them to be at least thirty feet or more in height. The Adorians who'd met them near the border arrived shortly after. The elder went into the room where Michael was.

Several of the men stood close watch over him. They'd been given instructions in Adorian, and though he could apparently conjure the tongue unwittingly, he couldn't understand it when he tried. He assumed their instructions were not to leave his side, but they looked afraid. Brave, but afraid nonetheless, and they stood as far away from him as possible. His patience for not being told what was going on with Ariana was wearing thin and he was in the midst of contemplating a run for the doors, when they suddenly opened and Michael emerged.

He was shaken, his eyes swollen and red, his complexion just as drained of life as his sister's had been. He staggered to where one of the others stood and sank to the floor with his back to the wall. When he spoke, his voice was low and hoarse. "The healer said it's irreparable … her wounds are too deep, she …" He bowed his face in his hands and breathed in a slow choked breath. "She will not live."

Jareth stretched out his wings and rose into the air, yelling down to Duncan, "Come on, old man, there'll be time enough for grief once we're home!" Then, after he was certain Duncan had shaken himself from his disbelief, Jareth flew ahead.

He could not get the image of Ariana, bloody and unconscious in Michael's arms, out of his head. She'd looked so pale, so lifeless. And Garren, riding beside Michael as if he had the right to still draw breath after what he'd done?

Flying was hard enough on an Adorian's body, but doing it with broken bones was excruciating. The muscles that created movement in his wings were attached to those that allowed for movement in his arms, shoulders and torso. It would be a mere mile, perhaps less, before he'd be forced to land.

Jareth hadn't been asking Duncan if he'd seen Kendall out of curiosity; he'd asked because he needed to know whether Kendall had made it to the western side of the dividing wall or not. If he hadn't, Jareth would need to find him, take the breastplate and continue as Michael's decoy. Three small groups of Adorian knights had volunteered to fly into Eidolon before the main party arrived, while the Ereubinians were too unaware to pay attention to the sky above them, and wait within the castle ramparts with enough crudely constructed bombs to take out more than a few Moriors. Explosives weren't a weapon of choice for either Adorians or Ereubinians simply because the resources to make them were scarce, but when they were used, they were undoubtedly effective.

The last of his energy gave out and Jareth descended. His intention was to walk, but once his feet hit the ground, he crumbled forward and was lucky to crawl to a nearby tree, where he could rest.

He came to with the smell of stale breath in his face.

"Did you know?" Duncan was bent over, his face bright red and puffy.

Jareth's eyes felt like someone had thrown sand in them and they burned once he was able to pry them open all of the way. "Care to be a little more specific?"

"Kendall! The others! Did you know what they were going to do?" Duncan roared.

Jareth cringed. His head was pounding without any help from Duncan. "Such a Braeden thing to ask. You piss and moan that you're done with the realm of man, that you're unwilling to reunite your men, and you've still got balls left to whine about not being included? If it makes you feel any better, Michael didn't even know."

Duncan laughed, but there wasn't anything jovial about it.

"Is it because you don't have wings, Duncan? Is that why Braeden are so arrogant, because you feel like you have to make up for something? You've got your ways of doing things and we have ours."

"Yeah, Jareth, that's it. I'm pissed because I don't have wings. You want to talk about wings? I'm pissed because Gabriel died ... because if Gabriel had kept his wings ..." His voice shook as it trailed off. Then, when he could no longer find the words to continue, he roared indecipherably and hauled Jareth to his feet by his good arm and began to walk toward his horse.

"I think I'll wait on the others, thank—"

"They've already left for Adoria, Jareth. I've been waiting on you to wake up from your beauty rest for over two hours. Now shut up and get on behind me."

Jareth briefly considered flying despite the pain in his body, just to avoid having to deal with Duncan's attitude, but the look in the Braeden's eyes told him the decision had been made for him.

"I should have told you," Jareth muttered as he struggled onto the horse.

Duncan reached back and helped him. "Kendall was the only one of you with any sense and he goes and does something stupid like this."

Before they rode off, Jareth flexed his wings full span for one good stretch. "He saved hundreds of lives."

"I didn't say he wasn't heroic. I said he was stupid."

The words did not immediately register. Then, as they did, the room felt like it was falling down on Garren and he fought to catch his breath. He heard Michael sobbing, but he couldn't see him for the tears that filled his own eyes.

"My Lord," an elderly man, perhaps human, gripped Michael's arm. "Let Garren go to her. Time is running out, you mustn't question why."

One of the other Adorians started to protest, but Michael put his hand out weakly. "Do as Bronach says, let Garren go to her. What's done is done." Michael barely got the words out, his voice cracking at the finish.

Garren paused in the doorway and Bronach placed his hand on Garren's back to urge him forward. "It's alright. You must go to her."

Garren stepped into the dimly lit room. He saw Ariana on a bed against the far wall, her face no longer showing any trace of pain or fear. Her cheek was cold when he touched it. He took her hand in his and placed it against his chest. "Forgive me," he whispered.

Bronach drew back and stood along the wall, unseen now, his heart frozen in his chest. The other immortals had already knelt, their heads hung, words spilling over their lips that couldn't hold a candle's worth of light against the darkness that purposed to take Ariana's soul.

It cannot end like this.

"She's dying," Onora looked up at Bronach, horror-stricken. "Can you do nothing?"

She already knew the answer to that — they all did. It was forbidden. He shook his head, remaining quiet. Bronach felt Garren's grief all the way to his soul and all he could think about was the past, how deep their love had been. He remembered the gatekeeper's words ... "that same unpredictable power means that their love is far greater than even you or I could ever have imagined."

All of Bronach's fears had been for naught if she died now, before she or Garren had even begun the real battle.

What have I done?

Garren couldn't breathe under the weight of his sorrow. He didn't just weep for a girl he barely knew, it was as though he'd always known her, as though he'd lived all of his life in shadow only to be brought into the light by that first touch. Something inside him screamed, raged that this couldn't be the end, that this wasn't what was supposed to happen.

What was supposed to happen, then?

He rose over her, touched her hair, swept his thumb across her jaw. Everything in him willed him to do something, but what? What could he do? Whispers, dark and taunting, swirled in his head from an unknown source, telling him that it was over, that he had lost, to let her go. The whispers turned to laughter and resonated through his whole body, made him feel as though he'd been robbed of his very soul.

Garren braced himself, knowing he was losing his grip on reality. He glanced down and saw her chest rise one final time, filling her lungs with air, before she stilled and he knew she'd breathed her last.

"No," he whispered, "it is not over." The fury in him reeled against the voice and rose against it, urged him to act. He leaned down and kissed her, keeping her hand to his chest, clutching against his heart.

It started there, with her hand, as it warmed to the touch. Then, a light swelled around them, so gradually at first that Garren didn't notice it. It intensified until it burst forth to fill the immense room, spilling into the hall. The force of it threw Garren several feet.

Michael and the others rushed into the room. Garren couldn't move, his whole body stiff and weak. He rolled to his side to catch a glimpse of Michael leaning over Ariana.

He saw everyone moving around, but couldn't decipher what was being said. His vision blurred and he felt himself losing consciousness. It was all he could do to lie back, facing the ceiling, before he blacked out. As the darkness took him, he heard another voice, this one strong but soothing.

Rest now, you will need your strength.

The Dark Lord Azrian clenched the chalice in his fist before hurling it against the wall, roaring as it shattered into pieces.

"So be it!" he snarled. "You wish it to come to this?" He lifted his gaze to the east and knew that though he couldn't see him, the Creator would hear his words. "You wager so much with so little!"

His breath came in short huffs, his face bright red with rage. "An Adorian healer's blood. Clever, though not clever enough. Do you think this changes anything? Do you think the Sword of Ereubus will call to Garren any less?" He roared indecipherably, debating whom to kill for this, and was about to act on his decision when he caught a glimpse of her face out of the corner of his eye.

His voice became a whisper as he leaned over the pool of water to gaze at her for the brief time he would be able to. "So beautiful, even in this fragile form he has chosen for you. I wonder, does it please him to see you so weak, so powerless. Mortal enough for a blade to drain the life from you. I would never have done this. I would never have allowed such harm to come to you had you stayed by my side."

He whipped upright at the sound of Usilet entering his chambers. "I didn't call for you."

She bowed low to the ground, "No, my Lord. Ciara wishes to speak with you."

He laughed, genuinely amused. "Tell her my answer is the same. If she wishes something from me, then she may ask it when her part of the covenant has been upheld. Then we will see."

Usilet nodded, "Yes, my Lord."

"Before you leave — " He held out his hand for her to kiss it, "I want you to go to Caedmon. In dreams if you must. There is darkness in him, I can see the hatred in his eyes and it pleases me. Remind him how much Garren has taken from him."

Dismissing her, he walked back toward the pool, tightening his jaw as he saw the water, now dark and visionless.

"Make him remember, Usilet!" he screamed. "Do whatever is necessary!"

CHAPTER THIRTY-ONE

NINE DEAD

Michael pulled up Ariana with one arm around her waist, the other at her shoulder. The color had returned to her face and her breathing had steadied. He moved her shirt from her shoulder, exposing unharmed flesh. Her wounds were gone.

"Ariana," he whispered, his voice wavering with emotion.

Her eyes fluttered open and she looked up at him, a dazed expression on her face. "Where am I?" Her voice was low, hardly a whisper.

"Adoria. You are home, dear heart." He half-laughed, half-sobbed with relief as he sat on the bed beside her. "Do you remember anything?"

"No." She reached up, noticing the injury on his arm. He'd forgotten about it himself. His wings were bleeding in several places, and he had a rather large gash in his leg, but he couldn't feel any of it now.

She gasped, her memory having returned to her. "I'm so sorry, Michael, I shouldn't have — "

He hugged her, stopping her mid-sentence. "Ssh. Don't be sorry. Had I been more forthright, you would've felt more comfortable confiding in me. I'm simply grateful that you are … Ariana, you were barely breathing."

Jenner was seated on the opposite side of the bed from Michael. "Child, I bore witness to this. It was he who entered and spoke life back into you." He stood, stepping aside for Ariana to see Garren.

To Michael's surprise, she recoiled into his arms at the sight of Garren.

"I haven't the desire to so much as look at him," she said bitterly.

Michael waved his hand, indicating for Garren to be taken from the room. He appeared to be out cold; whatever he'd done had drained him completely. Michael turned his attention back to Ariana as Jenner ushered everyone else from their presence. He didn't speak again until they were alone.

"I'm sorry about Sara. Forgive me, please, for not speaking with you more candidly. Know that she had no choice in the matter, her words were not her own."

"I know they weren't," she said, her expression wistful. "She's a hollow shell of who she once was. But she is among the living." Her countenance fell grave as she reached up to her left shoulder, rubbing where the sword had pierced her. It seemed to all be coming back to her. "What has he said to you?"

"It was not a short journey here. We discussed many things, least of which is his maternity. He is part Adorian; I saw this for myself as he entered without hindrance. The only thing that kept me from killing him in Eidolon were the Adorian words that came from his mouth. You were right on several accounts. He wasn't responsible for your wounds or the visions that you've been having. He has been experiencing the same, or so he claims."

The expression on her face as he spoke of Garren turned sour. While part of him wanted her to feel that way, the other part of him noted it as significant that her perception of him had changed.

"This is a new reaction for you."

"I heard things come from his mouth that felt untrue, yet seem without reproach. I recall well being wounded by one of his men and him coming to me as I lay bleeding on the ground, saying the only reason he wanted me alive was because I had knowledge of Adoria that the Ereubinians wanted. Did I dream that he stayed with me through the night? I felt his presence each time I regained consciousness, but at the same time I heard him say clearly as I speak to you now that he was responsible for the dead who were left outside of our borders. There was nothing but vile retribution in his tone, Michael. I witnessed evidence with Sara that he'd spoken for her as a breeder. Her lip was bloodied and her cheek bruised."

Michael brushed aside a piece of hair that had fallen into her face. "Where was he when he said these things, when you witnessed this interaction with Sara?"

"Observance."

It took him a moment to realize she wasn't being sarcastic. "You were in observance? How did you go unnoticed?"

"The humans wear white cloaks. I slipped in with them. It was easy enough. Besides, I didn't go unnoticed. There was a young boy who knew you, who discovered me."

"Micah. He was the one out of twenty-two men who we let return to Eidolon on our last run-in with Garren's men."

"Was this the ambush that Jareth mentioned? How many Adorians were there in the second party?"

Michael grinned sheepishly. "A little over a thousand. Give or take."

"My, it's a wonder you made it out of there alive!"

He squeezed her arm, smiling in return. "You don't know how relieved I am. The reason I asked where you were is because of some of the things that Garren disclosed to me on our journey here. I don't believe he had any reason to be dishonest with me when he said the humans who were slain were killed without his knowledge or consent. I also recall him saying that Sara was claimed by one of his other men. Aiden, I think."

She pondered this for a moment before responding. She reached for her necklace, only to remember that it was no longer on its chain. She felt for it in her pocket and realized, sadly, that it was gone.

"Your necklace?" Michael asked.

"That amulet belonged to Mother." She wanted to ask him about it being pulled, so oddly, from her neck, but thought better of it. "Sara called out for Aiden, while we were in the city. He's the one who chased me into the woods."

Michael recalled what else Garren had said. "He was also apparently the only one capable of catching you. Nine dead?"

Ariana smirked. "Did you doubt it? They may have the ability to selectively conceal themselves, but that doesn't aid them in their unwieldy choice of animals. Those horrible beasts are loud and awkward in their movements." Her face fell then, her distress visible in the line of her mouth.

"What is it?"

"You didn't come for me alone."

He shook his head. "No, I didn't, but Ariana, there are things that I've failed to tell you." He proceeded to tell her the truth about the day they'd found her in the old world.

"Oh, that. I should have told you — I've always been able to conjure a spinning ball of light at my whim." Her face held enough gravity that for a moment, however brief, he thought she was being serious. Then, her smile gave her away. "And you didn't think telling me something like that was *important*?"

"I've met many times with the council since your arrival, and the consensus is that you have powers that have yet to be harnessed. Father must have known. Whatever lives were lost in coming to your aid, they were given in service to Adoria. Whatever this is between you and Garren is not chance, but fate."

"Don't be mistaken, I still regard him as who he is. But I'm wise enough to see that there are greater things at work than what's readily apparent. He's saved your life now on two occasions. He was well aware of whose sister you are when he met you again in Eidolon."

She looked confused. "How is that possible?"

"When I took Micah back to his realm, I sent him with a message that warned Garren to leave you alone. I still believed him to be the source of your injuries from the dream."

"Michael, I didn't intend for any of this to happen. All I could think about was Sara and — "

"When Garren wakes, I'll speak with him, see what he can tell us about the humans. Find out what chances we have of saving her."

"Thank you." Ariana reached over to his sleeve again, shifting it slightly to expose the wound. "You're still bleeding."

He turned his arm to look at it. It really wasn't his arm that was painful; it was his leg, which had started to throb. "Yes and you need rest. I will walk you up to your room." He rose from the bed, holding out his hand to help her to her feet.

"Garren still believes me to be dead doesn't he?"

Michael nodded. He supposed so. From what he saw, Garren had fallen out just prior to Ariana coming to.

"Don't tell him then, that I am alive. I wish to tell him myself."

CHAPTER THIRTY-TWO

WHAT IF IT IS NOT A DREAM?

It was nearing afternoon. Ariana had slept most of the remainder of the dark hours and well into the daylight. She awoke to find Jareth by her side. He was battle-worn, with a broken arm and what he'd said he assumed to be several wounded ribs.

"I seem to recall you saying once that Michael wouldn't allow you in here no matter what hour of the day it was."

"I wasn't going to rest until I saw for my own eyes that you were all right. I think he'll allow me this transgression."

She propped herself up against the headboard. "I'm fine Jareth. Please go and rest. We can talk about all of this later."

He looked hesitant to leave. "Please assure me that you aren't naïve. Don't put your hopes on Garren. I say this not only out of my own interest, but also for your sake. I don't want to see your heart broken when it's decided that he'll be put to death. And he will be."

She reached out, taking his free hand in hers. "You risked much, riding into Eidolon. You've been a much-needed friend and confidant. Thank you for that." She could see the disappointment in his eyes as she said the words. She was still too unsure of how she felt about Garren to respond any other way. "I'll be prudent. I promise."

He brought her hand to his lips and kissed it before leaving her.

She rose to change clothes and saw Koen sound asleep in Kaitlyn's doorway. She hadn't seen the girl since before she left. Peering in, she found the room empty. Ariana considered leaving Koen to his dreams, but the sight of him made her heart ache and so she bent down and pulled him like an oversized rag doll into her arms. He'd been sleeping harder than usual and it took him a moment to wake up fully and responded to her affection.

"I suppose I owe you an apology too." She scratched him under his chin, laughing as he tilted his head back so she could better reach him. "Sara was there Koen. I saw her. She's alive."

Koen nudged her neck with his nose. If she didn't know better she'd think he'd actually understood what she'd just said and was giving his approval.

"I'm not giving up on her, don't worry. For now though, I have some questions that I'd like answered." She stood up. "And I'm not giving Garren a choice in the matter."

She chose a cream-colored gown, with a midnight blue velvet cloak to change into. The dress had white crystals sewn into the bodice, around the hem at the bottom, and on the sleeves. It would serve just fine for how she intended to greet Garren.

Once she was outside of his cell, she gestured for the guard to open the door. He carefully pulled a single silver key from his pocket and slipped it into the lock.

As the heavy wooden door opened, Ariana could see Garren curled into a ball on top of the small bed that was in the far corner. He hadn't touched the food that had been brought to him, but she could see that he'd had his wounds tended to. There were several cuts on his face, and a bandage was wrapped around his lower right calf. His boots were heaped in a pile on the floor, along with his breastplate and the rest of his armor.

She closed the door behind her as she walked into the cell. The temperature was comfortable to her, but Garren shivered as he lay sleeping. She moved into the shadows, standing just beyond the light that shone from the window.

"Garren," she whispered. He stirred at the sound of her voice. *"Uskori mathro lestre ave nouromai."* Her voice carried in the cell like the haunting echo of a ghost. He opened his eyes.

She stepped out of the darkness, the crystals on her gown shimmering as she'd intended, and continued to speak to him in Adorian. *"Istho exist aeloro ghant."*

He struggled to sit up and face her. Once he did, he lowered his gaze to the floor. He stayed quiet, making no move to address her.

"My blood is on your hands."

He raised his head as she spoke, tears in his eyes. It surprised her. This was not the same countenance that she'd witnessed in observance. His eyes were red and swollen, his handsome features stricken with grief.

"Can you say nothing in your own defense?" she asked.

"I cannot ..." the words caught in his throat. "I reached you too late. Had I known that you were right there beside me, in the sanctuary ..."

"You made claims that you were responsible for the deaths of the humans. Do you deny this?"

"Aiden was in the sanctuary. I believe he was responsible." It made sense to her now. He must have had his hand on Sara's shoulder to make sure Aiden knew who he was accusing of treason.

"You are not surprised by my presence?" As she spoke, he brought his gaze back down to the floor. He now sat on the edge of the bed, his legs bearing his weight as he leaned on them.

"I have seen you in this manner before. I assume it's either my delirium that's conjured you, or your spirit has come to release me from this existence. Or I'm dreaming."

She walked close enough to feel the heat from his body. She knelt down in front of him, cupped his chin with her hand, then rising up enough to reach him, she brushed her lips against his.

"And what if it is not a dream?" she whispered.

He remained motionless at first, his eyes still closed from their kiss. She moved her hand to the side of his face and he turned into her touch, bringing his own hand to cover hers. He sweetly swept his fingers along her skin, moving to her wrist. He lingered there for a moment, rubbing it with his thumb before reaching out and pulling her into him.

His kiss was deep, but soft. She let herself fall into his embrace, letting the strength in his arms hold her up. When he finally drew back, she was surprised to find herself in tears as well.

Garren stroked her cheek, smiling through his sobs. "You're alive." He sat back so he could see her. "I don't understand. I saw you moments from death with my own eyes."

She lowered herself to the ground at his feet and looked up at him. "I don't have an answer for that — I was hoping you might. You were the only one in the room."

Garren shook his head. "Whatever strength brought you back is not my own." He took her hand, held it to his chest. He looked weak and exhausted. "The look in your eyes when I caught up with Aiden — I wanted to tell you so badly that you were safe."

She smiled at him. "I know. I don't remember much, but I felt your presence. I knew I wasn't alone. You stayed with me through the night." Suddenly, she remembered it.

"What is it?" he asked, reaching down to caress her face.

"I dreamed of my father. It was morning. He came to me, held me in his arms and told me that Michael was almost there. I'd forgotten about it until now."

Garren withdrew his touch and sat back farther on the bed, a coolness abruptly spreading over his face. His change in demeanor was so sudden that it startled her.

"You shouldn't be here, Ariana." He looked away from her.

"I have nothing to fear by being with you. The decision is mine to make."

The tone in Garren's voice was more like what she'd heard in Eidolon and it chilled her to hear it. "I'm sorry for misleading you."

Words formed in her mind, but she couldn't get them past her dry throat. She reached out and tried to take his hand again.

He grasped her wrist, stopping her before she could touch him. "Don't you hear what I'm saying? Don't mistake my joy over your resurrection as anything more than what it is — a weight removed from a heavy conscience. I feel nothing for you."

At first, she could do nothing but sit, stunned. Finally, she wrenched herself free from his hold and rose to her feet, rubbing her wrist where he'd gripped it.

She stood before him, trying to say something, anything — but closed her eyes, reeling with shock. She swallowed back tears. "There isn't an ounce of truth in your words, but I *will not* plead for your affections."

She turned to walk from the room, pausing once she reached the doorway. "The council will convene in three days."

CHAPTER THIRTY-THREE

DON'T THANK ME

Aiden knew to keep his eyes to the floor, not because he'd ever been summoned to the Laionai before, but because of all the times he'd heard Garren reliving his first encounter with them. Aiden knelt down before them, his whole body tense with apprehension.

As the Laionai entered the room, a thickness entered with them. It was a corpulent dripping thing, tainted with the odor of decay. He felt his stomach turn. The closer they came to him, the more pressure he felt building up in his lungs, but he didn't dare breathe.

"And what of the girl?" The voice dumbfounded him. He raised his head enough to affirm his suspicions.

"But... you're... you're *dead*. I saw the blood on the ground where you were slain." The words fell clumsily from his mouth.

"Such little faith, Aiden. Did you think an ordinary Ereubinian would be able to gain favor with their eminence? With the Goddess? Did I not grant you back your speech by their power?"

"But — I don't...."

Tadraem rushed Aiden, grabbing his shirt, and pulled him within inches of his face. Aiden could see the sweat pooling in beads along the hardened lines of the priest's skin, the leathery look of his neck.

"Enough of your insolence," Tadraem growled. "You're blessed to be in this position, far more than you know. Why did you not tell me about the girl?"

"I was held in my chambers by Garren's men. I couldn't ..." Aiden sucked his breath in, trying to control his shaking, as Tadraem pulled a blade from his belt and held it against Aiden's throat. The smell of urine flooded his nostrils and Aiden realized he'd wet himself.

Withdrawing the dagger, Tadraem kicked Aiden in the chest with the sole of his boot, sending him sprawled to the floor. Above him, Tadraem spit, smiling as the Ordakai chattered and laughed.

"Dim, priggish, spineless and arrogant, you should count Garren's death as more than providential. I would kill you, but you serve too useful a purpose for now. Get up."

Aiden crawled to his knees, covering his crotch with his hands in vain. "Thank you, my Lord."

"Don't thank me. You may decide you would have been better off dead." Tadraem paused, and Aiden heard the dagger being re-sheathed. "You'll be granted Garren's title of High Lord Commander. But hear this — you answer to me and to their eminence."

"Yes, my Lord."

"Tomorrow night, as you are dedicated to the position of High Lord, all of Eidolon will see you bring me back from the dead, leaving no one to question your authority as the chosen one."

"You ... planned on dying?"

"I'd planned," Tadraem spat, "on Garren killing me. Not on the arrival of his burdensome little friend. Alas, dead is dead. Now, get up!" He waited for Aiden to find his feet before continuing.

"Until then, see that the human army is gathered as their eminence has decreed. I have a feeling Adoria will be too distracted with Garren's execution and celebrating its victory to ready their forces. Such a shame, I was looking forward to at least some resistance. No matter — they will find themselves slaves to the Goddess either way."

CHAPTER THIRTY-FOUR

RUIN OR REVELATION

Michael was sleeping when Ariana entered his chambers. He'd been asleep for hours as the day eased into afternoon. Light filtered through large, stained-glass windows that lined the longest wall, tinting the room in shades of blue and gold. His upper arm was wrapped in cloth, the cuts to his face cleaned up. He lay with his wings stretched out below him. She sat on the edge of the bed, next to Koen, who'd found a spot in the sun to nap.

She'd tried to go back to sleep, still feeling a little drained, but her exchange with Garren weighed too much on her mind.

"How long have you been here?" Michael's voice was groggy and fatigued.

"I didn't mean to wake you. I thought you were sleeping deeply enough that I wouldn't bother you." She started to move when he grabbed her arm.

"No, stay. It's alright." He struggled to sit up.

"Stay still." She turned toward him, inspecting a tear in one of his wings. "Do you need anything?"

He lay back down, shaking his head in refusal. "No. Just your company, though I should warn you, I'm not a very good patient."

She laughed and started to fidget with the edge of the beaded trim on her gown, rubbing her fingers over the crystals.

"That was one of Genny's favorites."

Hearing the name reminded her of what she'd said to Michael before she'd left Adoria. "What I said about your relationship with her, I'm truly sorry. I had no — "

Michael touched her lips, too tired to put much effort into the gesture. "I don't want to hear another apology. You've nothing to be sorry for."

She took his hand and gave him a slight smile in acknowledgement. "Are you sure it doesn't bother you — seeing her clothes again?"

"No. It's comforting. I remember soon after she died, having the oddest sense of grief over never seeing them worn again. It's hard to explain, but — I don't know. I suppose broken-heartedness displays itself in all sorts of ordinary things."

She nodded, knowing too well what he meant. "After Father left, I remember missing a pouch he used to carry in his cloak."

A curious smile appeared on Michael's face. He tried to move again, but found it too uncomfortable. He motioned to his night stand.

"Pull open the top drawer."

She reached over and slid it open. The first thing she saw was the leather pouch.

"He left it behind the day he died."

She took it from the drawer and brought it to her face, breathing in the scent of the leather. "I used to play with this all the time when he was home, fill it with all sorts of things — it was kind of our little game. He'd always ask what I'd found for him, and I would always tell him he'd have to wait and see. I eventually outgrew it, but it was the first thing I thought of when I realized that he wasn't going to come home." She couldn't believe that she held it again in her hands. The feel of the worn leather against her skin brought back so many memories.

"Keep it, please. I'm sure he would've wanted you to have it."

She smiled, but couldn't hold back her tears. When she opened the ties and peered inside, she saw that it was mostly empty, save one small object in the bottom, wedged in the corner. She pulled it out and realized it was an amulet, identical to her mother's.

Michael narrowed his eyes, but didn't seem to recognize it. "After he died, I glanced in it briefly, but never noticed that before. Curious looking."

"It's a key. I used one just like it to get into the Braeden tunnels — that amulet I mentioned earlier."

"Father mentioned a key to me once. We were in the Saeculum and I was begging him to take me farther, to show me what was behind this huge, intricate carved door we'd come to that was, of course, locked. I was fascinated by it — though I suppose any boy would be at that age. Maybe we'll go there soon, see if the key works on that door by chance, if it's the same key he mentioned that day. Have you spoken with Garren, does he know you're all right?"

She was hoping that he wouldn't ask. "Yes. I've spoken with him."

"I know that look well. What did he say to you?"

She briefly considered not telling him, but after what she had gotten herself into already by not being honest, she thought better of it.

"That he has no feelings for me — that his response and actions subsequent to discovering that I was indeed alive and not a vision were based on penance alone."

She knew what his next question was going to be and it was unavoidable. "What actions?"

She cringed. Kissing her brother's mortal enemy would probably fall into the category of general treason. She took a deep breath, but he spoke before she could get a word out.

"He kissed you." The words came out like the revelation of a grave illness.

"I won't lie to you, I kissed him first. But he reciprocated with more intensity than I. As mistaken as I have been in matters like these in the past, there was no confusing the passion behind that kiss. His relief was palpable."

Michael said nothing for a time, obviously mulling over what she'd just said. "I believe what he's said to me, having seen the truth in his words for myself. But as for his motives or what is behind his dramatic transformation, we may never know. We may never have the chance *to* know."

She felt herself getting upset again. "Then it's already been decided. He'll be executed?"

Michael's expression shifted without effort from concerned sibling to provident leader. "His death will benefit our people more than sparing his life, despite his recent change of heart — if that's truly what's occurred."

She looked down. She wasn't going to argue, what her brother said made perfect sense. It just wasn't what her gut told her. "What of the prophecy? What if this change of heart means he's the only one who can defeat the Oni?" Her question seemed to take him aback. "I've learned much since I came here, thanks to Bronach. There's never been an Ereubinian born with Adorian blood in his veins. Surely this must mean something."

"There's so much we don't know about the scrolls and the ancient texts. I can't base my decisions on such tenuous things, not when it comes to the good of our realm."

Ariana nodded. "I understand. Will the council even meet then?"

"Yes. There are still things concerning the matter that need to be discussed. You aren't fighting me on this?"

"I have faith in your decisions. I just wanted you to hear my thoughts on the matter. I could never get Father to understand that, either. I may not command an army of thousands or lead a kingdom, but that perhaps opens my eyes to things that would be of little consequence to you. Sometimes it is those very things that bring ruin or revelation."

"Your words shame my heart."

She reached over and took his hand. "Michael, your efforts weren't unmerited. Don't think for a moment that I am ungrateful. I love you as a brother who I have always known — as a sister who has always been watched over."

Michael had moved to sit up with his back against the headboard. "I love you, too," he whispered, squeezing her hand. "I always felt like something was missing, even before Father died." He looked to the side. "Speaking of the Saeculum reminded me of something. Before Father died, he asked me if I recalled the way to the Saeculum. In fact, it was the very day he died that he asked me. I didn't think anything of it at the time and didn't get the opportunity to find out why he'd asked, but the question does have a curious feel to it. And this," he pointed to the key, "makes me wonder if it isn't just one more thing he was keeping from us."

She worried the key in her hand, memorizing the lines.

Michael let go of her hand and tipped her chin to look at him. "Healed or not, you need rest — you're exhausted. Am I wrong?"

"No, I feel it. And I'm not the only one fighting sleep here. You should get some more rest yourself." She touched him on the shoulder as she rose. "Sweet dreams."

CHAPTER THIRTY-FIVE

YOU'RE TOO LATE

I t began as it always did. Michael stood facing the northern entrance to the city, feeling the tension in the air. His senses were clouded, everything carrying the fog of a dream, suffocating weight bearing down.

Their cries could be heard from a fair distance as they approached, echoing off the once-sheltering arms of the mountains. He stood motionless as they swooped down, talons bared. Helpless, he witnessed several Adorians ravaged by their hands. Claws tore into bodies, blood dripping down the Moriors' withered, hollow cores. One of them turned toward Michael, the same one as each time before, and grinned with glistening teeth, its man-like jaws sunken into a fleshless face. He tried moving his arms, and felt the familiar paralysis in his limbs. Frozen in place, he closed his eyes to the carnage around him, hoping with every fiber in his being to wake from the nightmare once again.

Suddenly, he felt a hand on his shoulder, digging in hard to his collarbone. It shook him awake. The illusionary film that had always pervaded vanished, and the sounds of his realm's fear grew unclouded. He turned to see Garren standing beside him in the city.

Garren pulled Michael behind him as he drew his sword. With one flowing movement he turned, blocking the Morior from Michael and plunging his blade deep into its chest. It fell to the ground, but not before clipping Garren. He howled in pain as he grabbed his leg. He jerked his sword free, raised it into the air, then swung down and severed the creature's head cleanly from its neck.

"Ariana's here, I can feel it, but I can't find her." Garren's words were rushed.

Michael glanced around him to gain his bearings, then motioned for Garren to follow him, but as he started toward the castle, Garren clutched his arm.

"She's not there. I just came from that direction." Garren hitched a breath as he shifted his stance. The injury to his leg was substantial.

"Are you able to walk?"

"I don't have a choice!"

They began to weave their way through the battle. Michael picked up a sword from one of the fallen. Following just behind Garren, he fought off several Ereubinians. The chaos was difficult to maneuver around, the casualties mounting on both sides.

It wasn't long until they reached the center courtyard. Everything had grown dark, the sky burdened with black rolling clouds. He could hear someone speaking, but couldn't understand what was being said. Garren ran ahead, Michael emerging through the hedge moments later.

Ariana was on her knees; a hollow expression on her face, her eyes fixed on the distance. She was clothed in a black gown, with the hood from her cloak draped over her head. Michael started to run toward her, Garren by his side, when it appeared.

Behind Ariana, a great white dragon materialized. The light from its presence was stunning. It glistened with iridescent scales. Great blue eyes peered down at them, shining fiercely.

"Ciara," Garren murmured. He stood motionless at her sight.

She was over forty feet tall, looming over them. Her shadow covered Ariana completely. Ariana remained still as Ciara reached down to her. Sharp claws pierced her chest, light streaming from the entry wounds. Yet, she did not lose consciousness. Instead she rose to her feet, a look in her eyes that drained the blood from Michael's heart. He watched as she raised her hand, a small ball of light forming above her palm, the same as he had seen in the old world. She parted her lips, and began to speak.

As the words spilled from her mouth, the earth beneath them began to tremble. The light grew in intensity, spinning faster and faster, until it had become larger in size than Ariana herself. Ciara snatched the ball into her clawed hand and held it in the air. She opened her immense jaw.

The sound that escaped from the dragon was indescribable. It was more than a scream. It was a cry that summoned every Morior to circle around her, matching the intensity of her tone. Michael could not have heard her, but he no longer saw Ariana's lips moving. Everything slowed as the light erupted, covering all of them, expanding out. A tremendous crack followed by a loud rumble echoed against the sudden emptiness of the landscape. Michael fell to the ground. When the light faded, he rose to his feet. Garren was still beside him.

There was nothing left. They stood in what remained of the courtyard, surrounded by a gruesome landscape. Nothing was as it had been. The ground itself was thick with an inky blackness. It wasn't mud or mire, but something else entirely. It started to wrap itself around his ankle, but he shook his foot free.

Everything was silent. Ciara still stood before them, motionless. Ariana had once again knelt down, facing them. He could barely make out her figure, her clothes blending in with the surroundings. But he could still see her eyes. They were even more intensely blue than Ciara's. He looked at Garren, who sank to his knees as well.

Suddenly, Garren began to speak. The words coming from his lips were similar in sound to those spoken by Ariana. He closed his eyes, and reached out his hands.

Michael could do nothing. Paralysis had returned to his limbs, holding him from anything but witnessing the events around him.

A wicked laugh unfurled from the depth of Ciara's belly. The loudness of it sounded across the empty expanse. He was surprised to hear her speak. He was even more surprised at the sylvan quality of the voice.

"You are too late. She is mine." She laughed again, looking down. Ariana's expression slowly grew into one of possession. Her eyes darkened as she threw her head back and screamed. Tears streamed down her cheeks as she wailed with pain. He barely heard himself crying out for her over the sound.

He awoke clutching his chest. Jareth was at his side, shaking him.

"Michael! Wake up!"

He couldn't move at first; his whole body stuck in remembrance of the paralysis it had just possessed.

"I heard you screaming for Ariana from down the hall. She's fine, remember, we're back home. Everything's all right."

Michael's sight slowly cleared, and his heart rate returned to normal, but he still couldn't find his tongue.

"This was no ordinary dream, my son." Jenner's words were a welcome sound compared to Ariana's screams, which still echoed in his ears. Not that he didn't appreciate Jareth's efforts.

"No, it wasn't. More tangible than any dream I've ever had." He saw then that Jareth's arm was bound in a sling. "Are you all right?"

"I'm not the one emitting such frightful wails. What in the world did you see in this dream?"

"Jareth, if you would please allow me privacy to speak with Michael for a moment?"

Jareth nodded, not giving his father an ounce of resistance. It was a respect that Michael had seen greatly mature over the last ten years. After Gabriel died, Jareth seemed to appreciate his own father more. He rose from Michael's side and slipped from the room.

"Ciara had Ariana, Jenner. Whatever powers my sister possesses, Ciara had complete domination over them, and it ..." He paused. How to explain? Everything in their world had rotted away, leaving only death and emptiness in its place. "The Oni is clearly referred to as a male, but could it have been written as to mislead?"

Jenner was hesitant to answer. "I don't believe so, but it would behoove us to assume that those who penned the prophecies may not have told us everything."

"And what does this mean for Garren? He was with me in this dream. Ciara said to him 'You're too late,' as if he had the power to stop her. Do we risk keeping him alive and lose the faith of our people — or do we execute him and risk losing what may be the key to saving Adoria itself? Do the scrolls say anything of this?"

Jenner shook his head. "No, but in addition to the scrolls, the ancients also left us with a very strong code of moral and legal laws. It does not appear they intended to contradict themselves." Jenner sat down in a chair near the bed. "The choice is yours to make. I have already met with the council and our will is that the decision will rest in your hands alone. We will not intervene."

He was surprised to hear this. He'd thought the council to be taking on a more involved role after the last time he had met with them.

Jenner seemed to sense Michael's confusion. "You know the laws and how they are to be applied. If you feel it necessary to your sister's safety to keep him alive, so be it. You wouldn't have been chosen as ruler had we not had faith in your judgment. The sole reason we conveyed our disapproval of your last judgment was because you made a call out of unfounded theory. Revelation of your sister's powers is something not to be taken lightly."

"I need to speak with Garren." Michael started to rise when Jenner stopped him.

"You believe him to have been privy to this vision as well?"

Michael looked past the windows. "I don't know what I believe anymore." He rose to his feet, stretching his wings. They were sore and felt heavy. He rubbed his shoulder and peeked at the bandage on his arm. His leg was wrapped, making it awkward to move. He reached for his shirt and pulled it over his head, maneuvering his wings painfully as he finished dressing.

Jenner headed toward the door before addressing Michael again. "I will see you when we meet with the council, assuming the world does not fall to pieces before then."

Jenner smirked and for a moment the tension was lessoned. Michael sighed. "The way things have been going, it very well might."

Michael grabbed his cloak. He never thought he'd see the day that he desperately needed to speak with Garren and it was this thought that ran through his head as he limped down several corridors. When he was around the corner from Garren's cell, he heard raised voices.

"Michael will see you when he feels it necessary," the guard's words were clipped and teeming with disgust.

"Please, you don't understand the weight of … I *must* speak with him."

The guard seemed to have heard enough of Garren. As Michael walked into the hall, he saw the Adorian lean into the door, pressing his face to the bars. Judging by the hatred in his expression, he was about to say something rather nasty when, unfortunately for him, he discovered that some of his shirt fabric was exposed through the railing, just enough for Garren to grab hold of.

"Believe me," Garren hissed, "he'll feel it …"

Michael stepped up before Garren could finish his sentence. "Let him go. I believe I know what urgent matter you're referring to." Garren released the guard.

"My Lord, I'm sorry. I should've summoned you." The guard knelt down.

"Rise. I respect your intentions to honor me." Michael tapped him on the shoulder, motioning for him to stand. "Garren and I need to speak in private. I'll come for you once we're finished." The guard bowed again, then pulled a silver key from his pocket and handed it to Michael.

Left alone, Michael turned the key in the lock and opened the door. Garren had reclaimed his seat.

"You were there," Michael rasped.

Sweat poured down Garren's face as he nodded. "Did you see anything before I reached you?"

Michael shook his head. "Do you know anything of my sister? Words again came from your lips that weren't Adorian."

"I knelt when I saw her, but heard nothing."

Michael believed him. "Then you didn't hear Ciara address you?"

"No."

"She said, 'You are too late. She is mine.' Do you have any idea where such a vision would have come from, or for what purpose?"

"I can't begin to imagine. No Ereubinian or anyone else living aside from the Laionai themselves has had an audience with her, though it appears the tide is changing."

Michael almost didn't say anything, but he felt his gut urging him to. "I can assure you that's not true."

Garren looked up. "What?"

"Ariana. The day you released her from Palingard. Ciara approached her in Arcadia. She was trying to persuade Ariana against going any further, which would keep her from crossing over into our borders. She appeared to her as a child."

Garren stood up from his bed and started to circle the room.

Michael thought for a moment that it was odd that he didn't feel the urge to pace himself. "I'm unsure what your place is in all of this is. You speak our language when it's never been taught to you, and in a vision you speak in a tongue that only you and Ariana posses. I can't ignore that." Michael knew his next sentence wouldn't be anticipated. "I'm requesting that you appear before the elders. The council may have questions for you that I want to give you a fair chance to answer. Perhaps if they see the difference in you, as I have seen, it will steer the course of things to come."

Garren turned his gaze to the ground. Michael could almost reach out and touch his remorse. It couldn't have been an easy choice to make — walking away from everything he'd ever believed. Michael had been wrong, Garren hadn't chosen Adoria based on her leniency, he couldn't have. He'd never known mercy.

"I don't know if in the pace of the last two days that I've thanked you for saving Ariana's life." Michael dipped his head to catch Garren's eye. "You don't know what it's done to change mine. And dream or not, you saved my life when you thought the threat was real. I felt the blood rushing through my veins at the same pace that it must have yours. While I cannot forget the wrongs that have been done to my people, I can personally forgive you for them. It's easy to be honorable and just when you've always been so. It's clearly another matter when it's against all that you've been taught to believe."

Garren's breathing quickened. "I don't deserve your forgiveness. All this time, I assumed my father's blessings upon my actions and I have done nothing but shame him."

Michael shook his head. How many times had he told Ariana that darkness flowed through the veins of all of Eidolon and here he was retracting that statement to his sworn enemy? Maybe the world had fallen to pieces. "You are everything that I would have been, had I been raised in your world, Garren. While our ideals and methods have been drastically different, our dedication to our beliefs is the same. That's why I want you to meet with the council. I want them to hear your words — see what I have seen."

Garren swallowed hard. "I would still be that being had I not found Ariana. Her presence, just the simple touch of my hand on her cheek, irrevocably changed everything for me."

Michael remembered what Ariana had told him about their conversation. "I have been relayed a very different version of your feelings for my sister."

Garren sat down on the floor. "Ariana dreamt when she was in Eidolon that your father came to her and told her that you would be there soon and I remember well her calling out for you several times in her suffering. My feelings for her are stronger than anything I've ever known. But I am at death's door and have no intention of leaving her with resentment toward you for what must be done. Selfishly, I want her by my side in my last hours. But because I love her, I cannot allow it."

Michael was speechless. He'd taken Garren for many things, none of which was selfless. "Then what changes have been wrought in you are not false. What I have witnessed is truth."

"Michael, you must listen to me. Merely being in close proximity with her, near her in any fashion, awakens emotions and experiences that I've never known. It's as if I've lived two lives, one of righteousness, one of depravity. But it may be a persuasion of one whom you cannot afford to trust, The Laionai or the Goddess herself. Do what you know to be right, and let fate be what it may. It was my introduction into her life that brought all of this on, so perhaps when I'm no longer breathing, it will cease."

Michael looked at the floor. Garren's words had truth behind them, but to what extent? He'd have to trust that he'd know what to decide when the time came. He had no other choice.

"We'll see. You haven't eaten anything. If you are ill, then I will send for our healer. If not, then give your body what it needs. Your judgment in our realm doesn't include your suffering needlessly." He gave Garren as much of a smile as he could given the circumstances. "I will send another plate of hot food and a blanket. If you change your mind, let the guard know, and he will summon Aulora."

Michael left the cell and stood in the hall for a moment with his back against the wall. He concentrated only on his breathing — everything else was far too overwhelming.

CHAPTER THIRTY-SIX

SEVEN KINGS

S he'd left Michael with the intention of resting, but her curiosity was too much, especially in consideration of all that had transpired. And of course in conjunction with Michael's revelation — she couldn't fathom having powers. There had been so many things throughout her life that had made her feel less than normal, but she couldn't conceive of what he'd described. Yet, she was hardly in a position to argue that what he'd said couldn't be possible. After all, her father had done what he had for a reason.

"How far is the Saeculum?"

Duncan, who'd met her in Michael's doorway as she was leaving, took a moment before answering. It seemed as though it had been awhile since he'd been there himself. "Not too far. An hour's ride or so."

He scratched his beard, his brows furrowed. "I chose to bite my tongue in Michael's presence, but if this ever happens again, I won't leave your scolding to him — I'll personally make sure that you understand the consequences of your actions. Many died in Eidolon to bring you back here safely. I know you care about Sara, but being whose daughter and sister you are, you must realize your actions have more weight than before. You may not consider it much to risk your life, but it means everything to Michael. And to me." He reached over, and pulled her to him.

"I'm sorry Duncan," she whispered.

He patted her back roughly with his hand, and then released her. Taking her by the shoulders, he leaned down to face her eye to eye. "I heard a rumor that you defeated a few of their men before being apprehended. Is this true?"

"Eight or nine? I wasn't really in a position to keep count." She rubbed her shoulder where Aiden's blade had pierced her, the memory lingered still.

"Nine?" He laughed. "That shouldn't surprise me. I'll give you this, you're brave. I have had grown Adorians twice your size cower in their boots at the sheer thought of going anywhere near Eidolon, and you ran off alone in the night to walk right into it. Did you see her? Was she still alive?"

"Yes. She's one of the breeders, as you said she might be."

He tilted his head to the side, his hands shoved into his coat pockets as they walked down the corridor. "So, you saw her in the outer courts."

She knew without asking where this conversation was going. "I followed them into observance. You didn't think I would go there unprepared to find her did you?" His eyes grew wide, as she expected. "I'm too tired to go over all of this again, do we have to talk about it right now?"

"No. You don't really want company today do you?"

She paused before answering. She felt guilty considering all that he had gone through for her sake.

"It's alright. You aren't going to hurt my feelings. We have been constantly by your side since you arrived here. I will tell you how to get there, just make sure you take Koen with you, please. Give an old Adorian some peace of mind at least."

She leaned down to pet him. "Of course, I'd be lost without him."

Duncan smiled and began to give her directions.

As she ventured beyond Cyphrus, out into the countryside, she thought of her conversation with Michael. Why would her father have asked her brother if he recalled the way to the Saeculum, had it not had a purpose? As soon as Michael had said the words, she immediately wanted to see it for herself.

She'd been riding almost an hour, when she saw the thick overgrowth on the rocks ahead as Duncan had described. At first she decided that she'd in fact stopped in the wrong place, but something caught her eye. Beneath the vines and foliage, she saw what looked like stone.

It was a stairwell, twined with ivy and twisting root. It lay beneath years of detritus. She pulled at the vines and after awhile she found that the stairs led to the mouth of a hall. She looked back at Koen.

"Well, I suppose this is it, are you coming?"

Koen stayed frozen in place near the horse.

"Koen, you coward! Fine, suit yourself. They'll come after you if something eats me in here." Taking a deep breath, she started into the hall.

She'd gone several yards into the darkness when Duncan's assurance of Aurora stones was made good. Except this time, they weren't randomly scattered about, they were gathered in groups and held in bowls carved from ordinary stone.

She continued further, running her hands along the walls as they led her deep into the ground, finding that it was nothing like she'd expected. The hall evolved into a complicated series of columned corridors.

The light from the stones became so intense it was as though it were daylight. Looking around, she found herself amazed that there were no signs of the years that had to have passed since anyone had been there. There were no spider webs, and just the lightest covering of dust upon the floor. Just like it had been in Arcadia.

Its beauty took her breath away. She'd already been told by Bronach that the Saeculum preceded Adorian record and she could see where their ancestry had been born. How could Michael have left out how indescribable it was? The deeper she progressed, the more ornate everything became. Sculptures stood esoteric along the length of the halls.

The immortals. Their eyes pierced her with the knowledge of things that she could scarcely dream of. She could feel it in her blood. The main throughway that she was following led finally to a dead end. A large wooden door with intricate carvings stood before her.

After trying the door and discovering it to still be locked, she looked for a keyhole and found none. She considered going down another hall, that maybe this wasn't the door Michael had been referring to, but as she ran her fingers over the roughness of the wood, she came to a shape she recognized.

She pulled the key from her cloak pocket.

"Is this what you intended?" She placed the key flat against the door and slipped it into place, where it appeared to merge with the wood. The door moved and resonated with what sounded like pins falling into place from a large lock. She lifted the handle and began to leverage her weight against it. Moving smoothly, the door opened to reveal an immense room. As she walked farther in, she realized there was no light beyond the doorway. She reached back, remembering her luck with the stones in the castle and picked up one of them. Without moving any further, she lifted the stone in her hand, shining the light around her.

It started slowly at first. Hundreds of sconces lined the walls. Holding the stones like torches, the sconces stirred to life. Once all of them were lit, she could see the room clearly. It was beyond majestic. It seemed similar in size to where Jareth had taken her, but this was a room that had been soaked in complicated forethought. Everything had detail. The floor was made of carved stone. A perfect circle, it reminded her a little of the sanctuary that she'd seen in Arcadia, yet a thousand times more spectacular.

At the top of the ceiling, words were carved into the border. The characters looked foreign to her at first. She walked out into the center of the room.

"What did you know that you couldn't tell us?" she whispered, thinking of her father. Though she knew what she'd intended to say, it sounded strange to her ears. She froze as she realized that she wasn't speaking either the common tongue or Adorian.

Everything around her began to shift. She turned her gaze toward the ceiling as she tried to regain her bearings. The words started to change shape. When the room stopped spinning and her vision cleared, the formerly unknown words were as known to her as her own flesh.

Her mind couldn't wrap itself around what she'd just read. It was too great, too much for her to comprehend. Could it be? Could they have known — even before mortal man had summoned Ciara into Middengard? Adorian history had given no such illusions, yet here upon the walls of those who breathed before all others — here it was inscribed in stone. Everything was there save one small detail.

Seven. It foretold of seven members of the Laionai, not six as she'd always heard. Jenner himself had spoken of them as six individuals now acting as one collective.

Seven kings of Man will rule in the last days. Darkness, long awaited, will appeal to them and they will open the gates between the realms and death shall pass over all created kind. A sacrifice will be offered — one life for many. A wager will be made against this sacrifice, the outcome of which will depend upon a battle born of blood and bone, immortal against immortal.

The souls will be gathered and a great age of suffering shall be ushered in. The Mortal Coil will grant power to the Oni, as the second prophecy is fulfilled and the souls wage battle against the winged ones. The six kings of men will then, in judgment, stand before the seventh. A second darkness, the beloved one, shall come forth to fight the final battle. This day shall bring with it either eternal salvation or immortal death.

"We've been waiting for you."

Ariana wasn't sure how long she had been there, staring at the words in mute awe, before she heard him speak. It was more than a voice. It was resplendent, unlike any mortal being. She turned and fell to her knees.

Light radiated from the beings before her, casting everything else into shadow. She felt a hand cup her chin and lift her face. "It is not you who should kneel." He lowered his hand to help her to her feet, bowing his upper body as he did so.

He had blonde hair and an ageless face, the vague physicality of a mortal man, but the similarities ended there. His skin might as well have been made of light itself.

"I don't understand," she murmured. "Why me?"

He smiled sadly. "I fear your questions must go unanswered for now. Garren will be sentenced to death by poison. You will see the vial brought to his lips, and then you must trust me — he will not meet death in this realm."

"What of the prophecy?"

The being shook his head, murmuring something below his breath as he touched her on the cheek.

Ariana bolted upright from where she lay. Looking up at the canopy of her bed, she took a deep breath, remembering that she'd changed her mind and gone to lie down after speaking with Duncan. She shivered despite the roaring fire at the foot of her bed.

... and then you must trust me.

CHAPTER THIRTY-SEVEN

I HAVE NOTHING
LEFT TO GIVE

G arren rose from his bed and walked into the hall to meet Michael. He was still as the guard bound his hands behind his back. As many times as he'd done this to another, it was the first time he'd ever experienced the helplessness himself. He kept his head down as they made their way to where the elders were waiting.

Two armed soldiers opened the double doors and he was ushered in. He noted the elders were dressed in dark blue and white. He was guided to a chair beside Michael.

"Garren, we meet as a council to decide your fate. It has been brought to our attention that there has been wrought within you a change of sorts. Do you feel this matter carries enough weight to keep you from your rightful penance?" It was the same elder who'd spoken to Michael at the border to Adoria.

When Garren spoke, his voice was low, still tired from everything that had transpired. "What has been done at my hands cannot be undone by any change of heart, no matter how sincere."

"You have come into this realm then, knowing that your death awaits you. You chose to save one of our daughters, yet you demand no payment for her return?"

Garren was taken aback by the question. "She is worth more than any payment my life could bring. I will make no such request, no matter what is leveraged against me. I go to my end willingly."

The elder rose, and began to walk around the room. "The Laionai have begun to train an army of men. This is the army that you were commissioned to lead? What purpose did it serve, considering that none aside from our own blood can enter our realm unaccompanied?"

"I have been in the presence of the Laionai. I believe Ciara's intentions were to wield what powers I possessed to breach the divide. She must have known that I was part Adorian. I naively assumed I was chosen for the powers I had, but it was my lineage instead. I will be of no use to her dead."

The elder stopped, and turned toward him. "You speak in past tense. Are you no longer carrying powers of your own?"

Garren took a stifled breath. "I have bare abilities, no more than any average Ereubinian. What had been granted by the Laionai was taken from me without my knowledge. I cannot explain what has happened save to say that it directly relates to Ariana. If I were any use to you at all, I would gladly offer my life in servitude instead, but it is my death that will bring you the most benefit. There is no punishment that will justify or right the transgressions I have committed."

The elder remained quiet.

Garren flexed his hands at his sides and looked at the ground. It wasn't death that frightened him, but the judgment of the Adorian people that surrounded him. The disdain was so thick it was tangible.

"Michael, what say you?"

Michael rose, and placed his hand on Garren's shoulder. "I say it is to be left to a vote. The Adorian people are whom the crimes have been committed against. It will be you who decides. A show of hands. Who among you says he shall live?"

The silence was deafening. Garren didn't lift his head, but he heard not a single shred of fabric rub against another. It was unanimous.

"Then so be it," Michael whispered.

Ariana watched as Garren was led up a wooden stairwell to stand before the crowd that had gathered. Muffled voices and whispers filtered through the crowd, hushing as Ariana made her way toward the front. Her eyes met with Garren's briefly as she passed behind him to sit beside her brother and Jareth.

"You shouldn't be here," Michael whispered.

"Don't think me faint-hearted, Michael, I fully understand the death he could have met with for saving my life. I owe him this much." She looked up to the opening in the roof, unsettled by the bright blue of the sky.

What if it was merely a dream and you have said nothing in his defense?

She drowned out the sound of his grievances as they were listed, ignoring the thrumming of her heart as the moment neared.

A hooded figure whose face was concealed by a plain white mask walked to where Garren stood. She saw Garren's lips murmur something, followed by a slight nod by the executioner. Slowly, as if time had paused in mourning, the vial was brought to Garren's lips.

And then you must trust me ...

"Stop!"

The voice startled the executioner and the vial slipped from his hands and fell to the ground in a violent crash, sending glass shards across the platform.

The voice had come from the back of the assembly. She watched in amazement as Roahn made his way to them. He leapt two steps at a time until he was standing breathless before Michael.

"You cannot execute him, not without knowing ..." Roahn bent over, trying to catch his ragged breath.

Jenner had come forward and was behind Roahn. "Roahn, what — "

"He is of Adorian royal blood."

An audible gasp was drawn in at once from all who heard him. He paused for only a moment before continuing. "He is Indeara's child, my nephew. Regardless of the trespasses he has committed, as it has been written since the age of guardians, it's up to the sovereign alone to decide his fate. Forgive me, Michael, I heard of the council's decision and couldn't keep his lineage a secret any longer." He looked at Michael, a deeply worn grief in his eyes pleading for Michael to grant Garren his freedom.

Every being held their breath — every eye was trained on her brother. Ariana watched Roahn, understanding now how torn he must have felt when he found out that Garren had spared her life in Palingard.

Was he the only one who knew?

She could tell without asking that her brother was weighing the consequences of his words, each second that passed representing the thousands of lives that would be affected by his decision.

"He lives."

"Your debt has been forgiven," Michael whispered into Garren's ear.

Garren was too overwhelmed to say anything.

Michael turned to Jenner, "I'll address the people of Cyphrus this evening. Please send messengers with the news and have a feast prepared."

Garren couldn't tell from the elder Adorian's face how he felt about it.

Michael turned back to Garren. "Turn around and I'll unfetter your hands." He could barely hear Michael over the scuffle of feet and the flurry of speech that erupted as the assembly was dismissed. No one left right away.

Garren, without lifting his eyes, turned to face the wall. He felt the binds loosen, and the cords fall. He rubbed his wrists were they'd been tied.

"I don't understand." He turned to see that it wasn't Michael who'd untied him, but Ariana. Michael, after making the offer, now stood off to the side of the platform with Jareth, whose anger was evident on his face, and Roahn, whose expression was indecipherable.

Ariana flashed Garren an insincere smile. "You should count yourself lucky." There was an unmistakable coolness in her voice.

"Ariana, I — "

"There's nothing to discuss. I wasn't the one who spoke for you. You have Roahn to thank for that."

He couldn't help the smile that tugged at one corner of his mouth. She was even more beautiful when she was flustered.

"I'm glad you find this amusing."

He grabbed her by the arms as she started to walk away. "Don't you understand the purpose behind what I said to you?"

"You believed me some frail creature, unable to wield her own emotions? Perhaps you were under the impression that I would wither into a deep despair over your loss, never regain the motivation to eat or drink or subsist again?"

"If your feelings were even half as strong as those I carry for you, then what your brother had to do as a sovereign of Adoria would have caused a rift between the two of you that I couldn't bear to leave you with. As your brother, you would've eventually accused him of knowing your heart more than any other, and ending my life despite its affect on you."

He could see the expression on her face change. This was something that she had obviously not considered. Still, she refused to answer him.

"If I didn't have affection for you, would I have stayed awake the night I released you in Palingard, worried for you? Or spared Michael his life after learning that he was within reach of our borders, simply because he is your brother? There hasn't been a single moment since my return from Palingard that I haven't thought of you. Even my wedding night, I couldn't …" He watched her expression change yet again as the words fell from his lips. He hadn't considered how they would sound to her.

"You *are* married."

He took a deep breath, trying to figure out how to respond to such a statement. "It's not what you …"

"It's exactly as I think." She pulled herself from his grasp and sat down on one of the chairs behind her. The color drained from her skin.

"How long — when?"

"I swear to you that I've never laid a hand on her, not in the way you're thinking. It was after Palingard's fall. My confession, though, is that I chose Sara for Aiden. The only consolation I can give you is that had I not, she would've been sent to the outer regions and would've been one of the humans left at your borders."

Tears had started to well in her eyes, though they remained unshed. He sat down in front of her and put his hands on her shoulders.

"I can't get the image out of my head — what she must be enduring. Garren, they are still aware of what's going on around them. They are still conscious. Every time he touches her … she can't even close her eyes to escape it. I can't …" She lowered her head again and he could no longer help himself.

He pulled her into his arms. "Micah, the boy who helped you in Eidolon — I swore that if I were allowed to keep my life I would go back for him. I fear for his life, just as you fear for Sara's. I don't know how, but we will find a way to bring Sara back here. As soon as I get a chance, I'll speak with your brother."

"But what of her soul? Will she re — "

Garren clenched his jaw. It wasn't a question he wanted to answer. "It's never been done, but because I was the one who took her soul, I may be able to restore it."

She surprised him by taking his hand in hers. "Then there's hope."

He placed his other hand over hers and rubbed her wrist where he'd grabbed her in the cell. "I didn't hurt you did I?"

She shook her head. "My pride maybe, but my wrist is fine. I knew you were being untruthful. I just didn't fully understand why."

"And how were you able to tell?"

She held her mouth in a tight line as he finished his question. "Wouldn't you like to know? You'll have to earn that next kiss, Garren. And considering that you had to save my life for the last one, I'd say you have your work cut out for you."

He smirked. "Indeed."

Roahn came to stand beside them and started to rest a hand on Garren's shoulder, but clutched it to his breast instead. His features turned in pain and he cleared his throat. "I adored Indeara and it's her life and love for you that's saved you. Please, don't ask anything else of me. I have nothing left to give."

CHAPTER THIRTY-EIGHT

JUST THE BEGINNING

Bronach sat in his chair in the library, the Book of Life open before him. He'd had no need to attend the execution, for he could watch words appear on the pages, as if penned by an unseen hand, recording everything as it happened. His presence there would have been for naught, since the covenant forbade him from interfering with the due consequences of Garren's actions. He couldn't have stopped it had he wanted to.

But what Azrian didn't know was that Bronach had already been told by the seventh Laionai, who had foreseen it, that Garren would be pardoned.

A draft swept through the room, flipping the pages of the book. Bronach glanced up to see the light from the candle flicker, casting shadows across what might have been the darkest mistake he'd ever made.

And so, with the covenant in place, Irial and Èanna were sent to the created realms; Irial born into the cursed lineage of the Ereubinians, Èanna born into the blameless blood of the Adorians. Unaware of who they really are, or of the weight that rests upon the outcome of their lives, they will come face to face as strangers in the mortal world.

He could hear the sounds of preparations being made to accommodate the crowd that would gather for Michael's address that evening. The elders had decreed the age of guardians had come to an end. They felt secure behind the divide, but Michael was right. This wasn't the end of anything.

"It is just the beginning."

CHAPTER THIRTY-NINE

A FAMILIARITY

A riana saw Michael braced against the wall with one hand on his forehead.

"Is it Garren that concerns you?"

"There are things that have happened in the past with some of our people that are not such simple matters to forgive. Adoria as a whole has fought for so long for righteousness' sake, that what is for the good of all is what's held with highest regard. This is not true for those who have spent much of their lifetime in Middengard. They weren't born of man, but their souls are accustomed to his ways."

"You're referring to the Braeden, but something in your tone tells me that you're thinking of someone specifically. Is it Duncan?"

Michael nodded. "He lost a wife and a stepdaughter, the latter at Garren's hands."

Ariana felt her stomach turn again. She had mixed emotions. Her heart felt one way, but her reason and experiences told her something completely different. "That's why they are not coming tonight? Is Jareth coming?"

"Yes on both counts. Jareth may be part human, but he has been raised in this realm. It's not in his character to dishonor me by going against my wishes. The Braeden may never be able to accept Garren. I almost, even despite my recent change in perception, have a difficult time trusting that what I have been shown to be true is true. This is my burden to bear. Please, don't worry yourself about it. I'll deal with Duncan."

"Okay."

He turned to walk back to the dining hall, saying below his breath, "I'll see you shortly."

She could feel the distress that Michael was trying so unsuccessfully to hide. She hoped Jareth would be able to provide him with some comfort or insight that she couldn't.

She came to the room that had been readied for Garren, and paused to brace her palms against the door frame. Her conversation had reminded her of home, what she'd once known as home. She still suffered vivid recurrences in her mind of the day Palingard had fallen. She regretted her last conversation with Bella. Her hand curled into a tight fist as she remembered dropping the cloak in spite to the ground. She had no idea what she'd say to Garren now that they were alone again. She lowered her head and exhaled. His voice caught her off guard.

"I'll leave you alone, if that's what you wish."

She turned to see Garren standing in the darkened refuge of a large beam that supported the hall. When he stepped into the light, she noted that he'd changed clothes. He looked so different, she almost didn't recognize him. No longer clothed in black, he wore brown, brushed suede pants and a light cream shirt. A cloak of the same color hung over his shoulders. The silver clasps on his clothing glinted in the light from the torch that hung on the wall.

"No ... I'm not — "

"Ariana, I can tell by the look in your eyes that you're uncomfortable right now. I don't want to be any more of a burden to you than I've already been."

Ariana leaned her back against the door. "I was thinking about Palingard." An expression of sincere regret fell over his face and she rushed to stop him from speaking it aloud. "I said things to loved ones that I can't take back, Garren. You aren't the only one capable of making mistakes. I was also thinking about my brother. He has a lot weighing on him and it frustrates me that I cannot help him bear it."

"That feels like a lifetime ago."

She could hear the helplessness in his voice; she could see it in his ey They appeared much darker in the shadows of the hall, where he r stood, compared to what she'd seen earlier on the platform.

"Why didn't you kill me?"

Stepping closer, Garren looked as though he was about to reach her, but held his arms against his chest instead. "I don't think that explain it. Something caught me. It was almost like being awakened a heavy sleep, as if seeing your face stirred something in me that ha slumbered."

"A familiarity," she whispered.

He nodded. "Yes, if there were but a thing deeper. It revealed everything in a light that I knew nothing of, stripped me of all the things I'd once called truth."

"When did you learn of your mother?"

"Tadraem, our High Priest — the man who raised me — told me right before Micah killed him." A grave expression darkened his eyes further. "Do you have any idea what you risked coming into that sanctuary?"

"No less than what you risked with your intent to take me to Adoria's border. Michael told me that's what you were about to do when they arrived." Garren opened his mouth, an incredulous look on his face, but she stopped him before he could disagree. "But, I'll admit, there is much about your world that I don't know — only what I've read from Adoria's history books. I have so many questions."

"Perhaps you could show me your world first. I've seen enough darkness to last me the rest of my life. There's nothing in my past worth salvaging."

"You aren't comfortable with tonight are you?"

"Would you be?"

"I suppose not. Are you still willing to go?"

'e nodded his head. "I won't do anything to disappoint Michael and asked that I be there." He reached for her hand as if he expected her se the gesture.

rinned as she took his hand but wasn't about to give him too much e. "You won't receive the reaction you're expecting. Not from o'll be present tonight." She started to lead him toward the dining

e ones without wings who concern me most."

raeden. You knew of their existence?"

ut we weren't sure how they came to be. Were they born without

ir wings are removed at birth. They're taken from their families — there are two houses — The Iidolis, where Michael was the Aidolis, where the Braeden were raised."

and his men were also schooled away from their families?"

"Our father was Braeden, so Michael couldn't have been. Traditional Adorian fighters are usually the children of Adorians like my father, though that's not always the case. Jareth is the child of one of the elders. Michael never knew our mother and was never told where Father was when he was away."

"Where is your mother now?"

"She was killed in Palingard, years ago."

"I'm sorry." He squeezed her hand.

"It was a long time ago. As my brother has said, you can't undo what's been done."

"You are a lot like him, you know."

She smiled. "I wish that he and I had known each other when we were younger." She laughed. "I've been told that we act alike on more than one occasion, which amuses me, because I don't think we could be any more different. I always felt too serious in Palingard, and yet here I feel so undignified, almost foolish. Sara would never believe that I'd ever be accused of such a thing …" Her voice trailed off as she thought of her friend.

Garren must have sensed her discomfort. He stopped walking, and stepped out in front of her, taking her by the shoulders. "We will save her. If I do nothing else to redeem myself, it will be that much that's accomplished."

CHAPTER FORTY

NO MERE LORD

Aiden rushed through the castle. His stomach still felt curdled with the rancid stench of the Ordakais' breath. They had breathed hot and heavy in his face and the mere sight of them had made him tremble. Had they free will, they would have been much more terrifying than the Moriors, simply for their likeness to children. He reached the doors to his chambers and smiled as he entered.

She was curled up on the floor in the far corner of the room. He had no interest in having to travel back out among the humans every time he wanted her in his presence.

The room was dimly lit. He walked over to her and leaned down to see if she was asleep. He could tell by her breathing that she was. Grabbing her by the arm, he pulled her to her feet. Slamming her hard against the wall, he began to laugh.

"You seem quite cold. Such a shame that you cannot go of your own accord and put on a cloak." He mocked her, making his body falsely tremble as he gripped his fingers around her arm, bearing down hard into her flesh. "I'm proud of you for pointing out such a foul being. That girl had no business being here. If it weren't for you, she might have lived. You have served me well, *wife*." He thought it humorous that perhaps she'd at one time had ridiculous notions of a real marriage. Humans were such pathetic creatures.

As he released her arm and left her standing against the wall, he took long strides, dramatically, around the room. "I will tell you this, you should be incredibly grateful to me. I've now saved your life on two occasions. Had you not been chosen as my beautiful bride, had you not been specially picked for me, then you would be dead along with the rest of those who were taken from your village." He rushed upon her and ran his hands up her bare thighs, then higher. He could just imagine the repulsion that screamed inside of her.

Laughing, he reached around her neck and loosened the ties that held the bare sheath she wore and it slipped to the floor. "I'm really not in the mood for company tonight, but seeing that you are already here and so eager for my advances, I suppose I cannot deny you such things." He took her again by the arms and threw her to the bed, then leaned down over her.

"What are you thinking in there?" Sara didn't respond, which infuriated him. "Answer me!"

Her eyes welled with tears and he sat up, horrified. He reached a hand back and brought it hard against her face. "You will not display such sentiments in my presence. Do you understand me?" Upon her subsequent lack of an answer, he grabbed her chin in his hand and shook her. "Did you not hear me?"

"Yes, my Lord," she whispered.

He sighed and said under his breath, "To you, I am no mere Lord. I am a God, and this night, you are blessed to worship me." He started to unbuckle his belt and saw something flash in her eyes. For a brief moment he thought he might have recognized it as anger, when he thought twice, and realized that it couldn't have been. He must be imagining things.

When he was finished, he stepped back off of the bed and stretched. He pointed toward the corner where she'd been when he had returned. "Out of my bed. You disgust me." She rose, the discomfort in her leg obvious. As she started to struggle, he reached over and pulled hard on her shoulder, hurling her away from him. "Stand against the wall." He walked over toward a basin of water that sat beside a large wardrobe, chilled from the air. The night had grown cold, and Sara's body reacted violently to the now-frigid temperature.

Grabbing the basin in his hands, he walked to where she stood against the wall. He forcefully splashed it over her, drenching her face and body. She choked, coughing uncontrollably as her body tried to clear her throat of the water. "You will relent, this ridiculous hold you have on your emotions, and we will continue this every waking hour until you do!"

He leaned over and pulled his clothes from the floor where he'd thrown them. He pulled his pants back on, then walked over to the light and blew out the flame, blanketing the room in darkness. He slid back into his bed, grinning.

"Daughter of man, you will be broken. Just like a horse, you will learn who your master is and will come to love me. Do not doubt this. You and I have a long life ahead of us and you have many sons to bear." He closed his eyes, welcoming sleep. "Many sons."

CHAPTER FORTY-ONE

THESE HANDS

G arren walked into the dining hall where the elders awaited him. He tried not to focus on the hundreds of Adorians who stood, filling the room, waiting to hear what would be said.

"Garren. Come forward." The same elder who had spoken to him earlier motioned for him to draw nearer. Ariana and Michael stepped back.

"You have been forgiven of your sins. No longer will you hold your head down in shame. You are one of us, not only by blood, but by creed." One of the other elders brought forth a sword. It was bright silver, the blade engraved with intricate carvings. The elder balanced it in two hands. "Do not fear us, Garren. By this sword, you are committing yourself a son of Adoria, and pledging your life in her service. Do you wish to do so?"

He nodded.

"Then kneel down." Garren obediently knelt before them. The elder with the sword walked closer to him, took the blade in one hand, and lightly tapped each of his shoulders.

"Arise now a child of our realm. No longer held in darkness, your eyes are now open to the light. *Existai domay enthro Adoria*." He reached down to help Garren to his feet.

The sword was held out to him. He took it, surprised by the weightlessness of it. He'd seen swords like it used in battle before, but had never managed to get his hands on one. The Adorians had been so swift in their movements during a fight, which made sense to him now. It would be nearly effortless with such a blade. The elder turned and spoke to those gathered.

"Please continue. Welcome our new brother as you would one who was raised in our realm. Tonight is a great victory for our cause, as Michael has said." He assumed that Michael had spoken before they arrived.

Servers emerged from a back room, carrying large trays. As they rounded the tables, the noise from various conversations grew.

The elder stepped closer to him, and gave a partial bow. "We have not been formally introduced. My name is Jenner. I am the leader of the council of elders, and on a lesser note, father-in-law to Michael and father to Jareth."

Garren bowed in return, unsure of what to say. The noise around them grew as the room swelled with the movement of a feast underway.

"Be careful of the blade. That is not a metal that exists in your realm. It will never dull, so don't let its weight fool you," Jenner said.

"I'm honored. Where did this sword come from?"

"That sword was given to me by my father. Consider it a gift."

Garren swallowed hard. He held his hand up in protest. "I can't take it. I wouldn't have even laid hands on it had I known." He started to give the sword back to Jenner, when he felt Michael step up beside him.

"You made a comment to me not too long ago. You said that our fathers had been allies. Your father would have wished it this way, and since we have no sword of his, this will have to do."

Garren looked behind him to see that Ariana sat quietly in the back of the room. He could barely make out her form in the shadows.

Jenner patted Garren on the shoulder. "Eat, Garren. The guards have informed me that you never touched your food, and it's been a long journey for you." He left Garren and Michael.

Michael gave him knowing look. "You're thinking about Ariana. Tomorrow morning, we'll need to discuss the matter of getting both Micah and Sara away from Eidolon, but tonight we need to put such things aside. Any man, Adorian or Ereubinian, no matter his training, will lose perspective if he doesn't rest."

Many Adorians approached them throughout the night. Garren was stunned, despite Ariana's warning that he wouldn't receive the reaction that he'd expected. There were very few who had any hesitation in their voices as they spoke with him. Was it possible that they weren't aware of what he had done? Yet, he'd heard his own crimes read aloud just hours before, so they had to know.

"You are wondering why they are so kind."

Garren nodded.

"They aren't human, Garren. They look human, many of them, but they aren't. Fallen man has darkness in his heart that is not shared by any in this realm. We are a people of simplicity and peace."

As the words left Michael's mouth, Garren saw a face that made his heart freeze in his chest.

Michael rose and approached the other Adorian, bracing one arm against his in a supportive grip. It was obvious how much it tortured him to be near Garren at all, let alone speak to him.

Garren rose from his seat, and knelt. "Forgive me," he whispered.

Caedmon placed his hand on Garren's head. It lingered there for a moment, a sob erupting from the Adorian's lips. His fingers shook as they pulled themselves together, gripping Garren's hair in a fist.

Garren's head pounded with the pressure on his scalp, but he stayed still — frozen, as Caedmon released his anger.

Sobs gave way to weeping as he let go, his hand still hovering over Garren for a moment before he reached down, his chest still heaving, and pulled Garren to his feet to face him. He held Garren's hands by the wrists. "These hands," he choked, pausing in his words, "these hands have taken flesh and blood from me! All three of those slain on that day left behind wives and children, who are now my wards to watch over. A senseless act of brutality, left for me to explain to their loved ones. All to deliver a message that had such little value in comparison to the lives you took."

Garren steered his gaze again to the floor, a lump in his throat. He could say nothing that would even begin to ease the loss that he'd caused.

Ariana, having heard enough, pried Garren's wrists free, taking Caedmon's hands in hers instead.

"It has not been in vain. Nothing will bring them back to us, but their deaths led to the downfall of Eidolon's most able fighter. The Adorians who lost their lives fought with the purpose of protecting man and defeating Eidolon, and what more of a victory can any Adorian still living claim? That Garren stands amongst our people as one of its citizens."

Caedmon squeezed her hands before releasing them. He cleared his throat, then looked back at Garren. "Know that though there is no longer a debt, the cost of your forgiveness was borne by our people. Its memory will not fade easily." Caedmon turned and left, walking alone away from the crowd.

"He'll heal." Ariana looked up at him, a sweet smile positioning itself on her lips. She motioned for him to sit back down.

Many others came to them throughout the remainder of the evening, some of whom were Michael's and Jareth's fellow fighters. Garren had never felt so insecure or humble in his whole life. His head ached, and all he really wanted was to lie down and close his eyes.

He leaned over and whispered in Ariana's ear, "Do you think it would offend your brother if I retired for the night?"

Ariana shook her head. "He looks exhausted still as well. Perhaps tonight was not the best time to do this. Go then, get some sleep. You'll be more comfortable in your chambers tonight than the last arrangements that were made for you."

Garren smiled. "Oh, I don't know. Cold stone does my back well."

"I'll walk you to your chambers." Garren turned to see that it was Jareth, who hadn't yet said a single word to him. Garren wasn't sure how to feel about the offer.

Michael leaned into the wall nearby with his palm holding his weight, listening with a doubtful look on his face.

Jareth smirked. "If I were going to do him harm, I wouldn't announce to the public that I would be the last one seen with him." He looked over at Ariana and laughed under his breath. "Why is everyone always assuming my intentions are malevolent? I seem to recall already having this conversation once, though in a much less crowded place."

Ariana shook her head and laughed as well. It was obviously an inside joke. It slipped under his skin, and idled there, irritating him just enough to outweigh his humility. He lowered his gaze to keep from scowling. Michael must have sensed it, because when Garren lifted his gaze he witnessed a look crossing between Michael and Jareth that made Jareth suddenly change his demeanor.

"I simply want a word with you. I don't think that too much to ask." His voice was much less abrasive and arrogant.

Garren nodded, and looked back over to wish Ariana good night, but she was already gone. He caught a brief glimpse of her hair as she walked out of his sight.

"I have no quarrel with it." He looked directly at Michael to convey his approval. Whatever it was that Jareth wished to say to him, it could not be unwarranted. He started out of the room, Jareth behind him.

They walked for a minute in silence. Garren heard the click of their boots echoing off of the walls, and down the corridor. He hadn't paid much attention to the stone of the walls before, but they were indeed resplendent, if anything definable. They were so pale in color they almost looked translucent. Slowly he realized he had seen it before — the temple.

His eyes truly hadn't adjusted to everything in their world. He had been so accustomed to the dark, desolate nature of Eidolon that he could not take in everything in Adoria at once. Jareth waited to speak until they stood outside of Garren's chambers.

"It doesn't interest me in the least that you have come across some sort of revelation, in which everything that you have been taught or trained has simply vanished from your consciousness. Don't be fooled for a minute by my kindness to you. I'm bearing your presence out of respect for my friend and my father — nothing more. It's no secret that I care about Ariana, and even if my feelings were unrequited, she's still Michael's blood, which makes her of even greater importance to me. If the thought even crosses your mind to do her harm, your fate would be better if you took your dagger, and plunged it into your own heart, for I will not be so kind. I'm not fully Adorian either, so what has been done to Middengard has been done to my people as well. I've heard mention of returning to Eidolon. Hear me, Garren. If you intend on leading him back into something to his detriment …"

Garren finally had to interrupt. "He has no need to accompany me. I understand every word that you speak, and would speak the same were I in your position, but you must understand that had I meant her harm, I would've done so long ago. I had her at sword's end and released her. Why would I have let her live?"

"Passage into this realm! How can you have been a leader and yet be so foolish? Why would I not believe that the Laionai or Ciara herself has conducted everything that's transpired? A human army is commissioned and miraculously you have a change of heart? You're either an imbecile, or you're under the impression that I am."

As much as Garren felt apologetic, it still took everything in him not to allow his temper to rise up at Jareth's tone. He exhaled slowly before responding. "I've never known truth, but now it's as if I have known it all of my life. I can assure you I will not harm anyone in this realm."

"I didn't come for assurance. I've come with a warning. Any step you make in the wrong direction will be your last and don't think I'm the only one watching you."

Garren sighed. "I wouldn't trust me either, Jareth. But what would you do if you were in my shoes? How could you possibly make amends for what I've done, gain honest respect and trust?"

"With an act I doubt I'll live to see. You can show me your repentance in a form more valuable than useless words. Only then will I grant you my trust."

CHAPTER FORTY-TWO

IRIAL

"**Y**ou are without allies. Had you but taken the right path, you would be at our side. You could have aided in her capture and saved the lives of nine of our men. Did you believe that you would be immune to the judgment of the Laionai?" Tadraem leaned into Micah, his sweat dripping down into the boy's eyes. Aiden stood along the far wall, watching. "Answer me!" he yelled, grabbing Micah by the collar and lifting him.

Micah's lower lip quivered and tears started to well up in his eyes.

Tadraem threw the boy to the floor. "I don't suppose you have the words to say." Looking down at him, Tadraem began to circle Micah, his boots making a shrill scraping sound as he bore his weight down onto his heels.

"High Lord, why don't you inform our young traitor what the penalty is for such a deed as that which he has committed?"

Aiden stepped forward, a smug grin on his face. He'd hoped Tadraem would include him in this. He walked over to where the boy lay. He leaned down close enough to hear the fear in the boy's breath and see the delicate lashes of his eyes.

"You will be given over to the justice of the Moriors. Your blood shall be spilled upon the steps of Eidolon. Such a pity, to die before you've taken your first soul."

Micah looked up at him, his eyes pleading for forgiveness. "Please." The boy's cheeks were void of color, having been without food for over two days.

Aiden crouched down beside him. "I'm sorry. What was that?" He bent his head down closer to Micah, already knowing full well what he'd said.

"I don't want to die."

Aiden sprang to his feet, and kicked Micah hard in the side. Even through the leather of his boot, he felt a rib give way to the force. The boy rolled over, grabbing his side, coughing.

"How amusing! You think your life worth that of nine fully trained men. Ten really, though Garren had his end marked out for him already!"

Spittle hung from Aiden's lip, a fury growing in his voice. "Surely you didn't imagine that he'd be allowed to live?" He started laughing, the idea having just crossed his mind. "You did, didn't you?"

Micah sat with his chest heaving, clutching his small hands to his side, moaning. Aiden stood up, walking back to lean against the wall.

Tadraem walked over to where he stood, and handed him a scroll wrapped and bound with a red tie. "Micah's execution has been set for Friday's eve. See to it that everything is set in place. You'll address those who will be present. Any — " Tadraem was interrupted by the sound of the door being thrown open.

A short man with a receding hairline and beady eyes stumbled into the room. Bits of food and drink were splattered across his shirt, which hung loosely about his wide midsection. He was out of breath and struggled to get his words out. Aiden felt his own impatience and was about to say something when Tadraem stepped forward.

"Spit it out!" he yelled. Taking the little man by his shoulders, Tadraem placed him squarely against the wall adjacent to the door.

"Something's happened with the humans. Something is very wrong."

Aiden furrowed his brow, and tilted his head. "What's happened to the humans?" The man swallowed, sucking in air through his stout, uneven nose. "There was singing heard."

Aiden looked at Tadraem and laughed, relieved. "You're an idiot. They do as they are told. I have commanded many times that my wife sing to me, and she does without question. Do you know anything a — "

The man interrupted him, and it took everything in Aiden's power to keep from reaching out and snatching him up by his neck.

"I heard of other things; glances, words spoken, things done that were not commanded."

Aiden's anger was replaced by an icy shiver. It worked its way up his spine, and rested somewhere near the base of his skull.

Tadraem whispered, "Nonsense. You see what you want to see."

Aiden listened to Tadraem, but recalled the night in the sanctuary that the humans turned to face Garren. Had Tadraem forgotten, or had he not witnessed it?

"Speak with the others if you don't believe me."

Tadraem stepped away from the man, cautiousness in his smile. "The wardens, I assume?"

He nodded, pulling his worn sleeve back onto his shoulder from where Tadraem had taken hold of him. "They've found something now. I couldn't get close enough to see what it was, but they're hovering around it in the outer courts."

Aiden pushed past the man, out to the hall. He heard Tadraem speak with the guard concerning Micah before turning to catch up with Aiden, both of them rushing to the human courts.

When they got there, Tadraem held out his hands and yelled above the noise. "Step aside!" The wardens shifted aside, making room for Aiden and Tadraem. Everyone eyed Aiden as they'd once eyed Garren, terrified of his power. The evening before had solidified that with Tadraem's dramatic return from the dead, seemingly through Aiden's powers.

As they came closer to the center, a hush fell over the crowd. Written almost illegibly, five letters were etched into the stone of the street.

Irial.

It couldn't have been a human. Aiden kept repeating it in his mind as he shook his head in disbelief and confusion. What was *Irial*?

"What does this mean, my Lord?" A tall, thin warden leaned toward Tadraem.

"It means nothing," Tadraem scowled. He grabbed the first human he saw, a fully grown man just a hair taller than Tadraem. The human's muscles were well defined, likely from a much earlier raid.

Taking a dagger from his belt, Tadraem lifted the man's hand, and delicately balanced the tip of the blade on his palm. "Let us see if he speaks of his own accord. If he says anything in his own defense, I swear upon Ciara herself, I will let him go."

Aiden could detect nothing in the human's expression indicating that he could act on his own. No fear. No malice. Nothing. Tadraem pushed the weight of the dagger through to the hilt. Some blood fell to the ground and pooled, while the rest of it traced the line of the human's arm and dripped down his side.

Still, the human was silent.

Tadraem, pleased, jerked his dagger from its position and spun on his heels to face the wardens.

"Nothing. Can you not see that one small fragment of a memory means nothing? A human risks his own life to scribble nonsense in a place where no one will ever see it? Meaningless. Let them sing; let them suffer to give even the slightest grimace. They are still slaves. They are still powerless, sniveling, useless, pitiless creatures that cannot even bathe themselves without our approval."

The wardens applauded at Tadraem's words, but Aiden barely grinned, his chest still struggling for breath. He felt his tongue tingle as he remembered the day he'd questioned Garren's decisions openly. He could still feel the burn, he could still taste the metallic salt of the blood in his mouth. They'd turned to him. The humans had felt his presence before he spoke, and turned to face him as he entered the sanctuary. Aiden had sensed something was amiss that night, but couldn't put a finger on it. He didn't know what had come over Garren since Palingard's fall, but Aiden wasn't even able to get a word in to warn him.

Garren is dead, what difference does it make?

Tadraem had continued talking to the crowd, but Aiden tuned him out. He looked up to see that everyone was scattering, and going back about their business.

"Stop looking so cowardly. The others may fear you now but they won't continue to fear you if you don't show them their rightful place — and their place is not to stand about reading into things that are of no consequence."

Aiden almost asked him about the incident with Garren, but thought better of it. "I haven't seen such things from the humans. Not when I've been in the outer courts to — "

Tadraem walked closer to Aiden. "Do I look foolish to you? Please tell me that you are not under the impression that I am an idiot as well. You may have thought Garren ill advised, but don't accuse me of such things. I know very well that Sara hasn't stepped foot in the outer courts since she was brought to you. I have chosen to overlook that transgression for now, but do not try my patience by acting as though I cannot see what is plainly in front of my face."

Aiden lowered his head. "I'm sorry my Lord, I didn't mean to offend you."

"Stop whining. One thing you will learn with me is that I will not tolerate juvenile behavior. I didn't allow it with Garren, and I'll certainly not bear it from you." Tadraem walked over to the man who stood, still bleeding.

"Go take care of your wound. *Hathride nortuk.*"

Aiden couldn't imagine what the humans would be like to manage had there not been a command created to instruct them to do whatever was necessary to survive. For most humans, that consisted of everyday things like hygiene, eating and sleeping. He found amusement in not giving Sara the command until morning, when he knew that he would generally be out of his chambers for the day. He would laugh to himself when he awoke to find her crumpled into a heap on the floor, her legs having given out on her in the night. This particular morning had been the worst yet. She was shaking so, he threw a blanket over her to spare himself from the irritation of seeing her. He supposed it was the chilled water that had done the trick. She would grow to appreciate his mercy when he chose to bestow it. When he did let her lie on the floor to sleep, she would be grateful, remembering the long, painful nights when she stood.

Tadraem left Aiden. Alone, he stood in the street for some time just staring at the ground. He knelt down to trace the letters with his finger. The stone was cold, jaggedly carved, each stroke of the instrument wrought with great effort. It looked like a child had written it, but there were no children in the outer courts. Only adults had been brought back to Eidolon, the children from the various regions were raised in captivity for servitude. No, definitely not by a child — if this word had been written by a human, it would have been an adult. He rose to his feet, and looked around.

Droves of humans walked past him. There was no need to separate males from females; they couldn't act upon any feelings or instincts they might have harbored otherwise. They were randomly placed alongside one another, except for the breeders, who resided in an entirely different part of the outer courts. There was a section close to the dividing wall where each breeder was granted his or her own quarters. It really wasn't for the human, but for the Ereubinian whom the human was married to.

Tadraem was right, he'd never stepped foot inside of the small house that had been set aside for Sara. It would have looked like all of the others to him, except that his name was etched onto the doorway.

He had started back toward the castle when he felt the hairs on the back of his neck stand on end. He pivoted to see what was behind him.

Nothing.

He surveyed the humans who brushed past him. Not a thing out of the ordinary. Aiden, feeling his temper flare, changed directions and walked further into the outer courts. Like a fish swimming upstream, he waded through the hundreds of humans going in the opposite direction. He pushed some of them aside, one or two falling as he began to pick up speed. Something was coming over him. He could feel it in every muscle — a prickly thing, piercing him in a thousand places all at once. Once he neared the edge, he slowed, then stopped next to the gates of the city. He stood there, his hands on his hips. His breath had started to come in halted pants and he cried out in frustration, running one hand through his hair. Again, he felt a chill race up his back. He turned, looking all around him. With wild eyes, he scanned the multitude of blank faces, searching for anything to explain what was raging in his head.

It was as if time slowed and the crowd parted to reveal, for just a hair's breadth of a second, a face. The stare that met Aiden's was enough to cool his blood permanently. The distinct jaw line and dark, knowing eyes had haunted him many times before, but not like this. Not in the light of day. Not outside of his conscious thoughts.

CHAPTER FORTY-THREE

STILL ALIVE

D uncan trudged through the snow-laden woods, his mind alive with memories that he'd long buried. It was dark, and the sounds from the feast inside the castle echoed among the trees. He kept his head down as he continued on into the forest.

When he'd first returned to Adoria, he'd walked this particular route countless times. He could trace every step blindfolded. Every rock and root had become familiar. It was all he could do to keep from thinking of what he'd left behind. It had been difficult not to return to Palingard once Gabriel was dead. He could still remember the first few months he spent in Ruiari, mourning the loss of his friend. He'd never been married, and had never expected to fall in love.

He met her daughter first. Lilly was a very bright, outgoing child, full of life and imagination. She reminded him just a little of Ariana, with perhaps a tad more restraint. He was in the marketplace when he discovered her following him. He dodged in and out of several tents, just to make sure that she was indeed on his heels, and not just coincidently taking the same path. He finally felt her eyes right on him, and twirled to catch her. She was still a girl at the time, not quite eleven years old. She stopped, openly surprised at his speed, and started giggling.

"What is it that you find so fascinating about me?" he asked, bending down to see her better. Her eyes were a deep brown with little flecks of gold.

"You have something in your pack that's moving," she said it as though he were ridiculous for not having noticed it himself.

He looked at her, wondering if she were trying to fool him, before he remembered that he'd indeed taken his furry friend along. He smiled and pulled his satchel around to undo the clasp. A small, black- and brown-striped head poked its way through the hole in the opening. Her eyes lit up as Duncan pulled the ferret from the bag and held him out for her to hold.

"Will he bite?"

"Only sour little girls, but you don't look sour to me."

She laughed and took the ferret with both hands, cradling him to her neck. "He's so soft. What's his name?"

Duncan thought about it for a moment. He hadn't named him, but the look in her eyes promised him utter disappointment if he didn't come up with one.

"Why don't you ask him?" He thought he would buy himself some time. He watched as the little girl leaned her ear down to the tiny cold nose and jerked her head up seconds later, a great revelation on her lips.

"Spoon!"

He laughed. "What?" He shook his head, not entirely certain that he'd heard her right.

"He said his name is Spoon." She shook her head. "What a silly thing to name a weasel." She then turned to address the ferret. "He should never have picked such a funny name."

"Well, I suppose you will just have to give him a new name," Duncan laughed.

She stopped stroking his fur and turned a serious glance toward Duncan. "Oh no. He says that he likes his name very much. I couldn't take it from him."

"Alright then," Duncan sighed, wondering how he'd become such a soft-hearted fool. "I do have a favor to ask of you. Do you think you could do something for me?"

She nodded.

"Spoon doesn't really have a home, and I think he would very much like to go home with you. You see I've been looking for a little girl, just like you, to keep him for me. Do you think you could do that?"

"Yes, I could. I would take very good care of him!"

Duncan patted the ferret on the top of the head. He would kind of miss him, having found him well over a year ago, but she took to him so well, that he didn't have the heart to keep such a thing for himself, not being a grown Adorian. "Run along then and introduce Spoon to his new home."

She smiled and threw one arm around him in a quick hug before running off back into the crowded market.

It was later that same day, well into the evening, that her very displeased mother found him and conveyed her disapproval for her involuntary adoption of the creature. He'd swung his door open with the idea that maybe the girl's father had come to find him, to question why Duncan had felt it necessary to give his daughter anything at all, let alone something living. But instead of the tall, dark-headed man he'd imagined, there stood a woman with one hand on her hip, the other holding out the ferret, who was struggling for solid ground. She was so perfect. Her smile had a slight crook to it, leaning down a little more on the left than the right, and her skin was like that of a child's doll. She opened her mouth to speak, but stuttered her words at first. She'd expected some strange, shady character to open the door.

"I meant no harm, my lady, and I'm sincerely sorry if I've caused you any trouble." He hadn't meant to greet her that way, "lady" wasn't a common term in the villages, but she'd struck him as having the regal nature of the Adorian women whom he'd grown accustomed to addressing upon his visits home. Aside from her clothing, there was nothing that could connect her to Middengard for him.

She smiled. "I just wanted to make sure that this wasn't a beloved pet that my daughter has somehow convinced you that she can't live without. She has a way of doing that."

He laughed, shaking his head. "No. Not at all, but I should have asked permission before telling her that it was alright. Really, I am sorry." Ironically enough Duncan had been moping about the remainder of the afternoon thinking about how he'd really grown quite attached to the little guy. Against everything in his usual demeanor, he reached out his hand for hers. "I don't believe that we have met before. My name is Duncan."

She smiled as he kissed the top of her hand. "My name is Jocelyn. I believe you have already met Lillian, my daughter." As she said the little girl's name, her head poked out from behind her mother, her eyes big and sad, and she'd no doubt been told that they were going to return Spoon to his rightful owner.

It was that night that she'd stolen his heart, that they both had. They didn't come in, or stay much longer, but in the following days and months he learned much about them. Her husband had been part of the human cavalry that had come to Palingard's aid in the siege that had killed Caelyn, Ariana's mother. He'd also lost his life that day, leaving Jocelyn a widow.

Before long, she and Duncan were married and he took Lillian as his own daughter. They tried for several years to have another child, but weren't blessed until right before Ruiari's fall. She'd just told him several days prior that she was with child. She believed it to be a son. He never had the chance to tell her where he was really from.

The day that they died was frozen in his memory. He breathed in the cold air, and stopped walking for a second. Closing his eyes, he could still see Lilly's face as she looked at him pleadingly from Garren's hold. Duncan had been trying to find her all morning.

Duncan shook as he remembered holding Lilly lifeless in his arms.

Jocelyn was already dead. She'd kissed him lightly on the cheek, as he was in between consciousness and dreams, whispering to him that she was going to the market for bread and would be right back. He awoke shortly after to the sound of horses' hooves and the screams of the Dragee.

Duncan never mentioned the unborn child to Michael. He would probably have never spoken Jocelyn's or Lillian's names again at all had it not been for Michael's keen perception. He'd approached Duncan shortly after his return to Adoria. They'd always had a sort of strained relationship since Michael had become an adult. Despite this, Michael had known something was different with Duncan. And Duncan couldn't lie to Michael any more than he could've ever lied to Michael's father. He told him of his marriage, and of their deaths and hadn't spoken of it since, including when Michael came to him earlier in the evening to tell him that it had been decided that Garren would live. *Not only that Garren would live, but that the elders were also presenting him with Jenner's sword.*

Duncan found his way to a large set of boulders that was fixed upright along the bank of a waterfall. Everything was pretty well iced over this time of the year, but it was still peaceful. He sat down and stretched his legs out in front of him. How could the elders be so foolish? What part of this didn't scream deception to them? Everything about it felt wrong.

He stopped breathing as he listened to the sound of something stirring in the bushes beside him. Holding his hand on his sword, he rose from his seat and was about investigate further when, from out of the ice-covered thicket, Ariana's dog emerged.

"What are you doing all the way out here?" Duncan asked, leaning down to pet him. "It's just as well. All who walk on two legs have lost their minds. Good thing you've got four."

Duncan returned to his seat as Koen lay down next to him. He noticed then that Koen was breathing hard and placed his hand on the dog's chest. His heart was beating furiously, as if he'd been running.

"Where have you been?" Koen just looked up at him. "I suppose it's silly to sit here and talk to a dog." He shrugged. If everyone else was allowed to go insane, he might as well follow suit. "Since we're speaking candidly here, what do you think Gabriel would've done?" Duncan let his hand lie still on Koen's back. "No, I don't suppose you *can* answer that, not having known him."

Koen let out a soft whine, almost as if he were sympathizing with Duncan.

"It's alright, friend." He rubbed the dog on the head. "I wouldn't have told Gabriel that his only son was being an idiot, either, even if he were still alive to hear it."

CHAPTER FORTY-FOUR

MY UNBORN SON

Duncan sat in the corner of the room beside Michael. The tension was palpable. Michael had paced most of the night, wondering how this morning's meeting was going to go. He was pleased to see that Duncan had at least come, considering that Michael had already written off help from the Braeden. Once everyone had arrived, at Michael's request, Jenner rose and spoke first.

"We have before us a choice. I assume Michael has spoken with many of you individually as to the reason that we're considering a return journey to Eidolon, but for any who are unaware, I'll briefly explain. Two individuals who are of importance to this realm need our assistance. Micah is an Innocent and will be condemned to death for his sympathies for Adoria. Sara, a childhood friend of Ariana's, is being held as a breeder."

Caedmon responded first. "Are you certain that he is still an Innocent?"

Michael hurt for Caedmon. His whole demeanor had changed since Reese's death.

"Garren has told us that Micah has yet to take his first soul. Michael saw it as well. This is the young man who was spared upon your last meeting with Garren's men."

"Respectfully, Jenner, I don't question who he is. I accompanied Michael and the boy back to Eidolon that day. What I question is all that has happened in his life since his return."

"He's an Innocent. After delivering Michael's message to me, I kept a close watch over him."

Michael watched as the others disregarded Garren's words. He rose from his seat to stand beside Garren.

"Do you think that I'm not aware of what transgressions Garren's committed? Do you think me a foolish leader who would send you head-first into harm's way? I'll go alone into Eidolon if that is what it takes, but after hearing claims of loyalty from so many of you over the years, it grieves me to hear you sound so resolute over your decision to abandon me when I need you the most."

Jareth started to say something in opposition, but Michael held up his hand to stop him. "What have we sacrificed so many lives for, if not for redemption? Was it vengeance that you purposed after, all this time, as you rode by my side in battle? I know some of you have lost loved ones at his hands." He looked at Duncan as he spoke. "But hating him will not bring them back, or lessen your grief. It will only kill any part of you that they loved."

Michael turned his attention back to the group. "Did you think this would be easy? What did you expect? What do you think will happen once Eidolon is defeated? It's much easier to hate than to forgive — but that's what separates us from them, the ability to choose. Hate darkness, but don't confuse those who are held captive by it with those who create it. Garren is of this realm. While his actions were dark, he did only as he was raised to do."

Caedmon's face grew tight. "How are you so convinced this isn't just another type of deception? Could he not have sensed that Ariana was your sister, and then used her as a source of weakness for you? It's purchased him free entry into our realm."

"He already had entry into this realm and could have used it at any time. There would've been no need for theatrics. All he had to do was simply walk past our borders. It's not my perception that has changed, but the circumstances."

An older woman, Juliana, with gray hair and a thin, distinguished face, spoke next. "If you deem it an acceptable risk to rescue these two, then I have faith that you'll not have to go alone. But I believe you will find it difficult to navigate Eidolon without the help of the Braeden." She was an elder of few words, like many of the other Adorian women, but there was a command to her voice that had always captured Michael's attention.

Duncan leaned with his chair tipped back against the wall and refused to respond.

"If you won't do this for me, then please consider it for Ariana. Did you not know Sara?"

Duncan was agitated already, but Michael needed his assistance and it seemed that eliciting an emotional response from him was the only way.

"Why do you think I'm sitting here? We should've talked about this already and gotten Sara out of Eidolon while we were there. This is yet another example of you being ill prepared. You concern yourself far too much with principles and manage to leave out common sense in the process."

Michael wasn't thrilled with Duncan's attitude and he could feel the shock emanating from Garren, who wouldn't have expected such outright hostility from those under Michael's command.

"Duncan, as I've already stated, I would appreciate your help, but it's not mandatory."

"It's quite mandatory. You won't be able to navigate your way through the tunnels. Our newfound brother doesn't even know they exist, much less where they lead. And now that we've made such a grand entrance, you can rest assured that Eidolon will be heavily guarded from now on."

Garren considered Duncan's words. He seemed surprised by any mention of tunnels. "My suggestion — "

"We don't need your suggestions. We've rescued our own from your castle's walls before, this is nothing new. Your mother was one of us, and you find that easy to believe, why does it shock you to learn that she wasn't alone?"

"What surprised me is that an Adorian made it to a cell in the first place."

Michael cringed as he heard the words. He knew Garren hadn't meant them the way that they'd come out, but Duncan's composure was starting to unravel.

"Not every Ereubinian has the exceptional sort of cruelty and malice that you carry for our people, for anything with a pulse. Your taste for blood is infectious and has been carried on into the hearts of your men. Things weren't always as they are now in Eidolon. Why do you think it was so easy for Gabriel to befriend your father?" Garren didn't respond. "Because he was nothing like you!"

"Wait," Michael clung to the vain hope that he'd misunderstood Duncan. "You knew Garren was Adorian before Roahn spoke for him?"

"Of course I knew. I was there." Duncan glared at him coolly. "Jareth was born of both Man and Adorian and yet he has wings. It's always been this way, being of no importance which side carries the blood of an Adorian." He turned to Garren. "Yet you were born without. More than a symbol, it means that you are not one of us."

Michael rose to his feet. "You said nothing to me when we last sat in this room, discussing the border. If you knew he was Adorian and could pose a threat to our realm by breaching the divide, why did you stay silent?"

"That's a question for your father."

"My father has nothing to do with this." His restraint was weakening. It was one thing to allow such talk to be done within this room, but quite another to place their realm in peril, no matter the excuse.

"He has everything to do with this! It's the same reason I couldn't tell you of your sister's existence. I made a promise to him, that the things we beheld and were privy to wouldn't pass beyond us. No one can make me break that vow."

"Even at the demise of your own people?"

"Beyond death, Michael. Gabriel asked if I'd be able to keep my promises, even after he was gone, and my answer to him was yes. For all the talk of ideals that you pretend to stand behind, I'm amazed that you're so shocked to find me loyal. I don't have to run my mouth to prove my allegiances."

Michael had heard enough. "It's not loyalty that drives your decisions or your promises to my father. I'm not sure what exact — "

Duncan clenched his hand into a fist and held it to his chest as he leapt to his feet. "It is my unborn son!" he screamed. "It is the child who was taken from me before I even beheld his face."

Michael's jaw fell slack.

"That is what drives this rage, Michael. Yes, you lost your father and mother, but you have lived most of your life within these walls, and that is quite a different matter from the daily torment that my men have endured. Gabriel understood that and knew that I wouldn't be swayed by lofty talk. He looked at me the day he asked for my allegiance with the same gravity that I would hold when I watched my beautiful stepdaughter murdered in cold blood. Gabriel had already lost Caelyn to the very being who was raising your newfound brethren and you want me to pretend that your father knew nothing of what Garren was capable of?"

Everyone sat in stunned silence. Michael, unsure of his words, whispered, "The Ereubinian who left her mortally wounded was Tadraem? He was also ..."

"He was responsible for Seth and Indeara's deaths as well."

Garren went pale.

Duncan shook his head, "Michael, you must understand, I cannot ..."

"Don't. You're right. My father had his reasons, though what they were, I cannot imagine."

Garren looked up. "Ruiari," he said slowly, reverently, as if he were just remembering. He closed his eyes and lowered his head. "Duncan, you have every reason to hate me. Know that could I go back and undo — "

Duncan forcefully let out a breath, interrupting him. "I offered you my own life for hers and unarmed myself in a good faith gesture, a foolish move on my part. You will not find me in that position again." He started toward the door, but stopped before he left the room. "Your chambers aren't but two halls down from Aiden's. The tunnels lead all the way into the castle itself. We were there, right alongside your lineage for hundreds of years. I had you at blade's end myself and it was the very fact that Gabriel didn't hate you that kept you alive. It was the first thing I did after Ruiari's fall. It was his words to me while he was still living that you should thank for your ability to take in breath, not the elders, or Michael, or archaic law. Had it not been for him, you would never have made it this far. I would have pierced you through that night as you slept, just as you mercilessly slay Lillian. She was merely a child, Garren. But just one of many for you. How many children have you slain since meeting Ariana?" He turned back to Michael. "I don't suppose you considered that."

Wordlessly, he left the room. Michael had trouble finding anything to say. He had been completely shocked by what Duncan had said, suddenly feeling very naïve. What else did he not know? What good was he as a leader when he knew so little of what was important? Duncan had known all along and yet Gabriel had told his own son nothing. Why? He tried to not let it hurt his feelings, but he was beginning to feel very much like Ariana had when she explained how left out she'd always felt, how unloved. He'd confided in his father about everything.

Jenner must have sensed his discomfort. "Then we will leave it as it is, the three of you will leave on first light. We will meet again tonight at the Torradh. Are we all in agreement?" Everyone nodded and began to leave, probably taking in everything that had just happened. Jenner walked over and placed his hand on Michael's shoulder.

"Walk with me. Garren, you may join us. I am an old Adorian and I am tired, but I still see things. I see that look in your eye, Michael, the same one that your father used to have, and I've sensed it in your sister. A lot has been said in the past few days."

Michael waited for the others to leave the room. Jareth lingered for a moment, until Michael raised his hand to let him know that it was alright to leave.

"Why would my father not tell me any of this? Do you have any idea how weary I grow of asking that question?"

Jenner opened the door, starting down the hall.

"Did the elders know of Garren's lineage?"

Jenner paused, rubbing his hands together to warm them. "We had our suspicions when Ariana mentioned him. Gabriel went to Eidolon without our blessing. I assume it had something to do with why he decided to keep your sister a secret from all of us. Do not be offended that he confided in Duncan. I would never have imagined that one of our daughters would have been able to capture the heart of an Ereubinian, but it seems that I have now been proven wrong twice." Jenner glanced at Garren and smiled, but Garren's thoughts were clearly elsewhere, his gaze was focused on the floor.

"I had been trying to place Duncan all of this time, I didn't remember until he spoke just now."

Michael stopped walking, and stepped in front of Garren to look at him directly. "Then you remember the girl?"

"I remember everything," Garren said, "as if it just occurred. What Duncan said as he left —"

Michael stopped him before he could finish his sentence. "We're well aware of what goes on in Eidolon. *Nech ordai neroman.*"

Garren looked at him, shocked, which Michael expected.

"Every child who is raised in the Iidolis and the Aidolis is taught the language of the Laionai. My father knew it well, as does Duncan, Jareth, Caedmon — all of us. Every time your men used such speech in our presence we were well aware of what was being said. Garren, what is important now, isn't the past — it's the future."

Jenner nodded in agreement. "Michael is right. I think to see even one human restored ... it isn't something that I expected to see in my lifetime." Jenner, usually an individual of great restraint, became overwhelmed as he spoke. He placed a hand delicately over his mouth in an attempt to shelter the trembling of his lips from their eyes. "Were it my own daughter who was enduring what this child is living through. Garren, I once rode as Michael does, as an Adorian knight, and I remember many were the days that I lived and breathed the calling of a shepherd of man. But it wasn't until I met Elspeth that I truly understood the depth of the sadness that the human race endures. The fathers who must watch their daughters and wives enter into a defiled marriage bed. The sons who toil for those very men who have stolen their brides and the wives who must watch them sire sons who will grow up to hate them.

"It may be the simplest of all things that destroys the darkness, so we mustn't overlook even the smallest of advances. For all of our efforts over the centuries, not one single human has ever had his soul restored."

Though Garren remained quiet, Michael could see the first signs of a new being emerging from the shadow of who Garren used to be.

Jenner stopped them. "I have promised the rest of the day, until this evening, to my sweet wife, so I will leave the two of you to finish discussing what needs to be done in order to bring them back here. We will see one another again tonight." Jenner bowed to Michael, then disappeared down a flight of stairs.

"We have much to discuss," Michael said. "While I know a good deal about Eidolon, I know very little of your former friend."

"The Laionai and the Moriors concern me, not Aiden." Garren flexed his hand at his side as he spoke. "Considering that Micah wasn't the only one to lay down his sword, I think it's a safe assumption that the Laionai will make his execution public, as an example. There is a gathering in honor of the Goddess, held every year on the 6th of Jessup. Let's hope that they've planned it for that event, and not any sooner." As Garren spoke, Michael remembered the Ereubinian who had approached them in the cell.

"One of your men came upon us as we were leaving the cell. He was loyal to you, and I assume by their reaction to you in the outer courts that he was not alone in his allegiance."

Garren stopped walking and looked out of one of the large picture windows that lined the hallway. His eyes were unfocused. "Malachai. I don't understand why any Ereubinian, knowing what they were risking, would do anything like what he did. Deceiving the Moriors is a serious offense."

"What are you not saying?" Michael asked.

"My men watched my reaction to Aiden's defiance — you wouldn't care to hear the details of it. I have a difficult time believing that any of them would concern themselves with anything but their own survival. They obeyed me out of fear, Michael. I've done nothing to warrant their loyalty."

"Yet they laid down their swords at the sight of your resistance. There is loyalty there, regardless of the reason. If we fail, what are the chances of your own men going against you?"

Garren shook his head. "We cannot fail. If we do, we won't live to see this realm again."

CHAPTER FORTY-FIVE
UPON THE
WAKING HOUR

The night was dark and cold. The wind blew as faint as an infant's breath across the surface of the lake, gently rocking the ice fragments that still remained from the harshest part of winter. Not all of the fallen could be brought back to Adoria, but pyres had been fashioned as symbols for all who had been lost. The landscape was dotted in the distance with great fires that had been lit in their honor.

Michael came before them, wearing a solid black robe. He carried a thin, leather-bound book. Duncan stood next to Ariana, who wore a simple white gown. The sleeves were loose at the elbow, billowing around her wrists.

Michael raised one hand into the air and held aloft his father's sword. He read several passages aloud in Adorian, then read the names of each of the fallen Adorians. Ariana closed her eyes, swallowing back sobs for what she'd done.

Duncan put his arm around her and pulled her to him. "What is done is done. Your heart was in the right place," he whispered.

She looked up at him, thinking that it sounded like something her father would have said. She mouthed the words 'thank you,' and bent her head back down.

As Michael finished reading the names, the elders came to him and lit their torches from the single candle that sat sheltered from the wind at his feet. They carried them out to the water's edge to set each of the flats alight. Ariana kept her eyes fixed downwards, listening to the muffled cries of loved ones. As she rose, she caught a glimpse of Garren through the sea of faces. He was next to Jenner, who had chosen not to stand with the other elders.

Michael walked to the largest pyre, and with the help of several others, pushed it into the frigid waters. As soon as it was afloat, he dropped his candle onto the kindling, setting it aflame. Soon after, the other pyres were set into the water and lit as well.

Michael had come to her earlier in the afternoon, telling her about what had happened after their meeting. It reassured Ariana for Michael to confide in her, asking her about Father, and revealing that he felt a little betrayed that he hadn't told Michael about Garren's parentage. She wasn't sure how much she had been able to comfort him, but she had tried.

Michael stepped back from the shore and motioned for Ariana to come forward. Duncan reached over and squeezed her shoulder as she moved through the crowd. Her heart fluttered as everyone parted, but it was something she needed to do. Michael had explained to her what would happen during the Torradh; when he mentioned a song that was sung in remembrance of the dead, she had offered to sing it.

Michael spoke a short prayer as she came to stand beside him, instructing all to kneel at the end. She was relieved when Michael had told her earlier that they would stay facing downwards until she was finished. Every time her father returned, he always asked her to sing to him, even when she was little. While she loved music, it had always been difficult for her to sing in front of others. She wondered how many times her father had heard the Torradh sung in his lifetime and if he'd ever imagined that his own daughter would one day stand before their people for that very purpose. She took the book from Michael's hands and took a deep breath, hoping she would remember the tune.

Upon the waking hour, I shall think of you
My heart grown still in sorrow
Till the setting of the future sun
When there shall be no morrow
Then we will meet again.

Upon the waking hour, I shall speak of you
Your memory etched in stone
Till the setting of the future sun
When all shall then be known
Then we will meet again
Upon the waking hour, I shall weep for you
My soul in longing waits

Till the setting of the future sun
When Adoria dances with Fate
Then we will meet again

Upon the waking hour, I shall sing for you
My voice grown weak in sound
Till the setting of the future sun
When victory resounds
Then we will meet again

Upon the waking hour, I shall wait for you
My home no longer here
Till the setting of the future sun
When I shed a final tear
Then we will meet again

She'd learned Adorian as a child, but the words, now sung from her lips, felt unfamiliar. When she finished, she knelt down as he'd instructed her. She could feel the chill from his body as he stood above her, shivering in the coolness of the night air.

"Go then, and speak unto our brethren who have left us. May the ancients bless and keep you."

Everyone then rose to their feet in reverent silence and came to the water's edge, lighting small candles from the torches the elders held. Ariana watched as all down the shore, tiny flames flickered to life like a thousand fallen stars. It was something to behold for certain, but more than anything, it broke her spirit to know that she'd caused their deaths.

Michael leaned down to whisper in her ear. "Had you not already stolen Garren's heart, I think hearing you sing might very well have done it."

She felt his absence as he left her to join the elders in their own private ceremony. Michael had told her their father used to lead them in the *Teirlith Eisla*, the old prayer, when he was alive. Michael now led the prayer.

Still kneeling, she closed her eyes and whispered a prayer that her father had taught her. She could still hear his gravelly voice reciting the words to her, before she was old enough to articulate them herself. She hadn't said anything to Michael about it, but wondered if it was the same prayer.

After a time, a hand on her shoulder pulled her from her solitude. She wasn't sure how long she'd been there, but when she looked up, she saw the landscape was dark, the candles having long blown out, the shore deserted. She hadn't heard Koen approach either, but he had come to her side while she prayed.

Garren leaned down and said, "The night grows much colder, and I don't want to leave you out here alone."

He reached out and helped her to her feet, then wrapped his cloak around her.

"It is chilly," she whispered, pulling it closer to her.

"You sing beautifully."

She looked at him and smiled, the darkness hiding the depth of her expression. "Thank you for the compliment, though I wish it were a different occasion."

Garren nodded. "As do I."

They stopped as they reached a gate that opened to a steep stairwell, edging its way up the mountain. She looked to the castle, and then to Garren. "I'm not quite ready to end this night. Walk with me?"

He reached out, taking her hand in his. "What are you thinking?"

She kept her head down as they walked back down to the shore of the lake, Koen following beside them. "I was thinking about my father."

Garren's hand felt solid against hers, as she shivered, both from her remaining grief and the cold. He placed his other hand on top of hers and brought it to his mouth, absentmindedly warming it with his breath, as if it were something he had done before.

Suddenly he paused, realizing his actions. "I never truly breathed, nor opened my eyes before I came upon you in the woods. I don't understand it, but I am hushed in its presence."

"I saw it in your eyes," she said. "And I saw the same fear and confusion in your eyes as I stood before you at the gate in Eidolon."

"The dream," he whispered, "I thought you'd cursed me, yet was terrified for you all the same."

She started to reach up to touch his face, but withdrew her hand, remembering his response when she had done so in the cell.

He grabbed her hand before it reached her side, and pulled it to his cheek. "I wanted nothing more than for you to be by my side. Had I been executed, I would have spent my last hours wishing, quite pathetically, for one last kiss, for one final glimpse of your face." He grinned. "And you, my lady, damn well know it."

Ariana ran her fingers over his skin, tracing every line until she came to the scar her brother had left on his face. He cringed and started to open his mouth to apologize again for the past when she interrupted him.

"Hush," she whispered. "Perhaps you should stop fretting over the life you've left behind and pay a little more attention to the one ahead you."

"You say that with an invitation in your eyes, yet wasn't it you who told me I'd have to do something akin to saving your life if I were ever to be granted permission to kiss you again?"

She shook her head in mild protest. "That wasn't what I meant by what's before you."

He closed the distance between them. "Isn't it?" he whispered.

Ariana cleared her throat and tried to appear disinterested, despite the heat in her cheeks. Why did he have to make this so awkward? This apparently amused Garren more than a little bit because when he laughed, it brought tears to his eyes.

"Your bark is so much worse than your bite. You can kill trained warriors, walk fearlessly into a room full of high-ranking Ereubinian elite, sass an Adorian sovereign who most wouldn't consider even inconveniencing, tell the High Lord of Eidolon to his face that you could care less who he is, then go to him, alone and unarmed, pretending to be a ghost come to torment him and yet," he lifted her chin with his knuckle, "you don't know what to do with yourself now, when things aren't on your terms."

"Perhaps you're stretching to say that things aren't on my —"

He framed her face with both hands and before she could say a word, he pressed his mouth against hers with enough passion to silence even her soul from thinking about anything but the warmth of his kiss.

Garren moved one arm to her waist to press her body closer to his, wrapping the other around her shoulders to caress the back of her neck. Her breath caught in her throat as she moaned against him, against the feel of his tongue teasing hers with gentle strokes.

He held onto her for a brief moment after she pulled away, lifting his head to kiss her brow. His once-steady hands trembled as he enclosed her hands once again in his. "I know not where our souls have met, but I have never loved another. I am more certain of it than I am of anything in this life."

Ariana closed her eyes, breathing in his scent. Her voice cracked as she tried to speak, finding that she'd lost the words.

Garren lifted her face to his. "It was not chance that led me to follow you into the woods, nor could it be an accident that you were hidden away in Palingard."

He reached up, brushing a strand of her hair aside that had fallen loose from the hood of the cloak. "You really didn't have any idea that you were Adorian?"

She shook her head. "I thought they didn't exist, that it was man's way of inventing something to have faith in, that the darkness had grown so great that even false light would illuminate it."

Thoughts of her father, words he'd said on the subject, came back to mind. "My father, who abhorred any mention of Adoria, left Palingard ten years ago and didn't return. I set out in the path that I watched him take when he last departed, not knowing where it led. I can still remember running barefoot in the night, following him as far as I could go. He never knew I was there. We'd argued and I wanted to apologize. He left sooner than he had expected to, and didn't say goodbye. Michael disagrees, but I think he chose to leave early because he was angry with me."

Garren shook his head. "Michael is wise, believe him. He treats you as if he has never been separated from you, so I doubt that he would outright lie to you, even to spare your feelings."

She leaned her head back against the warmth of his chest, her body shaking from the cold.

He leaned down and whispered, "It is too cold out here for you, let's go inside."

"I'm alright," she murmured. He was right, it was freezing, but her desire to be alone with him and away from the earshot of others kept her from agreeing.

"Shall we walk farther?"

She nodded, keeping her hand held in his, and they started back down the shore. "I saw a bandage on Sara's hand. I assume Aiden didn't put it there."

"I did. I hadn't seen Sara since … it had been quite a few days. I came across her when I entered Aiden's chambers. She wasn't supposed to be there." Garren's eyes went unfocused as he recalled it. "She faced the floor as she sat curled up along the far wall, near the window. When I lifted her face, I saw the bruises. She had a cut on her hand as well, and I tended to it with what I could find in his room. He came in before I was finished."

Garren exhaled sharply. "I want to — I have, but I can't rightly call him cruel, because of my own transgressions."

She squeezed his hand. "There are moments in your life prior to now that contain traces of the man who stands before me." She stopped him again.

He didn't immediately respond. "Maybe when I was a child. When I was still an Innocent, but none after that. Ariana, you have such a gentle spirit. I pray you never fully understand the weight of the blood that I have spilled."

"I watched my mother die before my eyes, and not a kind death. Michael told me earlier this afternoon that it was your mentor who took her from us. Do you not think that being raised by such a vile being would affect you?" Garren did not respond. "The human who was chosen for you to marry — were you unkind to her?"

He shook his head. "No. But I can't promise you that I would have been kind had I married her prior to Palingard's fall."

"I don't believe you would have treated anyone like Aiden has treated Sara. Your response to this girl is proof enough."

Garren brought her hand to his lips, and kissed it. "No, but some wounds go deeper than the surface." He glanced at the now motionless waters of the lake.

"Michael said you are leaving at first light?"

He nodded. "Don't be offended by what I am about to say. I just need you to know that Sara will be changed."

"I know that," she said softly.

He shook his head. "You know that she will be different, but what none of us can know is how long it will take her to heal from all of this, or if she will at all. I saw the blood on her gown. There were more wounds than I could tend to, Ariana. When we return, her hands will be bound and she will probably be under the influence of whatever the healer can provide to dull her senses. I didn't want that to take you by surprise."

"When … I mean, will you not return her soul sooner?"

"I won't even attempt it until we're well past our borders."

She smiled as he finished his sentence. As he looked at her, it was clear by his expression that he didn't understand the sentiment behind the gesture. "You said, 'our borders.'" She said the words slowly, each syllable precious. She wanted nothing more than for him to loosen the burdens that he carried, and while this was not a promise of such things, it was a hint of what could be.

"I didn't mean …"

She silenced him with a kiss. "You are one of us," she whispered, her lips still touching his. He smiled, but remained still. She leaned back, met his eyes, and found a trace of mirth in them. "If you would prefer your own company, I'd be happy to turn around and — "

He grabbed her just as she'd looked away. Then, with such tenderness that it made Ariana weak, he traced her lips with the pad of his thumb, as if to memorize every inch. When he kissed her, the world fell away beneath her.

The sensation was strong enough to make Ariana feel as though her heart were no longer beating. Her eyes were closed, but visions were before her. They were no longer in front of the lake, but in the temple in Arcadia, haunted by faint images of another embrace, another kiss. She heard both of their voices, hushed in the darkness, at first unable to understand the words, just that they were laden with sorrow and weighted by fear.

Then, Garren's voice, though she could still feel his lips unmoving on hers, said soothingly in the darkness, "I will find you."

She pulled away and looked at Garren, searching for any trace of what she had just experienced. He tightened his grip, letting one hand slide through her hair, and leaned down to rest his cheek on the top of her head.

She couldn't speak, hearing the echo of his words in her mind — the looming feel of darkness like the swell of warmth before a spring storm trailing along her skin.

CHAPTER FORTY-SIX

HOLLOW

Aiden was too afraid to move. He stood frozen, his eyes searching the crowd. He reached to his belt, fingering his dagger lightly to assure himself that it was still there, though if *he* … were out there, it would do Aiden little good.

After several minutes, he started to wade back through the humans to the castle. He couldn't look at them for fear of seeing him again so he kept his eyes to the ground until he reached the wall. Everything appeared as it should have; nothing out of place, no glances, no whispers. He laughed under his breath, having convinced himself that he'd been hallucinating. To consider anything else was ludicrous.

After he entered the south hall, he returned to his room and paused. Something was wrong. He couldn't quite place what it was. There was a stillness in the air, an absence of something perhaps, the lingering of something that had been there, but was now gone. He glanced at Sara, her eyes no more focused than her voice sounded whenever she spoke with him. *Hollow*. His head hurt, anger swelling inside him. He pushed his fear to the back of his mind. He had other things to consider. Things like Garren's sudden shift in perception. Aiden had been so angry with Garren that when he saw the girl Tadraem had described to him, he felt nothing but blind hatred.

Now, in the quiet of his room, Garren's absence became real. He felt discomfort in his chest and rubbed the tightness away with the heel of his hand. The room spun and he felt uneasy in his stance. He leaned over onto the bed, lowering himself down to rest on the very edge.

He looked at Sara. "I would never have suspected him of treason. Not him. When we were children we would talk of when everything would come to fruition, when the realm of man would finally fall. How weak he was to betray his beliefs so easily." His face warmed and he felt his eyes sting. "I hate him still, even as he lies dead and rotting in the ground."

His voice trembled as he spoke, his hand shuddering as he brought it to his face to wipe the sweat from his brow and the tears as they fell from his eyes. He rose from his seat and walked to the window, suddenly smelling the horrid stench of burning bones and flesh. Their cries had been drowned out by the sound of the all-consuming flames. As much as they deserved it, such a thing was not something he cared to see, the death of the very same men who'd just ridden with them into Palingard and had stood by Garren's side. They knew better. Garren had told them on many occasions that were he ever to falter in his decisions, to do what the faith would have them do —had he not faltered?

Then, hesitantly, he sat beside Sara. He leaned sideways and looked into her eyes. "There is hatred for me in those eyes." He gripped her chin with his hand, pressing his fingers into her skin and turned her face to his, truly looked at her for the first time since he'd met her. Her hair was dark blonde and fell thick at her shoulders. Her eyes were light in color, not quite blue or green. Her face was bruised in places, several cuts still healing along the outer edges of her jaw from where he'd hit her, not remembering to remove his metal-adorned gloves.

Sara's lip was cut at the lower right corner of her mouth. He watched her chest rise and fall with breath, the nape of her neck move where her blood flowed just beneath the surface of her skin. She was by far more beautiful than any of the other breeders he'd seen. He ran his hands through her hair, something that had never crossed his mind before now. It felt soft in his hands, sliding between his fingers. It reminded him of a moment that was nothing but a vague memory now, standing in the darkened hallway, resting along the wall next to her. He was but eight years old at the time. He'd kissed her. It was brief, but he remembered her hair more than anything. It was dark, like the color of night. It was nothing like Sara's, but it felt the same.

The tightness in his chest deepened, as though all of the muscles were contracting at once, making it impossible for him to draw a full breath. He closed his eyes, blinking away more tears. Then, before he'd considered his actions, he leaned into Sara and brushed his lips against hers. For a moment, he lost himself to the feel of her gentle mouth and a sense of comfort that he'd never known, but when he cradled the back of her head in his hand and deepened the kiss, pressing harder against her wounded lip, Sara whimpered in pain and woke him from his trance.

He withdrew, horrified that he'd kissed her. He wiped his mouth, cursing under his breath and rose to his feet. He had to repeat it in his mind to make certain of it. He'd kissed her — not something looked upon favorably by any Ereubinian, faithful or otherwise. He reached his hand back and struck her cheek, his palm scraped against her lip, splitting it open the rest of the way.

His hand shook as he stood and he held it in front of him, as if it weren't his own. He flexed it, watching his once familiar skin move as the joints bent to his will. Sara sat listless, her back against the wall, blood trickling down her jaw. It ran down the nape of her neck and stained the neck of her gown. He could take no more. Without a word, he turned to leave, pausing in the doorway. It was still there — whatever he'd sensed when he'd entered the room. But he shook it free as he crossed the threshold. There were greater things afoot and his rightful place at the right hand of Ciara was coming. He could feel it.

He resisted the urge to turn around as he made his way down the hall and around the corner, finally coming to the dining hall where he rid himself of it completely. This was his time, and he wouldn't let it escape him as easily as Garren had.

CHAPTER FORTY-SEVEN

DID YOU POISON HIM?

"I feel strange not going with you," Jareth said, leaning against the side of the stable as Michael finished securing his saddle.

"If anything happens, and we do not return ..."

Jareth stood straight again, interrupting Michael before he could finish. "I have no doubt in your safe return."

Michael nodded. "Your faith will be with us on our journey, but I need you to reassure me that you'll take care of them if things don't go as I intend."

Jareth sighed, moving dirt around on the ground with the tip of his boot. "Of course. You have my word."

Michael put his hand on Jareth's shoulder, and leaned in to give him a brief embrace before he turned to leave. "*Gahai werndt thanos.*"

"*Gahai werndt thanos,*" Jareth repeated the words as if he didn't want to say them.

Michael did not hear Jareth move as he left the stables, leading his horse out into the haze of the still dark morning. It would be another three hours before the sun rose.

Garren was already saddled and waiting for him. Duncan sat, already mounted, several feet away from Garren. It was obvious they hadn't spoken to each other. Without a word, they began their ride back to Eidolon.

Michael thought about the night prior. He hadn't had a chance to mourn his men who'd been killed in their attempt to intercept Garren outside of Palingard. So much had happened so fast since then that once Michael was finally behind closed doors, away from everything else, he felt a slight sense of release. He'd led the men in the *Teirlith Eisla* and felt his composure give way. He almost hadn't been able to finish, but Jareth had been next to him and it served to keep his focus. The faces of the widows and children who had been left behind haunted him, lit by the dim candles as they'd stood on the beach. Adoria had suffered much. It could not have all been for naught. His heart was heavy. Even riding next to Duncan was unwieldy. He wondered what Kael, the previous Archorigen, would have done.

There had been many times when Michael had wondered, if he would be able to do all that would be required of him as Archorigen. He remembered his father speaking with him when he was just a boy, telling him that one day he would lead. What secrets did he keep from them? What lay hidden in his mind that he would not release even upon his death? He had told Duncan not to reveal Garren's birth. Why? What purpose could it have had?

Michael tried to recall the instances where Garren had been present. He could not remember clearly what his father had said, but he had spared his life on more than one occasion. He supposed that was the real reason he had done so himself, when he had him defeated. The only real time that came to mind was right before his father's death. They were almost a week's journey from Adoria, far out into the furthest regions of the Northlands. Michael was twenty-three at the time. It had been one of the few times his father had accompanied Michael into battle. The morning was much like this one, the fog still rolling along the forest floor.

The beginning of the battle was a blur in his mind. He could not clearly recall where the Ereubinians had come from, only that they were without the Moriors. The fight ensued around him; the clang of sword upon sword pierced his ears, causing them to ring well after everything was over. He had seen his father fighting Garren. He rushed upon them just as his father had Garren pinned. Even as a young soldier, Garren had been swift and difficult to evade. He didn't recall everything that was said, but he did remember the look on his father's face, because it had confused him at the time. He had paid it little mind and tucked it away, forgotten until the day Michael heard Garren speak Adorian in Eidolon.

His father had Garren pinned against a tree, sword held against his abdomen. Michael fought those who tried to come to Garren's aid, but he could see what was going on from the corner of his eye.

Gabriel made Garren kneel in front of him. Keeping the sword in place, he pulled a small bottle from the pouch that hung at his belt. The same one that Ariana was so fond of. He forced Garren to drink from it. Michael turned his head to see Garren crumple to the ground.

"Did you poison him?" he shouted at his father.

Gabriel rushed to his feet, coming to Michael's side as an agile

Ereubinian approached him from behind. Piercing the man through, he then pulled a dagger from its sheath and slit the throat of another who had come upon him from the side.

"No. But I wasn't going to give him the chance to rise against me after releasing him. I know that look on your face, my son. You want to know why I didn't take his life. You'll understand some day. Perhaps when you're all he has left in the world. Just remember this — our tongue is a living tongue, spoken only by those whose blood is pure. Never forget this and show mercy accordingly."

The fight had continued to rage for a while, but everything else had faded in his mind. Now, thinking back upon that day, knowing all that he now knew, it would have made sense for his father to have been careful with Garren, having known and been allies with his parents. Seeing his friend's son being raised against everything he knew to be right and true would have been more than difficult. Michael couldn't imagine it. He began to have a deeper understanding of many conversations that his father had pulled him into over the years. Garren rode in silence next to him and Michael wondered if Garren would remember the incident, but thought perhaps with Duncan at such close range, it would be more thoughtful to bring it up at another time.

They stopped to rest their horses several hours into their journey, just outside of Adoria's northern border. The tall, thin trees loomed, very different from the large redwoods that scattered Adoria's landscape. The ground was thick with wet, rotting undergrowth.

All of Middengard was now dark, save a few areas of the Netherwoods. He'd tried to keep his thoughts positive while they continued to wage war for Middengard's protection, but now it struck him how desolate it all had become. Everything had seemed so much brighter when he was a young knight. Now, as Archorigen, Michael knew what it was like to fear for their safety and bear the concerns of the world that the younger generations would inherit. He finally understood the burden his father must have been carrying.

He shuddered as his mind wandered to his sister. He'd held her nearly lifeless in his arms. He surprised himself at how well he was handling her affections for Garren. What felt like just moments ago, he'd stood outside of Eidolon's castle doors, ready to kill Garren for even mentioning her name. He'd begun to learn that his own perceptions could be deceiving, his feelings apt to betray him. His father had warned him of this, but he'd never listened. He had been more tied up in the rush and fervor of his ideals, just as Duncan had said. Why did he have to learn everything the hard way?

Even with Genny he had regrets. He'd been so distanced from her at times. Ariana wasn't completely wrong when she'd spoken so harshly about his relationship with her. It was partly the fear of losing Genny and partly the frustration of being helpless. He could do nothing against her illness and it nearly drove him mad. He should have clung to her in those moments, but instead he busied himself with everything but her. She'd meant so much to him, but he'd never really told her, much like he'd never told his father. He thought perhaps it was the reason he had taken so quickly to Ariana. It felt like redemption for him.

The only time he had been able to voice everything to Genny had been in the letter he'd written and laid in her grave. It was poorly written, his emotions scattered and unconnected. Michael could still remember when he'd asked Jenner for Genevieve's hand in marriage. Jareth overheard it and came bursting into the room, interrupting what would have been a reverent moment. He sheepishly grinned at the two Adorians' lack of a response, murmuring an apology for interrupting. It made Michael chuckle to recall it.

That moment had held in its brevity all the possibilities in the world. His future had looked bright, as had hers. It reminded Michael of the way Ariana had described Sara — her innocence, her strength despite her gentility. There hadn't been a day that had gone by that hadn't brought with it stories of things Sara had done or said over the years. Michael felt as though he knew her and now, knowing she'd been in Eidolon, he regretted having not considered saving Sara sooner, just as Duncan had said.

"Please hold on," he whispered.

Garren, having somehow noticed Michael's sentiments, steered his horse closer. "Sara is strong, Michael. The last time I saw her, she had resistance in her eyes. Many of the others have given up hope and begun to adjust to their surroundings, but she had not. They give birth without so much as a whimper of pain, and yet she cried at the act of betraying her friend, showing strength that I've never seen in a human."

Michael hadn't considered that Sara could be with child. He prayed against it, though more for her sake than for his. "You said you chose Sara for Aiden. Did you mean that literally?"

Garren swallowed hard, and took a deep breath before answering him. It appeared to be a subject that he was afraid for Michael to broach. "Yes. She was among several others who had been taken from Palingard." Michael knew there was something that Garren wasn't telling him.

"You are uncomfortable with this. I shouldn't have asked you."

Duncan overheard the conversation, and addressed Michael. "What he is uncomfortable with is your response when you find out how they are chosen. They are lined up like cattle, and made to remove their clothing. It is humiliating. They are inspected like objects at auction. It disgusts me to even consider the thought. Sara will no doubt recall every excruciating minute of it. And what about the wardens, you ask? They delivered her to the slaughter in the first place; they have free reign over the humans until they are claimed. Even then, it is not always a promise they will leave the soulless humans alone. Garren, if it makes you feel any better about your sins, your own father had to endure watching your mother stand bare before the same lot of your breed, falsely pretending to choose her as his wife, when he was already well familiar with every inch of her, already willing to die for her sake. Pain is not the word I would use."

Michael felt both sickened by what he had said and furious at Duncan for having said it in such a manner. Garren would probably not have considered how his parents would have to have conducted themselves in order to remain undetected.

"Enough!" Michael roared. "Is there no sense of honor in your blood at all?"

Garren stopped his horse and dismounted to stagger behind a tree, sick to his stomach.

Michael faced Duncan again. "If you're going to continue to act out your hatred for him, go back. You're nothing but a detriment to me this way. Sara is counting on us and if you feel so deeply about saving her, as your mouth has just proclaimed, then behave in a manner befitting to Braeden. You dishonor the Aidolis and you dishonor me."

Michael softened his voice, leaning closer to him. "As Adorian Knights, we are called to a higher standard. Don't let your years of life among the humans persuade you otherwise."

Michael dismounted and found his way back to where Garren was standing. He was leaning against the tree, his chest heaving as he took in air in shortened breaths.

"I'm sorry, Michael." His face was pale. He leaned back over and threw up again.

"You owe no apologies."

Garren spit to the side and wiped his mouth with the back of his sleeve. "He's right. Everything he has said is true. I have become everything that my father hated — everything that brought loathing and dread into my mother's heart." He closed his eyes and rested his head against his hand.

"Your father shares your past, Garren. Do not forget that. He made the same change that you have made. He would know your footsteps intimately." Michael placed his hand on the tree next to Garren's face, and leaned in. "Who better to understand what you're going through?"

Garren rolled his head on his hand to look at Michael. He said nothing for a long time. "I couldn't have done it, Michael." He closed his eyes, and almost appeared as though he was about to be sick again, but let out a slow, purposeful breath instead. "I would rather die than even imagine Ariana in those circumstances. Why didn't my father force her to leave?"

Duncan's voice behind them surprised Garren, who still had his eyes closed, causing him to jump. "He tried." Duncan cleared his throat, and looked away from them. "He loved Indeara and had no interest in her suffering, but she was unwilling to leave his side, no matter the cost. Gabriel did everything in his power to protect her while they were in the outer courts, but his ability to guard her was limited once Eidolon became more familiar with our generation of Braeden. He couldn't save her from everything. I remember well the day your father died. Gabriel mourned him as if he were of our realm. Of our brethren."

Michael could tell that Duncan was only speaking out of respect for his wishes, but it was appreciated nonetheless.

"I know that Tadraem killed my mother. What I don't know are the circumstances behind it."

Michael was surprised to hear Garren ask. His words were faint, as if he did not want to hear the answer. Duncan glanced at Michael, almost asking permission to tell him. Garren spoke before Michael had a chance to give an answer. "Knowing won't change anything, but it will put such questions to rest for me."

"Indeara was given no preferential treatment and stayed mainly beyond the dividing wall. Tadraem discovered your father's connections with our realm, and came to your mother when she was alone. Gabriel halted Tadraem before he had chance to rape her, which was his intention after having savagely beaten her, but he was too late to save her from her injuries. Gabriel never told your father it was Tadraem who'd done it because he felt Seth had suffered enough, and to reveal that it was his brother would be too much to bear. Even then, Seth never recovered from it."

Garren sank to the ground, his legs giving way beneath him. He lowered his head into his hands.

Michael was almost too stunned to speak. "Tadraem is your uncle?"

Garren shook his head, still peering down to the ground. It appeared to be more out of disbelief than denial.

"Let me guess," Michael looked at Duncan, "something else my father asked you to keep to yourself?"

"No." Duncan's words were sincere. "Michael, I genuinely thought he knew."

Garren raised his head, a horrified look on his face. "I was always told that he was a close confidant of my father's."

Michael had more to learn about Eidolon than he thought. How could Garren not know this?

Duncan answered as if he'd read his mind. "Family is of little consequence in Eidolon, outside of simply dividing humans from the Ereubinians. Unless Tadraem or another family member told him, he wouldn't have known. I am guessing by your reaction that you don't have any other immediate relatives living?"

Garren again shook his head. "No. My grandmother was the parent of lineage, and she died before I was born. Tadraem told me she died while my father was still a child. I had no idea he was talking about his own mother. Why would he have kept this from me?"

Duncan dismounted as he answered. "Considering your birth and that he knew you were of our realm, I would say it was to keep you indebted to him. Taking you in out of obligation would have held different weight than believing him to have done it out of respect and admiration for Seth. He could have also been told not to tell you."

Michael turned toward Duncan. "What do you mean?"

"I am not certain that Tadraem is the only one who knows about Garren's true lineage."

Garren nodded. "As I said in the council meeting, Ciara must know. Why else would she have thought it possible to take a human army beyond your borders if she didn't know that I am able to pass through unaccompanied? There has been talk of the chosen one."

Michael rubbed his chin with his hand. "Then Ciara believes the time of the Oni has come?"

"It's not a prophecy that is widely read in our realm, but I have read it and at one time believed it to be true. And there are sects within Middengard that have revived the old faith." Garren looked away. "But what does she want from Ariana, from me?"

Neither Michael nor Duncan had an answer for this. Michael walked back to his horse, taking the reins in his hands. "Perhaps she fears Ariana could defeat the Oni? I truly don't know."

Duncan walked over to Garren and, to Michael's wonder, he reached out his hand to help him to his feet.

"I won't offer my hand again if you refuse it."

Garren took his hand, uncomfortably rising.

"We're lingering too long here. I can feel it." Michael said, looking around them. The air felt thick and stiff. They mounted their horses and continued on, a shadow of things to come looming in the distance.

END OF BOOK ONE

GLOSSARY

Adoria: Realm of the Adorians, it is protected by a mystical divide that allows entry only for those of Adorian blod. All others pass over it as if Adoria did not exist.

Adorian Divide: The divide between the realm of Adoria and Middengard. Little is known about when it came into existence or how the magic works. Only those of Adorian blood, be it full or half, are able to cross over without aid; all others pass through it as if Adoria didn't exist.

Adorian Knight: Winged Adorian warriors, trained in the Iidolis.

Aidolis: Home of the Braeden.

Arcadia: Twin city to Eidolon, once ruled by Irial and Èanna. The first human soul was taken just beyond the gates by Ereubus, who was then banished to the Immortal Labyrinth by Èanna.

Arch Elders: Elected leaders of the twenty-four provinces of Adoria who reside in Cyphrus and convene with the Archorigen.

Archorigen: Elected sovereign of Adoria. This position was created by the last king at the dawn of The Age of Guardians.

Artesh: Home of Adoria's main university.

Azrian: The Dark Lord of Hothrendaire, he once ruled the realm of light. His fall tore an irreparable hole in the fabric of existence.

Bedowyn: Orphaned Adorian children, most of whom serve in Cyphrus.

Braeden: Elite Adorian warriors, chosen at birth for service to Middengard, whose wings were removed at birth. Trained from infancy, they were taught in the art of warfare and the customs of the human realm. Deadly accurate in their ability to both wield a sword and shoot a bow, they held off the total depravity of man for centuries.

Braeden Underground: Tunnels forged below Eidolon that are protected in the same way as Adoria itself. The tunnels origins are also unknown.

Breeders: Humans, both male and female, chosen to continue the lineage of St. Ereubus.

Creator: Also referred to as Father, Father of Light or His Beloved. He is never referred to by name because legend holds that his name is unspeakable by all but his own child, Èanna. Both Adoria and Middengard once worshipped him as the creator of all life, but after Ciara's entrance into Middengard, all mention of the "Adorian God" was forbidden.

Cyphrus: Capitol of Adoria

Dark Goddess: The immortal Ciara who betrayed the creator by siding with Azrian.

Èanna: The Father's only daughter.

Eidolon: Once the heart of Middengard, Eidolon became home to the Ereubinians after Arcadia, its twin city, was destroyed.

Ereubinians: Gifted by the Dark Goddess with the power to steal the souls of other men, they rule Middengard. Also known as the blessed or The Lineage.

Garden of Dedication: Winter Garden in Adoria where a statue is erected in memoriam of every fallen city in Middengard.

High Lord: The Laionai's chosen servant, the High Lord holds dominion over every Ereubinian ruler in Middengard.

High Priest: Considered the voice of the Goddess, the High Priest is the position directly below the High Lord. Directs the activities in Observance and holds power over the vessels who have been chosen in service of the Goddess at the Temple.

Hothrendaire: The Dark Realm, opposite of the Realm of Light and home to Azrian.

Iidolis: School for the Adorian Knights.

Laionai: Once kings of Man, they chose sides with the Dark Goddess upon her entrance into Middengard and were cursed by the Father. Now they speak and act as one consciousness. They see through the Mortal Coil and the Moriors.

Lycus: Northern realms of Middengard.

Middengard: The realm of Man. Ruled primarily by the Ereubinians who took control of it at the end of the first age of war. Eidolon is its capital city.

Morior: Creatures ruled through command of the Laionai, they are rumored to be gifts to the Goddess from the Dark Lord.

Mortal Coil: Made of collected human souls, the Mortal Coil is held beyond the inner sanctum of the temple in Eidolon. In it is every memory, every feeling, every instance of pain or pleasure felt by any stolen soul.

Observance: Ereubinian religious ceremony.

Old World: Adorian structures that predate the first Age of War.

Oni: The Chosen one, prophesied to take his place at the right hand of Darkness once the whole of Middengard has been enslaved to the Goddess.

Ordakai: Servants to the Laionai, they are childlike in stature and appear to be genderless.

Palingard: Once Èanna's favorite place for solitude, it became a city after the first age of war and is eventually the last stronghold of Middengard.

Realm of Light: Home of the Father.

Ruiari: Known once for its attention to the arts, Ruiari was once a thriving epicenter of culture and trade.

Sacred Chalice: Blessed by the Goddess herself, it holds the sacrificial wine used in Observance.

Sacrificial Garments: Worn by the vessels and The Lineage, each color signifies role and rank. White is reserved for Breeders, red for vessels in service to the Goddess, black for Ereubinian hierarchy, gold for sacrifice.

Saeculum: Temple in Adoria, partially underground, that predates any known Adorian history.

Saint Ereubus: Gave up his soul in exchange for the power to take the souls of all others: Known as the father to The Lineage.

Sword of Saint Ereubus: Known by the immortals as the Sword of Eternal Death, it has the power to kill an immortal. Created by Azrian.

Temple of the Goddess: Forged of Adorian stone, it was once a place for worship of the Father. After Eidolon is taken over it becomes a place for worship of the Dark Goddess.

The Ancients: The first Adorians in recorded history.

The Fall: Refers to the forging of the Sword of Eternal Death by Azrian and the event where he took the life of his brother's beloved and thereby created the second realm of substance, Hothrendaire, by tearing a hole in the fabric of existence.

The Immortals: Immortal beings placed in the created realms by the Father to tend to the creatures who inhabit them. Each of the immortals was given a gift that aided in the forming of the created worlds.

The Lineage: Also referred to as the Blessed—any human of Ereubinian descent.

The Prophecy: Origin unknown and feared by humans and Adorians, The Prophecy speaks of the coming of the Oni.

Torradh: Adorian funeral.

Vessels: Soulless humans.

Wardens: Ereubinians chosen to live among the humans and oversee their servitude.

White Dragon: Depicted throughout Ereubinian and Adorian history, The White Dragon is assumed to be another form of the Dark Goddess Ciara.

Look for books two and three in the
Guardians of Legend trilogy to be released
Winter 2011 and 2012.

BLOOD OF ADORIA, BOOK TWO

NOVEMBER 2011

ETERNAL REQUIEM, BOOK THREE
NOVEMBER 2012

AUTHOR BIO

J.S. Chancellor, whose personal motto is, "woe is the writer who mounts their merit on the masses," started writing stories when she was still in grade school, and finished her first fantasy novella at the age of 14. She drafted chapter one of the Guardians of Legend trilogy when she was a freshman in high school, sitting on a stool in front of a piano bench, in her parents' den. It wasn't until she was 25 when a resident at the apartment complex where she worked lovingly made a casual remark about her procrastination that her passion for fantasy fiction took center stage. Since then she's focused all of her efforts on writing, to include leaving her full time job in September 2009 and actively maintaining a blog dedicated to the art of crafting fiction (www.welcometotheasylum. net). You can find her there, or her official website, www. jschancellor.com. She currently resides in Georgia with her husband and two beloved dogs.